Andrew Waterston has thas seen and grasped new ow they might look on a Ca Chartered Building Surved, folded it away and hid it in a shed. Information Technology seemed to offer greater rewards, variety and a good reason not to crawl around roof spaces hunting woodworm in a suit. He did not look back, other than to design and build offices and data centres for large companies, and house extensions for friends and family.

In parallel, he enjoyed 20 years serving as an Officer in the British Army (Territorial) and still misses the camaraderie and indefatigable humour of soldiers whose imagination, low boredom threshold and cunning could be relied upon to create amusement in the most unlikely situations. Battlefield tours and Staff College stimulated an interest in military history. The brilliant Richard Holmes, another TA Officer, inspired him to see how political will translated into military strategy, Regimental action and ultimately individual stories of courage. Discovering his Great Grandfather had a fascinating and untold story that linked several great, and sadly forgotten, characters resolved him to research and tell the tale. The First Batman series tells an incredible true story that may even inspire readers to discover more from the proper history books contained in the bibliography.

Royal Horse Guards Trooper in State Uniform

THE FIRST BATMAN OUTSIDERS

Andrew Waterston

The First Batman – Outsiders

This edition published in 2017 by Andrew Waterston

001

Copyright © Andrew Waterston 2017

ISBN: 9781549904202

All rights reserved. No part of this publication may be reproduced, or utilised in any form or stored in or introduced into a retrieval system, or transmitted, in any form, or by any means (electronic, mechanical, photocopying, recording or otherwise) without the prior written permission of the publisher.

Front Cover - The Royal Horse Guards charging at Kassassin and returning to Albany Street Barracks via London Docks

Back Cover – The day after the battle at Kassassin

All illustrations are taken from prints in The Illustrated London News 1882

Maps created by the Author

To Hilary

Those who do not learn from history are doomed to repeat it

Habit is stronger than reason

GEORGE SANTAYANA
POET, PHILOSOPHER, HUMANIST (1863-1952)

OUTSIDERS

Are we all outsiders, our lives spent searching for somewhere we fit in?

Or driven by the desire to change the world to one where we do?

Is human happiness measured by our ability to find somewhere we belong or by our ability to compromise, to accept and cherish differences?

To my dear Aunt Jo for asking me to clear out her cellar and in rediscovering her grandfather's travel chest, inspiring me to share her interest in family history. Like your beloved brother, you departed this life far too soon and are very sadly missed.

I am deeply indebted to those who read the drafts and provided such constructive criticism, Peggy Ewart, Robert Smithbury and Julien Dixon. Thank you too, the experts, Ewan Carmichael, Angus Campbell, Mark Boden, the staff of the Household Cavalry Museum, the National Army Museum and victorianwars.com.

Finally, thank you to everyone who heard me tell my Great Grandfather's story, urged me to write it down and convinced me that they would read the book.

To John Waterston DCM, and the combatants, I hope I have done your memory justice.

CHARACTER LIST

General Sir John	Adye	Lieutenant General, Chief of Staff to Sir Garnet Wolseley in Egypt
General	Alison	Commander of the British Highland Brigade in Egypt
Ted	Ankers	Trooper in the RHG - a fixer
Colonel	Arabi	Egyptian officer and Minister of War
Cornet / Lieutenant	Baillie Hamilton / The Lord Binning	Baillie Hamilton, Troop commander in the Royal Horse Guards
Valentine	Baker	Disgraced former Colonel in the 10th Hussars, General in the Turkish Army, friend of Fred Burnaby
Colonel Creed	Baker Russell	Friend of General Wolseley, Commander of 1st Cavalry Brigade in Egypt.
John	Bright	Cabinet Minister, Chancellor of the Duchy of Lancaster, Quaker.
Captain	Brocklehurst	Officer in the Royal Horse Guards
Colonel Fred	Burnaby	Lieutenant Colonel, officer commanding the Royal Horse Guards
Prince George / Duke of	Cambridge	Cousin to Queen Victoria, Commander in Chief of the British Army

Joseph	Chamberlain	Cabinet Minister, Liberal MP for Birmingham, President of the Board of Trade
Hugh	Childers	Secretary of State for War
Lieutenant	Chilvers	(F) Riding Master in the Royal Horse Guards
Vice Consul	Cookson	Vice Consul / British diplomat in Alexandria
John	Crook	Trooper in the RHG - an old soldier
Samuel	de Kusel	Controller General of the Egyptian Customs Service
General	Drury Lowe	Commander of the British Cavalry Division in Egypt
Lord	Dufferin	British Ambassador to the Porte /Turkey
Prince Arthur	Duke of Connaught	Favourite son of the Queen, Commander of the Guards Brigade in Egypt
Angus	Duncan	Trooper in the RHG - the joker
Harry	Evans	Trooper in the RHG
Colonel Henry	Ewart	Colonel of the 2nd Life Guards, Commander of the Household Cavalry composite Regiment in Egypt
Edward	Finch	Trumpeter in the RHG
Robert	Gibson	Trooper / shoeing smith in the RHG

William	Gladstone	British Prime Minister
General	Graham	Friend of General Wolseley, Commander of 1st Infantry Brigade in Egypt.
The Earl	Granville	Foreign Secretary
Coxwain	Gray	(F) Coxwain / bodyguard to Captain Molyneux RN
Charles	Gwinnell	Troop Corporal Major in the RHG
General	Hamley	Commander of the British 2nd Division in Egypt
The Marquess of / Lord	Hartington (Spencer Cavendish)	Cabinet Minister, Secretary of State for India.
Khedive	Ismail	Former Egyptian ruler, exiled to Italy. Father of Khedive Tewfik.
Major / Lord	Kilmarnock	RHG Officer
Samuel	de Kusel	British born Controller-General of the Egyptian Customs Service
Robert	Laidlaw	Trooper in the RHG – an old soldier
Omar	Lufti	Turkish born Governor of Alexandria
	Mahdi	Muhammad Ahmad – "al Mahdi". Self professed prophet and leader of the rebels in Sudan

Sir Edward	Malet	British diplomat and Consul General in Egypt
John / Jock	McIntosh	Lance Corporal, section second in command in the RHG
Donald	McLeod	Trooper in the RHG
General	McPherson	Commander of the Indian Contingent in Egypt
Major	Milne Home	Major, second in command of the RHG, Conservative MP, commander of the RHG contingent in Egypt
Will	Mitchell	Trooper in the RHG
Captain RN	Molyneux	Captain of the ironclad battleship, HMS Invincible
James	Morice	British born Inspector General of the Egyptian Coastguard Service
Catherine	Nairn	(F) Daughter of a linoleum maker in Kirkcaldy
Lord	Northbrook	Cabinet Minister, First Lord of the Admiralty
Tom	Parris	Trooper in the RHG
Sir Henry	Ponsonby	Major General (retd) Private Secretary to Queen Victoria
Prince Albert	Prince of Wales	Eldest son of Queen Victoria and the future King Edward VII

Melton	Prior	War Correspondent for The Illustrated London News in Egypt
Joe	Proudlock	Trooper in the RHG
Leslie	Robertson	Eton Schoolboy and friend of Gordon Wilson
Albert	Robeson	Lance Corporal in the RHG. 2ic of the recruit section
Ewan	Rogers	Corporal of Horse in the RHG
Colonel Suliman	Sami	Commander of a disciplined Egyptian Regiment
George	Scott	Lance Corporal of Horse in the RHG. Section Commander
Sir Beauchamp	Seymour	Admiral, Commander of the Mediterranean Fleet
Joseph	Simmons	Civil Engineer and Aeronaut
Colonel Herbert	Stewart	Friend of General Wolseley, Quartermaster to the Cavalry Division in Egypt.
Henry	Storey	Trooper in the RHG - Batman / Soldier Servant to Fred Burnaby
Ivy	Storey	(F) Wife of Henry Storey, clothes washer, cleaner and occasional cook to John Waterston's Section billet

Khedive	Tewfik	Egyptian Leader son of the exiled Khedive Ismail
John	Waterston	Railway guard who becomes a Trooper in the Royal Horse Guards (RHG, or "The Blues")
Captain	Watson	Royal Engineers, Intelligence Officer in Egypt
General	Willis	Commander of the British 1st Division in Egypt, friend of the Duke of Cambridge
Cornet John	Willoughby	Troop commander in the RHG
Gordon Chesney	Wilson	Eton Schoolboy and aspiring RHG officer
Sir Garnet	Wolseley	Major General and commander of the British Army in Egypt.

F denotes fictitious name and character

With the exception of John Waterston and Henry Storey, little is discoverable about the Troopers in the RHG. Real surnames taken from the medal rolls have been used though their forenames and characteristics are fictitious.

THE RIVER NILE 1882

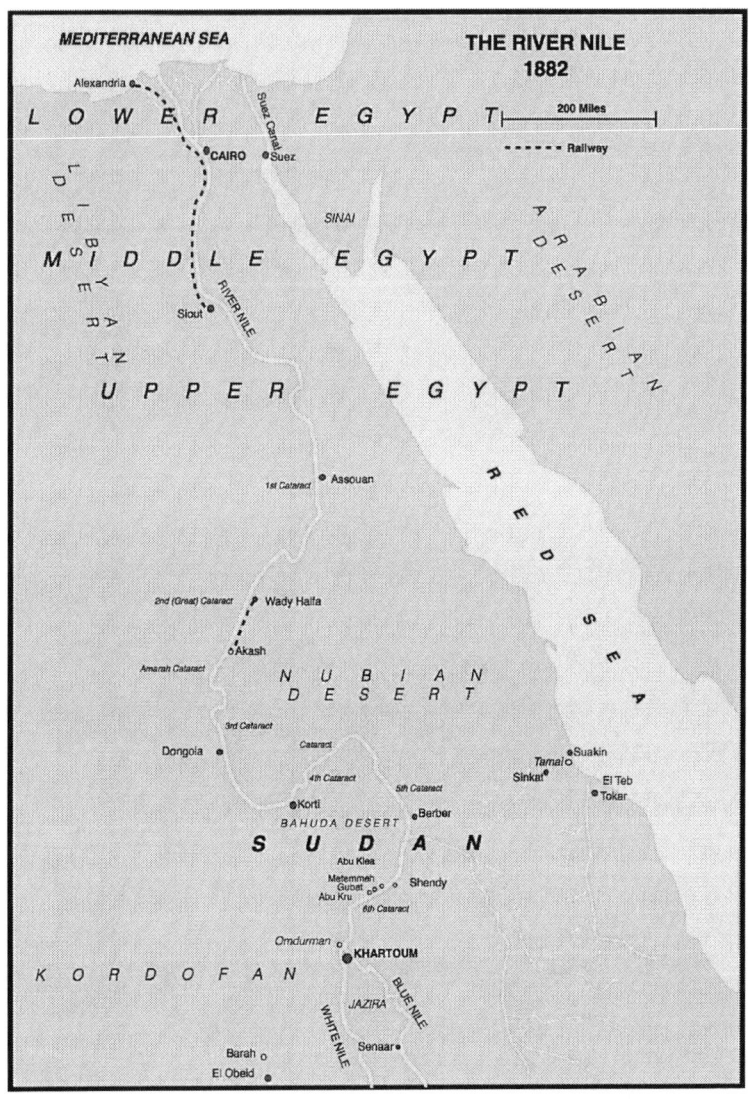

	Character List	8
	The River Nile 1882	14
1	Burntisland Station	17
2	Langerenong	20
3	Burntisland	21
4	Kirkcaldy Station	23
5	True Blue	28
6	The Marlborough Club, 52 Pall Mall, London	31
7	Near Aba Island, White Nile, Sudan	37
8	Recruit Training	38
9	Passing Out	54
10	Aba Island, White Nile, Sudan	57
11	Wimbledon Common	59
12	Windsor	74
13	Politics	81
14	Annual Manoeuvres	85
15	Lured to water	90
16	Christmas 1881	91
17	Assassin	101
18	Flying to France	105
19	The Trouble with Egypt	114
20	Reversals	120
21	Riot	121
22	A Delicate Matter	136
23	Damned if we do, damned if we don't	139
24	High seat	141
25	Losing control	144
26	Bombardment	149
27	Aftermath	164
28	Preparation for War	168
29	Feint	183
30	Ismailia	187
31	Magfar	196
32	Mahsama Station	212
33	A Moonlight Charge	220

34	Consequences	230
35	The Administration of War	235
36	The Price of Honour	238
37	The Second Battle of Kassassin	247
38	Reversals	252
39	Tel-el-Kebir	253
40	Cairo	268
41	Little Victories	274
42	The Khedive's Parade	274
43	Homecoming	281
	Epilogue	293
	Explanatory Notes	295
	Royal Navy Ships in Egypt	298
	British Cavalry in Egypt	300
	Bibiography	301

1
BURNTISLAND STATION

February 1881

Flustered, the young woman stepped from the second-class carriage and pressed through the steam. Burntisland Station bustled with passengers invisible to each other as they hurried through the columns fronting the main building towards the ferry that would carry them south to Edinburgh. A stiff breeze raised white horses on the Firth of Forth, while in the shelter of the outer harbour, grey gusts chased each other across the filthy water.

John Waterston watched as a crane scooped coal from a rail waggon and fed it into the expectant belly of a coaster. In the distance he could just make out the recently abandoned support pier for the Forth Bridge, discarded in the wake of the Tay Bridge disaster not two years before. He shuddered at the thought of the 75 souls, several colleagues included, who had vanished into the estuary that stormy December night.

His grey eyes were drawn back to the girl. She was pretty, with auburn hair, fair skin, freckles and large blue eyes; a fellow Scot. Her dress was simple, dark blue and elegant; what he could now see of it under her travelling cloak. She was not one of his regular passengers but for several months he had looked out for her among those alighting at Kirkcaldy. He would inspect her ticket and attempt a brief conversation, though she did not appear to have noticed him any more than his North British Rail colleagues, and avoided his eye. He caught a last glimpse as she threaded her way past a bear of a man in a bulky brown overcoat who had suddenly slowed his walk to search his pockets. A scruffy, weasel faced lad walking back towards the station, changed direction to avoid the bear, and bumped lightly into the girl. There was a muffled apology from the lad and the girl walked on. In that brief moment, John had seen the other movement, the quick hand dipped into the girl's bag, and the transfer of the purse from weasel to bear. Bear walked on, the purse now in his pocket.

John signalled to his friend, James, nodding towards the weasel while patting his uniform pocket and mouthing 'dipper'. James nodded back and set off after the weasel. John followed the bear, watching carefully to see if he contacted anyone else. Bear appeared to have abandoned his plans to board the ferry and was now walking up Harbour Place toward Smugglers Inn. John increased his pace, the Inn may not be busy at this time but there were folk in there he would rather not become involved. After twenty yards, the bear became aware of him, and suddenly turned.

"Are you following me?" The challenge came from a man in his late thirties with watery eyes and the complexion of one who had spent a lot of time outdoors, or in his cups. He seemed surprised to find himself facing a man as tall as him. The bear looked John up and down, sizing him up. When he took a proper look, the railway guard uniform, designed on the basis that one size fits nobody, actually looked smart on him. Events didn't appear to be unfolding in the way the bear expected. Worryingly the guard did not seem intimidated by the bear's sheer size and presence. Alarm bells began being ignored in the bear's over inflated and under equipped brain.

"I'm sorry if I startled you sir. I believe someone may have slipped an item into your pocket while you were not looking." The guard was polite, softly spoken and with the quiet confidence of one who successfully confronted aggressive passengers on a regular basis; and had done so for years.

"What the fuck are you talking about?" the bear stepped forward into the guard's space. The bear was used to aggression, and the threat of imminent violence, to get his way. The Guard stepped back, but only slightly.

"I'm sorry sir, I have reason to believe a lady's purse has fallen into your pocket. Would you mind checking?"

"You have t'be fucking joking? There is no way I am going through my pockets for you." The bear's eyes were narrowing, his gaze fixed on John and spittle appearing at the edge of his mouth. A couple of passers by were taking an interest and he was not going to back down, reputation was all.

"Sorry sir, are you certain I am mistaken? John smiled, and paused, suppressing the desire to mirror the bear's aggression. "Without even checking?"

"Yes, now fuck off back to your trains". The bear glared at the guard, facing him down. Then his eyes flickered over John's shoulder and momentarily widened slightly. Whatever he had seen, he did not like. John knew better than to take his eyes off of the bear. With any luck James and some of the other guards were coming to provide some support.

"I am sorry, sir. I am sure this is a simple misunderstanding we can clear up in a few minutes in the office. Can you come with me?"

The bear smiled and leaned back slightly.

"Of course."

In a flash the bear brought his head forward and smashed it into the guard's nose; or where he was sure his nose had been half a second before. Rather than feel the satisfying crunch of bone breaking under forehead, his own nose exploded on an iron fist. Stunned, his legs buckled; kicked from behind and he was face down on the mucky cold cobbles, a heavy knee in the small of his back. Adrenalin flooded his veins and engorged his muscles, but they were useless. He could not move without pain searing through shoulder, elbow and wrist, locked in a vice-like grip behind his back.

Looking through a myriad of tiny stars he could see the polished boots of two more guards. "It would appear more than one purse has fallen into your pocket sir. I am surprised you had not noticed the additional weight."

"Fuck off". The bear cursed his luck; a young smart arse that knew how to fight.

2
LANGERENONG

Gordon Chesney Wilson watched a camel wander past a lush cheese tree on the far side of the creek; a humped legacy of the Burke and Wills expedition to explore the interior. A swan serenely ignored a Ceylon Peafowl as it coasted across the smooth brown water towards its mate. Everywhere he looked was a verdant green; how different from the parched red sandscape he remembered as a child. It had been a scorching couple of summers and even the hardy merino sheep had suffered. Now, the wool trade was booming and his father, Sir Samuel, was immensely wealthy. His Irish father had moved to Australia in 1852. With his brothers they had bought the Station for £40,000 after selling some land they owned in Ballymena. Now Sir Samuel had bought them out and continued to acquire more land.

Today, Langerenong Station boasted 153,000 acres of sheep on a total estate of over a thousand square miles. Gordon looked back at the homestead, a grand brick built six bedroom house. He had been born in the master bedroom 15 years ago and, other than the trips to Melbourne, 200 miles South East of the house, knew nowhere else. Tomorrow the family was moving thousands of miles to England. He would go to school at Eton to prepare him for Oxford and then, hopefully, Sandhurst. His sister would marry an impoverished Englishman with a title. His father would campaign for election as a Member of Parliament. Their lives were planned out, and for the next six weeks they would be living aboard a steam ship.

3
BURNTISLAND

John stepped on to the 2 year old paddlesteamer *William Muir*, his eyes already searching out the girl, his right fist stinging as the adrenalin wore off. He found her in the rear cabin, seated on a wooden bench and looking out towards the smoky skyline above Edinburgh. "You want to see my ticket again?" her eyes hinted at a smile but it was gone in an instant.

"My name is John Waterston. I am one of the guards for Northern British Rail and regret you may have been robbed, Ma'am. I hope I can reunite you with your purse if you could come with me?"

Her eyes widened in surprise and then darted to her bag, hands frantically fumbling through the contents. "It's gone. Where is it? How did you know?" Tumbled from her lips in quick succession in the shock of the sudden departure from her normality.

Recovering, she stood at the moment the ferry moved slightly as a mooring line was cast off in preparation for departure. He caught her elbow as she almost fell, and held a moment longer until he was sure she was stable. Her composure and balance returning she glanced at the shore, and then at the hand holding her elbow.

"Don't worry, they know the situation and won't leave until we are back ashore" he said, releasing her arm and hoping the captain had received the message. "We have apprehended the thieves. If you could just come with me to the stationmaster's office we can have this settled in a few minutes. You, and your purse will be able to catch the next sailing at 11.00."

"My father will be furious. He is always warning me about thieves on trains." She followed him up the companionway toward the waist where the deck officer waited with a seaman, impatient to secure the gangplank and cast off.

"How did you know I was the victim?" she asked as they walked back to the station building.

"You were lucky and I just happened to see the young lad who bumped into you lift the purse from your bag and pass it to an accomplice. They clearly knew what they were doing. They had a well-worked routine. I doubt you even noticed."

"You're right, I didn't" she replied, "'So how did you?"

"Training and experience." He watched her reaction as they reached the stationmaster's door. "We have had a few passengers report losses on this line recently so we have been keeping a special watch for outsiders, those who don't quite belong. But I must admit it was mainly luck." Damn, why had he admitted that?

"You just happened to be watching me?" she smiled, watching him closely. "Was I deserving of special attention?" The smile in her eyes showed she was playing with him, gauging his slightest reaction. "Am I suspected of being part of the gang?"

"No, Ma'am." He quickly looked away, hoping to conceal his growing embarrassment at being accused of paying her special attention. Why was he unable to talk to girls? He was twenty-three for crying out loud, and had sisters that he could talk to without any problem – though they, and his brothers, were all younger than he. He could even talk to the girls at the kirk every Sunday, but he did not fancy any of them, even if they seemed to like him. Maybe it was easier to talk, when you were not trying to impress them into walking out with you.

Sorting out the paperwork did not take long. James was both a railway guard and county constable. He took a statement from John, who described the involvement of the weasel faced man and the chain of events. The girl, he finally discovered was Catherine Nairn, daughter of one of the largest linoleum manufacturers in Kirkcaldy. She identified her purse from among the haul, found in the bears' pockets, and confirmed she had not given it to the man. An hour later John escorted Catherine to the paddlesteamer, *John*

Stirling. "Thank you for saving my purse. You were very brave to tackle that man, he was huge." She looked him up and down, as if seeing him properly for the first time. "But then you are not exactly small, and you look very smart in your uniform; it suits you." She paused and turned to board the ferry. "Almost as smart as those dashing Horse Guards at the Castle."

4
KIRKCALDY STATION

Catherine's final words played on John's mind for days afterwards. By chance, he had seen her again later that day, returning from Edinburgh with a small box and some brown paper packages, but the train was busy and he was unable to speak to her alone.

A week later he saw her again. This time she was in the company of another young lady and, as he checked their tickets, Catherine introduced him as 'the guard who had rescued her purse'. John quietly enjoyed the recognition, but the moment was lost as he realised she had forgotten his name, and dashed as they turned their conversation back to excited speculation about how many handsome cavalrymen they might see on their trip to Edinburgh.

He had hoped his guard's uniform would attract the girls. It was one of the reasons he had joined the railway in the first place – that and the need for a wage that would help support his three sisters and seven brothers, the youngest of whom was barely two.

Generations of Waterstons had been oatmeal millers in Linktown, now a borough of Kirkcaldy, with a mill powered by the burn that burbled down through the sparse trees to the North Sea less than half a mile away. His early childhood was filled with the creaks and groans of machinery and the rumble of heavy stones turned by the water that never ceased its race under their home. His memory could still smell the sweet drying days when the oats were spread over the iron plates and the hot coals scattered under them. He had revelled in the early freedom to dispense small sacks of oatmeal to the local shops and hotels. Later he had learned to drive the cart; riding out into the countryside delivering meal to the farms and shepherd huts.

His childhood had been accompanied by a more exciting sound too. Screaming, smoke shrouded trains thundered over the mill on a brick built viaduct that had not blocked the burn, but signalled the slow strangulation of the family living. Steam powered mills, fed from the local coalfields were far more efficient and reliable than water. New jobs had to be found to feed the family. The new flax spinning and linen weaving mills swallowed some of them.

John had long been fascinated by the railway; running errands for the stationmaster from an early age. After a spell as a porter his desire to travel the line, and the prospect of a smarter uniform, led him to apply to be a guard. For several years it had been a dream job, but being a guard was not enough; he knew that now. He craved excitement. He did not think himself a violent man, and was proud of the way he had dealt with the bear, a man who was clearly no stranger to violence. His reaction to the head-butt had been autonomic. Time had slowed as instinct and experience had predicted the threat and fed adrenalin into his system, preparing it to fight. A youth spent hefting large sacks and a diet of porridge, brose, haggis and mealie puddings had made him strong, even if he was too thin to look it. His technique had been honed in waste ground and backstreet brawls. His height and strength had long made him a target for the local toughs, eager to prove themselves. He had been forced to learn fast or take a beating. One to one he had not lost a fight in eight years and it was the confidence so derived that had enabled him to unleash the adrenalin fuelled fist into the bear's nose, just at the moment it was needed.

Reflecting on the fight, as he always did, he did not believe he could have handled the situation differently, nor hone his performance. He just needed more.

With a limited education, he had learned to read the weekly newspapers that were now cheap enough for the masses to buy, though he occasionally was lucky enough to find The Times discarded in the first class compartment. For years he had bought the special editions of 'The Graphic' and 'Illustrated London News', with their etchings of battles and daring acts of bravery in far off lands. Last September the 72nd and 92nd Highlanders had fought with great distinction at the Battle of Kandahar, in Afghanistan, that had brought the war to a close. He kept the pictures in his trunk.

That evening he and James shuffled closer to the pot bellied stove in the Kirkcaldy Station staff room, hands wrapped around huge enamelled mugs of cocoa. The room smelled of coal, and slightly damp clothes. Dribbles of condensation chased each other down the windowpanes, briefly clearing channels through the steam obscured glass and hinting at the raindrops illuminated by the gaslights outside.

The topic had come back to a familiar theme, fighting Zulus at Rorkes Drift almost two years before and the eleven Victoria Crosses and four Distinguished Conduct Medals awarded there. They had noticed a small piece in the newspaper about another DCM that would have been awarded to a private in the Army Hospital Corps. He and James had enjoyed a good crack about that, speculating on why the recommendation had been made almost a year after the battle. Their discussion redoubled when the recommendation was then withdrawn after the man absconded and was discovered to be a thief.

"I can't abide thieves, but is it really fair to take away a medal awarded for valour on the battlefield, no matter what you do afterwards?" asked James.

"They didn't take it away, they just didn't give it to him" said John. "I bet he was a real troublemaker and they couldn't bring themselves to give him a medal no matter how brave he had been."

"Did you see that comment from General Wolseley?" asked James.

"The very model of a modern major general?" chuckled John. James looked quizzically at him. "Apparently the funny song about the General in that new Gilbert and Sullivan musical 'The Pirates of Penzance' is about Wolseley."

James' face cleared. "Yes, him. He doesn't reckon any of the VCs and DCMs should have been awarded to those at Rorkes Drift."

"To be fair, he didn't quite say that" said John. "He said it was monstrous to make heroes of soldiers who were shut up in a building and fighting like rats for their lives. After all, what else were they going to do?"

"Which is a point, but rather harsh. So why did they award them then?" James was curious, and often found John had some interesting ideas that had not occurred to him.

John paused before saying, "Clearly, we don't know, but notice we are talking about the bravery of one hundred and fifty men who successfully defended themselves against four thousand Zulu warriors, rather than how a force of two thousand was heavily defeated by twenty thousand the day before at Isandlwana."

"Do you think Wolseley tried to get all the medals taken back now he is Quartermaster General?" asked James.

"I don't think even Sir Garnet has enough clout to do that, Her Majesty would never allow it."

They both took great swigs of cocoa and John used the back of his finger to clear a small section of window and look out at the deserted platform and steady rain. "In the light of recent events, I have made a momentous decision."

"You are going to quit mooning over Catherine Nairn and find someone in your own league?" asked James, smiling.

John grimaced. "Possibly, but with the Russians causing trouble in the Balkans and the fighting in Afghanistan and South Africa, they are looking for unmarried men to volunteer for the Army. I am going to volunteer for the Royal Horse Guards in the hope that I will have more luck with women wearing an even smarter uniform".

James looked at him in surprise before turning back to the red glow of the stove. "Have you told your mother? She won't be at all happy with you going off to visit foreign countries, meet strange people and then kill them."

"I am a big boy now, and don't need mother's permission," John replied

James looked up at him and chuckled. "You haven't told her yet, have you?"

"Not exactly." He grinned. "I've told her I am going for a new job in Edinburgh. It comes with a great uniform, use of a really good horse, and they provide all my board and lodging so she will get a bed back for the new bairn. It's not as though it will be dangerous, the Blues haven't been in a battle or even abroad since Waterloo. I can learn to ride properly, shoot and spend my days sitting on a magnificent horse, fending off pretty women."

5
TRUE BLUE

April 1881

A few days later, John Waterston walked into the Royal Horse Guards 'recruiting' office in Edinburgh castle. It was a small room tucked out of the way by the portcullis gate and was probably used as a private space out of the sight of the officers for most of the time. Recruitment into the Blues appeared to be a half-hearted affair. He supposed that without the need to replace casualties from active service, they could afford to be choosy.

"You want to volunteer to join the Household Cavalry?" The slightly overweight and ruddy nosed soldier seated behind the battered desk looked John up and down, the mild disbelief evident in his tone.

John noted the three stripes and the crown on the soldiers arm. "Yes, Sergeant." The soldier bristled. It was Sergeant wasn't it?

"Don't call me 'Sergeant', I am a Corporal of Horse in Her Majesty's favourite regiment, not some chicken livered ponce serving in the poor bloody infantry." The retort was practised, he was evidently used to the three chevrons with the brass crown above being confused by new recruits. His voice softened slightly. "There are no Sergeants in the Blues. Sergeant is a Frog word meaning servant and we are all gentlemen in the Blues, not servants. You will address me as Corporal of Horse, or Corporal of Horse Rogers, are we clear?"

"Yes, Corporal of Horse."

"So, why do you want to join Her Majesty's finest regiment?

"Because it is Her Majesty's finest regiment and has the smartest uniform, Corporal".

Rogers almost smiled. "At your age?" He paused. "What have you done? On the run? Broken the law? Got a girl pregnant and need to escape her father?

"None of those, Corporal of Horse."

Rogers did not look convinced. Few volunteered for service, most joined because it was preferable to prison, or starving on the streets and the Blues would not accept those. Even the uniform was far from attractive to the general public. "A gentleman then, as befits Her Majesty's finest regiment. How old are you exactly?"

John had been warned about age by the 'bringer' who had introduced him to Corporal of Horse Rogers, he suspected in return for a fee. He was actually twenty three last Christmas day, but that was clearly considered old in the Blues who liked recruits aged less than twenty as it was easier to teach them to ride. "I was nineteen last Christmas, Corporal of Horse."

"You don't look it."

"I've always been told I look older than my years, Corporal of Horse."

Rogers was convinced there was more to this recruit than met the eye "What work do you do?"

"I'm a railway guard, Corporal of Horse." Instinct told John to keep his answers brief. The less Rogers knew the better if he was going to have to hide four years of his life.

"You don't look like a railway guard. You look as though you have been lifting heavy loads all your life."

"My family were millers, Corporal of Horse. I have been hefting mealie bags since I could walk. I then worked as a porter on the railway before becoming a guard."

"All that and only just 19, eh?" Rogers did not look convinced, but seemed to let the matter go. "Where are you from?"

"I was born in Auchterderran and lived most of my life in Kirkcaldy, Corporal of Horse." The lack of recognition confirmed Rogers was not local. "They are both about 20 miles North of here, in Fife" he added.

Rogers moved on. "Religious?"

"I'm Presbyterian, Corporal of Horse."

Rogers raised an eyebrow. "Not a Catholic then? Don't worry, we have all sorts in the Blues. Do you go to church regularly?"

"Yes, Corporal of Horse, every Sunday when I am not on duty."

"Good, the officers like volunteers who believe in God." The questions continued for a while until the Corporal of Horse appeared satisfied. He was required to strip down to his underclothes and his height and chest were measured and noted. He was three eighths of an inch short of six foot tall with a 37 inch chest. He would have been weighed too if they had a scale. Rogers explained 2 or 3 in 10 recruits were too undernourished to be accepted, but he met the requirements laid down in the book and was fit to be medically examined. He was handed a shilling and a notice to appear before the doctor.

That afternoon a civilian surgeon engaged by the Blues asked him to strip and extend his arms above his head. The doctor walked around him, carefully inspecting the whole surface of his body. He was asked his age again and the doctor shook his head in disbelief.

"You're older than twenty one, but in good physical shape so if you want your regulation age to be nineteen then so be it".

It was established John could walk, jump, stand on one leg without falling over and had good teeth. He was carefully examined for evidence of scrofula, phthisis (Tuberculosis), syphilis and defective intelligence. He was not branded as a deserter or man of bad character, could say loudly "Who comes there?" and so received the signature of approval.

John then swore allegiance to 'Her Majesty the Queen, her heirs and successors, and the officers and non-commissioned officers set over him'. He swore on the bible in front of a Magistrate, and on 22nd April 1881 became a soldier, 'aged 19 years and 3 months' and committed to twelve years service. He was then slightly shocked to discover that the Blues were only recruiting in Edinburgh and he would soon be travelling south for his training at Windsor.

6
THE MARLBOROUGH CLUB, 52 PALL MALL, LONDON

Late April 1881

"Good evening, Sir Garnet." Major General Sir Garnet Wolseley, Quartermaster-General closed the pocket book of psalms he read each day and smiled, his hand indicating welcome and the seat beside him.

"Good evening, Sir Henry. How are you?" he replied as Major General Sir Henry Ponsonby took the wing backed leather chair beside him. "I hope Her Majesty is in the best of health?"

Sir Henry smiled sadly. "She is as well as can be expected given the passing of her dear friend and advisor, the Earl of Beaconsfield."

"A tragic loss to both the country and the Conservative party," replied Sir Garnet. "I gather it is far from clear who will replace him."

Sir Henry, private secretary to the Queen looked appraisingly at Sir Garnet. "There may be no single leader. Disraeli is a tough act to follow. I believe the Marquess of Salisbury will now lead in the Lords, and Stafford Northcote will continue in the Commons."

Sir Garnet replied, "An interesting situation. With each vying for control, the party will fragment. Gladstone's Liberals must be delighted that the opposition is in such disarray."

"As must you, Sir Garnet" said Sir Henry. "Surely it must enable Mr Childers to proceed apace with his reforms at the War Office, knowing that the Duke of Cambridge lacks the parliamentary support to oppose them?"

They were seated in a quiet corner of the Marlborough Club in Pall Mall. Members sat in groups of two and three around the room, deep in conversations that were unintelligible across the smoke filled room.

"I hope I can count on Her Majesty's support in opposing Sir Edward Watkin's channel tunnel folly?" Sir Garnet asked. "Now the Liberals are in power he believes there is nothing to stop him and they have started trial digging at both ends." He paused, gauging reaction.

"While France is an ally today, events in Suez show their support cannot be counted upon and the speed with which Prussia was able to march into Paris not ten years ago gives me great cause for concern as to their ability to defend their end of it. The Channel has been our primary means of defence since time immemorial and we cannot afford to compromise that in the cause of a high speed railway from Liverpool and Manchester to Paris."

Sir Henry raised an eyebrow. "I am sure you have discussed the matter with His Royal Highness the Duke of Cambridge?" he asked.

"It is one of the topics on which we agree" Sir Garnet replied.

"I am gratified to learn you agree with Prince George. I am sure he will raise the matter with his cousin, the Queen. Are there other topics on which you disagree?"

Sir Garnet frowned slightly. "I am sure you will be aware of those, Sir Henry."

"Please remind me."

Sir Garnet paused, unused to losing control of a conversation, before reluctantly continuing. "I believe he is concerned at the amalgamation of Infantry Regiments, the creation of a reserve army and the abolition of the Regimental numbering system and facing colours. He is of the view that the latter in particular will degrade regimental spirit. He is also firmly of the view that the only place an officer can and should learn his trade is in their Regiment."

"Is he right?" asked Sir Henry.

Sir Garnet grimaced. "Her Majesty agrees that reform of the Army is necessary?" he looked at Sir Henry for any reaction, and grateful to see the slightest affirmation, continued. "For myself, I attribute much of my success to the fact that I have learned my trade in several Regiments and through attachments to the Royal Engineers and the quartermaster general's staff. This has enabled me to gain experience in numerous campaigns in Burma, Crimea, India, China, Canada, West Africa and South Africa. I even have experience of the American Civil War and believe I am one of very few British officers to have met General Robert E Lee and Stonewall Jackson. I wonder what I would have learned had I remained with the 12th of foot, who had barely stepped outside Suffolk in almost 30 years until their recent foray into Afghanistan?" He realised he was talking with passion and softened his tone. "The only way officers can learn their trade is via experience abroad, which is not always possible or practicable, hence attachments and attendance at Staff College is key. Do you not agree, Sir Henry?"

Sir Henry considered for a moment before replying. "I certainly learned a great deal about the need for an effective quartermaster's department and medical chain from my experience in Crimea; and like you, found my time in Canada during the American Civil War to be valuable."

Sir Garnet noted that the General had not actually voiced support for the staff college, an institution still regarded with suspicion by the old guard, and only attended by 40 officers a year. He considered pressing the point but Sir Henry had moved on.

"And what of amalgamations and the creation of a reserve army?" asked Sir Henry.

"As you know Sir Henry, we simply cannot afford the standing Army we need. Compromise is necessary. Reservists represent a cost effective solution that has proven to work in successful modern armies such as Prussia, who incidentally have a flourishing staff college that is personally instructed by their Chief of the General Staff, Field Marshal von Moltke."

Seeing no signs of reaction or objection, he continued. "A reservist may have served under the colours of the 22nd of Foot, but if he settles into civilian life in Reading, needs to be part of a locally raised and trained regiment; amongst his friends. He will not travel to train or be mobilised. He is more likely to identify with the Berkshire Regiment than the 66th of Foot."

"Particularly if he was previously associated with the 49th of Foot?" Sir Henry asked pointedly.

Sir Garnet looked distinctly uncomfortable at how well informed Sir Henry was, before recalling that Sir Henry had been commissioned into the 49th before transferring to the Grenadier Guards. "I am acutely aware that the 49th are lobbying hard against amalgamation with the 66th, but the reality is that they cannot recruit their establishment in Hertfordshire and the 66th will struggle to replace their recent losses at Maiwand. We cannot afford the overhead of two headquarters and two understrength Regiments" he replied. "Compromise is an unfortunate necessity in these straightened times". An opportunistic thought occurred to him and he continued. "Of course it would ease the situation if Her Majesty would be gracious enough to grant the new Berkshire Regiment the honour of being the 'Royal' Berkshire Regiment?"

"After the 66th lost the Queen's Colours?" Sir Henry looked aghast.

"Severely outnumbered by the Afghans and deserted by the Indian Infantry, the 66th fought a rearguard action in the finest traditions of the service. Several officers and NCOs died trying to keep those colours aloft. Indeed, the Colours became the focus of the enemy's attack." Sir Garnet's words were measured but there was an underlying passion as he warmed to the debate.

"As well as the rallying point for the men?" responded Sir Henry.

"Quite, Sir Henry. However weapons have moved on. Our enemies are increasingly armed with rapid firing rifles capable of killing at ranges of a mile, rather than muskets requiring them to close to 100 yards to fire one or two shots a minute. On balance do you not question whether continuing to carry the Colours into battle is appropriate, particularly in colonial conflicts?"

In the silence that followed he signalled to an attendant standing discretely by the door. "I would like a brandy, Sir Henry, can I offer you one?"

"That is most kind, thank you."

"Two brandy's then, please, George." They waited for the servant to return from the drinks' tray and Sir Garnet to sign the chit before Sir Henry resumed an earlier theme. "Could these reservists be used in colonial conflicts do you think? Could they be mobilised to further our interests abroad when there is no direct threat to Great Britain?"

Sir Garnet paused before replying. "If the general public and Parliament is sufficiently behind the action, if it is the right and proper thing to do, then I have no doubt they will mobilise," he replied. "I have found that volunteers make extremely effective soldiers, and am increasingly of the view that those with faith are the bravest of the brave."

Sir Henry glanced at the pocket book of Psalms. "An interesting observation, particularly from a protestant born and bred in Dublin, whose bravery is beyond question," said Sir Henry.

"The Lord is my light and my salvation – whom then shall I fear?" replied Sir Garnet.

Sir Henry smiled at the quote from Psalm 27. "Does the faith make a difference? Could your reservists be deployed to suppress Republicans who are almost entirely of the Catholic faith?"

Sir Garnet positively bristled, controlling his temper with difficulty, he replied. "There is considerable intelligence to support the view that Catholic priests are intrinsically involved in stirring up dissent in Ireland."

"Quite." Sir Henry paused before continuing. "While I understand faith, in the form of Pan-Islamic spirit, is also being used as a tool to rally the poor to rebellion in Egypt. Poor beggars, as with any revolution the poor will die to elevate a few to power, while ultimately remaining as downtrodden as before."

Sir Garnet nodded. He was very aware of the potential problems in Egypt and had commenced contingency planning for invasion. The tiny, fledgling, Military Intelligence Department was already collating maps and reports from officers who travelled incognito, often with their wives, during their winter leave.

7
NEAR ABA ISLAND, WHITE NILE, SUDAN

Muhammad Ahmad ibn al-Saiyid 'Abd Allãh awoke from his drug induced stupor. The dream had been vivid. He had been summoned to Al-Hadra. At this gathering the Prophet Muhammad, surrounded by the other prophets, had drawn light from the centre of his heart and given it to him, declaring him to be al-Mahdĩ.

The Prophet had given him 8, no, 40 years to lead a host of His Ansãr, His most devoted followers, from Khartoum to Constantinople via Cairo, Damascus, Mecca and all the other great cities of the Arab world. He, Muhammad Ahmad, would subordinate orthodox Islam to his personal will. Nothing could stop him; it was God's will. He was al-Mahdĩ, the 'divinely guided one', and successor to Muhammad Himself.

This had of course been written from his birth in Dongola in Northern Sudan. His family of poor carpenters and boat builders was descended from the Prophet Muhammad's grandson, Hasan. It was written, even if his family tree was not. His lifelong piety had been rewarded.

He would lead the impoverished and disaffected against the rich Turkish Egyptians who governed his Sudan. He would unite the tribes of Kordofan, the Hadendawas, the downtrodden poor of the Nile Valley and the desert dwelling Bĩja clans of the Red Sea Littoral. He was al-Mahdĩ and all his followers would know it when he preached this day.

There would be difficulties. The 'Ulema, the orthodox Islamic leaders, were loyal to the rich Turkish Egyptians and would try to discredit him. He would prevail. He was al-Mahdĩ and he knew how to rally the tribes to his cause. While the Egyptians were distracted by their internal squabbles he would use his wives' family connections and his position as a holy man to spread the word; to prepare for Jihad and a return to the ways of the past, when the unbelievers were slaves.

8
RECRUIT TRAINING

At Cavalry Barracks, in Spittal, Windsor, John was medically examined again and inspected by the officer commanding, Lieutenant Colonel Burnaby. The inspection was perfunctory, but gave John his first view of the legend that was Colonel Fred Burnaby. Burnaby was huge, at lease 4 inches taller than he, with a large moustache that balanced a long nose, and with a barrel chest that supported the stories of his enormous strength – the strongest man in England. This was the man who had travelled 300 miles across the Russian steppes to Khiva, with minimal equipment, in a winter so cold his beard snapped off. What all the stories failed to convey was his thin piercing voice, or his warmth. There was a smile in the Colonel's eyes, even as they appeared to bore into John's soul, curiosity without malice. John did not know why, but there was something about this man that engendered trust. He felt he could follow him to the ends of the earth.

John must have satisfied the Colonel as he was then issued his recruit uniform of dull grey coveralls, perfectly suited to life as the lowest of the low. A real uniform had to be earned.

He was billeted in an imposing three storey rectangular brick barrack block that overlooked the main parade square. It had a slate roof and cast iron covered veranda that ran along one long side and each end of the block at first and second floor level. Their billet was on the first floor above the stables with access via a stone staircase with simple iron balustrade. At its entrance a small room was home to their section commander Lance Corporal of Horse George Scott, and his second, Lance Corporal Albert Robeson. John guessed Scott was about four years older than him, perhaps twenty seven, well built and just over six foot tall. He was bright but hid it well behind the veneer of a regulation issue Lance Corporal of Horse persona John suspected he had purchased from one of the new mail order catalogues. This was the first recruit section he had been given, and he was determined to do well. Robeson was a couple of years older than Scott but in both looks and actions seemed considerably older. An enormous moustache dominated his thin face, the waxed ends giving the appearance of ear supports.

The recruit's room contained ten iron-framed beds that could be folded in half with the palliasse rolled to create more space. The beds were set five to each side of the room. A central walkway was dominated by two tables, benches lining either side. Most of the floor was made up of polished wooden floorboards though there was a concrete hearth by the cast iron oven and hob located at the far end of the room. The windows did not appear to have been opened in a considerable period so there was an all pervading aroma of damp clothing, lamp oil, coal, dish cloths, pipe clay, tobacco smoke, soft soap, butter and cheese.

The whitewashed ceiling was almost ten feet high; suspended by iron straps from which were three, two foot wide shelves that ran almost from one side of the room to the other. John presumed they were to provide storage for all their equipment, when it was issued. He was partly correct; they also stored their food, mugs, bowls, cutlery and everything else needed to live. For now they also provided something else to keep clean.

Another shelf was attached to the wall above their bed space and this was where their meagre personal belongings could be stored, extremely tidily in a trunk. A clothes rail was suspended under the shelf.

Each day, before reveille was sounded, he was gently roused by the sound of a gun being discharged in the stable below, followed by Corporal Robeson screaming in his ear "the sun's burning holes in your blankets. Rouse yourselves you insanitary frequenters of the casual ward." The gunshot reminded John that it was not just the recruits who were being trained, and below him the young horses were being acclimatised to the sound of gunfire and the smell of black powder.

Washing and shaving in cold water in a wooden tub, that had only just been emptied of the urine that had collected overnight, he folded his bed in half, his palliasse into three and his blankets and sheets into an exact block that was then placed on top of the folded mattress. The finished effect reminded him of a first class railway carriage seat, and made him wonder, briefly, whether he had been right to volunteer.

In the cool dawn he paraded outside with the nine other recruits who shared his billet, suppressing shivers. Corporal Robeson called them to attention and for once appeared satisfied that they had moved as one. Turning to the left they double marched to the stables to start their working day.

They cleaned out the stalls and then prepared and provided the first of the three feeds of mashed corn, beans and peas the riding school chargers would be given each day. At 7am the trumpet would call for the horses to be exercised 'led to water' and then returned to their stalls, heads all turned out to face each other so they were able to breathe fresh air. The result was that walking into the stables you were met by two rows of curious, intelligent long faces that turned as one to look at you.

At 8am the recruits were able to take a light breakfast of bread and butter and the first mug of coffee of the day; not that they had much time to drink it.

Life for the recruits was spent running or marching all over the barracks at the whim of their 'elders and betters', which was everyone. Much of their first few weeks seemed to revolve around manure as if to reinforce the point that they were barely more than horse muck, and the slightest transgression would result in being lowered beneath it. Whenever they were not on other duties or training they would patrol the barracks with buckets and shovels, clearing away any manure they could find.

They were introduced to all aspects of stable management and care for the chargers that would one day carry them into battle or, more likely, through the parks and streets of London at the head of a parade. Many of the horses had been out to grass over winter at Melton Mowbray, returning to their barracks at Windsor, Hyde Park and Albany Street in March. Days were spent, washing, clipping and manicuring as well as learning basic veterinary skills that would enable them to keep their mounts fit and healthy in the field.

They learned how to make hoof ointment, to treat brittle feet and sand cracks, out of equal amounts of tar and train oil; how to treat mange and the correct way to clean and sew up sword cuts and bullet holes.

The horses were shod once a month by the Regimental farriers and shoeing smiths. From them they learned how to inspect and clean the hooves, how to soothe kicks and sprains and the approved method of shoeing a horse using the two spare shoes each horse carried.

Each recruit was allocated a horse to look after, those belonging to A Troop having a name beginning with 'A', B Troop 'B' and so on. John's horse, 'Alfie' had his number 'A27' placed on a card over his manger. Alfie was ten years old, nearing the end of his service, and typical of all the recruit chargers with a small lean head, a flat, broad forehead and fine full nostrils. He had a good, clean throat and thin neck supported from a deep, wide chest, and short, broad back and loin designed to carry the 23 stone each trooper would weigh once fully equipped. At almost 17 hands, his legs were well shaped with long pasterns between the fetlock and hoof. His coat was black with a white blaze running from his fringe to the end of his nose.

The work was hard, long and so far as John could tell in the early weeks, often pointless. In particular, standards of cleanliness were ridiculously high and applied to everything. Cpl Scott revelled in discovering dirt in the most obscure places and the billet inspection carried out every morning after breakfast was a trial that, even after five weeks, they failed every day. Long after they had been dismissed for the evening they would labour into the small hours pressing clothes and blankets, dusting and polishing in the vain hope Scott would be satisfied.

John stood rigidly to attention in front of his bed and stared, unseeing, at a point six inches above Tom Parris' head. Scott's white glove was still pristine after three bed spaces had been inspected for dirt and he was presently inspecting Parris' blanket block with a ruler. John could sense Scott's irritation rising as he failed to find fault and moved on to James Freeman's bedspace. For five minutes the absolute silence in the room accentuated every sound made by Cpl Scott as his frustration and colour rose like a tank engine with a sticking pressure relief valve. John could not see him now; he had moved on to Harry Evans's bed and, from the sound of tins rattling, appeared to be rooting around in his wash kit.

Harry Evans was a gangly Welshman with soft features and sad eyes who did not find anything easy. However his gentle nature, quiet determination and willingness to volunteer for the most mundane of tasks, meant that his fellow recruits rallied around to support him. John and Parris had spent two hours last night helping Harry prepare his bedspace and Donald McLeod, the recruit's blanket block expert had ensured Evans would pass that test.

There was a shriek as Scott finally exploded. "What's this?"

Silence. Not even the fly they had vainly failed to remove this morning dared move. Cpl Robeson standing to attention by the door, smiled imperceptibly.

"Evans, what the hell is this?" roared Scott.

Out of the very corner of his eye, John could just make out the slightest quiver in Evans's leg as his sleep deprived mind attempted to determine the best course of action. Act dumb and do nothing was favourite, but it was fighting a losing rear-guard action against the instinct to rush to Scott's side and at least have some idea what he was incandescent about this time.

"Come here you disgusting glocky git". Scott's order removed the final inhibitor in Evans's mind and he dashed to Scott's side.

"What the hell was that?" Scott was warming to his task and Evans had gifted him another reason to see if his voice could carry to the Officers Mess. "Get back to your mark and come here like a soldier not some moocher with a bad case of the trots". Evans jumped back to attention in front of his bed, did a smart about turn and marched the two paces to Scott's side, halting with a clatter of boots on polished floorboard.

John was dying to discover what the fuss was about, but his only clue lay in Tom Parris' face. Parris' eyes were similarly fixed on a point above John's head, but his peripheral vision should enable him a 'view' of Evans's bedspace. From his vantage point by the door, Cpl Robeson would leap upon the slightest movement in any of them.

"Look in this soap box and tell me what you see?" Scott told Evans.

"S…s…s..soap, Corporal?" asked Evans. The silence was palpable.

"And on the soap, Evans?" Scott's voice had dropped to very dangerous levels. John hoped Evans had spotted the warning, though was unsure what could be done even if he had.

"A hair, Corporal?"

"What type of hair?"

There was a long pause. "A pubic hair, Corporal?"

"A pube!" Cpl Scott exploded. "A Pube?"

John's eyes flickered and met Parris' for less than half a second. Parris was desperately trying not to laugh. John smothered a snort. Too late. Cpl Robeson charged down the room and brought himself to a halt inches from John's face. "Something funny, Waterston?" he screamed and whirled on the spot to face Parris. "Do you think this a joke?"

"No, Corporal". Parris and John exclaimed as one. Robeson bounded down the room and stood to attention in front of James Freeman, staring into his eyes, his nose inches away from James' nose.

"What are you looking at?" Robeson screamed. James must have made the mistake of looking back. "Do you fancy me or something? Don't you dare look at me."

"No, Corporal." John could hear the stifled smile in James' response and knew the sleep deprived recruits were on the verge of hysterics. Fortunately, at that moment Cpl Scott started throwing the contents of Harry Evans' bedspace out of the window in a ritual that normally started at the first bed rather than the fifth. They were getting better.

After six weeks, Scott and Robeson gave the recruits a little more slack on the room inspections and the military training started in earnest. They were issued their Undress Uniforms and some of the scrutiny moved from the billet to their attire. They still wore coveralls for the pre-breakfast mucking out, and now, after the room was squared away, had less than ten minutes to change into their uniform and grab something to eat before forming up outside ready to march to their first lesson. Undress uniform comprised a short fitted navy blue 'shell jacket' with silver buttons up the front, two braided cords for epaulets, and slim fitting high waisted overall trousers with a red stripe up the leg. Just above their right ear they wore a round forage cap with a narrow chin strap worn just below the lower lip, except on mounted parade when it sat under the chin. They wore leather wellingtons that finished just below the knee, and which occupied them with polishing and buffing for many hours of an evening. They were not entitled to wear the spurs that slotted into the heel yet.

For five and half hours a week the recruits were required to attend the Regimental school and learn basic sums, reading and writing. Every recruit was required to achieve a fourth class certificate of education. While John did not find this part of the training particularly difficult, many of the other recruits had not had any schooling at all. Cpl Robeson was not spared the education either; he was studying for his second class certificate, necessary for promotion to Corporal of Horse. Cpl Scott had been educated as a gentleman and was alone in not needing to attend school. The youngest son of a Selkirk landowner and farmer, he had joined the Blues in the hope of earning his commission.

Once deemed comfortable and confident around the horses, the recruits were introduced to the Riding Master, Lieutenant Chilvers, and taught to ride. Chilvers had risen through the ranks before being appointed Riding Master, and his pedigree showed. While now a member of the Officers' Mess, he could summon a healthy stream of vernacular when the need arose. He was supported by Rough Riders, selected from the ranks to assist in the instruction and to break and train new horses.

John had ridden a little before and was used to being around horses from the trips with the cart out into the country delivering meal to the farmers, but he found he had to unlearn all he knew. Riding was totally different with straight legs and on such massive black chargers. They started with flat work, building from a walk to a trot to a canter and slowly learning to ride alongside each other as a group. All this was carried out in the enclosed riding school and out of sight of the public. For weeks no saddle was allowed and they rode bare back.

Mounting the huge horses was exhausting. John did not find it easy but James Freeman really struggled to master the technique. While he repeatedly tried to mount each day, the rest of the recruits were forced to continually mount and dismount with growing fatigue and impatience.

They rode single handed, using their legs to control the horse. After six weeks, they were allowed to use a saddle, though no stirrups, and deemed fit to start jumping. They started low and gradually worked up. Harry Evans and Tom Parris proved to be natural riders, able to jump with confidence almost immediately. All the recruits took numerous tumbles in the early weeks and John became familiar with the chiding from the instructors "Waterston, what are you doing on the floor? Who gave you permission to dismount?" Bruised he would remount, thankful he had not landed on his head, and carry on.

For the first three months they were regularly medically inspected. Anyone who, in the view of the officers or instructors, appeared to be lacking in stamina was sent to the medical officer. If rapid improvement was not seen then the recruit would be discharged 'as not likely to become an efficient soldier'.

Recruit training was focussed on discipline, drill and horsemanship; skills that would enable them to parade in public. John forgot the 'Blues' more serious purpose, as soldiers designed to project the power of the British Empire, until one morning they were marched to the rifle range. They were introduced to the Martini-Henry cavalry carbine and were told to first check it was neither cocked nor loaded. Cpl Scott was also keen to ensure they only pointed it at someone they intended to kill.

Cpl Robeson showed them the approved positions for firing the weapon while standing, sitting, kneeling and lying prone. They were not expected to fire while riding. Cpl Scott explained how the sights worked; how to line up the target with the front barleycorn and the rear 'V', and how to adjust the rear sights for various ranges up to a thousand yards – not that it was any use above 700 yards. Finally they were able to practise what they had been shown at a circular target one hundred yards away. The object was to fire five rounds into the bull from the prone position, though the instructors made it clear they just hoped the recruits would hit the target. The red danger flag by the target was lowered and Cpl Scott gave them the command to fire when ready.

John settled down as he had been shown with the carbine resting in his left hand. He cocked the lever to open the breach and fed the first ugly .45 inch brass cartridge into the chamber. Checking it was pressed home he closed the breach and noted the position of the cocking indicator. He pulled the stock into his shoulder and sighted along the barrel towards the target. The stock felt slightly cool against his cheek as he tipped his head to look down the sights. The foresight was not quite on the target so he shuffled his hips until it was. He took a deep breath noting how the barrel dipped down away from the target as he did, and then slowly exhaled. As he breathed out the foresight came up onto the target and slid past it. He adjusted his hips again and repeated the process. To his right, Donald McLeod and James Freeman had both already fired their first shots.

"Come on lad, we haven't got all day" muttered Cpl Scott, standing behind him.

Satisfied, this time when the sight came up onto the target, John pulled the trigger. The carbine roared, kicking back into his shoulder and bruising his cheek. Smoke obscured the target and filled his nostrils with the acrid sweet smell of black powder. He worked the lever, ejecting the cartridge and inserting a new one. Closing the chamber he noted the smoke had cleared sufficiently to be able to see the target again. He could see a white arrow on a stick being pointed at the centre of his target, about a hands width to the right of centre. To his right, an arrow was showing Donald's shot was almost two feet high and right of the bull, while a wildly waved arrow showed Parris had missed entirely.

"Good shot, lad!" said Cpl Scott. "Next time, don't pull the trigger, squeeze it."

He had managed to maintain his position and the second shot was away as soon as his breathing was settled. This time the arrow showed the shot was dead centre. "Well done," said Scott. He fired without further comment from Scott until all five rounds were gone. To John's surprise, and everyone else's amazement, all were in the bull with a grouping of about eight inches. "It appears we have either a very lucky man or, with a lot more practice, a potential marksman" said Cpl Scott. "Freeman, Evans, Burston, you're next."

Later they learned to fire the heavy Enfield revolvers each Trooper was issued for close protection in the event they were unhorsed. It soon became clear the Enfield was a weapon of last resort as the .476 inch black powder propelled rounds were far from accurate at anything other than very close range, and once the five shots had been fired, reloading was painfully slow.

At the end of a long day they were taught how to field strip and clean the weapons.

With smoke blackened faces and oily hands, they marched back to the barracks, for the first time feeling like soldiers.

Arms training was also introduced. Drill, that up to that point had been limited to marching and riding, was now expanded to include the use of the sword. They were taught to hold, swing, point and parry with the issue swords that were kept blunt to avoid accidents. It now became clear why they had been taught to steer with their knees as cutting an enemy's reins meant they were otherwise unable to control their mount.

John was surprised to discover that it was more effective to use the point of the sword than to cut with it. They were taught to point to the left and right of the horses neck, hands high and low depending on whether the target was a mounted or dismounted enemy. "Keep your guard twisted high, Waterston, it will protect your head and arm from an enemy sabre. The way you're doing it at the moment, the enemy will be on your point, but your head will be detached from your body!" Scott's warning rang in his ears. At ever-increasing speeds and almost lying down on their mounts, with their arm straight they practised picking up tent pegs on the point, allowing their arm to swing back through the strike as they passed.

Fitness training was carried out in the gymnasium and ensured that any muscles not tired out by the running, marching and stable work were exercised. There were trials for the football team; Donald McLeod narrowly missing selection for the Regimental team and attracting the attention of the Squadron scouts. The gym training included boxing and wrestling. John excelled at the fighting, though suspected that Tom Parris had a similarly interesting upbringing to his, as he was the only recruit who came close to giving him a bloody nose.

John's instinct was to hold back while fighting Harry Evans. Evans's wild and increasingly frustrated swings were easily avoided and signalled more determination than skill. He landed a couple of gentle jabs to Evans's head and midriff when Cpl Robeson called out loudly "Hit him properly. How will he learn if you hold back?"

Avoiding another wild swing John ducked to his left and landed a heavy punch in Evans's side. Off balance, Evans tumbled to the floor and lay there panting.

"That's more like it," said Robeson. "Evans, nobody can doubt your effort but you fight like a demented daisy. Parris, you fight Waterston and show him where he is going wrong."

John and Parris sparred, with Robeson and Scott interjecting comments and observations they hoped would be helpful to the other recruits. Occasionally the fight would be stopped and a move one or other had made, that Scott or Robeson liked, would be re-enacted and analysed. The recruits were then paired off and told to practise the moves. It became apparent that almost everyone had experience of violence and knew a particular move, usually underhand, that had proven useful to them in the past. The experience was shared for the benefit of all. The recruits were developing into a close knit team.

Teamwork was essential to meet the exacting requirements of Cpl Scott. Every third evening at six, a pair of recruits would be told off to carry out 'night guard' duty and look after the horses. They would reappear at reveille ready to start the working day. The rest of the recruits would have prepared their kit for the day, but it did add to their exhaustion.

With the arrival of the August heat, the recruits were finally judged ready to ride out in public. Each day they would exercise through Windsor Great Park, riding with ever-greater confidence and speed. One day as the temperature climbed into the high 80's they turned left out of the Barracks rather than right and made their way North to the River Thames. There they were greeted by the unusual sight of several NCOs dressed in shirt sleeves and standing by wooden punts.

"Right you lucky chaps, the good news is that today we will practise river crossing," said Lt Chilvers. "The bad news is that none of your mounts have swum before and if you don't encourage them to get it right, the next time you will do this is December."

"I can't swim, Sir," said Harry Evans, a slight pleading evident in his voice.

"That's fine, it will encourage you all the more to hang on to your horse," said Lt Chilvers.

"But sir, you just said he can't swim either," said the unhappy Evans.

"Ah, but the difference is that he does not know that," replied Lt Chilvers. "So I suggest you don't tell him and ride like you go swimming all the time. If he so much as suspects you're nervous he will panic and you'll probably drown."

"Is that what the boats are for Sir?" asked James Freeman. "To rescue us if it all goes horribly wrong?"

"The boats are to recover your bodies so as your mother has something to bury, and the Regiment does not get into trouble for polluting the water," said Cpl Scott. "As it is we'd better hope nobody sees grubby Evans in there or we will get complaints from the water company. Now, dismount, remove saddles and strip down to your cacks."

John dismounted and after removing the saddle, hobbled his horse while he undressed. The sun was almost overhead, the sky a cloudless pale blue. A slight breeze rippled the leaves on the nearest tree and disrupted the flight of a mayfly as it skimmed over the water. He piled his clothes on the saddle and placed it in a neat line alongside the others. Out of the corner of his eye he saw movement and, turning, saw two Eton College boys, one wearing a straw boater peeping through a bush a few yards away. He smiled and winked at them. They ducked down, out of sight.

"Mount up," Cpl Scott's order cut through the heat and the calm. John felt his horse quiver with excitement and gripped hard with his knees to steady him. They formed in line abreast facing the river.

"Waterston, Evans, you first," said Scott. "Waterston, can you swim? We already know Evans will do his finest impression of a brick."

"Yes, Corporal," John replied. "We were taught almost from birth so we wouldn't drown if we fell in the mill pond."

"Lucky," said Evans under his breath. "Any top tips?"

"Relax and let the horse do the work, he will know what to do regardless of what Lt Chilvers says" said John, quietly. "All the mounts are taught to swim by the Rough Riders as part of their six months training. Just follow my lead. You're a far better rider than I so this should be a piece of cake."

Evans smiled and nodded slightly at the vote of confidence.

"Get on with it then," said Cpl Scott

John looked back at Evans as he urged his mount towards the river. Evans was all right, far from bright but a good horseman and he could always be depended on to complete a task, regardless of how mundane or unpleasant; provided it was clearly explained to him first.

They made their way down the grass bank where the turgid brown water was gently lapping on a shallow sandy beach. His horse, A21 "Alfie" needed little encouragement to walk out into the water, though Evans needed rather more and Cpl Scott had to tell him to stop holding back. The bank suddenly shelved and he and Alfie lurched out into the sluggish current. He allowed his legs to float up and lay along Alfie's back, his head alongside Alfie's neck as the stallion kicked out strongly in the deep water. Looking back again, John could see Evans 's horse following him, its head raised out of the water, eyes wide and nostrils flaring with excitement.

"Nothing to it, " said Cpl Scott from his punt. "Take them over to the other bank then circle back to the shallows 50 yards down stream."

John acknowledged and reined Alfie towards the bank 30 yards away. "Well done, Evans, keep it up".

He revelled in the tepid water, noting how they would sometimes pass through cold patches as they made their way across the river. The sun was hot on his back and the reflected light from the surface made him squint. He was taken back to those rare hot and sunny days at the mill when he was allowed to swim with his friends in the millpond and play on the races. Alfie was swimming strongly, eager to make it to the other side and revelling in the weightless exercise. As they neared the shore he steered the black charger back towards the point Cpl Scott had indicated and was surprised how quickly it came towards them now the current was helping them. Donald McLeod and Tom Parris were now in the water too, grinning as their mounts swam across the river.

As they arrived at the bank he realised the river bottom shelved far more steeply than where they had entered. He had to grip hard with his legs to avoid slipping down Alfie's back as the horse struggled to find a footing and reach dry land.

"Good job, Waterston, well done, Evans". Lt Chilvers's praise was unexpected and all the more welcome for it. "Once the section have all done the swim, take your mounts back into the water by the beach and give them a good rub down."

The rest of the afternoon was the first relaxation they'd had since arriving in Windsor over three months earlier. The sun dried their underclothes, though the heavy cotton was still damp as they dressed again for the ride back to the barracks. John could feel the sun had scorched his exposed flesh, his tunic collar rubbed his neck, making it sore and encouraging him to keep his head facing forward as they rode up the Alma Road. As they passed the Lord Raglan public house, he wondered whether he would ever take part in a battle that warranted a road to be named after it.

9
PASSING OUT

September 1881

The following day Lt Chilvers formally tested their riding. All the work they had done in the previous weeks was rigorously examined both individually and as a group before he declared them fit to be seen in London. In a small formal parade they were awarded their spurs by Major Milne Home, the Regimental second-in-command.

After packing their few possessions into a baggage waggon, they rode their horses the 26 miles to Albany Street Barracks near Regents Park. It was the longest ride they had done and the recruits swelled with pride as they entered the outskirts of the 'big smoke'. Excited children pointed at them and ran alongside waving. John had not seen the streets of London before as the journey from Edinburgh almost five months previously, had been by train and the capital was wreathed in smog.

The streets were coated in a dark brown dust that rose in a haze around the horses' hooves. The air became increasingly thick, flakes of coal soot descending like volcanic ash, dulling the brick and stone of the buildings to a uniform grey. A sulphurous smell emanating from numerous fires and furnaces was mingled with the odour of rotten fruit and vegetables, stale tobacco and beer, rank cart grease, damp straw, unwashed people and manure.

John had never seen so many people, carriages, and carts and marvelled at how they moved around each other, like a single gigantic ants' nest.

Their new barracks comprised a series of three story blocks set in the space between Regents Park and the railway lines into Euston station. Their new billet was almost identical to the one they had left in Windsor, though the stables were in a separate block.

The recruits chattered excitedly as they gathered by the Regimental Quartermaster's Store to be issued with their full dress uniform, or 'State clothing'. Jackboots, leather breeches, silver cross belt and cuirass were all sized and handed out. Each recruit spent some time having their helmet with its red plume fitted to ensure it would not slip off or be the cause of an unbearable headache. For many this was the reason they had joined the cavalry, though John was not sure they had appreciated how much polishing would be required.

The next four weeks were entirely focussed on learning to ride in full State dress. First they were taught how to clean it to a brilliant shine that clashed with the grime of the surrounding streets. Fitting the saddlery to all to their horses was an art. The black leather head kit with its bright chain and Peninsula bit, stainless steel collar chain and black leather surcingle traps; all 11 pieces of leather and 25 pieces of brass needed meticulous cleaning and polishing, then special care when fitting to ensure that the hours of bulling and buffing were not destroyed. The girth webbing was white rather than blue and required pipe claying. Over the saddle was a black sheepskin flounce, secured by black leather straps with the front arch underneath; they were told this was warm in winter and cool in summer. Looking at one of the soldier servants preparing an officer's charger made John grateful that theirs was relatively simple in comparison.

Now they were allowed stirrups, silver-plated and bar topped with brass slides. All that they had learned about seat and position finally made sense, enabling them to control the horse in the straight jackboots and ensuring they did not rise to the trot.

They concentrated on troop drills in Regents Park and Hyde Park, and in the outdoor riding school. As the day of their passing out parade neared, a Cornet appeared to lead the troop and take part in the final preparations. A Troop Corporal Major (TCM) became involved in preparations and added his voice of displeasure when any mistakes were spotted. John was pleased to see that Cornet Sir John Willoughby was not immune to criticism, though only realised this when he returned to the stable office to pass a message and stumbled across the TCM vigorously 'debriefing' the young officer in private.

When the TCM was satisfied, the Regimental Corporal Major (RCM) watched a rehearsal. John found the RCM's silence gratifying, though suspected any criticism would be provided in the Corporals' Mess. At the end of the week long hours polishing into the night ensured their equipment and uniforms were as perfect as they could possibly be. There was a frisson of nervous tension as the recruits helped each other tighten and adjust their kit in preparation for departure through the gate and into Hyde Park. Cpl's Scott and Robeson fussed over each of them and John realised that the next hour would be as much a final test for them as it was a passing out parade for him.

At the appointed hour the Regimental band struck up and the order to advance was given. As they rode out of the gate and wheeled left to the sound of the slow march of the Blues, John was surprised to see huge numbers of people lining the ride cheering and clapping. His chest swelled with pride, or would have done, had it not been constrained by the brightly polished cuirass. Passing through Green Park and Birdcage Walk they arrived at Horse Guards Parade where a small crowd had gathered. Alfie was an old hand at parades but his ears pricked up nevertheless and he had more bounce in his step than usual. Lieutenant Colonel Burnaby, officer commanding, rode down the two ranks followed by the RCM. He looked at each recruit in turn and occasionally said a few words. He stopped in front of John.

"Trooper Waterston," he said. "I have been hearing good things about you, not least of which is an ability to shoot. Well done on a smart turnout."

"Thank you, Sir."

The inspecting party moved on. John was surprised the Colonel even knew who he was as he had barely seen any officers during their training. Indeed, the subject of officers was rarely raised during conversations; they lived in another world.

10
ABA ISLAND, WHITE NILE, SUDAN
11 August 1881

As expected the 'Ulema had been spreading lies about him, denying he, Muhammad Ahmed, was al Mahdi, and accusing him of spreading false doctrine. What did they know? They were the puppets of the Turkish Khedive and everyone knew that the Colonel Arabi had sent messages to the people of Sudan telling them not to follow the Khedive. As it was written, the time was right for the people of Sudan to rise up against their Turkish Egyptian rulers.

The 'Ulema and the Turkish Egyptian rulers were afraid of his power and would do anything to put him down. Fools. They would bow before him, but first he must show them his power. He had rejected the emissaries from Khartoum and declined to return with them to hear their lies. It was a trap. Now they would be sending their Egyptian soldier puppets to arrest him. He must stand ready, ambush and defeat them. They had no idea how powerful he had become, how many Anṣār he had.

He considered his followers for a moment. Before becoming al Mahdi he had been a Fakir, had taken vows of poverty and worship, and this had brought him fame. Such fame had enabled him to marry well. He carefully selected daughters of Baggara sheiks, men who traded cattle and slaves, and who had thus bought him wealth and even more fame and influence. In accordance with the law he had only married 4 times. This law had proved inconvenient when he needed to marry again, but he had divorced some of his wives when they were no longer needed, to ensure he complied. Yes, he now had wealth and influence and soon, God willing, he would have guns.

Muhammad Ahmed finished placing his 4000 supporters so they were concealed. The steamer with the Egyptian troops would be here soon and he must be ready to receive them.

Later, that day al Mahdi reflected on his good fortune, the hashish dulled the exhilaration but the feeling was there nevertheless. He had won a great victory. Fools! They had sent only 200 men. His followers had driven them back into the river. 120 of those men were now dead and he had their rifles. One of his supporters pulled a rifle from the death grip of an Egyptian soldier's corpse, and pushed the body out into the sluggish current with his foot. To the left the body of one of his Anṣār was pulled from the mud for burial. Yes, some of his supporters were dead, but he had won a great victory and now others would flock to his banner. He watched as the body of his now divorced second wife's brother was wrapped for burial, determination and the surprise at his sudden death still evident on the young man's face.

Al Mahdi must be careful though, he must send out emissaries from amongst his faithful to spread the word, and the word was Jihad. Jihad against the Turkish rulers who had corrupted Islam and who had banned slavery and their way of life. The Turkish Egyptians would send more men against him here, so for now, he must move and build more support. He would fulfil the ancient prophecy. He would march south to Jabal Qadir in the Nuba mountains. In the mountains he would defeat them and his fame would grow and his followers would become more numerous. He was al Mahdi, he would unite all Islam to his single version of the faith.

11
WIMBLEDON COMMON

Returning to the barracks the recruits were able to celebrate their acceptance into the Regiment. On the noticeboard the part one orders showed John as posted to A Troop under the command of Cornet Baillie-Hamilton, the Lord Binning, a fellow Scot who had been commissioned into the Blues less than a year earlier. John was pleased to see that his friends Tom Parris, Harry Evans, Will Mitchell and Donald McLeod were also posted into A Troop and noticed that it appeared to be mainly established with fellow Scots. Their new Troop Corporal Major, Charles Gwinnell, was waiting to welcome them and re-acquaint them with his second, Corporal of Horse Ewan Rogers, the man who had recruited them last April.

A Troop was based at Albany Street Barracks so John, Parris, Evans and Donald were shown to new billets with members of the Troop. John and Parris were soon moved to a room with eight other troopers, their section commander and second. Their 'new' section commander was Cpl Scott, who had a new second in Lance Corporal John 'Jock' McIntosh. Lance Corporal Robeson was staying on with a new intake of recruits.

Once they had removed and carefully stored their State dress they were given leave to relax and take the following day, Sunday, off, too. It was the first time off that they had enjoyed since joining six months before and they were almost at a loss as to what to do.

In their undress uniform, forage cap and swagger stick, that evening they walked out into London in search of somewhere to wind down, and girls to impress. They strutted down Regents Street and into the public houses, but in the nicer, fashionable areas it was clear they were not welcome and they were quickly asked to leave. "This is a reputable establishment, Queen's men or no, we don't want your type in here causing trouble".

Shunned, they gradually made their way into the grimy back streets and alleys looking for somewhere they could drink. Once they found a Pub that seemed to be filled with soldiers, as well as women of negotiable affection, but found they were not welcome there either. Rough looking soldiers who had too much to drink jeered, "look lads, some of the Queen's tin soldiers have been let out for the night."

"Does your Mother know you are out?"

"Better run along home just in case there's a fight. You wouldn't want to break decades of tradition."

John supressed the growing rage he felt with the recollection of Cpl Scott's warning, that the Queen took a very dim view of any of her Household Cavalry caught fighting in public. Others clearly did not operate under the same restrictions and in several bars he saw raised tensions and brawling between soldiers in different Regiments.

They ended up in The Volunteer at Baker Street, which was friendly to the Household Cavalry and hence packed with them. They walked back through Regents Park to the barracks wondering if all the training had been worth it, if they were barely tolerated by the public.

The following day, John, still in uniform, went to church. He had been unable to find a Presbyterian service and attracted by the number of attractive young ladies of the congregation as much as the religious content, he went to the Methodist hall at Hinde Street, known locally as the 'Dutch Oven' due to its distinctive shape. Later he found a temperance society meeting room where he played games, mainly dominoes and draughts, and read the papers. As a 'Blue' he found he was tolerated rather than welcomed, though was gratified by some of the glances he received from young ladies and he resolved to attend more frequently in the hope he could strike up more than a passing acquaintance.

Life as the newest members of 2 section in A Troop was in many ways not much different from life as a recruit. John and Parris were still the outsiders and the lowest of the low so far as the Troop was concerned. They had not been initiated. The following week, as they gradually learned their new routine, the Troop members wound the new members up about their initiation ceremony, to take place in the canteen on Friday night.

"He looks like he has the makings of a future Troop champion that one, Cpl Scott," said Corporal of Horse Rogers nodding at Tom Parris. "A good thick skull and strong neck. He might take your crown."

"Nah, he does not have the teeth for it. I am more concerned about young Evans. Far more determination and stamina that one, and a tough skull," replied Cpl Scott. "How are you getting on finding the subject for the maiden's kiss?"

"Oh, I have found a real looker, and never been touched and no mistake."

Curious, and not a little concerned, the former recruits continued about their work while trying to elicit more information from the other troop members, which they pooled in the evenings.

"You need a strong tongue. Angus Duncan gave me some exercises to try to strengthen it before Friday," said Harry Evans enthusiastically. He demonstrated by sticking his tongue out and then straining to lift a grubby hand. "It all looks a bit odd but is guaranteed to work."

"Work for what?" asked Tom Parris.

"Quite", said John. "I overheard Cpl Scott and CoH Rogers saying Evans here is the only one who concerns Cpl Scott, who is the defending champion. They made no mention of tongues, just about stamina, determination and a thick skull."

"Perhaps the tongue is needed for the maiden's kiss?" suggested Donald McLeod lasciviously. Evans suddenly looked very thoughtful and the others all cheered up considerably.

"Yes, I heard they have apparently found a real looker," said Tom.

"A dollymop?" asked Will Mitchell

"I don't think so. I heard she had never been kissed before."

It was fair to say that when Friday arrived they were none the wiser and their imagination had peaked. Cpl Scott gathered them outside the canteen, formed them in a line and stood them to attention. "Everything I have taught you to date has brought you to this point. If you survive this, you will be fully fledged members of the Troop, one of the band of brothers." He grinned. "Don't worry too much, keep your wits about you and I am sure you will do well. Now, I will march you in to face the president. Form up on LCpl McIntosh. Right turn, quick march."

The canteen had been re-arranged into an arena formed from a ring of chairs and tables upon which the whole troop sat at attention with a mug of porter in their right hand. TCM Gwinnell presided from an armed chair that had been placed on a table overlooking the arena. On one side, on a slightly lesser chair, sat CoH Rogers. The former recruits lined up on LCpl McIntosh facing the TCM. They could not help but see a very pretty girl sat on the table to the TCM's right.

"Who brings these men before me to be initiated?" thundered the TCM.

LCpl McIntosh answered, "I bring them, Troop Corporal Major."

"How dare they see my magnificence before being initiated." The TCM was warming to his role. "Poke out their eyes, damn them." There was a roar of approval and laughter from the troop, but CoH Rogers spoke in the TCM's ear, who feigned surprise.

"It appears this is no longer allowed. Very well, cover their eyes."

Troop members stepped forward behind them and John felt a cloth tied around his head so he could no longer see. The troopers returned to their seats.

"Have they drunk of the bowl of chargers' piss?"

"They have not Troop Corporal Major." LCpl McIntosh's words were almost drowned by laughter, jeers and cries of "shame."

"Then how can they know that their charger is fit to fight in A Troop?" John shuddered slightly at the TCM's words. "Bring forth the chargers cup so they may drink in turn."

To John's right, he became aware that someone had approached Parris and then he heard the sound of someone drinking and then gagging before spraying out whatever they had drunk. "He must finish it," roared the TCM. Silence, then laughter and cheers and then it was John's turn. His nose was pinched so he could no longer smell. A wooden bowl was placed against his lips and tipped until he felt the liquid against his top lip. It was slightly warm. He had no choice but to drink. He steeled himself and opened his mouth. No matter what, he would not spit it out. The liquid filled his mouth and tasted familiar, he guessed at rum and porter and grinned. He finished the cup amidst cheers. So that was the game.

The other recruits drank from the cup of life, some in silent acceptance and, in Harry Evan's case, amidst much gagging and spluttering.

"Now they have drunk, they may kiss the maiden," boomed the TCM. "Maiden, are you willing?"

"I am willing," answered the unseen maiden. John steeled himself again. The induction was getting better, he was going to enjoy this bit. There was a cheer and a few ribald laughs as Parris kissed the maiden, then it was his turn. He felt lips pressed to his, but they were not the warm and willing lips he remembered from the girls back home. And there were bristles and the faintest aroma he did not recognise. He kissed the lips fleetingly and they were removed, as was the blindfold. With a shock he found himself staring into the unseeing eyes of a severed pigs head, its tongue slightly protruding from between its lips. The pretty girl was nowhere to be seen.

The head was taken away and he was motioned to keep silent as it was proffered to Donald McLeod. He must also have suspected something as his kiss was cursory too, though his surprise on seeing the pig was a picture. Harry Evans on the other hand, kissed the 'maiden' very enthusiastically amidst much mirth. Before his blindfold was removed, the TCM, desperately trying to suppress laughter, asked, "Did I see you use your tongue, Trooper Evans?"

Evan's answer of "yes" was almost lost in the cheers and howls of laughter, and his face on having his blindfold removed was something John would remember for many years to come.

"And now, the final trial. Bring forth the spoons," roared the TCM. Two large serving spoons were brought forward. "Now, before the initiates are allowed to compete against the reining master, Cpl Scott, we have a challenger. Trooper Duncan, step forward."

Angus Duncan came forward, flexing his neck, and wearing a serious and determined look. Cpl Scott stepped down from his throne and with LCpl McIntosh carrying the spoons at his side faced off against Angus.

"Gentlemen, select your weapons. Trooper Duncan as challenger, you may select first."

Duncan weighed the spoons carefully, checking them for weight and balance as he would a fine sword, before nodding and selecting a spoon that to John's mind looked identical to the other. He flourished the spoon and the rest of the troop nodded and cheered.

"Gentlemen, take your positions." The 2 adversaries faced off against each other with determined looks.

"Cpl Scott, as defending champion you will strike second. Prepare yourself." Cpl Scott took the second spoon and then stood at the 'at ease' position, hands and spoon clutched behind his back. He then bowed low to Trooper Duncan, and remained bowed, his chest and head parallel to the floor. Duncan placed the spoon between his teeth and bent low until his head was almost touching Cpl Scott's, the heavy spoon dangling toward the floor.

"Ready. Strike!"

Duncan lifted his chest and head, and with the spoon still clutched between his teeth and hands clasped behind his back, brought the spoon down on the back of Cpl Scott's head. There was a soft thud and a roar of approval from the crowd. Cpl Scott rubbed the back of his head. The recruits grinned with relief.

"A fine hit, Trooper Duncan. Cpl Scott, ready, strike!"

Cpl Scott clearly had a better technique and there was a more solid thud as the spoon hit the back of Duncan's head. Duncan made a muffled "ahh" sound and the room erupted with cheers. Duncan hit again, to John's way of thinking, without much improvement. Cpl Scott's second hit was again more solid. Duncan cried out, dropped his spoon and rubbed his head. The bout was over and Cpl Scott remained champion.

"Initiates, prepare. Trooper Duncan, please take them outside and brief them on the finer points of technique. There may be a new champion among them."

The initiates went outside where Duncan gave them a few hints and they drew straws as to who would go first. John drew the short straw and was taken back into the room by John Crook who was to be his second. He liked Crook, he was one of the old soldiers with a 'worn' pockmarked face and a tendency to mother the newer members of the troop.

The two seconds, John Crook and LCpl McIntosh shook hands and then stood by the spoon duellers' sides. The two combatants bowed to each other and then remained bowed. "Trooper Waterston, ready, strike!" The spoon was heavy and John did not find it easy to manoeuvre with any power onto Cpl Scott's head, but the crowd seemed pleased with his attempt.

"Well done lad, that was a fine strike, now, head down and be ready." John Crook seemed to think he had done well. He bent to receive the first strike. He fixed his eyes on a knot in the floor and gripped the spoon with his teeth and lips.

The hit when it came was far harder than he expected, making his eyes water and it was only with effort that he held on to the spoon. He rubbed the back of his head and then on the command, struck again. Better he thought, John Crook agreed and the crowd egged him on. Cpl Scott's second hit was hard, very hard and came with a solid crack. There was no way he could have delivered that much power with his teeth. Was there? It had to be another trick. John dropped the spoon and rubbed the back of his head to groans and cheers and laughter from the Troop. Cpl Scott removed the spoon, grinned at him and shook his hand. "Trooper Waterston, welcome to A Troop. Grab your reward and take a seat." He indicated a chair with a pint of porter on it. John was no longer the outsider, he was part of the family. He grinned and went to his seat while the rest of the section shook his hand and patted him on the back.

Tom Parris was next to duel, and now John was able to relax and see how the game was really played. Parris' hit on Cpl Scott was determined but no better than any of Duncan's or John's attempts. Parris bent to receive the blow, spoon dangling, eyes fixed on the floor. Cpl Scott lifted his head to strike, and as he brought the spoon down, stopped with the spoon slightly to one side. In that moment, LCpl McIntosh brought a second, larger spoon out from behind his back and brought it down on Parris' head with a solid thump. The spoon was concealed behind McIntosh's back in an instant as Parris rubbed his head in disbelief.

John laughed with the rest of the troop each time Parris was hit. Parris conceded defeat after 3 blows and took his seat with a relieved grin. Each initiate lasted 2 or 3 blows before taking their seats. Harry Evans was last to go and approached the challenge with his usual bloody-minded determination. LCpl McIntosh's blows became progressively harder as Evans refused to give in, tears of frustration and pain falling from his eyes onto the wooden floor. The Troop cheered him on with increasing disbelief. Finally, after 6 strikes from the incredulous McIntosh, the TCM took pity on him.

"Trooper Evans! Are you always this daft or are you making a particular effort today?" He grinned at Evan's dismayed face. "You are the most stupidly persistent bastard ever to have played this game. I declare this bout a draw and that you are joint champion. Congratulations, and welcome to the Troop. LCpl McIntosh please show him how the game is played."

Evans' face, when he realised the whole bout was a trick, was a mixture of surprise, shame, embarrassment and a rueful grin. He could not believe he had fallen for it. The recruits had all made it into their new family. They were still the lowest of the low but were now considerably higher than any Trooper in any other Troop.

Military training now started in earnest with a week long exercise on Wimbledon Common during which they would prepare for a Squadron and then Regimental Exercise at Aldershot in October.

John was delighted to discover that he was to continue to ride Alfie. They had become quite attached to each other during the past six months. While Alfie was a little older than normal, John felt that was something they had in common.

Under the direction of Cornet Baillie-Hamilton they practised troop manoeuvre drills, becoming familiar with responding to the trumpeter as one formed body. John noticed that while Lord Binning was in charge he paid a great deal of attention to the advice he was given by TCM Gwinnell and Corporal of Horse Rogers. The Troop was far happier for it.

"Thank God the boss is listening to the TCM", Ted Ankers commented. "Cornet Willoughby in C Troop is so sure his TCM knows nothing he is ignoring everything he says. I popped over to their camp last night and the boys are being run ragged jumping at everything Willoughby says for fear of spending their life in the Guardroom on extra duties if they don't. Things keep going wrong and Willoughby is blaming everyone else. He has threatened to have all his NCOs on a charge if things don't improve, but won't listen to their suggestions. Bloody Zounderkite."

John was becoming familiar with the characters in the Troop and Trooper Ted Ankers was certainly a character. He was the person who seemed to have friends and connections everywhere; people who could provide all manner of hard to find items for a very reasonable price, even in the middle of Wimbledon Common. At the end of each day he would have a quick word with CoH Rogers and then disappear, returning on one occasion with four fresh rabbits. This was just as well as John discovered that administration in the field was not something the cavalry seemed to be particularly adept at. While the horses were supplied with oats and their normal mash, the men had neither equipment nor experience to prepare food, tending to rely on foraging from local vendors to supplement their meagre rations. He wondered how they would fare if the locals were neither willing nor able to feed them.

They camped on the common or on Putney Heath, moving to a new location each night. Each evening they would muster as a troop to debrief on the lessons learned during the day, prepare for the next and allocate troops to tasks for the night. The new Troopers were detailed off with the more experienced men for sentry duty. While there was no enemy threat, there was always the risk that an enterprising member of the public, or worse, a rival unit might be tempted to steal some of their equipment in the night. The loss of a horse or weapon did not bear thinking about.

Ted Ankers roused John at one thirty in the morning. They were camping in the open and in the moonlight John could make out the dark, sleeping forms of his section around him, weapons by their side. He slipped out from under his blanket and put his leather belt and pistol holster on over his tunic. Finally placing his forage cap on his head and picking up his carbine, he followed Ankers towards the picket line where the horses were hobbled and standing silently. He could see Alfie was standing asleep, ears relaxed, head and neck drooping.

John made to start patrolling, but Ankers shook his head and motioned him to stop. "Stand still and use your ears," he said quietly. "Sound carries a long way at night and highlights movement. If you see movement, don't look straight at it, look to one side or other. You can see far more that way."

They stood back to back and listened in silence. After about fifteen minutes Ankers signalled for him to move and they quietly made their way to another position the other side of the picket line. The grassland around them was silver in the moonlight; the trees and bushes, marking the edge of fields, dark and uneven. The night air was cool and damp as autumn approached. A horse coughed, breaking the still, and so human like John was startled for a moment. In the distance they could see a single light in a cottage window and for an instant John longed for the normality of a night in a home surrounded by family. He caught himself; this was his normality now, the Troop his family.

At two thirty he roused LCpl McIntosh, and Ted Ankers returned to his 'pit'. They stood in silence, periodically moving to a new randomly chosen position, and occasionally splitting up. As the hour crept towards three, John noticed the horses move in a way they had not before. The movement was slight, the difference from the previous hour minimal. McIntosh, new on watch, did not appear to have noticed and was standing twenty yards away. John tapped the stock of his carbine with his hand and McIntosh looked towards him at the soft sound. John motioned towards the horses, thumb down, the signal they had been taught to represent 'enemy'. Suddenly on the edge of his vision, John saw movement. Two human shapes moving stealthily towards the nearest sleeping form, about fifteen yards from where he stood. The shapes did not appear to be armed but were clearly up to no good. He realised that with the dark mass of the horses behind him he was invisible to them. Adrenalin heightened his senses and pushed aside any fatigue. He silently moved towards them, McIntosh following and still twenty yards behind. The first of the intruders had made it to the sleeping form of Harry Evans, his kneeling accomplice watching out for guards but looking in entirely the wrong direction.

In a rush, John strode the last two paces and used the butt of his carbine to hit the first man on the side of the head, knocking him senseless. In a continuation of the same movement he drove his knee into the back of the accomplice sending him sprawling into the grass with John's weight and the stock of the carbine against the back of his neck, forcing him down.

"Keep down if you know what's good for you," he growled.

LCpl McIntosh, carbine raised, swept the area looking for additional threats. All was silent and still. Harry Evans, slumber disturbed, sat up and rubbed an eye with the back of his hand. Seeing John and LCpl McIntosh so close he looked around and saw his assailant unconscious by his side.

"Evans, go and wake Corporal Scott, Corporal of Horse Rogers and the TCM and bring them here, quietly," said McIntosh, looking at the unconscious man.

A few minutes later, Scott, Rogers and Gwinnell were inspecting the intruders who had now been tied hand and foot and were sitting looking disconsolate.

"Bloody 'C' Troop out causing mischief" said the TCM quietly. "Well done Cpl McIntosh, Waterston. Evans, go and rouse the Cornet, we have to decide what to do with them."

The TCM then asked the 'C' Troop men what they thought they were up to. It appeared Cornet Willoughby had ordered them to come and 'borrow' a carbine as a joke on Lord Binning. When the Troop commander arrived there was some discussion about a retaliatory raid, but the conclusion was that there was more to be gained from waiting for C Troop to come looking for their missing men. Losing two men was almost as embarrassing as 'losing' a carbine.

"Well done, John," said Cpl McIntosh later. "That was nicely done back there, it's good to know you can keep a cool head about you." John was filled with an inner glow at his Christian name being used for the first time.

First thing in the morning they took the horses to water at Rushmere, one of the many ponds found on the common. Returning to their overnight camp for a light breakfast of bread and cheese, they saw CoH McLaren from 'C' Troop talking to the TCM before riding away.

"Cornet Willoughby can come and clear up his own mess, rather than sending others to do it for him." John overheard the TCM saying to Lord Binning.

They met up with 'C' Troop at the rifle range later that morning. Cornet Willoughby conversed with Lord Binning and, looking distinctly unhappy, retrieved his men. John could see him berating them for being caught as they returned to their lines.

Wimbledon common offered the opportunity to shoot up to one thousand yards, though the shorter, lower velocity carbines were only effective at less than five hundred yards. The range existed through the auspices of the commander in chief, His Royal Highness the Duke of Cambridge who allowed the shot to fall on his lands located behind the butts. All the men were cautioned to keep their shots low as a stray shot over the butts on a previous shoot had narrowly missed the head of a lady pruning the roses in the garden of her villa. "The Duke of Cambridge may be very fond of the Blues, but I really don't want to have to explain it was one of my men who accidently killed someone on his land," said Lord Binning as they prepared to shoot.

Today they were going to shoot a 'falling plate' competition against 'C' Troop. The officer commanding, Lieutenant Colonel Fred Burnaby, would be looking on. The competition involved running as a half section from 300 yards to the 200 yard point then knocking down five metal plates about a foot square before the half section from 'C' Troop could.

John lined up with Cpl McIntosh just behind the 300 yard point. All the carbines were empty, they would only load once they arrived in the firing position.

"Ready," shouted TCM Gwinnell. "Go."

John sprinted over the 300 yard point, his cartridge pouch bouncing on his belt, carbine by his side. Harry Evans was just ahead of him and to his right he could see they were both ahead of the 'C' Troop team. The ground was uneven with tussocks of long grass and rabbit holes forcing him to keep his eyes peeled for trip hazards as he ran.

Arriving at the 200 yard point he dived to the ground, retrieved a round from his pouch and fed it into the chamber. His heart was pounding and he struggled to control his breathing as he pulled the carbine into his shoulder. With no time to make sure of his aim or adjust his position he moved the sights onto the white plate he could just make out in the distance, highlighted against the grass bank that protected the range crew in the gallery. As soon as the sights were on the plate he squeezed the trigger and felt the recoil from the heavy bullet thump into his shoulder. His shot was moments behind Evans's. There was a clang and a thump as the bullet hit the right hand plate and pushed it over.

John reloaded as several more shots rang out and there were a couple more clangs indicating falling plates. Behind him he could hear the rest of the Squadron cheering on the teams. He fired again and was sure he had hit another plate, though with so many other shots he could not be certain. Eject, reload, aim, fire. He worked the carbine like a machine, just missing with his next shot but knocking the final plate down with his fourth.

"Cease fire!" shouted TCM Gwinnell. "'A' Troop win." Looking across, John could see two of the 'C' Troop plates were still standing. They unloaded and walked back to the 300 yard point as the butt party replaced the plates ready for the next round. John enjoyed watching the competition unfold, honours between the two troops being about even. Then he had to shoot again against one of the successful 'C' Troop teams. They won again, this time he only had time to knock over two plates, the rest of the section warming to their task. Then it was down to the final three teams, two of which were from 'A' Troop. In the next round the final 'C' Troop team was knocked out and John was surprised to find himself in the final against a team that included TCM Gwinnell, CoH Rogers and Lord Binning. It was clear they were determined to win.

After the sprint, they all reached the firing point at the same time and each side dropped four plates in the opening volley. TCM Gwinnell reloaded and fired first, with Cpl McIntosh and John less than a second behind. The final plate fell and Lord Binning's team had won; it could not have been closer.

Lord Binning's team was magnanimous in victory; delighted that 'A' Troop had prevailed for the second time that day. The officer commanding was generous with his praise, commending the teams on some fine shooting. It was then that John noticed another senior officer he had not seen before, wearing a Grenadier Guards uniform as Colonel Burnaby's speech drew to a close.

"So I am delighted the standard of shooting is so high, h'yar" said Burnaby looking pointedly at the Guardsman. "You are cavalry, not that cavalry of poverty known as mounted infantry, and have today demonstrated your utility as the elite of Her Majesty's troops. I look forward to demonstrating this to Horseguards in our annual manoeuvres in Aldershot."

"What was all that about?" asked Cpl Scott of the TCM as they returned to Cavalry Barracks.

"I don't know but I aim to find out," replied TCM Quinnell.

12
WINDSOR

'A' Troop returned to Cavalry Barracks in Windsor in preparation for the annual Regimental exercise, after which many of the horses would be sent to Melton Mowbray for the winter. John's maturity and performance at Wimbledon had accelerated his acceptance into the Troop family, particularly by the older soldiers who could make new recruits lives difficult. It helped that Cpl Scott knew him, and Tom Parris, well, and seemed determined to integrate them as quickly as possible but the recruits still felt like outsiders.

John and Parris had moved into the section billet, not far from where they had lived as recruits. Their lives were still full, but there was now a routine and they had a little more time to themselves.

Reveille was at 0630 and the following thirty minutes were spent washing, shaving and folding blankets for inspection. First stables were at 7 when John would muck out and clean Alfie before saddling him for riding exercise and to take him to water, after which he would be fed. At 8 o'clock the section would all breakfast in their billet, with coffee, bread and cheese. Training commenced at 9 with a troop parade on the main square during which any notices and orders would be given. This would be followed by an hour of mounted or foot drill before they were released for school or fatigues. At 1145 they would return to the stables to groom their horses and clean saddles, straps and other horse furniture.

They were released for an hour for lunch at 1pm. This was the main meal of the day where they would consume the bread and three quarters of a pound of stewing beef or mutton they were rationed. This was usually provided in a stew supplemented with vegetables they paid for via 3 pence stopped from their wages of a shilling and tuppence a day. There were very few cooks, minimal equipment and the fuel supplied for cooking was too little to ensure adequate preparation.

At 2pm they reporting to the armoury to draw weapons for shooting or sword practice. This might be combined with more drill, though increasingly shooting was prioritised. Tea was at 4.30 after which they would have the third stables of the day. They were released at 6, though it was often as late as 8pm before they had finished their work.

Room inspections were less regular and rigorous. They ate, relaxed and slept in the billet. The windows were rarely, if ever, opened resulting in a steamy fug on rainy days when wet clothes were hung next to the coal fire to dry. Personal administration was also reduced as the section each paid a penny a day for Trooper Storey's wife, Ivy, to wash their clothes and clean the room. John had not really thought about married life for a soldier.

"Corporal, could I ask you about Ivy?" he asked Cpl Scott when, for a rare moment, they were alone in the billet one evening. "I'm curious about all the other soldiers' wives, and where they live."

"Why, do you have a haybag in mind as the future Mrs Waterston?" Scott chuckled. "You're a dark one. I've not so much as seen you go into town alone, let alone going out on the randy."

John suppressed his embarrassment. "No, nothing like that Corporal. I know Ivy is Trooper Storey's wife, but have not seen many other wives around the barracks. I was just curious as to where they all are." John paused, gauging Cpl Scott for a reaction before continuing; he was not sure whether he was on personally sensitive ground with his section commander. "A few of the older

NCOs have wives and children living in rooms dotted around the barracks, but what about the soldiers?"

"Well, you know that any of us wanting to get married has to ask the officer commanding's permission, don't you?"

John didn't, and shook his head. Cpl Scott looked surprised, but continued. "Well, there are a few reasons for it, but the main one is that there are only so many married quarters available in the barracks so they are allocated by the OC on the basis of rank. Remember it is not just the room, the wives and children are also fed, schooled and doctored at the Regiment's expense. There are other conditions too. You need more than 7 years service, 2 good conduct badges and £5 in the bank."

"So you can't get married unless you are a Corporal of Horse or above?" asked John, sounding surprised.

"I didn't say that" Scott smiled at John's reaction. "Soldier servants to the officers can usually get permission with the support of the officer they are looking after. Trooper Storey is batman to Colonel Burnaby, which is why he was able to marry Ivy and get a room on the floor above us."

"OK, so a handful of soldiers can get married then, if they are selected to be servants," said John. "What about the rest of us?"

"Well, according to your records, you're only 19 so far too young to be interested in settling down," said Scott looking for a reaction from his new trooper. He was far from convinced John was as young as his record stated. "But quite a few of the men have wives out in the town. So long as the soldier is in barracks to do his work, then a blind eye is turned."

At that moment Ted Ankers, Angus Duncan and LCpl McIntosh returned from the Lord Raglan in town, slightly the worse for drink. They must have caught the tail end of the conversation.

"What's up, John?" asked Duncan. "Marriage is for nickeys. What you need is a pretty dollymop to take your mind off that sort of nonsense. I'm sure Ankers can set you up with a nice girl of negotiable affection. Why don't you come into town with us on Friday?"

"That's kind, but I don't drink," John replied. "And the last thing I need is a dose of glim. I think I'll stick to the club. Cocoa, anyone?" He swung the pan over the fire and searched for his huge enamelled mug.

A few of the section, John included, would make regular forays out to the temperance society tea room in the Barracks where they could read the weekly papers, drink tea and play games; mainly cards and dominos with other members of the Regiment. It was often the only chance he had to meet up with their friends from the recruit section and find out about life in the other troops.

The following day, after lunch, there was a football match between the Blues and the 1st Life Guards, played on the green inside the barracks. The game was eagerly awaited, all inter-troop rivalry set aside in the face of the common enemy, the Life Guards. The verandas were crowded with spectators roaring on their team. Late in the second half, with goals even and the game finely poised, the Life Guards were enjoying a few moments on top, threatening the Blues' goal. Colonel Burnaby, dressed for London in a frock coat and tall hat with a cigar in his mouth, came out of the officers' quarters and proceeded slowly across a corner of the ground, apparently oblivious to the fact that a game was in progress. Suddenly, Bates the full back, a gigantic Yorkshireman, charged wildly for the ball and crashed into Burnaby. The impact was terrific and Bates was thrown backwards to the ground as though he had collided with a building. Burnaby's hat and cigar did not move and, acting as though he had not noticed that a collision had taken place, he calmly removed his cigar, smiled and said in his high-pitched voice, "Dear me, I do hope I am not interfering with the game". The crowd roared their delight.

Back in the billet later that afternoon, the section drank tea and discussed the game. The Life Guards had won by the narrowest of margins and, so far as the Blues were concerned, mainly by luck. Ivy Storey had joined them and was sitting with her husband on the long bench nearest the fire. As they finished the all in one stew and supped at their mugs of tea, the conversation turned to the Colonel.

"Is he human?" John Crook asked. "If Bates had run into me there would have been a splat and a Crook shaped hole in the ground covered in studs."

Henry Storey smiled and lit his pipe. "He's human like the rest of us. I'm just not sure he cares to admit it. He has always pushed the boundaries of what is physically possible. You must have heard about the dumbbell he uses to build his strength? It weighs 150 pounds and he can hold it out at right angles from his body for a minute at a time."

Cpl Scott said "And not just one dumb bell at a time. You heard about that incident during the hustings at the Agricultural Hall in Wolverhampton a year or so back?" John and a couple of others looked blank. Events in England did not always get reported in Scotland. Scott continued, "Well, the Colonel was speaking as part of his campaign for the Conservatives to win the seat of Birmingham from the Liberals, and was relaying his experiences in India and Kandahar."

Storey chipped in. "He stood no chance of course, Joseph Chamberlain was far too strong, but the Conservatives selected him and he gave them a really good run for their money."

Scott resumed his story. "So the Colonel has his speech memorised and is determined to give it, but the audience is rowdy and some at the back start poking fun at his accent. All those 'h'yars' and 'lawdidaws' that the officers are so fond of. Well, the Colonel is having none of that, so identifies a couple of the hecklers at the back and with a big smile calls for them to be brought forward. The crowd sensed some fun so they oblige and these 2 men are pushed to the front. The Colonel bends down from the stage, grabs both of them by the collar and, holding them at arms length so everyone can see, hoiks them up on to the stage and carries them to the back saying, 'Sit there, little man, and you, little man, sit there'. Well, the audience loved it and let him give his speech, in no doubt that he is not an easy man to intimidate."

Amid much mirth and not to be outdone, Storey said, "It was before my time but there was a great story about Burnaby and a couple of ponies in the Windsor officers' mess?"

Seeing he had their attention, Storey continued. "Well, a horse dealer had come into possession of a couple of miniature Shetland ponies that were of interest to Her Majesty, so she summons him to Windsor. The officers heard about this and before he has been to the castle, asked to see the ponies too. They invited him in to the mess for lunch and, while he was eating, a couple of the Cornets thought it would be a great joke to coax the ponies up to Burnaby's room on the first floor."

"Horses in the Officers' Mess?" Tom Parris was incredulous.

"Oh yes," said Cpl Scott. "It is positively encouraged by the Duke of Cambridge. They have been known to use the billiard tables and wing back chairs to set up steeple chases through the ante rooms."

"But what about the damage?" Parris asked.

"The Officers pay for it all out of their mess bills." There was a hint of sadness in Cpl Scott's words. Despite his ability, upbringing and desire to be an officer, he knew he could never afford it. "It is just one reason they say you need £500 a year on top of your wages to be commissioned into the cavalry. The officers also have to pay for their horses, equipment and servant's wages.

"But, sorry Henry, we interrupted your story. The Cornets have led the ponies upstairs."

Storey continued. "Well, there is the Colonel, sitting at his desk and his door ajar as usual when these ponies push the door open with their noses and walk in, bold as brass while the Cornets and several of the other officers loitered outside his door, waiting for the explosion."

"Did he explode?" asked John Crook. "I would have done if I was the Colonel and was cheeked like that."

"He was actually a Captain at the time, not that it makes a difference," replied Storey. "But he has a great sense of humour and I am sure would have played similar pranks when he was a Cornet. So there was a moment's silence and then he laughed, and all the other officers piled into his room to much general amusement.

"The trouble is that while they had been happy to trot up the stairs, nothing would convince the ponies to go down again. The horse dealer couldn't get them down either. Carrots and apples were fetched from the kitchens to induce them but they merely added to the mess the ponies had already made in Burnaby's room and," Storey paused momentarily, labouring the word, "the Mess landing."

Angus Duncan laughed with the others. "I can picture it now, the ponies running around the mess in panic. They must have been cacking themselves."

Storey smiled. "Too right. They were not alone in being rather panicky. The thing was that they were running out of time for the audience with the Queen, and the Colonel, sitting calmly at his desk made it clear the Cornets would have to explain to her why she was unable to see the ponies. He told them she would not be amused. As the hour approached, the dealer and the Cornets became increasingly desperate. Burnaby watched them squirm to the last minute, then simply picked the ponies up, one under each arm, and carried them downstairs as if they were cats."

They sat in stunned silence for a moment contemplating the sight, and the feat of strength.

"I get it now," said John Crook. "Far better than an explosion. Those Cornets sure learned their lesson."

"And that is how men become legends," said Cpl Scott. "There is more to him than strength. He speaks about 7 languages, flies balloons for fun, and will do practically anything to irritate the Russians."

"That's true," said Storey. "In the action he fought with Valentine Baker alongside the Turks a couple of years back, the Russians were so fed up with him they issued an order that any British soldier over 6ft tall was to be shot on sight."

"And he's ours, a true Blue," said LCpl McIntosh. "The bloody Life Guards don't have any officers like him."

13
POLITICS

Albany Street Barracks, October 1881

It was late and the other officers and the mess staff had retired for the night. Major David Milne Home MP watched his officer commanding, Lieutenant Colonel Fred Burnaby, light a cigar from the one remaining gas lamp and return to his chair. Burnaby had just returned from his dinner at the Junior Carlton Club and subsequent conversations at the Marlborough. They sat alone by the fireplace in the Albany Street mess lounge, silently watched by the portraits of disapproving long dead cavalrymen; talking shop was banned in the mess. The clock in the hall struck one thirty.

The cigar glowed red in the dim light as Burnaby drew deeply. Milne Home was curious as to what his OC had learned.

"I think we can safely say, David, that your intelligence has been corroborated," said Burnaby through a cloud of smoke. "With regard to both the size, and more particularly the cost, of the Army, Lord Randolph Churchill is loudly criticising Gladstone's Liberals and quietly engineering a war with his own front bench for not being critical enough.

"While I can understand the concerns about our ability to afford our armed forces, if he succeeds in splitting the Conservatives and reducing opposition we can only assume that the Navy and Army will continue to battle for an ever declining allocation of funds from the Treasury.

"Now that Gladstone's Liberals are back in power, Army reform is back on the cards and consolidation of the Foot Regiments will continue with the Secretary of State for War and Sir Garnet Wolseley pushing hard in the face of opposition from the Duke of Cambridge, the conservative front bench and the rest of those Wolseley calls 'Wellington's men'. Once they have consolidated the Infantry there is a risk they will try the same with the Cavalry. If you can buy 4 infantry Regiments for the cost of one heavy Cavalry Regiment, how long do you think it will be before questions are asked about Regiments that have not been deployed since 1815?"

Burnaby paused to draw again on his cigar and gauge reaction. He realised that his second in command was in a difficult position. Milne Home had been re-elected Conservative MP for Berwick-upon-Tweed at the 1880 elections. It had been a close run thing, Milne Home had only been re-elected after the original result was declared void and a by-election called a few months later. In the traditionally frugal Scottish Lowlands his success had in part been due to public recognition of the need for austerity at the War Office. Now that austerity had the potential to threaten the Regiment he had served in for almost 20 years. It almost made Burnaby glad that his own audacious attempt to dislodge Joseph Chamberlain from the Liberal constituency of Birmingham had failed. He had come closer than any other Conservative though and actually increased their share of the vote in Birmingham, while it had declined in the rest of the country.

Milne Home frowned, both at the content of the speech, but also the fact that talking shop was breaking mess etiquette. "The Regiment can of course count on the support of the Royal Family, but that does not make us immune from the effects of reform, Colonel. Just because it would be uncomfortable for the Prime Minister to present plans to amalgamate Her Majesty's Household Cavalry, does not mean that he wouldn't. Her Majesty already complains that he addresses her as he would a public meeting."

"It is an outrageous suggestion, but I agree," replied Burnaby. "Gladstone is a Russian appeasing menace whose policies are surely aimed at a peace dividend. We need to ensure we are not turned into a bargaining chip. We cannot underestimate the enemy, or their potential to disrupt the status quo."

"Agreed, Colonel" said Milne Home. "We are heavy cavalrymen first and foremost. Heaven forbid they suggest our use as that 'cavalry of poverty', mounted infantry."

Burnaby nodded. "We must continue to demonstrate why we are the elite Regiment in Her Majesty's Army; in addition to sword work and massed charges let us redouble our shooting training and introduce light cavalry tactics, too."

Milne Home was horrified. "Shooting? Patrolling? Whatever next? Fighting on foot?"

Burnaby responded with a fierce smile. "We need to surprise those who might suggest we don't offer value for money and place us in the vanguard if Wolseley creates a new expeditionary force. When we prove our worth abroad, Gladstone and Childers will have no ammunition at all, and we will have avoided the need to fight in Parliament.

"We need to be careful though, old mutton chops would have an apoplectic fit if he thought we were acting in anything other than the finest traditions of the Household Cavalry. Heaven forbid introducing professionalism to the Regiment when, in his view, enthusiastic amateurism and sporting prowess has done us splendidly for centuries!"

Milne Home, grimaced at the reference to the Duke of Cambridge. Had Burnaby really not learned that the Commander in Chief had no sense of humour? Experience told him that he would never be able to joke at the Duke's expense. You never knew who might be listening. Burnaby really had gone too far. He simply did not seem to understand what it meant to be an officer in the Blues. After all these years feigning disinterest in actual soldiering like the best of them, now he was in command he appeared to want to turn his back on years of tradition and actually introduce professionalism into the Regiment. The man really did not understand. The last thing they should do was compete with the rest of the British Army, they might lose, and then where would they be? He changed the subject. "An expeditionary force? Was there any talk about Egypt, Colonel? What is the outcome from the mutiny in the Egyptian Army last month?"

"Ah, depending upon who you talk to, some good news for Gladstone's policy of non-involvement in Egyptian affairs," replied Burnaby. "The latest from our man in Egypt, Consul General Malet, is that the mutinous Colonel Arabi, having had his demands met, is speaking in terms of moderation, calmness and conciliation. On the other hand, I have spoken with my friend, Val Baker, who is serving with those intimately acquainted with the politics in the region, and he sees this as the calm before the storm."

Milne Home grimaced again. Valentine Baker was not someone mentioned in polite company. He was the former commanding officer in the 10th Hussars who the Queen had insisted be dismissed from her service after conviction for indecent assault on a young lady in a railway carriage. Even his friend, the Duke of Cambridge had been unable to save him. It really was too much; Burnaby would need to be sent to Coventry, again. He would speak with his likeminded fellow field officers. There was little point talking with the junior officers, they were too inexperienced to yet understand the finer points of being an officer in the Blues, and all worshipped Burnaby.

14
ANNUAL MANOEUVRES

October 1881 brought the final exercise of the year, with the Regiment moving to the huge tract of open land, spreading south west from Lightwater through Pirbright, to Aldershot. The training was similar to the troop exercise on Wimbledon common, and at a much larger scale with infantry, artillery and engineers all involved.

The Blues manoeuvred over the gently rolling grassy hills that were criss-crossed by sandy tracks and interspersed with thickets of gorse, heather and copses of pine. Occasionally they would pass near small hamlets and John proudly ignored the small boys and admiring girls who raced to vantage points where they could watch the cavalry thunder over the soft ground. This was part pride and part practicality. The horses were excited to be away from the barracks and in the company of so many, while riding in full equipment Alfie was now carrying over 23 stone and he approached jumps differently. John needed to maintain his concentration. The last thing he wanted to do was fall off and let the Troop down in front of the entire Regiment.

Administration in the field was better than it had been on Wimbledon Common. The officers dined on mess silver in a large tent, waited on by the mess staff and their soldier servants, while the soldiers collected food, cooked and prepared centrally by the commissariat. Ted Ankers, though, continued to make his own private arrangements and carried a small cook set that he used to make tea and even delicious smelling rabbit stews whenever they stopped long enough to light a fire. Where he sourced all the ingredients was a mystery, though John did see him setting snares for the rabbits. "Any fool can be uncomfortable," he said. John watched with interest and resolved to buy his own set when he returned to Windsor.

The Troop revelled in the change of routine and the freedom they felt when released from the main body to carry out reconnaissance patrols to search out the enemy, this time played by the Guards and the Royal Dragoons.

Once again, there was an emphasis on shooting and, according to the older soldiers, the intensity of the exercise was higher than normal. However, this did mean that John was able to demonstrate his consistent accuracy to the senior officers and, together with a few other troopers, was rewarded with the presentation of the crossed rifles badge of a marksman.

Inter troop rivalry was at fever pitch with some Troop commanders competing fiercely under a thin veneer of indifference while others remained indifference personified. The change was the subject of considerable discussion as the soldiers sat around their campfire drinking cocoa in the evenings.

To the casual observer, all the officers maintained the traditional façade of a cavalry officer, a proud, dashing gentleman of leisure. For the Household Cavalry, who had not been in action or even abroad since Waterloo over sixty-five years before, war was unlikely and soldiering a sporting pastime that enabled them to ride and shoot while wearing fancy uniforms that impressed the Ladies. For some officers, soldiering was something a gentleman should do, ideally in a proud and historic Regiment, to occupy a few years before settling down to a life on their estates.

In the past ten years however, there was an increasing emphasis on professionalism. To the consternation of senior members of the Royal family, such as the Duke of Cambridge, officers could no longer purchase their commissions and even had to pass tests to be accepted into the Royal Military Academy at Sandhurst.

"You can put them into one of two camps," said Cpl Scott leaning forward. He pulled a smouldering stick from the camp fire and used it to light his clay pipe. He turned to look at John McIntosh. "Officers who see soldiers and soldiering as a distraction from the serious business of polo, racing, hunting, shooting and generally impressing women. And officers who enjoy all that but want to be professional soldiers too."

"So which camp would you put our Troopy in then?" asked Angus Duncan. "He seems to be taking it all pretty seriously to me."

"Yes, his Lordship seems keen to learn the trade and takes more than a passing interest in us," replied Cpl Scott.

"He actually appears to listen to what the TCM is advising him," said Cpl McIntosh. "Which is more than can be said for some."

"Which camp would you put Cornet Willoughby in then?" asked Robert Laidlaw. "He seems to be taking it seriously too, but I don't think he is in the same camp as Lord Binning."

"That's true," said Angus Duncan. "He listens to nobody but himself on the grounds that he knows best. The man's an idiot."

"Careful, 'Trooper' Duncan," said Cpl McIntosh. "That sort of talk would have got you flogged last year, especially by men with influential families. Now that they can't order that, you would be stuck in the guardhouse over Christmas. You may have a point though. Perhaps there is room for a third camp containing officers who want to be professional but haven't the foggiest idea how, and are too arrogant to ask."

Changing the subject, Ted Ankers asked "So what is with all the shooting and recce patrolling rather than our traditional shock and awe of sabre rattling charges? I joined the Heavies to cut people in half not shoot holes in them from half a mile away."

"I overheard some of the officers asking the same question," said Robert Laidlaw. "Since when does Heavy cavalry get close enough to the enemy to need to use a carbine, without being asked to charge?"

"Yeah," said Robert Gibson. "I understand why we might need to use a pistol if we fall off while hacking too enthusiastically at the enemy, but these carbines kick like a mule with a burr up its backside, and I can barely hit the butts let alone the target." He looked at John. "How you manage to hit the bull all the time is beyond me. It's unnatural."

John smiled at the complement. "Just lucky I guess, but you are the best shoeing smith in the Regiment and I know who the officers value more." He paused and looked back at Robert Laidlaw. "Laidlaw, did you happen to overhear what the officers speculated the answer to be? Why all the shooting and patrolling?"

Laidlaw paused to think. "Well, they were saying that a cavalryman costs about four times more than an infantryman."

"Quite right too, we are reassuringly expensive, a sure sign of quality" said Angus Duncan. He puffed his chest out and felt his bicep like a circus strongman.

Laidlaw smiled with the others and continued, "and that some of the politicians are asking why that extra money should be spent on cavalry who haven't been used since Waterloo, and who are only any good for parades."

"Suggesting they want to get rid of us?" asked Tom Parris.

"No, it's those politicians posturing again" said McIntosh. "They could not get rid of us. Her Majesty would never allow it."

The section nodded agreement, as one, indignant at the very suggestion.

Cpl Scott responded. "That may be, but who are we to know what game is being played?

"With the Empire so large now, and the British Army so stretched trying to pacify it all, they might want to send in the Household Cavalry to save the day. Colonel Burnaby, is well connected and knows what he is about. He wants to show off our shooting and ability to be used in a recce role, as well as being heavy cavalry to demonstrate our utility. He is making the point that while we may be more expensive than an infantryman, we are far more valuable to a commander, too. He is showing we can be used as mounted infantry, light cavalry and heavy cavalry."

He paused to let this thought sink in. "This is purely speculation, but I have had heard talk of them creating an expeditionary force to be sent to calm trouble spots."

"They won't send us abroad," said Ted Ankers. "It costs them too much to transport the horses."

"That's true," said Scott. "Cost is a factor, as is distance. Horses don't travel long distances by ship and still retain their condition at the other end. And if we are sent without our mounts then not even you could find hundreds of battle trained 16 hand chargers capable of carrying our great weight in the country we are invading."

"So that means they must be planning for us to fight the French again. Hurrah!" joked Angus Duncan amidst chuckles.

15
LURED TO WATER
Jabal Qadir, South Sudan, 9 Dec 1881

Muhammad Ahmad, al Mahdi, smiled. It was a great victory and almost 300 Turkish Egyptians lay dead around him. There were over 100 prisoners and he now had another 400 rifles. The soldiers had thought to surprise him with a night march and dawn attack, but the local people had warned him of their approach. Knowing they would be thirsty, and all discipline would be lost when they saw water, he had laid the ambush at these wells.

The battle had gone as he had planned, his followers charging from their concealed places to overwhelm and hack down the soldiers before they could reform and defend themselves.

Another prisoner was brought before him and forced to kneel. He could declare allegiance to al Mahdi and do God's work on earth, or he could meet God. The choice was offered and made.

So it was to be the latter. Al Mahdi looked at the headless corpse with a feeling of? He searched his drug-dulled soul for a feeling; nothing, it was irrelevant. It would be good for his followers, who had surrounded him during the battle, to see that he had fought alongside them. He wiped his newly bloodied sword on his garments and proudly paraded through the battlefield giving orders for the dead to be buried in their clothes. The weapons and ammunition were piled and then issued to his most trusted followers, to be kept to further God's will, al Mahdi's will. He was al Mahdi.

16
CHRISTMAS 1881

Christmas Day was coming amidst much expectation and excitement amongst the men, for whom it represented as close to a day off as possible, given there was still the need to look after the horses.

Following the Regimental exercise many of the horses and three of the eight Troops had been sent away to winter in Melton Mowbray. The shorter daylight hours limited training and riding opportunities so the workload was reduced considerably.

"Where have all the officers gone?" John asked Cpl Scott one evening. "We don't see much of them, other than the occasional inspection, but I haven't seen the Cornet for weeks."

"Oh, most of the officers take 5 months leave a year," replied Cpl Scott. "Lord Binning will be hunting, shooting and fishing on his estates in Scotland. Some are off to visit sunnier climes like South Africa and countries around the Mediterranean: Turkey, Italy, North Africa, places like that."

"It's a tough life but someone has to do it," said Angus Duncan, taking a swig of tea out of a huge mug.

"Some go abroad in search of action and adventure," replied Cpl Scott. "You will recall Colonel Burnaby has used his annual leave to learn new languages and cultures and generally cause mischief for the Russians. Three years ago he was determined to pay the Russians a visit on the basis that they had specifically banned him from their country. He tried to cross the border from Turkey, but was caught up in the Russian invasion of Turkey instead. He ended up fighting alongside Valentine Baker, who commanded a division in the Turkish Army.

"Valentine Baker?" asked John. "The colonel who was fined £500, thrown out of the army and spent a year in prison for trying to kiss a young lady he did not know on the railway train?"

Surprised, Scott turned to John. "That story made it up to Kirkcaldy then did it?"

"Well, as a Railway guard I was interested," John replied slightly defensively.

"It was a rather strange case. The newspapers made much of it, but nobody knows what really happened because Colonel Baker refused to allow her to be cross examined," said Cpl Scott. "According to someone I know in the 10th Hussars he was a cracking commanding officer though. When he was released from prison he had to join the Turks and was offered divisional command."

"I think I heard something about that," said John Crooks. "When the Russians attacked through the Balkans, Baker was ordered to provide the rearguard and was denied reinforcements despite being outnumbered ten to one."

"I think it was closer to 20 to one," said Cpl Scott. "Anyway, Baker fought with great skill, determination and personal courage and they won the day. Burnaby and his soldier servant, Radford were with him throughout the retreat. The cold was intense, rations were minimal and it was so cold some nights 40 men would freeze to death. They finally made it back through Greece where Baker and Burnaby were poisoned with arsenic at dinner with an Archbishop and were only saved by the skills of English doctors."

"What happened to Radford?" asked John. "After that kind of adventure I imagine he'd had enough."

"You could say that," said Cpl Scott. "He contracted Typhus during the retreat and died at the Artillery Barracks in Dover less than 2 days after returning. The Colonel was devastated. Radford had been his closest companion through years of adventures and they had saved each other's lives on numerous occasions."

The men sat in silence before John asked, "Did Radford have a family?"

"He did," said Cpl Scott. "Colonel Burnaby set Mrs Radford up in business, got two of the children into schools and found a place in service with a good family for the eldest girl."

"What of the Colonel? We see rather more of him than normal, did his adventure in Balkans cure his desire for action?" asked Laidlaw.

Cpl Scott considered a moment. "According to Storey the birth of Burnaby's first child, a boy, last May has rather curtailed his trips abroad. His main interest at the present seems to be as an aeronaut. He has decided that the next great adventure is to be the first person to cross the English Channel by air and is currently searching out a suitable balloon before the bloody French can successfully cross."

"Someone is mad enough to attempt it every year," said Cpl McIntosh. "However, rather than talk about officers floating about the countryside in bags filled with nothing but gas, I want to see how heavy your dimmocking bags are. Duncan, if yours is still filled with nothing but air you are going to have to ask the TCM to place you on stoppages."

"Quite right," said Robert Laidlaw. "Last Christmas your contribution to the section pot was barely enough to pay for the bung in the ale cask and you spent the day drinking at our expense."

"Come on! Let's be seeing them," said Cpl Scott.

The dimmocking bags, carefully sewn over the course of a couple of evenings in early November, were brought out and placed on the table. The contents counted, and a couple of the section admonished for failing to save enough, discussion turned to preparation for the festivities themselves. While they talked Ted Ankers brought out sheets of coloured paper, string, glue and a pair of scissors. Cpl Scott was on the verge of asking where these items had all been sourced before deciding that he might not like the answer.

There followed a discussion about suitable decorations and, following a brief but amusing competition, it was discovered Tom Parris had the artistic ability to draw shapes for others to cut out. Several evenings were then spent creating paper chains and decorative patriotic shapes of rose, thistle, shamrock and crowns, to be suspended from strings on the wall. While the creation of a suitable ambience for the day itself was important, ensuring the section, and Angus Duncan in particular, stayed in of an evening rather than spend money and cause trouble in town, was the primary benefit. The barracks was in fact unusually quiet with the entire Regiment all on their best behaviour to avoid any reason to be charged. The last place anyone wanted to be was in the guardroom over Christmas.

Three days before Christmas day, TCM Quinnell entered the barrack room as the section was preparing their uniforms and equipment for the Christmas parade and service. The smell of beeswax and boot black challenged metal polish for supremacy. Brightly bulled boots and white leather gauntlets, freshly pipeclayed, stood immaculate by each bed. Sparkles of gaslight chased each other across the walls and the faces of the men as they burnished the gleaming helmets. A tin lid clattered to the floor as the men stood, almost as one.

"As you were chaps," said the TCM, and they returned to their seats. "Our worthy Captain has asked what you will have for your Christmas feast? Plum pudding of course; game or venison is out of the question, so what is it to be?"

The question was traditional and expected, the debate that followed likewise. Beef and mutton were swiftly discounted as everyday fare with the result that they eventually settled for two geese and a couple of legs of pork. They were also to be given a quart of porter each so Cpl Scott accompanied the TCM and the other section commanders to the Royal brewery in Peascod Street. There they were able to negotiate the purchase of a 24 gallon barrel of the dark brown bitter for each section.

Official duty over, Cpl Scott met up with Ted Ankers and the contents of the dimmocking bags. The couple spent a happily productive hour with some of Ankers' connections to procure chestnuts, whisky, brandy, oranges, apples, flour, tobacco and new clay pipes. These were brought back to the room and secreted about the place ready for the preparations to begin in earnest the following day.

Saturday 24th December dawned cool, and, standing in the frigid air, the men gently steamed from their exertions cleaning the stable block in double quick time. The focus today was on preparations for Sunday. All the promised ingredients were collected from the cookhouse and recovered to the barrack room where all hands were turned to making stuffing, puddings and mince pies. Ted Ankers' ability in the cooking department set him apart but every other man had a role drawn from the hat, whether festivity related or finishing the preparation of equipment for the parade.

Fruit was cleaned and stoned, suet chopped, breadcrumbs and pastry made. The hated meat ration was minced and mixed with fruit and brandy before being added to the pastry that Ankers had made and rolled out. More fruit and brandy was added to the suet pudding mixture that was constantly being stirred or tested by boot-blackened fingers. Tom Parris spent much of his time gathering firewood or running errands, at one crucial point having to dash to the canteen to acquire more allspice for the mince.

Clean towels were turned into pudding cloths into which the mixture was placed for each man. The corners were then gathered and tied before all being taken to the canteen to place them in the mighty bubbling copper caldron. John Crook drew the short straw, 'man of time', and was tasked with watching the caldron bubble until morning, though he was provided with a large jug of beer to comfort him through the night.

Finally, before retiring to bed, they all decorated the barrack room with the paper chains and patriotic symbols. Liberally draping them above the fireplace and around the windows and gas pendants, by the time they had finished the barrack room was transformed.

Christmas day dawned without reveille being blown. The men luxuriated in bed until 15 minutes before stables. At a quarter to six, Ivy Storey entered the room with a bottle of whisky and dispensed a dram for each of them, starting with Cpl McIntosh as the eldest. The youngest and last to receive, Tom Parris, was unusually quiet as his whisky was poured. Ivy diagnosed the problem almost instantly.

"Homesick, eh?" she said quietly. "Well, you're not the first, certainly won't be the last and are in good company today. It might help if you consider the Regiment your family now. They certainly know how to celebrate Christmas."

After stables the men changed into their blues for the church parade. Full state dress, with cuirass and swords, was fortunately not the order of the day, significantly reducing the time it took them to change and prepare. They paraded on the main square with plumed helmets, silver cross belts and overall trousers that mainly covered their best riding boots. Marching north out of the barracks to the Holy Trinity Garrison and Parish church John reflected on how different this Christmas was from his last, at home in Scotland. He wondered what the girls would make of him now in his best uniform, and his eyes searched for pretty faces in the crowds that lined the streets as they passed the silent Lord Raglan public house.

Ted Ankers and Robert Gibson remained in the barrack room to prepare the feast. Immediately after stables they had collected the meat from the canteen and now this was being roasted on an improvised spit above the fire. Three bedframes had been upended, covered with blankets and strategically positioned to throw heat back on the meat. Gibson, dripping with sweat, was tasked with regularly ducking inside the blanket tent to rotate the spits. Ankers had acquired 2 additional clean sheets to act as a tablecloth for the barrack room table and this was now set ready for the meal. Ankers was now in the cook-house supervising the puddings, preparing vegetables, and baking the mince pies and stuffing.

Returning after the church parade the section quickly changed back into their working clothes to feed and water the horses. John and Tom Parris then went to the Corporals' Mess with a wheelbarrow to collect the barrel of porter and carry it up the stairs to the room, mouths salivating at the delicious smells now emanating forth.

Finally, all the preparation and work was done. The men assembled in the barrack room, dressed in their overalls and anxiously awaiting permission to proceed with the festivities. At the due hour, Captain Brocklehurst, who had almost certainly upset Colonel Burnaby in some way, entered the room with the TCM. To John, Captain Brocklehurst looked slightly uncomfortable; as though he feared the men all knew whatever transgression had resulted in his being made orderly officer on this of all days.

"Merry Christmas 'A' Troop," he said, his eyes scanning the room and taking in all the decorations. He smiled and his face took on a thin veneer of bewilderment. "A fine display of decorations. I particularly like the pictures of broomsticks crashing into a bat, and the elephant heads, though I confess to being at a loss as to their relevance to Christmas."

Tom Parris, outrage overcoming inhibition, blurted out. "They're patriotic thistles and shamrocks, sir!"

Captain Brocklehurst's smile broadened as the TCM and the men laughed. "Of course they are, I can see it now, amazing likeness, well done." He paused. "Any complaints?"

There was a chorus of "No, Sir" and then the eldest Trooper, Robert Laidlaw stammering and blushing at being the centre of attention, thanked the Captain for his kindness and wished him a Happy Christmas, and many of them, on behalf of all the men. As the sound of three cheers for the Captain died away, Brocklehurst made his escape to the next barrack room.

The bung was removed from the barrel and the dark beer poured into a pail set on the hearthstone. This was then decanted into pint basins. Meanwhile, the feast was served. The table and each plate groaned under the weight of goose, pork, vegetables, porter and plum pudding. The section took their places at the table, Cpl Scott at the head, next to Robert Laidlaw, with John at the foot as the most junior present. John felt a pang of guilt thinking of Tom Parris, who had drawn the short straw for the Troop and was now on watch in the stables. A minimum establishment from the other Troops was on guard and fire picket duty.

Cpl Scott broke the expectant silence. "John, Grace if you please."

John thought of home and in his best highland accent said, "Some hae meat and canna eat, And some wad eat that want it; But we hae meat, and we can eat, Sae let the Lord be thankit."

Cpl Scott looked at John with approval and in his finest voice of command. "Section, draw swords," and after the briefest pause, "Charge!"

They ate without speaking; all concentration was on the feast of the year. In John's case it was the feast of a lifetime; he had never experienced anything so delicious. He had been brought up in the Presbyterian community where faith brought redemption and the only form of worship was as defined in the bible, specifically in the Book of Psalms. Christmas and Easter celebrations were inventions of the Catholic Church and, in the view of the members of his, and most other Kirks, unbiblical. Throughout his life Christmas day had been no different from any other Sunday. Regardless of the religious context, John reflected that in his family's case, poverty prohibited feasting.

After 20 minutes of fierce assault, the men surrendered, too stuffed to eat all the plum pudding, which was removed to a shelf for later.

John carefully prepared a plate of pork, goose, vegetables and plum pudding. Accompanied by LCpl McIntosh, who carried a basin of beer, packet of tobacco and new clay pipe, they walked down to

Tom Parris in the unusually silent stables. The horses turned to look at them as they walked down the stalls and Alfie nuzzled John as he passed. "Happy Christmas, Tom," said McIntosh. "All well?"

"Yes, Corporal." Parris had eyes only for the plated feast and set about it with the same relish as the rest of the section only minutes before. John kept him company while LCpl McIntosh satisfied himself that the horses were in fine fettle and then returned to the barrack room.

When John returned to the room with the empty plate an hour later he found the beds, folded into divans, had been drawn up around the fire. The section were merrily tucking into whisky, brandy and mince pies, while chestnuts roasted in a large frying pan on the fire.

Later, as dusk descended, Ted Ankers prepared a bowl of currants and warm brandy. John, who had otherwise eschewed spirits, reached for one of the delicious fruits.

"Not so fast, John," said Ankers, slapping his hand away. "They are not ready yet, for it is time to introduce you to the game of 'Flap dragon'." The men all grinned and ushered him to a seat at the head of the table. As one, they began to chant as Ankers lit the brandy and reverently carried the bowl, wreathed in an eerie blue flame, to the table.

"Here he comes with flaming bowl, don't he mean to take his toll, Snip! Snap! Dragon!

Take care you don't take too much, be not greedy in your clutch, Snip! Snap! Dragon!

With his blue and lapping tongue, many of you will be stung, Snip! Snap! Dragon!

For he snaps at all that comes, snatching at his feast of plums, Snip! Snap! Dragon!

But Old Christmas makes him come, though he looks so fee! fa! fum! Snip! Snap! Dragon!

Don't 'ee fear him but be bold — Out he goes his flames are cold, Snip! Snap! Dragon!"

As they chanted, they grinned and motioned to John to take some currants and pop them into his mouth.

"You have to be joking," said John, horrified.

Amidst much mirth, the men shook their heads and with even greater enthusiasm repeated the chant.

"Go on, hurry up before it goes out," said Cpl Scott.

John took note of the final line of the chant and boldly reached into the blue. As his friends cheered, he grasped a couple of flaming currents with his fingers and popped them into his mouth. They were not as hot as he had feared, but he could smell that the hairs on the back of his hand were singed.

His initiation complete, the rest of the section tucked in and John watched with amusement as each, by turns, plucked at the flaming currants. Devilish flames curled around their lips as they closed their mouths.

Everyone laughed as Tom Parris cried out and hastily drank from his basin of beer. "No more than three at a time!" he gasped, fanning air into his mouth.

Despite the day there were still duties to perform. The more sober soldiers, John and Parris included, carried out the evening stable under the direction of Cpl Scott.

Later, the plum puddings were finished off and the men told stories and sang around the fire. The songs began patriotically with "Rule Britannia" and the National Anthem, but later became quieter and more soulful - "The Soldiers Tear", "There came a Tale of England", "Shells of the Queen" and "Ben Bolt".

John retired to bed at midnight, feeling more than ever that Ivy was right; he had a new family.

17
ASSASSIN

Windsor, 2 March 1882

Gordon Wilson nudged his friend Leslie Robertson and indicated the crowd by Windsor & Eton Station. "What do you think is going on there?"

Robertson shrugged, "Her Majesty returning from London?"

The two 17 year olds smiled at each other and decided that a sight of the Empress was worth being late for classics. In their top hat and tailcoats they edged their way to the white picket fence at the front of the crowd. Around them the crowd swelled and more Eton College boys joined them. Gordon hooked his rolled umbrella on the fence and looked to his right for a glimpse of the waiting Royal carriage. A large man in his mid thirties, with a bushy moustache, unkempt beard and wearing a battered brown bowler hat and coat, obscured his view. He craned his neck and could just see several men in black coats and top hats bustling between the door to the Royal train and a black Clarence carriage drawn by a pair of Windsor Greys. A uniformed policeman with a bushy beard, ten yards to Gordon's right, was watching the Royal party as the crowd fidgeted and chattered in expectation. Several other men, who could only be plain-clothes detectives, surrounded the carriage. An outrider, also in black coat and top hat, was seated on another grey just in front of the carriage. All eyes were on the most powerful lady on Earth. The horse whickered, impatient to be away from the crowd.

After a few minutes, the postilion, in top hat and dark coat, urged his mount forward, and the carriage began to move. The crowd clapped and cheered. In the dark depths of the carriage, Gordon could just make out the Queen, dressed in black with a white lace cap. She was seated next to her youngest daughter, Princes Beatrice, a serious looking lady in her early twenties.

The carriage slowly made its way off the platform. As it passed the uniformed policeman, the man who was obscuring Gordon's view suddenly moved, drawing a small revolver from his pocket and pointing it at the carriage.

Time slowed. Gordon did not think, he pushed the man, hard, with his right hand, while reaching for the gun arm with his left. Just as his hand made contact with the man's arm, the pistol fired and a cloud of grey smoke shot from the barrel, fogging the air and filling his nostrils with the acrid stench of black powder. Where the shot went, Gordon did not know, his only thought was on pushing the gun arm into the air. The man's focus was entirely on the carriage. His left arm swept back, trying to fend Gordon off and bring the pistol to bear. Gordon gripped the man's wrist, suddenly aware of the fact that the man was considerably larger than he, and pushed the pistol into the air. He heard another crack and realised that Robertson had hit the man over the head with his umbrella. Unhooking his umbrella from the fence he tried to bring it down on the man's head, but only succeeded in hitting another man who was trying to help them. He was dimly aware of the postilion pressing his mount forward and the carriage driving off at speed.

In seconds, the assassin was surrounded by policemen who pulled him to the ground. Gordon, his hand still gripping the assassin's wrist was dragged down with him; his top hat fell off and rolled away to be stamped under the feet of the panicked crowd. He found himself on the ground with a policeman on top of him staring into the mad eyes of the assassin; a man who was clearly insane.

"Well done, lad, who knows how many shots he would have fired at the Queen if it had not been for you," said a plain clothes detective, helping him to his feet.

Gordon felt his heart racing, hands shaking and for a moment did not know what to respond. "Is she alright?" he asked eventually.

The detective nodded, "Thanks to you."

Robertson passed him his top hat. "Sorry, Wilson, I'm afraid this looks beyond repair."

The detective took their details and asked them to attend the police station later that day to make a statement. As they turned to leave, the man they had accidentally hit over the head with their umbrellas approached.

"I'm most terribly sorry to have struck you, sir," said Gordon.

"Think nothing of it. I wanted to add my thanks and congratulations." He held out his hand. "William M'Closkie; Landlord of the Star and Garter in Peascod Street. Come in any time and I would be delighted to stand you a drink." He looked at their slightly embarrassed expressions and then at the detective. "Lemonade or soda, obviously." He winked.

The boys murmured their thanks and walked back to the school where they had to apologise profusely to their classics master for being so late that they had missed the entire lesson. They suspected there would be consequences for their tardiness and those fears were realised when summoned to the Headmaster's study a couple of hours later.

"Wilson, Robertson, what on earth have you been up to?" Mr Hornby sat behind his desk and looked at them over his spectacles. Gordon tried to analyse his expression to determine the depth of the hot water they were in and gave up. Hornby had been Head for over 12 years and had mastered the ability to strike fear and respect into his pupils long before that.

"Sir?" Gordon decided that a question could do no harm. He was wrong.

"Don't play dumb with me, boy.

"And don't look at each other. Why did you miss your classics lesson this morning?" Hornby's tone was level, but no less threatening for it.

"We wanted to see the Queen arrive at the station Sir," Robertson replied. "Wilson has never seen her, Sir, being from Australia, Sir."

"And she was late?"

"Well, there was a bit of an incident, Sir," Robertson continued. "A man shot at her, but Wilson jogged his arm so he missed, Sir."

"I see." Hornby smiled, and the boys realised they had either been played by an expert, or the Headmaster had genuinely not heard about the events of the morning. "That explains this note," indicating a letter on his desk.

"You have been summoned to the Castle for tea at 4pm. Far be it from me to decline Her Majesty's invitation on the grounds that you are now behind with your Latin. You had better go and get cleaned up."

18
FLYING TO FRANCE

March 1882

Fred Burnaby presented his card at the entrance to the Traveller's Club in Pall Mall. "I understand I might find Mr Simmons here today? Would you be so good as to ask if he would have time for a few words with a fellow Aeronaut?"

A few minutes later, he was shaking hands with a delighted Joseph Simmons, civil engineer and aeronaut. Simmons' round, youthful face was matured by a bushy moustache that extended down to the line of his strong jaw and appeared to hang from a pointed nose. "Colonel Burnaby, I am delighted to meet you. Mr Wright speaks most highly of your ability as an aeronaut, while your courage is already well known. How do you do, Sir?"

Burnaby smiled as they took their seats. "I am well indeed, and very pleased to see you looking none the worse for your adventure in the German ocean last week. I wondered if you would be so kind as to tell the story? One can never gather the technical details from the papers, yknow."

Simmons grimaced. "It really was the most confounded luck. We really thought ourselves well set for the first crossing of the Channel by air. Colonel Brine and I took off from Canterbury at 11.20 on the 4th March and were blown south, south east. We crossed Shakespeare's Cliff at 12.50 watched by the good people of Dover and for a while looked set to make it to France. By half past two we were almost half way across the channel when the wind suddenly veered from a nor 'westerly to the south and we found ourselves being blown north east towards the North Sea."

"How high were you when this happened?"

"We had ascended to almost 2000 feet."

"Were you able to calculate your speed?"

"It was approximately 7 miles per hour up until that point. But the wind increased as it veered so we were being pushed out into the blue yonder at a great rate of knots."

"A very worrying state of affairs. Do you think the wind veered as you ascended, and what did you do next?"

"I don't believe it was the height that determined the wind speed or direction. We were very concerned, of course. Colonel Brine was of the view that we were both dead men, but I was sure the car would float long enough for us to be rescued. Fortunately, we could see the Calais – Dover mail packet below us so we signalled to her. Once we were sure she had seen our situation, we put on our cork jackets, I pulled the gas release valve and we rapidly descended."

"You were lucky she was able to pick you up. I understand you were able to save the balloon too?"

"We were, indeed, lucky. The car leaked and the water was above our knees by the time they reached us. You will recall Mr Powell lost both the balloon and his life attempting the crossing in a storm last December."

"He was courageous to believe that flying in 85 mile per hour winds would carry him swiftly across the channel, particularly when snow was threatened. His companions were extremely fortunate to have been able to jump out at Bridport. I believe no trace has been found of Mr Powell or the balloon."

"Indeed, no, though I believe Mr Powell was also trying to get out, but the balloon rose suddenly as his companions jumped out and he was carried away." Simmons reflected before continuing. "We were very fortunate the steamer 'Foam' was able to recover my balloon and brought us back into Dover with the car hanging over the side."

"As it happens, I was returning from Tunis that day and arrived in Dover on a later boat. Everyone was talking about your attempt. A great many people had watched you from the cliffs and all thought you lost when they saw your balloon descend into the sea. I believe the cheer when they saw you alive could be heard in Folkestone." He smiled. "Will you try again?"

"I will, of course, though believe I would be pushing my luck to attempt it again this year."

Full of resolve, Colonel Burnaby left the Travellers' Club and repaired to his home at 18 Charles Street, Mayfair. He immediately wrote to his friend, Mr Wright, requesting the loan of a balloon with which to make an attempt to cross the Channel.

Mr Wright immediately responded to the effect that, for a man of Burnaby's experience, he had a nearly new balloon that would hold 86,000 feet of gas. This would be far more suitable for the attempt than Mr Simmons' balloon, which was, in his view, old, small and leaky. He added that he would be delighted to accompany Colonel Burnaby on his attempt.

Burnaby replied, politely declining Mr Wright's offer on the basis that he did not believe a balloon of a mere 86,000 feet of gas would carry two men for the many hours the crossing would take. He added that he needed as much ballast as possible to gain the height needed. He would of course be happy to make an ascent again with Mr Wright on any inland excursion.

It was eventually settled that Burnaby would make the attempt on 22nd March from Dover. The Dover gas works was prepared to fill the balloon, the newspapers had announced the event, and there was much excitement throughout the country. Burnaby's only concern was that the Commander-in-Chief might summon him back to London. An eager correspondent from the Daily Telegraph offered to accompany him, but was declined. Burnaby did not want to share the glory; this was his adventure.

Burnaby and his batman, Henry Storey, travelled to Dover on the evening of the 20th March. The following day Mr Wright prepared the balloon, carefully laying out the silk on the ground and covering it top and bottom in tarpaulins to protect it from the weather, particularly frost. Burnaby was particularly grateful for this attention to detail, as such preparation had not occurred to him.

At first light on the 22nd, with light winds blowing towards Calais, Burnaby was ready to go, but for reasons he could not fathom, the Dover Gas Light Company could not be induced to fill the balloon. Perhaps they were worried about their reserves. Frustrated, Burnaby, Wright and Storey walked around Dover town and visited the cemetery to pay their respects at Radford's grave.

That night, the wind howled through the chimneypots and Burnaby fell asleep in his hotel room, certain that he would have to delay again.

Henry Storey woke him at 0430 with a cup of coffee. "The wind has dropped Sir, and all the weathervanes in Dover are pointing to the north."

Burnaby leapt out of bed and dressed rapidly in a striped coat and a close skullcap. "No time to lose." He downed his coffee.

Rushing outside he pelted Mr Wright's window with small stones until the man's head appeared. "Wind's fair, come on, hyarr."

They hurried to the gas works where Wright removed the tarpaulins from the balloon, noting with satisfaction that they were caked in ice. In the distance, the pennant on Dover castle streamed towards Boulogne. Wright removed his boots and walked over the silk envelope, checking it for any damage before he was satisfied and signalled to the gasmen to commence filling the balloon.

The red and yellow striped envelope gradually filled as a crowd gathered to watch the spectacle. All the town dignitaries were present and, amidst much clapping and cheering, Colonel Burnaby took his place in the car, his elbows resting on its edge. Storey passed him a package of sandwiches and a flask. Burnaby waved away the offer of a cork lifejacket and a buoy.

"If you come down safely, you will be careful packing her up," said Wright grinning at his friend. "Remember you just need to pull this line here to open the neck of the balloon and release all the remaining gas."

"And I am sure you would like a receipt for your balloon in case I don't come back?" Burnaby's eyebrow rose slightly as Wright smiled and nodded. With a rueful grin he wrote on the back of the bill from the gas company 'I agree to be responsible to Mr Wright for all damage or loss incurred by him through any accident happening to his balloon, in which I ascend today.' He signed, dated it, and handed it to his friend.

"I am afraid you think a good deal more of the safety of your balloon than you do for me."

"If, sir, I had not the greatest confidence in your experience as an aeronaut, I would not trust you with it." He paused. "I am lending you what I refused to Colonel Brine."

Turning to the gas men he said "One more puff and I think we're done." Wright looked up at the envelope critically. Finally satisfied the balloon was as full and symmetrical as possible he ordered the pipe to be removed.

At 10am the ties were cast off and the balloon leaped into the cool air, to cheers from the crowd. Burnaby waved, and then, to cries of alarm from below, had to hastily duck down and throw a bag of ballast out of the car in order to clear the gasworks chimney.

As he rose out of the smoke shrouded town, the sun broke through the thin cloud. In the windless tranquillity of the car the heat scorched the back of his neck and he fashioned a puggaree out of his handkerchief. Looking back at the castle he could see the flashes from the heliograph on the tower and wished he had learned the code so he could understand what the soldiers there were saying. Below him the harbour bustled with fishing vessels heading in with their morning catch. He counted four, three masted warships, without their yards crossed, in the docks and two packet steamers alongside Admiralty pier.

By 1115 he could no longer see England and Boulogne came into view. Looking down at the shipping passing along the Channel he congratulated himself that his crossing was free of the stomach churning movement he normally associated with travelling to France. The sun slid behind a bank of clouds and as the temperature suddenly dropped, so did the balloon, the gas condensing. He felt his ears pop with the change in pressure and was alarmed to see that some scraps of paper he threw over the side, rose up. In two minutes he dropped almost 2000 feet and he realised with alarm that the sea was rapidly rising to greet him.

He threw a bag of ballast overboard without effect. Two more bags followed but it was only with the fourth that the car began to rise. He realised that with the change in altitude he was no longer travelling towards Boulogne and was instead running south west and parallel to the coast. And then he stopped. Looking down he could see the shadow of the balloon, a dark grey hole in the becalmed water into which he would be sure to descend as the gas escaped. He reasoned that he had about three hours. Two fishing smacks appeared and signalled for him to descend so they might rescue him. He declined and, when they persisted, threw his rolled copy of The Times at them. Stomach rumbling he ate a sandwich while urging the barometer to signal a change to his fortunes.

Suddenly he saw a ripple on the water. A breeze. He let out some gas to descend but as he reached 500 feet he realised the ripple was a shoal of fish. He remained motionless and in the middle of the Channel. It would be dark in five hours but he would have sunk into the water by then. The smacks approached him again, the crews merrily offering to rescue him. For perhaps the twentieth time he reasoned that there would be no shame in descending, he need not even get his feet wet.

"No!"

The determination that had carried him across 300 miles of Russian Steppe in the middle of winter came to the fore. He still had five bags of ballast and, as a last resort was prepared to cast off the car and perch on the wooden ring. It was time to test his theory that the wind blew in different directions depending on the altitude. Throwing all caution to the (non-existent) wind and, ignoring the 86,000 feet of slowly leaking explosive gas above him, he lit a cigar. Mr Wright was not there to see him.

He threw two bags of ballast overboard and the balloon rose seven thousand feet, but resolutely refused to move sideways. He was left with two small bags and a large one filled with stones. He threw the two small ones and rose to ten thousand feet. It was dreadfully cold now.

The warmth of hope surged through him; he was moving South. In a few minutes he was merrily passing high over Dieppe. He sketched it in his pocketbook.

As the danger passed he decided to have some fun. Passing over a man ploughing with two oxen and a horse he dropped a little fine sand. The man started, at a loss to know where the dust had come from. As the shadow of the balloon covered him he looked up and fell on his back in astonishment, arms to the sides and feet in the air.

Burnaby carefully controlled his descent and made a perfect touchdown in a field near a large Chateau ten miles South of Dieppe. Remembering Mr Wright's words he pulled the neckline and the balloon deflated. Amazed French peasants soon surrounded it, flocking from the surrounding fields to assist him. They could not have been more friendly or helpful. Burnaby chattered fluently with them and soon a cart was brought to enable him to recover the balloon and car.

At the first opportunity he sent a single telegram to Mr Wright.

"Your balloon uninjured. Wind changed mid-channel. Afterwards for a time becalmed over sea. Eventually found southerly current at high altitude. Descended Chateau de Montigny, Envermeu, Normandy. Voyage difficult, but very amusing."

The contents of the telegram were leaked so that news of Burnaby's feat of daring was in the following afternoon's newspapers, much to the irritation of Wright and Burnaby who made sure that questions were raised in Parliament about the scandalous lack of privacy. In the event it was determined that the British telegraphic service could not be held responsible for the security of any service overseas, but the men had made their point.

The following Saturday, Burnaby returned to Windsor to a hero's welcome. The Duke of Cambridge was less impressed and in an interview, without coffee, reprimanded him for quitting England without obtaining a leave of absence from Headquarters. As he left the interview, Burnaby saw the Duke smile and heard him mutter "Valuable lives ought not be risked in such freaks."

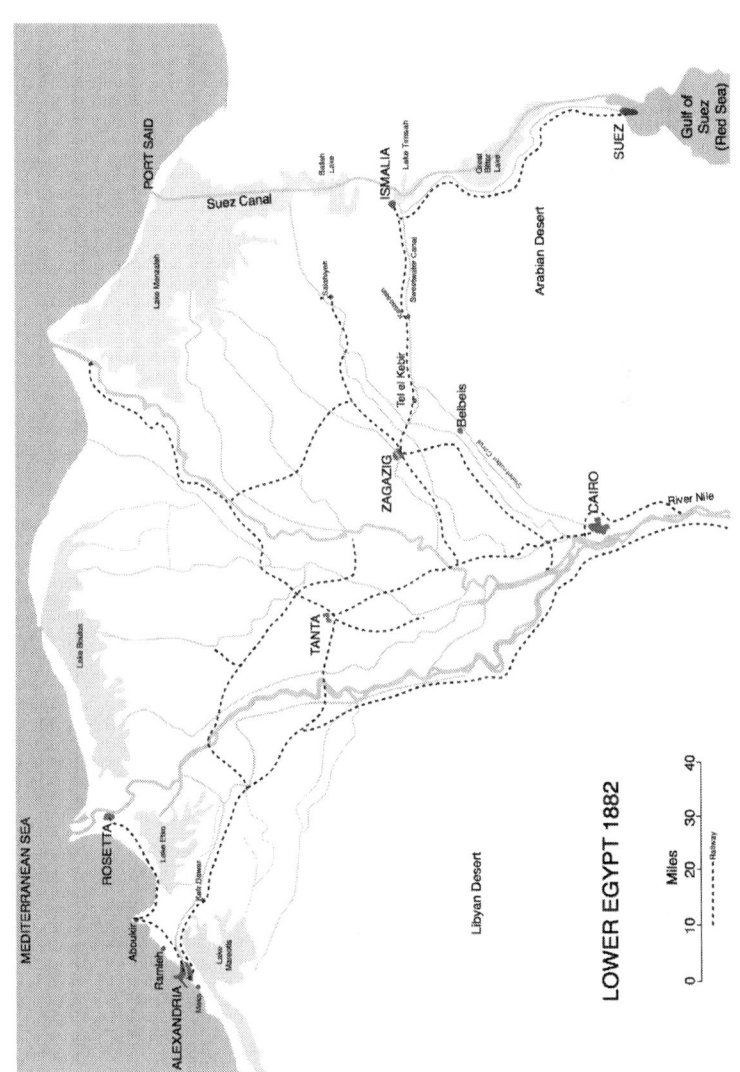

19

THE TROUBLE WITH EGYPT

Cabinet Room, Downing Street, London, May 1882

William Gladstone, the septuagenarian British Prime Minister, sat with his Cabinet in 10 Downing Street. It was his second premiership, electoral success coming on the back of a new form of political campaigning centred on mass rallies and lengthy, well reported, speeches. His theme, reinforced by evangelical Protestantism that was particularly popular in his Scottish constituency, majored on the mismanagement of foreign policy by his predecessor, Benjamin Disraeli. He was fervently committed to a world community, governed by law, protecting the weak. Events in Egypt were a worrying example of how difficult it was to execute such a policy in a complex world filled with self-interest. The room was restless, the tension palpable.

Gladstone glanced at his briefing paper and turned to the Marquess of Hartington. "Before we begin, I am sure I speak for the entire Cabinet in expressing our horror and sorrow at the murder of your brother, Lord Frederick, at the hand of extreme nationalists in Dublin last week. You can be assured that every effort will be made to ensure the men are found and punished."

Around the cabinet table there were murmurings of "hear, hear" and nods of acknowledgement. Hartington grimaced and nodded, the pain at the loss of his younger brother evident in his eyes.

After a moment's silence, Gladstone turned to his Secretary for War, Hugh Childers, "First item on the agenda, Egypt."

"Prime Minister, the situation in Egypt is deteriorating and a policy of non-intervention, while laudable and cost effective, may not remain possible."

Gladstone raised a quizzical eyebrow. Childers continued, "General Arabi, who is now both a Pasha and Egyptian Minister of War, is operating as the effective dictator in Egypt. Officers loyal to Arabi's nationalist party now command the entire Egyptian Army. The Khedive, Tewfik, is reduced to a figurehead, his European advisors now powerless to protect our interests."

"He does still have European advisors?" Spencer Cavendish, the immensely wealthy Marquess of Hartington, Secretary of State for India, was arguably the most influential man in the room, his comment just discernable as a question.

"Indeed, while they remain in place, are there circumstances in which they could influence the situation?" Joseph Chamberlain, MP for Birmingham and President of the Board of Trade, was a formidable radical politician in his mid forties. "Several of the Banks and bond holders have expressed concern about the security of their substantial loans in the event Tewfik is overthrown. Our 44% stake in the Suez Canal is also at risk. If we lose access to the canal our trade with India, the Far East and Australia is all threatened." He paused before making his key point. "We cannot ignore the fact that the majority of the British population, spurred on by the patriotic Press, is supportive of intervention."

The room was silent for a moment as the Cabinet contemplated the significance of this to the Liberal Party.

"And what of France and Turkey? Where do they stand Foreign Secretary?" asked Gladstone of his close friend and ally.

The Earl Granville sighed. Now in his mid sixties he was a suave man with considerable diplomatic experience that told him that a policy of having no policy was often the more successful course of action. "France has long had influence in the region and their banks and bond holders share the same risk as ours. Their shares in the Canal would also be at risk were Arabi to usurp the Khedive and declare all foreign interests void. When Gambetta was President his aggressive interest in Egyptian affairs, supportive of French expansion in North Africa, did much to inflame matters. Indeed, it is their annexation of Tunisia last May that is reported to have spurred Arabi into action."

He looked about the room and noted the Prime Minister's nod of approval. Gladstone was opposed to the European scramble to establish colonies in Africa, but was increasingly at odds with Nationalistic fervour and public opinion on the matter.

"Fortunately, President Freycinet is far more cautious. Our assessment is that Turkey remains the key to Egypt. Turkey can continue to claim Egypt part of their Ottoman Empire via its control of both Arabi and the Khedive. The Khedive's power has historically wrested in the Turco-Circassian Pashas and officers in senior positions in the Army. The Khedive grants them rank, decorations, money, fertile lands and spacious houses. They use their power to maintain the Khedive's authority, and he provides the cohesion that keeps the Turco-Circassian minority at the top; the pashas and officers are regularly moved about to govern different areas in order to ensure they do not build a power base that threatens the Khedive. It is a virtuous cycle that remains so long as the money does not run out. The fact is that the money comes not from Egyptian taxation but from European, mainly British, but also French and German, bank loans. The taxes barely cover the 40% interest charged."

"So, the Khedive's power comes from European money, giving us power over the Khedive," surmised Joseph Chamberlain. "It's a wonder the Turks allow us so much leverage, though I suppose, why would they want to fund Egypt?" He paused. "So what has changed this delicate status quo?"

"In short, Arabi and impending bankruptcy," replied Granville. "Arabi has pledged his loyalty to the Sultan of Turkey as his Master under God. However, that loyalty is tested by the Khedive. Despite Arabi's charisma and leadership ability he is a native Egyptian and as such has for years been kept in his place by the Circassian officers promoted over him based solely on the Khedive's patronage."

Childers chipped in, "In essence, the system I replaced in the British Army less than 10 years ago."

Granville politely smiled acknowledgement at the interruption. "Though in this case the Turco-Circassian population is outnumbered by the Arabs 70 to one. The Khedive cannot ignore the Arab population and for decades has showered the sheiks with minor honours and administrative positions, constantly moving them so they do not build a power base. It was only when the Khedive's new Circassian Chief Minister, Riaz, pressed to have Arabi and three other Arab Colonels replaced by Circassian officers that they mutinied last September. The Arab rank and file soldiers that comprise the four Regiments concerned are loyal to their Arab Colonels and effectively prevented their replacement.

"I have spent weeks trying to convince the French to support an Anglo-French-Turkish Commission and to back the idea of Turkish troops landing in Egypt to restore order. Unfortunately the French recall the recent Turkish atrocities in Bulgaria and have completely rejected that idea."

"Indeed, thousands of men, women and children were massacred. So, a complex and delicate situation where any action we take could have far reaching and unexpected consequences." Gladstone looked around the table, searching for any reaction to his words.

"Yes, Prime Minister. On balance a policy of non intervention remains the most prudent position," replied Granville. The room relaxed slightly, reversals in Ireland, India and South Africa needed to be overcome and the Empire was already stretched to breaking point without Egypt flaring up.

"How might this escalate?" asked Lord Hartington, not yet prepared to let the matter lie. The murder of his brother by extreme Irish nationalists, was fresh in his mind. He was determined not to let another nationalist, Arabi, get the upper hand.

"Arabi's supporters are threatening riots and attacks on Europeans, who are predominantly based in Alexandria," replied Granville.

"What will such instability gain?" asked Chamberlain. "To date, despite the nationalists replacing all the Circassian's in positions of power, all the European advisors have been kept in their posts."

"His aim appears to be to unite the Egyptian people against European control. The European advisors will fear for their lives and return home and if he provokes Britain and France to invade then the Arabs will rise up and fight. While a Franco British invasion might overcome the Egyptian Army, maintaining order in the face of civil insurrection would require far more troops than we could possibly find." Granville noted the nods of agreement around the table.

"Quite," said Childers, "Half our Regular Army of 190,000 is in India and the colonies, and the lions' share of the remainder is subduing the Fenians in Ireland. Without mobilising our Reserves we could not put more than 15,000 men in the field."

"Yet we have to do something, if not to protect British financial interests, then to assuage popular opinion," Chamberlain returned to his earlier theme.

"While effectively doing nothing that will inflame the situation further," Granville replied. As if it had just occurred to him, he added, "The French have suggested that a joint Anglo-French fleet should be sent to Alexandria." Seeing Chamberlain's quickly suppressed look of hope he continued. "While I am not advocating the deployment of the Mediterranean Fleet, could we not send a couple of ironclads to protect the life and property of Europeans?"

"All in agreement?" Gladstone looked around the table, grateful that the debate he had orchestrated with Granville had gone as planned. "Then, Childers, make it so. Warn the commander that we wish to remain on the best terms with the Turks and other powers. If we are forced to land troops to protect British subjects, then they are not to leave the protection of the ship's guns without instructions from home."

Three weeks later Lord Granville regarded his cabinet colleagues and the Prime Minister. "It is with regret that I report that the arrival of the Anglo French fleet in Alexandria harbour on 20th May was seen as a direct threat to both Egyptian sovereignty and the Islamic faith. The Khedive is being portrayed by nationalist agitators, and in the popular press, as having sided with the Christians and of being unworthy of office."

"And how did General Arabi respond?" asked Chamberlain.

"Arabi stated that the Europeans are welcome and safe, and even commented that the naval officers and men would be welcome to come ashore and spend money in the bazaars and clubs. Unfortunately he, and the Egyptian Ministry, then resigned as a body in protest against European interference. The resulting protests from both the Army and the religious leaders have actually strengthened his position. The Khedive was forced to back down, re-instate them all and has formally requested that the Turks send an Imperial Commissioner. This has reduced tension in the streets as it has re-asserted the Sultan's rights and the position of Egypt in the Ottoman Empire."

The Secretary of State for War looked up from his Admiralty briefing notes. "Admiral Seymour, commanding the flotilla in Alexandria, is concerned that the Egyptians are now re-building their forts and earthworks overlooking the harbour. New guns and mortars are being delivered daily. He requested we increase his force with *HMS Alexandra*, *HMS Monarch* and a gunboat. As you know, we sent Monarch and a couple of gunboats in reply and the French are sending 2 additional ships. Given the time it would take to get reinforcements into the area I think it prudent to be prepared."

"What do you suggest?" asked the Prime Minister.

"Most of the Mediterranean fleet is now concentrated in the area of Greece, Turkey and Egypt. The nearest troops are in the fleet home port at Malta, but there are no ships available to transport them to where they may be needed. I therefore suggest we move the Channel squadron from Devonport to Malta."

"Agreed," said the Prime Minister, "though keep them out of sight. We do not want to inflame matters further."

20
REVERSALS

Sudan, May / June 1882

Was this God's plan? This was not as it had been written. How could God be on the side of an infidel? Giegler Pasha, a German, had replaced Ra'ūf Pasha as the Khedive's Governor General to Khartoum in March and at first this had meant nothing. Al Mahdi had sent his great commander, Ahmad al-Makāshfī to lay siege to Senaar in the Jazīra, the broad swathe of fertile land between the blue and white Niles south of Khartoum. He had captured 150 more rifles, continuing al Mahdi's great work, but then a new Pasha had been sent to be Governor General and Giegler Pasha had taken any army into the field. The German had defeated his divine soldiers, his Anṣār, at Abu Haras on the Blue Nile and again near Senaar. People had doubted his divinity. He had needed a big victory.

And now God had given him one. At Massa, south of Kawa, his Anṣār had defeated Yūsuf Pasha and the strongest Egyptian force yet. His Anṣār had captured 4000 more rifles and now tens of thousands of Kordofanis were flocking to his standard. He would unite the poor and disaffected, crush the Turkish Egyptians in the Sudan, and then march on Cairo, Damascus, Mecca, Constantinople and all the other great cities of the Arab world. He was al Mahdi.

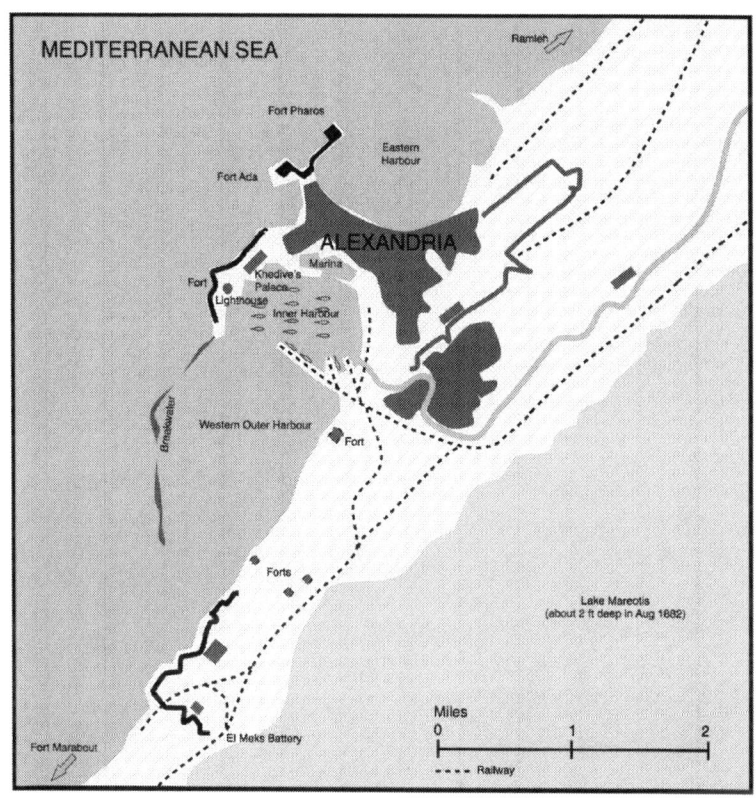

21
RIOT

Alexandria, Egypt, 11th June 1882

Captain Richard Molyneux, resplendent in immaculate white tunic and trousers, settled his pith helmet and stepped from his barge and on to the Alexandria quayside. At 44 his youthful looks belied a thickening frame that spoke of too little exercise, confined as he was to walking the decks of his ship when time permitted. Beneath the tunic, he felt the sweat prick his skin at the slight exertion and momentarily wondered whether he might have been cooler had he shaved his bushy side-whiskers.

The waterfront was thronged with porters, fishermen, merchants and beggars going about their business under the blazing late morning sun. Fellaheen boys in their distinctive white jellabiya whipped grossly overladen donkeys along the quay. Italian sailors jostled with native beggars, while Greek merchants shouted at Nubian guards, and Maltese shopkeepers mingled with fishermen, Arabs and Turks. His coxswain, Gray, a well-built Cornishman, made a hole in the throng and the pair slowly climbed through the narrow streets lined with small shops and stalls. Looking back across the inner harbour, Molyneux could see a myriad of boats beetling across the glittering blue water, plying their trade with the larger vessels, his ironclad battleship *Invincible* included, anchored in the three deep water channels beyond the pier. To the North West, set atop the Pharos islet, a spectacular lighthouse marked the eye in the head of a hummingbird's beak of breakwater, that created the outer harbour. The lighthouse and Pharos islet was connected to the city via a broad artificial causeway, dominated by the three storey Khedive's Ras-el-Tin Palace that extended down to the inner harbour.

The multiple forts and other defences looked less formidable from the shore than his quarterdeck; the soft limestone walls and simple barracks shoddily built and now practically obsolete. That was not the true picture though. He had seen in the intelligence reports that the Egyptians now had 44 modern rifled guns as well as over 200 old smooth bore weapons.

Not far from the quayside, in an avenue that ran parallel to the waterfront, they found the British Consulate. It was only distinguishable from the other small, whitewashed villas by the elite Turkish guards stationed outside and the gated side entrance for carriages. On meeting his hosts, Samuel de Kusel, the 34 year old Controller-General of the Egyptian Customs Service, and James Morice, Inspector-General of Coastguards, they took an open carriage to Ramleh with Morice riding beside on a horse. Ramleh, with its beach and cool sea breezes, was a favourite haunt of the idle rich, a handful of miles North East of the City. Kusel maintained a running commentary for his guest. As they continued away from the harbour, the streets and boulevards became progressively grander until they entered the City's central piazza. This well kept rectangle, shaded by trees, contained an oval pond and central green lawn; the central hub of the City, it was dominated by a huge statue of the former ruler.

"This is the Place Muhammad Ali where most of the Europeans live." Kusel pointed to the statue. "I often wonder what he would have made of his heir's management of the country he created. Y'know, he was a Macedonian small-time tobacco merchant? Almost 70 years ago he skilfully overthrew, well massacred, the Marmeluke Princes who had ruled the country for centuries. By all accounts he was as intelligent as he was cunning and ruthless. He died at the age of 80 having fathered 95 children and, advised by the French, transformed Egypt into a more European model. He also tamed the Nile floods and created the canals – not the Suez Canal obviously, that was started in 1869 by Said Pasha and finished by Ismail, Khedive Tewfik's father. That was a party when they opened that! It went on for days with no thought as to cost.

"Now, Ismail is a fascinating character. Everyone blames him for the huge debt Egypt now owes to the Europeans, which is true, and he was certainly profligate and totally out-negotiated by the financiers; but he was also charming, intelligent and responsible for most of the modern infrastructure you see today. Over 100 bridges, hundreds of miles of railway track and telegraph lines, over 4500 schools, including the first one for girls in the Ottoman Empire, postal services, courts and the customs service." He nodded at James Morice who was trotting beside the carriage. "Unfortunately his palaces and dreams of an Egyptian empire were the ruin of him. Military forays into Abysinnia, Somalia and the Sudan were far from popular and ruinously expensive."

"I heard that General Gordon resigned from his position as Governor General of the Sudan in protest at Ismail being deposed?" said Molyneux.

"As I say, Ismail has his admirers," Kusel continued. "Unfortunately for him, the Sultan was not one of them. So now he resides in a very comfortable exile in Naples and watches his son Tewfik try to clear up his mess. Y'know, Ismail was rumoured to be behind a recent assassination attempt on General Arabi?"

Over an excellent lunch of fresh fish washed down with a refreshing Italian wine, they told amusing stories and discovered mutual acquaintances. Molyneux discovered Kusel was born in Liverpool of naturalised German parents. Aged 34, he had been in Egypt for years and seemed to know everyone of importance; hosting the rich when they visited Alexandria in their yachts and helping to organise the customs formalities when antiquities were purchased.

"So what of recent events?" asked Molyneux as they drank sweet tea at the end of their meal.

"Well of course there is always tension in Alexandria," said Morice. "The Italians loath the Fellaheen donkey boys, the Greeks hate the Nubians."

"Sounds just like the Navy," commented Molyneux. "The crews of the *Alexandra* and *Colossus* are never allowed on shore at the same time as the enmity between them means they fight like wildcats."

Kusel smiled. "And the Maltese dockers hate your customs workers" he added. "These rivalries and tensions have existed for decades."

"Centuries, even" said Morice. "It doesn't take much for a riot to break out in the port cities, where East meets West."

"Hmm, men and women live on the sides of an active volcano, blissfully hopeful that if it should erupt it will go downwards and bypass them," said Kusel.

"True," said Morice. "Last week the city was perfectly calm, then about 1000 Arabs attacked 30 Greeks with sticks. Most worrying though was that the soldiers ordered to break up the affray joined in against the Greeks – their officer was not able to control them. With the rule of law breaking down I have had to tell people that they have the right to defend themselves."

"I am sufficiently concerned to have sent my wife back to her parent's home in Italy over a month ago," said Kusel. "You need to bear in mind that the Suez Canal has extended some of these tensions further inland and has added a religious component. The orthodox Greeks detest the pious Muslims, who in turn are intolerant of Europeans and Christians. The flash points are Suez and Port Said where the people of Al-Hejaz, and those on their pilgrimage to Mecca, connect with Europeans."

They decided to show the Captain the city, starting with the public gardens on the outskirts of Alexandria.

"Beautiful," commented Molyneux, sharing a carriage with Kusel. "I am surprised they are so deserted. Come to that I have also been surprised by how normal the City appears today."

"Indeed," said Kusel, "but this place is normally packed with carriages on a Sunday."

The local men looked at each other ominously. There was only one other carriage in the park and 3 uniformed British naval officers occupied that. Molyneux recognised Pibworth, the 32 year old engineer of the *Superb*.

"It's far too quiet," said Morice. "Let's head back into the City and see what is going on."

By the edge of the gardens they were able to stop a harem carriage and Morice asked the Arab diver if he had any news. He returned to the carriage with concern on his face.

"There has been a big fight near the Sikka Sabah Benat between natives and Europeans. Several people are dead."

"If you will excuse me, I think I had better return to my ship," said Molyneux looking at his Coxwain, Gray, whose eyes were constantly monitoring for threats.

As they hurried back through the streets they passed small groups of Arabs who cursed them, shouting "Infidel. The faster the better, you are only going to your death."

Arriving at the Rosetta Gate that marked the Eastern entrance to the City, they found soldiers lounging at ease in the shade of the dilapidated stone walls, arms piled, and the officers sitting at the roadside, smoking.

Kusel gave them a salaam, and they all returned the salute.

"Well, this doesn't look too bad," he commented. They continued down the Avenue Rosetta and their optimism faded as they saw all the houses and shops closed and barricaded.

The balconies were crowded with people urging them to stop and not go any further.

Turning into the Place Muhammad Ali they were met by a screaming mob, many of whom seemed to be high on drugs and baying for the blood of any Europeans they could find. Standing up, Molyneux could see bodies lying in the street. A shoe-blacking boy kneeled over a prostrate man, calmly caving his skull in with a rock until the brains were exposed. A European man in a black coat ran towards a soldier, hands extended in supplication. The soldier's sword flashed, slicing the top off the man's head; he sank to his knees before toppling forward into the gutter.

Ahead of them, the carriage containing the 3 naval officers they had seen earlier was surrounded by a large crowd of Arabs armed with knives and sticks. He watched in growing horror as Pibworth was stabbed to death. His companion, a furious petty officer, rammed his walking stick into the mouth of the main assailant, so hard that the end erupted from behind the man's ear and he fell back, dead.

The crowd was stunned for a moment by the ferocity of the attack and the petty officer was able to get away.

"Forget the harbour, make for the Consulate" shouted Kusel to the driver, Giovanni. With the horse, Bessie, rearing and plunging, and the men beating the crowd back with their canes, they forced their way out of the square and back to the Consulate. They were fortunate to be recognised by the gatekeeper, who opened the carriage gates just in time, and they lurched into the relative safety within.

They were met with total confusion. Terrified women and children were crowded throughout the building. Mr Calvert, deputy to Vice-Consul Cookson, had collapsed with stress and there did not appear to be anyone in charge. At that moment, Cookson arrived, his head bleeding profusely having been bit by a stone. As he stepped out of his carriage one of the staff passed him a note. Reading it, he frowned. His face lightened slightly as he saw Molyneux and beckoned him closer.

"I have been summoned to return to the Police Station for a meeting of the Consuls." There was barely a hint of irritation in his voice. "I have just returned from there, meeting the Governor and the sub-prefect of police. I thought things calmer until I neared the Consulate and was stoned by the mob."

He did not appear surprised that Calvert was indisposed. "The quayside is a hotbed of dissent, Captain. I do not think it safe for you to return to your ship and believe you would be of far greater value here. Thank the Lord we managed to install that phone line to *Invincible* last week. Can you take command of the Consulate and keep the Admiral informed? We can agree the best course of action when I return but for now I suggest you strengthen the Consulate defences."

Molyneux nodded and Cookson leapt back into his open carriage, gesturing for one of the Turkish guards to drive him back to the police station in Rue des Soeurs. The gate was opened and the carriage drove through at speed, heedless of the crowd gathered outside. The gate was immediately closed and barred.

Molyneux turned to his Coxwain. "Mr Gray, inventory of the weapons. Mr Morice, can you assess and strengthen the Consulate defences? As a former Navy man, I'm sure you will know what to look for. Mr Kusel, can you round up every able bodied man who is not doing something you deem important and send them back here to be re-deployed? Report back here in 15 minutes." The men went to their tasks without a word.

A striking lady in her mid thirties and in an elegant dress approached. "Constance Turner." She held out her hand. "Captain, may I be of service? Perhaps to gather the women and children into a place of safety away from the walls and to establish somewhere to tend the wounded?"

Molyneux regarded her with respect and shook her hand, lightly, "That would be most helpful, Ma'am. Are there many wounded?"

She nodded. "Quite a few. They are the lucky ones. There are many stories of Europeans being stabbed and beaten to death." Her eyes filled with tears at the recollection. "I even saw the animals club a five year old child to death."

Cookson relaxed slightly as his carriage left the Consulate behind for the short drive to the police station and he saw that the crowd had thinned. The wound on his head throbbed but at least the bleeding seemed to have slowed. The streets seemed quieter though he noted that Europeans were unusually absent. As he passed some of the European shops he noticed that the shutters had been broken down and the contents looted. Whether it was long held grudges being satisfied, or opportunistic thieving, he did not know.

90 yards from the police station the carriage crossed a four-way junction on the corner of the great square and was immediately brought to a halt by a shower of stones. A nasty mob immediately surrounded them and, as Cookson rose to his feet, a large native jumped up onto the carriage behind him. Before he could react he

was felled by a single blow from the man's quarterstaff. He was dimly aware of the driver trying to defend him before he too was brought to the ground under a hail of blows.

Cookson half fell and was half dragged from the carriage. Somehow he managed to get to his feet and with blood streaming down his face and his ears ringing, he stumbled towards the police station. Blows rained down on him as he dizzily made his way across the square. He tried to protect his head with his arms and felt the strikes sting his hands and forearms. A finger broke. Adrenalin surged and forced strength into his legs, driving him towards safety and dulling the pain. He almost welcomed the blows to his back as they pushed him forward. He was also grateful the mob was so close as it did not given them space to swing their sticks. He just hoped they did not carry knives.

As he neared the station he was driven to the ground and had to crawl the final few yards. All the time he was conscious that the soldiers that protected the police station were making no attempt to come to his aid or protect him. Fortunately the crowd did not attempt to enter the station and once inside he achieved some form of safety. He was greeted by a hugely apologetic Governor of Alexandria, Omar Lufti.

"I am so sorry, Vice-Consul, both for your treatment at the hands of the mob and that you did not receive the second message before you had already departed the Consulate."

Cookson, blood streaming from multiple wounds to his head looked askance at the Turkish born Governor.

"I cancelled the meeting as soon as I realised it would be too dangerous for you to travel here, which was when the Italian Consul was attacked crossing the square." Lufti looked guilty.

"Your soldiers appeared too distracted to assist me, sir!"

"I regret. You were fortunate. I understand some Europeans, who have sought assistance from the military, have been bayoneted."

Cookson was unable to conceal his look of horror at this news. "Why, sir? Have they taken leave of their senses?"

"Some look on while the mob does its worst, and some join in." Lufti's normal confidence was gone. He had lost control of his City. "Events deteriorated when the Greeks and Maltese barricaded themselves in their houses and started shooting from roof tops and balconies. A couple of police were killed."

"But what started this? What was the trigger?" asked Cookson.

"I doubt we will ever know. There are reports it started in the Rue des Soeurs; that a Maltese boy started beating a Fellahin donkey boy who was stoned on hashish. The Fellahin stabbed and killed the Maltese boy. Some Greeks ran to the aid of the Maltese and murdered the Arab. An angry crowd gathered. The Greeks and Maltese took to their houses and shot at them. Arabs were killed, more shots were fired, police were killed. Police and soldiers joined the mob." He shrugged, the simple action demonstrating his confusion. "I ordered the police to disperse the mob and was cursed for trying to help the Christian dogs." There was no doubting the regret in the man's voice.

A clerk approached with some cloth and a bowl of water. Cookson shook his head. "Thank you, no. I must find a way back to the Consulate. It is almost time for the afternoon call to prayer and I would hope many will hear that call and the streets will empty of this madness." He looked at the Governor. "Could you lend me a carriage and an escort that you can trust, sir? I fear I would fall off a horse in my current condition."

He returned to the Consulate via a circuitous route littered with sights he hoped in time to expunge from his memory; a pile of three bodies, one with a bullet through its head, the others broken and barely human. Outside a looted shop, the pathetically small body of a girl, still clutching a doll, face smashed to a pulp.

In the centre of town the boulevards were littered with broken furniture and household items, bottles of brandy, flour, linen.

Strange sights; spread across the street a shattered snake of squashed straw sunhats. He saw a soldier sway down the street with a chandelier balanced on his head, and an Arab caper into the lengthening shadows on a toy horse.

The streets were emptying, the sounds of carnage gradually replaced by the familiar cry of the East 'Allah el Akbar La Illah, illa Allah wa ashhadwar Mohamadur Rasul il Allah'.

He arrived without further incident at 6pm to find the walls and windows of the Consulate filled with armed men. He wondered where they had found all the weapons. Molyneux answered that. They had done some looting themselves, raiding a nearby gunsmith and helping themselves to his stock of shotguns, revolvers and ammunition. The Consulate was far calmer than when he had left it, each person had a purpose and he was soon being tended by a Doctor who dressed his wounds.

Sunset was at 7pm, with tension in the streets seemingly dissipating with the light. Shortly afterwards Governor Lufti and Colonel Suliman Sami, the commander of a disciplined Regiment of the Egyptian Army, arrived at the Consulate. They sought out the Vice Consul.

"Vice Consul, I am pleased to see that you arrived safely and have had your wounds dressed. I was concerned," Cookson was surprised that the Governor appeared to have regained his normal confidence and composure. It soon became clear why. "I am pleased to report that Colonel Sami's men are now in control of the city. The riot is over. Numerous people are under arrest, including, I regret to say, soldiers and policemen."

"Thank you for your concern and for troubling yourself to let me know, sir," replied Cookson.

"We now need to ensure that nothing is done that might re-kindle the flame," said Lufti.

"Indeed, sir" replied Cookson. "We shall ensure that the guards we place around the Consulate are instructed not to fire unless ordered to do so, by me."

"Quite, Vice Consul. Were they to fire I fear a large mob would storm the building." The Governor once again looked slightly uncomfortable. "There is, however, another source of ignition."

Cookson said nothing but looked quizzically at the Turk.

"The Anglo French Fleet?" asked Lufti.

Cookson said nothing but at that moment the telephone rang. Captain Molyneux answered and had a brief conversation.

Molyneux then reported privately to Cookson. "That was Admiral Seymour calling from the *Invincible*. He is sending a party of sailors and marines to guard the Consulate. He needs someone to guide them from the quay."

Cookson was horrified. "A British force landing in the harbour? Yes, that would start the riot again."

Molyneux looked aghast "But surely a small party sent to protect British subjects and sovereign territory?"

"Would be the only antagonism required, by whoever is orchestrating the troublemakers, to justify another riot," Cookson continued. "Come, we need to see what more Governor Lufti had to say." They returned to their guests.

Governor Lufti and Colonel Sami were both looking increasingly worried. "Vice Consul, I have just been told that a large body of men have been launched in the dark from the British Fleet and are at this very moment rowing towards the harbour quay," said Lufti.

Colonel Sami looked stern. "The Egyptian Artillery has been ordered to fire on any British that try to land out of the water."

"I think we can agree that this will be a massacre with terrible consequences," said Lufti.

"Agreed, I will call the Admiral at once," said Molyneux.

He was fortunate in being able to get through to the Admiral immediately. He returned a few moments later. "The Admiral agrees that the landing has to be stopped somehow, but the boats have already launched and there is no way to call them back." He hastily grabbed a signal pad, scribbled a few lines and signed the note. He turned to Morice, grateful that their lunch together had given him a reasonable view of the man's capability.

"As the Khedive's Inspector General of Coastguards, could you take this note out to the boats in the dark and get them to turn back?"

"Night navigation was one of my better subjects at Dartmouth," he replied. "I can give it a very good try."

Molyneux nodded.

Colonel Sami looked slightly relieved. "Good. I will send a couple of my best officers with him. They will be able to get him past any patrols or difficult areas."

They would also be able to report back that the boats have turned around thought Molyneux.

"No time to lose," said Cookson. "Captain, I suggest you go with Colonel Sami down to the quay just in case Morice misses them in the dark."

The men hurried to their tasks.

Debris covered the streets but there were no signs of the crowds as they made their way to the harbour. The bodies appeared to have been removed. They met two sections of well ordered soldiers who recognised Colonel Sami and saluted before continuing their patrol.

Arriving at the harbour, Morice discovered the coastguard cutters were nowhere to be found and nearly every boat that could float was anchored away from the quay. He eventually found a small skiff that would float for long enough to row out to one of the fishing vessels. The Egyptian officers were not happy at joining him in the leaky boat but eventually agreed.

Morice rowed out to a Greek fishing vessel he recognised. He knew the skipper and hailed him when he was twenty yards away. The Greek hastily stowed a shotgun as soon as he recognised Morice, and they were able to pull alongside with an uncomfortable amount of water already in the well of the skiff. It sank shortly after they boarded the Greek vessel.

The Greek was none too pleased at seeing the Egyptian officers but on learning the task, and with assurances from Morice, weighed anchor and they pulled out into the bay. The water was calm and ink black with barely a breath of wind. There were few lights showing in the town and only a riding light showing on the larger yachts, merchant vessels and warships lying darkly at anchor. Above them, the heavens were filled with a spectacular array of stars that provided a pale peaceful light, oblivious to the violent events of the day. The lighthouse beam swept the horizon behind the breakwater.

Morice directed the skipper to steer a line that bisected the *Invincible* and the breakwater and tasked the Egyptian officers with keeping watch. The crew, glad to be away from the town, pulled steadily at their oars. Every few minutes they stopped rowing and listened for any sounds that might give away the location of the British boats. Nothing was heard bar the lapping of the water against the boat.

"This is hopeless," said Morice after a while. "Show a light and let us hope they respond."

A lantern was uncovered and answered with a blue light. "There they are." Unfortunately the blue light was also seen from the shore and they heard the blare of bugles sounding the alarm. They pulled towards where they had seen the light.

"Ahoy, *Invincible*" he called. "I have an urgent message from Captain Molyneux."

After a tense few minutes they were able to pull alongside the lead cutter and Morice was able to pass Molyneux' note and explain the situation. The officer commanding the boat party was distinctly unimpressed at having his opportunity for action denied him, but eventually returned to his ship.

Dawn revealed a fractured City with frightened Europeans grouped behind barricaded Consulates urgently seeking passage away from Egypt. The streets were at least quiet. Colonel Sami's soldiers were in control and the clean up had begun.

Molyneux and Cookson sat in the Vice Consul's office on the first floor, drinking tea. While the streets had been quiet the tension remained and neither had slept for more than a few minutes at a time. Molyneux was used to disrupted sleep patterns and having washed and shaved was ready to return to his ship for a hard day's work. He inspected the Vice Consul over the rim of his teacup. Cookson, head and one hand bandaged and with livid welts and bruises apparent in all exposed areas of his body, understandably looked very tired.

"In a City with such a transient population I don't suppose we will ever know how many died," he observed.

Cookson glanced at a note on his desk. "Reports from the hospital say there are 44 European bodies there and another 36 wounded. I gather something over 200 locals are dead too, with many more wounded."

Molyneux grimaced, "Morice saw many more bodies that had been thrown into the sea. I have no doubt many old scores were settled yesterday. I had better return to my ship and prepare for the mass exodus. By next week I doubt there will be many Europeans left in Egypt."

22
A DELICATE MATTER
HMS Invincible, Alexandria inner harbour, 14 Jun 1882

"Come," Captain Molyneux did not look up at the knock on his door and continued to read that morning's intelligence reports. His clerk placed several more papers on his desk and stood to one side as Samuel de Kusel stepped past the Royal Marine guard and entered the Captain's stateroom. The Clerk departed for his small office next door, already distracted by the prospect of reconciling the wardroom accounts before lunch.

Kusel approached the mahogany desk and waited as reflections from the azure blue water beyond the windows danced across the ceiling.

A few moments later Molyneux placed the paper on his desk and looked up. A warm smile of recognition spread across his face and he rose to his feet, extending his hand. "Kusel, my dear chap, please forgive my lack of attention. Take a seat, do. Can I offer you a coffee or tea?"

Kusel smiled and shook his head, taking a seat across the desk from the Captain. "Thank you, no. I appreciate how busy you must be and will not detain you long. I wanted to share a dilemma that I thought might be of interest."

"You will, of course, be aware that as the Controller-General of the Khedive's Customs Service I am responsible for ensuring that dangerous goods are not transported into Egypt? You may also have noticed the unusual American built ship that entered the harbour yesterday, bound for service in the Khedive's Navy?"

Molyneux raised a quizzical eyebrow.

"I have taken it upon myself to impound the vessel after finding that it contains a new form of device that I am unfamiliar with. I worry that Egyptian sailors will lack the knowledge and ability to handle the device safely, or, God forbid, mutiny and endanger the vessels currently residing in Alexandria harbour. The damage that such an event would do to the Khedive's fragile trading status would be irreparable."

"I see," said Molyneux. "I am sure you have every reason to be concerned and impounding such a device is in the best interests of the Khedive. Is this device something that Her most Britannic Majesty's Navy might be able to assist you with?"

Kusel smiled, relieved that Molyneux had recognised the game and the dilemma that the arrival of the ship had given him. He was, after all, employed by the Khedive, and Arabi had no doubt ordered the weapon on the Khedive's authority. "You are too kind. I do not suppose you have any engineering officers familiar with ships that appear to be designed to lay torpedo mines? Or indeed who might know how such mines might be disabled so that they do not present a danger to Alexandria's shipping?"

Molyneux' fought the desire to smile.

Kusel continued, his face impassive but a smile lingering about his eyes. "Though I fear the loss of face to the Khedive's Navy, were British experts to be seen to assist them, would be embarrassing, particularly in the current, unfortunate circumstances. It would, of course, be necessary for any assistance you might provide to be given in such a way that it was…. not discovered? Do you think this might be possible?"

Molyneux considered. "Well, all our engineers are extremely busy during the day, but might be able to assist the Khedive when they are out of uniform and have a little time available in the middle of the night?"

"That would be most kind of you. My customs officers are rather short handed at present so are unable to keep a watch on the ship between 2200 and 0500 tonight. I do fear that, since there is no moon, thieves may make off with key components. Would your engineering officers be able to keep watch too?"

Molyneux lost the battle to suppress his smile. "I am sure that can be arranged."

Kusel smiled. "And I am sure the Khedive would be most grateful. Thank you, Captain."

"How is the Khedive?" Molyneux asked.

"Well, you will be aware that he arrived in Alexandria by train only yesterday. I am afraid that after the riots the people were not at all happy to see him. Regretfully, he was booed and jeered in the streets. He has now repaired to his palace and is considering how the Sultan may be able to assist. I imagine his hope is that the Sultan will send Turkish troops to re-assert his authority."

"And do you believe the Sultan will?"

"I have no more information than you, but I cannot see what the Sultan would have to gain by sending troops. Arabi and his allies have sworn loyalty to the Sultan and have done nothing to suggest an intention to break Egypt away from the Ottoman Empire. I think the Khedive is on his own so far as Turkey is concerned. Of course, the Sultan has to provide some support for the Khedive. I would not be at all surprised if he sends an envoy to support the Khedive's negotiations with Arabi."

23
DAMNED IF WE DO, DAMNED IF WE DON'T
Cabinet Room, Downing Street, London, 21 June 1882

The Foreign Secretary, the Earl Granville, looked down at his notes. "As expected, following the events in Alexandria and some smaller riots elsewhere, there has been a mass exodus of Europeans from Alexandria and Cairo. All infrastructure works have stopped, the shops and hotels are closed and the streets are deserted, except for those fleeing to the harbour or railway station. The situation is not helped by the fact that with 14,000 Europeans gone, there are 30,000 natives in Alexandria alone that are now without jobs or pay. Our Egyptian Consul-General, Sir Edward Malet, is of the view that since the French fleet will not land any troops, and we could only land 1000, our Fleet is now a threat to stability in the region and should be withdrawn."

"How would that look if the most powerful Navy in the World were to withdraw in the face of native insurrection?" asked Joseph Chamberlain.

"The knock on effects throughout the Empire would be disastrous," said Lord Hartington.

"Malet was the man who requested the Fleet in the first place!" exclaimed Gladstone. "And now we have Lord Salisbury stirring up the House and the Country, telling everyone that my pacifism has led to British subjects being butchered under the guns of the Fleet which has not budged an inch to save them!"

"I agree," said Joseph Chamberlain. "We are damned if we pull the Fleet out and damned if the Fleet remains and does nothing."

"The Fleet is doing something," said Lord Northbrook, First Lord of the Admiralty. "It has been swamped with refugees and officers have been heavily engaged chartering merchant ships to repatriate

British subjects. Admiral Seymour assures me his fleet could hold a beachhead to enable evacuation in the event of more rioting, though not in the current weather conditions. There is too much surf and too little sea room."

"And what of the French?" asked Hartington. "They have a similar interest to us in Egypt, yet their Fleet did nothing during the riots; they refuse to land troops to support us and they refuse to consider the idea of Turkish troops landing to support the Khedive. What is the use of such Allies?"

Granville grimaced slightly. "I would point out that the rule of law has not totally broken down in Egypt. The Khedive has created a new joint ministry and when he returned to Alexandria yesterday was even cheered in the streets"

"Though that may have had a great deal to do with the fact that his Minister for War, Ahmed Arabi, was seated next to him in the carriage?" Hartington chipped in.

Granville smiled at the interruption. "I am assured the authorities are tracking down the rioters, as well as the policemen and soldiers who took part, and will be prosecuting them."

"So the Khedive is publicly reconciled with Arabi," stated John Bright, the Chancellor of the Duchy of Lancaster.

"For now, though for how long?" said Chamberlain. "This latest development is no doubt because the Sultan has refused to send troops to support the Khedive. Without that support the Khedive has to appease the Arabists.

"We understand that as a Quaker you will always look for the God in all people and that nothing could justify war, but we have seen these reconciliations collapse time and again. The only thing that maintains stability in Egypt is power, and that power lies with Arabi, not the Khedive. For so long as Arabi needs a figurehead, the Khedive will remain. But he is on borrowed time."

"Indeed," said Hartington. "Despite the imminent Constantinople conference, several of us around this table believe war is inevitable and we need to be prepared for it. While a Turkish expedition is preferable it would not happen fast enough. The French will not invade without the Turks." He paused to allow these thoughts to settle before continuing. "We cannot ignore the possibility that, if we do nothing, the French will do a sly deal with the Turks and the Khedive."

At this statement, Gladstone noted the nods of agreement from around the room and determined to execute his contingency plan. "Very well." He looked at Childers. "With the First Lord of the Admiralty you will look at the best ways of protecting the Suez Canal, with the French."

Lord Northbrook nodded agreement. "Prime Minister, while this is considered I do not believe we can avoid the need to be seen to do something and for troops to support the Fleet. It would be prudent to send 3 Battalions to the Mediterranean so they can be immediately available to execute any plan we might agree?"

Once again Gladstone noted the temperature of the room and glanced at Childers, before responding. "Very well, though 2 Battalions will suffice."

24
HIGH SEAT

HMS Invincible, Alexandria inner harbour, 4 July 1882

Breathing heavily, Captain Molyneux climbed onto the main crosstrees high above the deck below and nodded acknowledgement to the two lookouts as, surprised, they made space for him. The exertion of the climb had raised a sweat beneath his tunic and his arms and legs burned from the unaccustomed exercise. He resolved to make the climb on a regular basis; it would do his fitness no harm and help to keep the ship's company on their toes. Their previous Captain had been far too relaxed about such things.

Without speaking he took the large telescope from one of the lookouts and trained it towards the Khedive's palace. Desperately trying to slow his breathing, and squinting through the glare, he stared at the warships from Austria, Germany, Greece, Italy, Russia, and the USA; all anchored as if to watch a show. In a few days, they would probably witness the first bombardment the Royal Navy had carried out in decades. Looking North, Molyneux could see workers scurrying over the earthworks at the lighthouse fort, and he wondered, not for the first time what the risk was that the Egyptian gunners would dare to open fire on the British Fleet without warning.

His breathing had slowed and he now felt able to speak.

"So, Able Seaman Higgins, what news of the natives?"

Higgins, surprised at the unexpected sight of his Captain climbing to the highest point in the ship, was astounded that Molyneux knew his name. "They are working day and night, Sir; though what use it will be against our high explosive shells I have no idea. As we already reported to Lieutenant Smyth, we think they mounted another 2 guns in Pharos Fort last night, but they look small and old." Molyneux nodded and trained the scope on the Fort. He could just about see the guns poking through the embrasures.

"We keep a sharp lookout for native craft, too, Sir, but have not seen any sign of them laying any mines, just fishing. That boat over there," Higgins paused and pointed out a scruffy looking vessel anchored off of the breakwater to the far West, "stops in the same place each day but never seems to catch much. Her skipper spends a lot of time looking for fish with his telescope though."

Molyneux smiled grimly. "We look at them, and they watch us. But they won't be able to see the rest of our Fleet from there."

He didn't add that they could no longer see what was happening in Alexandria. Intelligence from the city was difficult to obtain. A couple of British officers disguised as locals had risked all to establish there were probably 10,000 Egyptian troops in Alexandria now with hundreds of Bedouin camping just outside, though to what purpose no one appeared to know. The Khedive had taken the 130 mile, five hour rail journey North from Cairo and was now in residence in his Ras-el-Tin Palace, overlooking the inner harbour. His arrival had been greeted with great fanfare, the visiting warships bedecked with flags and each giving him a 21 gun salute. Arabi was last heard of staying at a nearby arsenal.

Their other information source, the flow of Europeans out of Egypt, had reduced from a flood to a trickle. The latest were the US Embassy staff, though the French, Austro-Hungarian, Danish and German Consulates were apparently still manned. Last week the British Consul, Sir Edward Malet, had departed his mission on the grounds of ill health, though had made a miraculous recovery soon after stepping aboard ship. Cookson was recovering from his wounds and had also departed the consulate; his deputy, Mr Calvert had resigned, leaving the British with no diplomatic representation, merely a large naval presence.

Molyneux considered the pile of paperwork on his desk and the climb down but there was nothing more to be gained from remaining in the pleasant isolation of the maintop. There was a fresh offshore breeze that hummed amongst the rigging as she pulled at her mooring. While it would take several hours to raise enough steam to weigh anchor and turn the propeller, the breeze ensured that they could loose topsails and escape if they had to. The officer of the watch had been briefed on the action to take in the event the Egyptian gunners took leave of their senses. He turned to descend.

"Well done. Keep up the good lookout and do not hesitate to sing out if you see them making ready to fire. I don't think it will be long now before we are in action.

25
LOSING CONTROL

Cabinet Room, Downing Street, London Wednesday 5th July 1882

The Cabinet Room was close, the books that surrounded the Ministers on all sides, added to the feeling of stuffiness, and the Earl Granville wished one of the windows could be opened. The agenda had once again turned to the subject that dominated the Press. He cleared his throat. "The European conference in Constantinople, as expected, ended without any way forward. The French confirm they will not participate in any action in Egypt without the consent of Chambers; which they will not obtain without a commitment from Turkey to send troops. Turkey will not send troops.

"The Sultan's private secretary did offer us sole control and administration of Egypt if Turkey retained sovereignty. We turned the offer down flat. Even if the Sultan were to offer Egypt as a gift with all of Europe consenting, we do not want the burden or responsibility."

There was consternation around the table with several Ministers muttering words to the effect. "Surely that would solve the problem?"

Lord Hartington sighed. "Far from it. The offer was informal and easily dismissed had we accepted. The Sultan fears and loathes the French and, after Tunisia, does not want them to gain a bigger foothold in North Africa if they invade with Britain. Such an offer, informal or otherwise, was probably designed to drive a wedge between Britain and France."

He paused to allow his colleagues to consider. "If the offer were genuine, and even if we had the support of Europe, we would still be faced with Arabi in effective control, and, so far as the people are concerned, he has the support of Turkey. To remove him we would need to deploy sufficient troops to nullify his power base, without any military support from Turkey who would still claim sovereignty and the moral high ground with the Egyptian people. It was the kind of clever ploy we have come to expect from the rulers in the region."

"If Arabi is the key, can the Sultan not remove him?" asked John Bright.

Granville answered. "We believe they have tried. The Sultan's envoy has been trying to entice Arabi to Constantinople but without success. Most recently, the offer was to be personally awarded the Order of the Medjidieh by the Sultan in recognition of his recent conduct. Arabi knows his power rests at home in Egypt and will not leave."

"So what do you suggest?" asked Chamberlain of the Foreign Secretary. "We cannot maintain a policy of inaction; our Fleet, the greatest symbol of our power throughout the Empire, will look impotent."

"I disagree," said Granville. "Egypt is an incredibly complex and unpredictable environment. This situation was triggered by French intervention in Tunisia generating nationalistic pride. To the South, all it takes is rebellion by some Islamic fundamentalist in Sudan and you can add religious fervour and a clash with the Sultan to the mix. Any action we take could, and probably will, have dire and unforeseen consequences."

"Is Egypt more complex than India?" asked Hartington. He paused to provide his Cabinet colleagues with a moment to contemplate the implications of the question. "Would we have an Empire if we followed a policy of non-intervention? Strong leadership, and the desire to improve lives for all, have proven a successful formula for decades. Why abandon it now?

"It is clear that Arabi's strong leadership carries the population. While we cannot know who instigated the riots, they, and their subsequent put down, have cemented Arabi's position as the most powerful man in Egypt. What happens when he unilaterally decides to ignore European interests and stop repaying the bonds? Will anyone ever risk investing in Egypt again? And where will that leave the Egyptian people who cannot understand the consequences? I suspect they are beginning to feel those consequences now that most of the Europeans have left and most of them are out of work and hungry. Four fifths of all Egyptian commerce is driven by Britain. Do we write that off too?

"Ignoring its obvious strategic importance, what of our 44% stake in the Suez Canal if we do nothing? What is to prevent Arabi nationalising it? Our stake would be worthless but the millions of pounds of British Government bonds we issued to buy it would still need to be honoured. What message would that send to the rest of our Empire?" The Secretary of State for India looked around the room, aware that he had won the point with most of his colleagues.

"You argue your case very eloquently," Granville responded. "The French, who as you know manage the operation of the Canal, have given Arabi every assurance that it is neutral territory. Were Arabi to nationalise it, such would be in contravention of international law."

"Hah!" exclaimed Chamberlain. "Are you suggesting that were Arabi to take control of the Canal, the French Chambers would vote to take it back by force?" He, and many of the others around the table, chuckled. "Arabi must look at the French Fleet in Alexandria harbour with the same disdain with which he regards ours."

"So what do you suggest?" asked the Prime Minister, irritated by the discussion and clearly still minded towards a continued policy of inaction. "What action do you suggest that does not risk the canal?"

"The presence of the British and French Navy in Alexandria has not dissuaded Arabi from his belligerent course," said Hartington. "Nor has it caused him to fire the first shot in a conventional war.

Meanwhile he rebuilds the forts, buys new mine laying ships from the Americans, no doubt, modern rifled guns from the Germans and all paid for with British loans. Soon, there is a risk Arabi or an excitable gunner will open fire and force our hand and our fleet would be unable to prosecute our wishes. I propose we bombard the forts before they are rebuilt."

The Quaker, John Bright, responded, "Surely as a sovereign State the Egyptians have every right to build up their defences? Such an unprovoked attack would surely endanger the canal?" It was not so much a question as a statement, and seeing he had the attention of the room, he continued. "Surely if the attack on the port endangers the Canal, and it is the protection of the canal that is the primary reason the Fleet is in Alexandria, the attack should not be made?"

Lord Northbrook, First Lord of the Admiralty, spoke for the first time. "I agree with the Secretary of State for India. If the forts are rebuilt, and offshore mines laid, there would be a risk that the Canal would be nationalised and our 44% stake would be worthless while the Government would still be liable for the debt incurred in purchasing it. A bombardment now, before they are rebuilt, reduces that risk. If we want to bring on a fight we can instruct Seymour to require the guns to be dismantled."

Gladstone realised he had lost the room. He knew only Granville and John Bright supported the policy of inaction, and had been warned that several of the ministers would resign if he continued the policy. Those resignations would make the governments position untenable. He seized the opportunity to give the Egyptians a chance to come to their senses. "Agreed. Instruct Admiral Seymour to demand the guns be dismantled." If they had to resort to a bombardment he hoped it would bring the Egyptians to their senses and destroy the Nationalists without invasion being necessary.

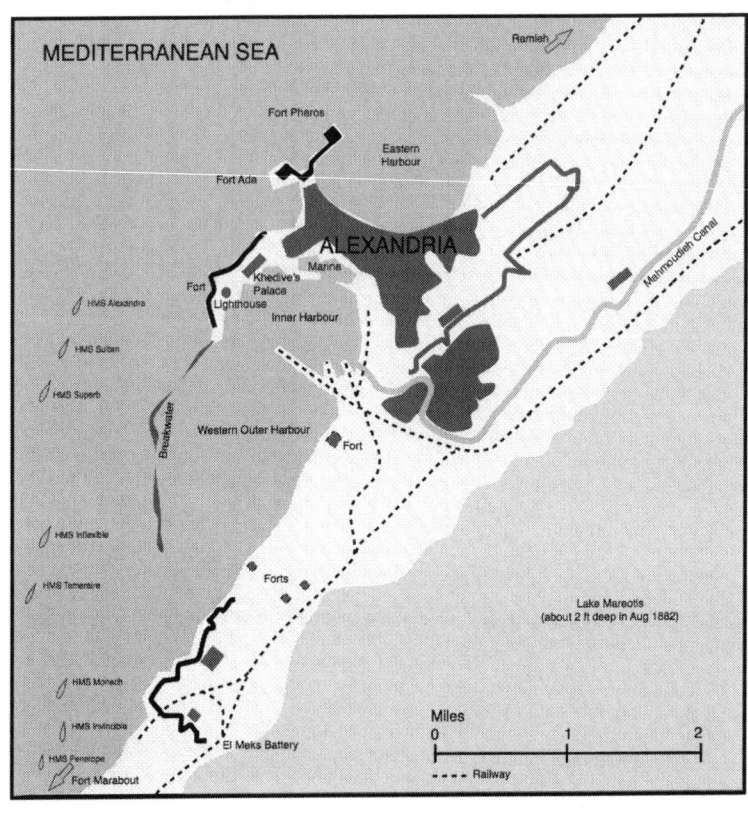

Alexandria, 11 July 1882 – Royal Navy ships shown in their positions during the bombardment.

26
BOMBARDMENT

Alexandria, Monday 10th July 1882

Admiral Seymour regarded all the Captains of the Mediterranean Fleet as they sat in his stateroom on board *HMS Alexandra,* looking out of the windows at the Lighthouse Fort. Their eyes shone with excitement. "As you know, I gave notice to Arabi on 6th July that he must disarm the batteries or face bombardment. The following day, the Turkish envoy returned to Constantinople in his yacht so we can take it that he has given up hope of encouraging Arabi to return with him.

"On Saturday I ordered the ships we had held back over the horizon into the outer harbour. While their appearance was undoubtedly a shock for the Egyptians it was a sign of our ability and intent to follow through with our threat.

"Yesterday I gained intelligence that new 32 pounder guns are being mounted at Fort Silsileh and also at Fort Pharos. I signalled this to the Admiralty and asked for confirmation from the Prime Minister that I am to carry out our threat. I have now received that confirmation.

"At 11 o'clock this morning I sent notice to Arabi and the Khedive that as hostile preparations continue, I will commence bombardment at sunrise tomorrow unless the forts on the isthmus, and commanding the entrance to the harbour, are temporarily surrendered for the purposes of disarmament. I have received no reply.

"I have sent word to any remaining British subjects and the remaining Consular staff to take refuge on the P&O ship *Tanjore,* together with all the war correspondents who have now gathered here, and who seem determined to ensure this will be the first naval action reported, first hand, in history. Word has also been sent to the other Consulates."

"I have informed the French fleet of our intent and invited them to join us in the bombardment. They have politely declined, citing an unavoidable prior engagement and were last seen steaming for Port Said." The officers smiled and there were a couple of tense chuckles at the unexpected humour.

"Gentlemen, Battle Orders. Your mission is to destroy the forts and emplacements in accordance with the instructions you are now being handed." He looked at Molyneux. "I will be transferring my Flag to *Invincible*. With her shallower draft I wish to command the bombardment from closer to the shore."

On returning to their ships the orders were disseminated and the men sent into a flurry of activity, excited and nervous in equal measure. The top masts, top gallant and royal yards were sent down, reducing the elegant profile of the ships to a squat, menacing black form. The ships were cleared for action with screens and personal belongings removed below so that the decks were clear from stem to stern. Hammocks were slung around the wheel and around the maintop where the 10 barrelled Gatling and heavier 2 and 4-barrelled Nordenfeldt machine guns were positioned. The dense rolled canvas would protect the helmsmen and gunners from flying splinters, though there was no expectation that the Egyptian gunners would actually hit anything, as they had not fired a shot for 25 years.

In the inky black of a moonless night *Invincible* steamed very slowly into the shallow water near the entrance to the outer harbour. The navigator, sweating under the scrutiny of both his Captain and Admiral, could barely contain his relief when they dropped anchor without running aground. HMS *Penelope*, the smallest battleship in the Fleet, dropped anchor alongside, while *HMS Monarch*, drawing another foot, came to a halt about 500yds further out.

A wire hawser was run from the stern capstan to the anchor chain to act as a spring that would enable *Invincible* to present her broadside to the chosen targets. Unseen, 1000yds away on their starboard side, the 31 guns of Fort Meks lay silent.

At five the following morning, the bugle call to action sounded through the Fleet and 450 men in *Invincible* made their way through the half light to their battle stations. In the centre of the ship, on the 2 gun decks, the ten 9 inch and four 6 inch rifled, muzzle loading guns were made ready and more ammunition drawn up from the magazines in the bowels of the ship. Most of the men were stripped down to their flannel jerseys despite the cool morning. The surgeon removed his coat and set out tables, pillows, mattresses and instruments to treat the wounded. The men screwed cotton rags in their ears to protect them from the sound of the guns. The gunners laid the guns onto their designated targets as they slowly appeared through the gloom of the approaching dawn.

An expectant silence settled over the ship.

A small boat cautiously approached *Invincible* and hailed the Flagship; three rather nervous Egyptian officers requested permission to come aboard. Molyneux advanced to the waist and leaning on the rail looked down into the boat as it bumped against the side of his ship. He did not recognise any of the men.

"How can I help you? If you want breakfast, I'm afraid you've missed it." Some of the men nearby chuckled. The leader of the three men, a lean Captain with a prominent nose and moustache, looked up.

"Captain, praise Allah we have found you at last. We have been looking for you all night. May we come aboard and speak with Admiral Seymour?"

"Unless it is to tell him that you are surrendering the forts on the isthmus and commanding the entrance to the harbour so they can be disarmed, I am afraid he is busy."

The Captain looked uncomfortable. "Captain, we have dismounted 3 guns in the Silsileh, Caid Bay and Salah forts." He knew it was not enough, but fired up with patriotic zeal, it was all the Egyptian War Council had been prepared to concede in the face of the British aggression that they believed was contrary to International Law.

Molyneux did not need to look back to Seymour on the Quarterdeck. He looked the Egyptian in the eye and replied with a dismissive wave of his arm towards the shore. "The time for talking is over. Run along."

The Egyptians glanced briefly at each other and then hurriedly turned their steam launch back to the shore. Molyneux returned to his Admiral's side on the bridge. Seymour nodded approval but said nothing.

An expectant silence settled over the ship as the hour for action approached. In the outer harbour they watched as the offshore squadron of *Alexandra*, *Sultan* and *Superb* formed line of battle and steamed towards the batteries that stretched from Ras-el-Tin, by the breakwater, to Pharos. Mid way between *Invincible* and the Offshore Squadron, lay the huge *Inflexible* with her four 16 inch guns, and *Monarch*.

At 7am the signal was sent from Admiral Seymour to *Alexandra* "Fire one shot", then a signal to the Fleet, "Attack the enemy's batteries".

From the other side of the breakwater a dull thud from *Alexandra* heralded the start of the bombardment. "Open Fire!" Molyneux' words of command were barely past his lips when the ship shook with the recoil from the first staggered broadside. A deafening roar and a cloud of smoke belched from the side of the ship before ascending. Above them, monstrous 16 inch shells from *Inflexible* rumbled in the air like a dozen trains racing through tunnels. Moments later, explosions flowered on the Fort Meks emplacements and then the sound of tap-tapping as the Gatlings and

Nordenfeldts opened fire on the Egyptian gunners, whose embrasures offered little cover.

Looking at the other ships, Molyneux could see columns of powder smoke rise above the masts and men waving and pointing as they would during gunnery practice. *Invincible* quivered with the concussion of the heavy guns, and then with a dull clang, the first Egyptian shell hit her iron side just below the waterline.

"They're going to make a fight of it then?" Seymour said as columns of water rose around the three ships and rounds screamed over the deck. "It was as though they had been told not to return fire until we had fired our first few broadsides."

Molyneux watched through his telescope as an Egyptian gun crew was swept away by a direct hit, only to be replaced and the gun brought back into action.

"Brave buggers," he commented, and was surprised to see one of the sailors who clearly had the same thought leap up onto the top rail, one hand gripping a stay, and shout "Well done, Gippy!"

For an hour the guns roared out and the British sailors cheered direct hits on the forts and laughed and jeered the misses. One miss landed in the Arab quarter at 0800, causing panic. By 9am many of the locals were barricaded behind doors or huddled in coffee shops where rumours that two ironclads had been sunk and 5 others disabled were greeted with joy and then growing dismay as the rate of fire increased. Shells that missed the forts started to fall on the town at the rate of more than 2 a minute.

"Wheeeeeeee!" yelled the sailors as the Hales war rockets were launched, trailing long haphazard tails of smoke towards the shoreline that was barely visible through the ever-expanding smog that clung to the deck like wool to a brier.

Above Molyneux, in the maintop, Midshipman Hardy directed his 1 inch, crank handled, Nordenfeldt and called out each fall of shot to Lt Bradford, the gunnery officer below. They were firing deliberately now, each shot aimed at the Egyptian guns that had now got their range and were trading blows with his ship – albeit without much effect; most of the shots were ducking below the water line and bouncing off the iron hull or sailing overhead.

"*Penelope* is taking rather a pasting, Admiral," he commented. "I have seen her take several shots above the waterline and among her yards. The crafty Egyptian's have hidden a gun in that house over there. Our chaps are on it though." A few moments later they noted with satisfaction that the house had been hit and the gun stopped firing.

At 0830 a magazine at Fort Marsa-el-Khanat exploded under the weight of fire from *Monarch*. A few men cheered but after taking casualties it was no longer a game and the men had settled into a serious workmanlike rhythm. He winced slightly as he saw a sailor struck down by an unseen splinter of hot shell that had come from a different direction, and another collapse clutching his belly. *Invincible* was now taking long range crossfire from the 24 gun Fort Marabout to their stern.

"What the Devil is Beresford up to in *Condor*?" asked Admiral Seymour as they watched the gunboat steaming towards Fort Marabout. "She is so small and with only 3 guns I thought her best kept out of the fight."

"She has done well, Admiral," said Molyneux. "She towed *Temeraire* off that reef earlier and now appears to be taking on Fort Marabout."

"One direct hit from one of those heavy guns and she will be matchwood," replied Seymour.

"True, but with the angle of approach Beresford is taking, the heavy guns cannot get a bearing on her. If he can navigate through the shoals and get up close, the Egyptian guns won't be able to depress their barrels sufficiently and will be firing over the top while he can rake their embrasures."

They watched as Condor made it through the shoals and started peppering the fort from about 1200 yards. As the other four Gunboats joined them the fire from the fort decreased.

"Yeoman!" called Seymour. "Send a message to *Condor*. Send, 'Well done, *Condor*.'" He seemed to consider for a moment and then said, "Send 'Well done, *Inflexible*,' too".

The signals officer looked surprised, but the messages were sent and a few minutes later messages were flashing, "Well done, *Condor*," through the fleet.

Suddenly Molyneux saw a shell land on the deck below him. He braced himself for the explosion but fortunately the fuse must have fallen out as nothing happened and a sailor tossed it overboard a moment later. "That was a close call," he commented to Seymour and called down to the deck; "Well done, that man."

"The offshore Squadron is anchoring off Ras-el-Tin, Admiral."

"Quite right, too, they have been steaming at full speed back and forth and firing for over 2 hours but seem to have had little impact on the forts. Perhaps with a steady platform they will have more success."

The guns continued to roar out from both sides all morning as the sun climbed into a clear blue sky and the heat became intolerable. The anchored ships were hidden behind the pall of powder smoke, through which could be seen the occasional orange flash of the guns. Below, on the gun decks, the men were stripped to the waist, caked in powder residue and choking on sulphurous fumes. The sailors laboured, lifting the heavy shells and powder up from the magazines to be consumed in the potbellies of the guns. Poorly aimed rounds from the Egyptian guns flew overhead or skipped across the waves before disappearing in a plume of spray. The odd shot found its mark, fragments clanging down the hollow of the mast, ripping through funnels and tearing splintered fissures through the wooden decks. Casualties were light.

Molyneux wondered how much worse it would be in the Forts with the dust, smoke, flying splinters from shells and fractured stone, the tearing crack and thump of machine gun rounds, and the ever present risk that the magazine might be hit and explode at any minute. His respect for the bravery of the Egyptian gunners grew as each hour wore on.

Stray shells had hit several buildings in Alexandria, including an Anglican church, the German consulate and a synagogue. The damage and casualties were limited as many of the shells did not explode, but the remaining 1500 Europeans became the target of the mobs that became progressively angrier and bolder as the bombardment wore into the afternoon. Egyptian soldiers cut the telegraph lines and checked the flat rooftops to ensure Europeans were not reporting back the fall of shot.

Large numbers of horribly wounded artillerymen, accompanied by the stripped and bound bodies of the fallen, rattled up the streets in carts towards the main hospital in the Avenue Rosetta; a sad indicator of the power of a modern fleet. The medical staff, comprising only three doctors, was overwhelmed; the wounded lay on the bare stone floors covered in blood and dust, pitifully crying out for water.

The Lighthouse battery was finally silenced under the fire of the Offshore Squadron at 1230. In an incredible display of courage, the Egyptian officer commanding appeared on the parapet in a grimy white uniform and red fez hat, and shook his fist in defiance at the British Fleet.

The Inshore Squadron, supported by the Gunboats, continued to concentrate fire on Fort Meks with *Monarch* targeting a barracks to the rear that was reached by a bridge suspended over a deep, dry ditch. Unexpectedly, Egyptian soldiers rushed in panic from the barracks and over the bridge at exactly the time a shell broke the supporting chains on one side. The bridge collapsed and a great many soldiers were thrown to their deaths in the ditch. Others grasped at the remaining timbers while shells and machine gun rounds rained about them. The fort ceased fire shortly afterwards.

At 1330 there was a sudden flash with a bright upward burst of flame in the distance beyond the lighthouse. Fort Ada, bisecting the Lighthouse Fort and Fort Pharos at the end of the Isthmus, exploded under fire from *Superb*. The men raised a huge cheer as a dense black column of smoke, dust and debris shot into the air and gradually spread outwards like a giant fungus, followed by a great wall of sound. Fort Pharos ceased fire shortly afterwards and then in mid afternoon the lines at Ras-el-Tin hoisted a white flag, though one gun continued to fire every ten minutes for a considerable time afterwards.

"Fort Meks has been quiet for some time now, Molyneux. I propose we send a small landing party ashore to spike the guns," said Seymour at 2pm.

Amidst much vying to be included, Lt Bradford, the ship's gunnery officer, was selected to lead a party of 12 bluejackets as well as Major Tulloch of *Invincible's* Royal Marines, Seymour's Flag Lieutenant, Lambton and Lt Poore. Under the cover of the Gunboat *Bittern*, they found the fort deserted and Bradford blew up its two biggest guns with dynamite. Lambton and Tullock, armed with hammer and nails, quickly drove spikes into the vents of the smooth bore guns. They returned without contact with the enemy, though the heavy swell smashed their boat on the rocks and they had to be picked up by the spare.

By 4pm the Forts had fallen silent and the bombardment subsided, enabling the residents of Alexandria to stream out of the city along the banks of the Mahmoudieh Canal or follow the railway line towards Cairo. The mass exodus was only halted by the approaching darkness that shrouded the City. Gaslight, symbol of European progress, remained unlit; the only illumination the flickering flames consuming the Khedive's palace.

At 5.30pm Admiral Seymour signalled cease-fire and *Invincible* fired a last, experimental shell that exploded on the upper works of the windmill fort. As the dust cleared an old woman emerged from an outhouse and chased some chickens into their coop before disappearing inside again and slamming the door. An occasional Egyptian gun spat defiance, but the action was over.

Later that evening Molyneux sat with Admiral Seymour analysing the after action reports. Molyneux summarised the situation.

"We fired almost 3800 shells from the guns, though over half appear not to have exploded. I think we can conclude that armour-piercing shells are not suitable for shore bombardment, particularly of earthwork emplacements.

"Over 33,000 rounds were fired from the machine guns, though the effect of these cannot be confirmed. Initial reports from the landing parties suggest the Egyptians suffered hundreds of casualties.

"With the exception of the Gunboats, who have been able to resupply from *Hecla*, the Fleet is very short of ammunition, Admiral. *Alexandra* has only 15 shells left. None of the other ironclads have many more and we cannot be resupplied until *Humber* arrives tomorrow evening.

"Casualties in the Fleet have been light with 5 killed and 28 wounded, one grievously. The Egyptians were not using armour-piercing shells and most of their roundshot bounced off the armour plate." Molyneux considered *Invincible* very fortunate to have only 6 wounded, mainly from splinters. He put down his notes and picked up a separate dispatch.

"We have a recommendation for a Victoria Cross from *Alexandra*," he said. Seymour looked up with interest. "At 0800hrs a 10 inch shell hit portside, shot through a cabin and onto the deck where it struck an engine room hatchway and narrowly missed some officers. It then bounced backwards against some rifle racks and rolled over to the starboard side hatchway leading to the magazine where men were hauling up powder for the gunners. A warning was shouted and Gunner Harding, one of the old hands, rushed up, seized the shell and threw water on the burning fuse before dumping it into the bucket of water. The incident was witnessed by Melton Prior of the Illustrated London News."

"Brave," replied Seymour. "Had it exploded the damage and loss of life would have been considerable, but hardly worthy of a VC."

"I beg to differ, Admiral. I recall the first VC ever awarded was to Midshipman Lucas for an identical act in 1854."

Seymour regarded Molyneux for a moment before replying. "Very well, send it up to the Admiralty with my support."

They were interrupted by a knock at the door and Lt Poore, the officer of the watch appeared. "Excuse me, Sir, I thought you ought to know that Ras-el-Tin is on fire and more fires are appearing across Alexandria."

Dawn on Wednesday 12th July revealed a leaden sky and a strengthening offshore wind that raised a choppy sea and caused the offshore Squadron to roll.

Molyneux looked across the quarterdeck to where Seymour stood, deep in thought and staring towards the City where a few tendrils of smoke arrowed down to the scenes of overnight arson. Familiar with the loneliness of command he was glad he was not in the Admiral's shoes. Seymour was very much alone and in a difficult position. He had neither authority nor the troops needed to invade. The only instruction he had been given from the Admiralty was to disarm the Forts and he had already been rebuked by the Prime Minister for going so far as he had. He did not want to exacerbate the situation by raising the Union Jack in Alexandria. The only action he could take was bombardment; a demonstration of shock and awe that would hopefully cause Arabi's followers to submit. Once the Khedive was back in power, British interests would be protected. But he had almost run out of shells. Many of the shells they had fired had faulty fuses, exploding too early or not at all, and he suspected a more determined enemy could have brought many of the Egyptian guns back into action with little effort. There was no firing from the Forts but neither had they surrendered.

At 1045 *Inflexible* and *Temeraire* fired a few of their remaining shells at Fort Pharos, which promptly raised a white flag.

Carefully briefed, Flag Lieutenant Lambton was dispatched to determine the position and relay the Admiral's terms. At 2pm, he stepped aboard the Khedival yacht just as Toulba Pasha, commander of the City's defences, arrived on his steam launch. The Khedive was in Ramleh and, fired with patriotic fervour, had ordered that the Egyptian soldiers defend the Forts and prevent a British landing. Lambton relayed the terms to Toulba - namely that the British occupy Fort Meks on condition they did not display any flag, and that the defences in Fort Adjemi be destroyed.

Toulba Pasha was not empowered to agree and needed the truce extended to provide time to consult the Khedive. He was given an hour, during which time, 1800 Egyptian soldiers loyal to Arabi, smartly marched out of Alexandria towards Ramleh, leaving behind a leaderless rabble of uniformed looters who fought with the

Bedouin for the spoils. The City was descending into a chaos that Arabi was unable to control, despite several attempts.

Flag Lieutenant Lambton returned to the Fleet and later in the afternoon, a single shot at Fort Meks brought about its surrender. When Commander Morrison of the Gunboat *Helicon* was sent to investigate, he found the Khedival yacht deserted and, as darkness fell, an ominous glow from the European quarter of the City.

Aboard *Invincible*, Seymour needed information but could not risk the ire of the Prime Minister by exceeding his orders and landing a British military reconnaissance party. His dilemma was solved by a local merchant, John Ross, and the Press; John Cameron of *The Standard* and Frederick Villiers of *The Graphic* were determined to be the first to file reports. Lieutenant Forsyth took them to the marina by *Invincible's* steam launch.

All along the waterfront the wharves were on fire, flames reaching high into the sky and casting ghastly shadows. The marina was choked with abandoned boats that bobbed up and down against the jetty, fended off by the blackened and gas bloated bodies of men, women and children, mainly Syrian Jews slain by the Bedouin marauders. Occasionally the smoke would clear to reveal the scurrying scum of society, arms laden with booty, mad with greed.

Ross, Cameron and Villiers slipped ashore and, avoiding the main avenues, crept up the narrow side streets as far as the Place Muhammad Ali. Bodies lay scattered outside looted stores that smouldered, crackled and creaked as weights changed along newly unstable walls. Roofs and floors collapsed into the sparking ruins, vomiting limedust and smoke. Molten lead pipes spat jets of water that steamed into the smouldering cinders. Cats mewed piteously for water, the mains having burst, their cries mingling with the screams of frightened humans and animals alike.

The Place Muhammad Ali was a square of fire, the trees in the centre shrivelling away from the tongues of flame that poked from the windows and licked the walls of the once grand houses. In the deserted centre the men recoiled at the sight of blackened headless and armless corpses, only to grin with relief on realising they were dressmakers' dummies, abandoned by the ravaging hordes.

The three men returned to the marina where they came upon the first disciplined troops they had seen. 160 American sailors and marines under the command of Lieutenant Commander Caspar Goodrich were soon busy fighting fires around the American Consulate. They were too late to save the French Consulate, which collapsed, but St Mark's Anglican church was spared.

It was not until the following afternoon, the 13th, that Seymour finally received authority from the Admiralty to land 'seamen and marines for police purposes and to restore order'. That morning he had in fact already landed men at several forts to spike guns, 250 sailors and 150 marines to secure the western end of the Ras-el-Tin peninsular, and a small party of marines and a gatling gun crew from *Monarch* that pushed into the City to fire on looters.

At 4pm, after receiving British assurances for his safety, Khedive Tewfik, escorted by cavalry and 50 infantry, whose loyalty had been bought with jewels from the Royal harem, arrived back at Ras-el-Tin.

Arabi was furious that his attempt to escort the Khedive back to Cairo had failed. Tewfik, leader of a Moslem state, had slipped from his control and back to the British who were attacking that State. To do so was contrary to all that was honourable and the law. He denounced Tewfik and declared martial law. The British were aggressors and the Khedive a traitor who at night remained afloat with his women among the British, and by day returned to the shore to order the unnecessary slaughter of Moslems in the streets of Alexandria. He gradually assembled half the Alexandria garrison into a camp at Kafr-Dawar to wait.

The next few days were incredibly tense. A multinational force, assembled from the ships in the harbour and led by Captain Beresford of the *Condor,* gradually established order in the City. Looters and arsonists were shot on the spot, or captured, tried and executed; their bodies buried in Place Mohammed Ali. The multinational force was disbanded when it was found the Europeans, particularly the Greeks, were more inclined to shoot first and ask questions later. The arrival of the Channel Fleet enabled the force to be reconstituted by the British and a few American marines.

Captain Fisher of the *Inflexible* was tasked with defending the City from Arabi's substantial forces and the Bedouin camped outside. He was woefully equipped to do this but fortunately Arabi's force was too disorganised and demoralised to consider attack. 150 Bedouin did attempt a thieving raid but were driven back by a twelve man Gatling crew, with heavy losses and only a pillaged donkey to show for their effort.

By nightfall on the 18th July, the arrival of the troopship *Tamar* from Cyprus and HMS *Agincourt* and HMS *Northumberland* from Port Said meant there were almost 3700 British troops on Egyptian soil.

27

AFTERMATH

Cabinet Room, Downing Street, Thursday 20th July 1882

Lord Northbrook, First Lord of the Admiralty, was in his element. His Cabinet colleagues hung on his every word as he described some of the unreported details of the bombardment at Alexandria and the subsequent events. The newspapers were full of details with engraved prints of the naval action drawn for the very first time by artists who were actually there – though Melton Prior on board *Alexandra* had been unfortunate in having his luggage and many of his sketches destroyed by an Egyptian shell. Northbrook concluded with a report on the latest position.

"The fires are now generally out. Captain Beresford has taken control of policing the City and a Corps of Arab policemen has been created. Courts have been set up and arsonists have been tried and executed, as have looters caught for a second time – the first time, they are flogged."

"Dangerous walls have been identified and are being pulled down, by locally employed labour, to make buildings safe. Work has today commenced in burying the bodies.

"Arabi has set up a formidable defensive position with between 15,000 and 30,000 troops at Kafr-Dawar. It is an area of marshland south of Ramleh, south east of Alexandria, where the railway and canal to Cairo pass between Lake Aboukir to the East and Lake Mareotis to the West. For the moment he seems content to wait for us to attack him, rather than re-take the City"

"Thank you, Northbrook," said the Prime Minister. "And the broader position, Granville?"

Lord Granville cleared his throat. "Secure under our protection in Alexandria, the Khedive is now demanding answers as to our intent, and that Her Majesty's Government take action, without delay," he paused. "Before his entourage leaves him."

"While it was our hope that the bombardment would bring Arabi to his senses, this does not appear to be the case. Reports are now reaching us that Imams throughout the region are calling for Holy war against the foreigners. This has resulted in some atrocities against the few remaining foreigners but these have been swiftly punished by Arabi."

"News from our allies is encouraging and we are now hopeful of French and possibly even Italian support." He turned back to the Prime Minister.

Gladstone's expression was unreadable. "Let me make this clear. Britain is not at war and the wider consequences of further action are considerable. You are aware of the note I have received from Arabi, but I will read it again: 'I repeat again and again that the first blow struck at Egypt by England or her allies will cause blood to flow through the breadth of Asia and of Africa. England may rest assured that we are determined to fight, to die martyrs for our country, as has been enjoined on us by our Prophet; or else to conquer, and so live independently.'"

"While I could be pushed to accept a police action, with France, to protect the Suez Canal, we cannot go any further."

There was silence for a moment, as Gladstone confirmed his fear that he did not have the support of his Cabinet. Popular sentiment supported more decisive action to defend the interests of the Empire. Lord Hartington, Secretary of State for India, led the opposition to his position. "Prime Minister, I totally agree that we need to protect the canal, it is the artery through which 82% of British trade passes. That is why we agreed to fund its construction.

"I am particularly concerned at the religious component in this situation. Some believe parties in Turkey have been stirring up Moslem fanaticism in the hope of dividing the European powers and banishing Western influence from the region. This would enable the Sultan to extend his influence into other areas after their recent losses in Europe." He paused for a moment, allowing his colleagues the opportunity to consider where the Sultan might try to extend his influence.

"I would draw your attention to the large Moslem community in India. Differences exist between the different communities but the Sufi Wahabi in the Punjab need very little encouragement to rise to violence in the name of Allah. I therefore believe it vital that, in any police action, we should be decisive, with sufficient troops to be sure of the outcome, and that some of those troops should be native Moslems from India."

"We should act with anyone who will act with us," he paused, noting he had the full support of the Cabinet, except the PM and the Quaker, John Bright. "And if need be, alone."

Childers, Secretary of State for War, was clear in his support. "We have been considering scenarios in Egypt, as we do for all potential trouble spots, for some time. The Duke of Cambridge is in agreement that an army under the command of Lieutenant General Sir Garnet Wolseley, with Lieutenant General Sir John Adye as his Chief of Staff, be deployed to Cyprus where they will be available for operations in any part of Egypt. The estimates have been done for manpower and transportation. We would need the House to vote £2.3m to pay for the expedition which would be funded by raising income tax to 3.5p in the pound."

Joseph Chamberlain injected his support. "Such is the feeling in the House, and indeed the Country, such a vote is a formality."

The vote was a formality on the 24th July, with the Prime Minister supporting invasion, not to preserve the security of the Suez Canal, but to settle the root cause of Egypt's malaise. The resolution was passed with 275 for, and 19 against. John Bright, one of Gladstone's oldest political friends, resigned.

The French Premier, M de Freycinet called for a similar vote and was heavily defeated in the Chamber. He resigned immediately afterwards. Britain was alone.

28
PREPARATION FOR WAR
July/August 1882

The sun beat through his dark tunic, uncomfortably roasting his back, and burning the nape of his neck. Trooper John Waterston settled his cheek onto the warm wood of the Martini-Henry rifle and drank in the sweet smell of the oil and powder residue. His elbows sought comfort in the short cropped turf and he fractionally pulled the butt further into his shoulder. He was barely breathing, his pulse slowed to half its normal rate. With a soft blur in his left, he allowed the focus of his right eye to travel from the 'V' in the sliding ramp leaf sight through the fixed post of the foresight and on to the miniscule speck of the target, before settling on the tip of the foresight. The flag above the gallery range stirred in a desultory breeze and he fractionally adjusted his point of aim and gently squeezed through the second pressure on the trigger. The 480 grain bullet, propelled by 85 grains of black powder, corkscrewed down the barrel and began its 800 yard journey. Smoke mushroomed and the rifle thumped up and back into his black and blue bruised shoulder. He winced and worked the lever to eject the spent cartridge. There was nothing more he could do.

To his left, Cpl Scott lay with his eye pressed to a telescope and a fierce look of concentration on his face that ten seconds later resolved into a warm smile. "Bull! I really don't know how you do it. Without this telescope I can barely see the target at this range, let alone hit it plum in the middle. Great bit of shooting, let's go and see whether it is enough to make it through to the next round?" He noted the shot on the score card and stood up.

"Its certainly easier to hit the target using a rifle and a heavier round than it is using our carbines, the 410 grain bullet and 70 grains of powder." John replied. "Thank you for getting one for me, Corporal."

"A pleasure. We can't have you trying to use a 480 grain round down a cavalry pea shooter. Your shoulder would never take it, and there is a risk neither would the carbine. It's Ted Ankers you really need to thank, though I was surprised when he told me I had to give it back. That's not normally his way."

John slung the rifle over his back and the pair made their way around the brow of the hill towards the cluster of cottages, windmill and the temporary clock tower that marked the National Rifle Association headquarters on Wimbledon Common at this time every year. To their right, shooters continued their practise at the wooden targets 500 to 1000 yards away on the other side of the valley. The Queen's Prize of £250, and its accompanying gold medal, had been won by Sergeant Lawrence of the 1st Dumbarton Rifle Volunteers. Several other prizes were still in play and they passed crowds of spectators, many of them ladies and young girls, sheltering from the sun under multi-coloured parasols.

Bell tents in neat rows were already being vacated as the Army prepared to return to their barracks and make way for the civilian meeting where the real prize money would be won. They handed their scorecard in to be validated and retired to the Regimental lines.

Ted Ankers, his eyes glowing with excitement, greeted them. John reluctantly passed him the rifle, but he brushed it away. "Later...... once you've cleaned it. Have you heard?"

"Heard what?"

"We are going to Egypt!"

"All of us?" asked Cpl Scott. "The whole of the Household Cavalry is going to war? Who is going to guard the Queen?"

"They have created a composite Household Cavalry Regiment. Each of the three Regiments has provided one Major, a Captain, two Subalterns and 153 non-commissioned officers and men. Actually, the Blues are providing more officers than that because there are some staff appointments, too. Lord Binning is going, and so are we! We are all on the list for a pre-deployment exercise in Aldershot next week. The quartermaster is frantically busy preparing all the stores and kit issue."

A smile spread across the faces of all three men.

"We get new uniforms then?" asked Cpl Scott. "I have been hearing about the new khaki that the Indian regiments use to hide from the enemy?"

"A disgraceful notion! Oh no," replied Ankers. "It has been decided that the Household Cavalry Regiment will continue to fight in colour, the Queen will not allow anything else. We are to get blue serge Mediterranean frock coats, the Life Guards will be in red. The QM is also laying out dark trousers and laced 'high-low' ankle boots. We will wrap blue puttees around our calves to protect them."

"More comfortable than knee length riding boots in that heat," said John. "What else do we get?"

"Bright white pith helmets, …..without spikes," he grinned, "and wound round with a puggaree." He noted their confused looks and explained, "It's a thin muslin scarf you can use to protect your neck from the sun, or shield your eyes. The Colonel has instructed the QM to make them less visible and stain them with tea or tobacco juice. We also get blue tinted goggles that protect us against the desert glare, knives, water bottles, lanyards and some strange green and blue 'veils' that supposedly keep mosquitos away. Even the horses get new kit, too; there are special fringes to keep the flies out of their eyes." His excitement was palpable, like a child armed with thruppence in a sweet and toyshop. "Someone in the QM's department has been thinking about this for some time."

For John, the highlight of the pre-deployment exercise centred on Colonel Creed Baker Russell, a cavalry officer of the old type, who was to command their 1st Cavalry Brigade in Egypt. The Brigade would comprise a Squadron from each Household Cavalry Regiment, the 4th Dragoon Guards, 7th Dragoon Guards, and a company of transport and commissariat.

Baker Russell was larger than life and almost as great a legend as Colonel Burnaby. He had seen action in several continents, leading the 13th Hussars in India (obviously they had called themselves the 'Baker's Dozen') and had been with General Wolseley in Ashanti. Indeed, he was a trusted friend of General Wolseley, one of his Ashanti Ring. The troop was looking forward to seeing this man for the first time during a ride by salute to the General commanding the Aldershot area.

"What on earth happened?" Cpl Scott asked as they drank tea around the fire at the end of an eventful day.

"Yes, what is he like?" asked Angus Duncan.

All eyes turned to Trumpeter Edward Finch. A huge grin spread over Finch's face. "Well, it was as we thought. Colonel Baker Russell is not one for the rule book. I don't think he knows all his bugle commands."

"Well, there are over 80 of them," said John Crook. "Which one doesn't he know?"

"Canter," replied Finch.

"But there isn't a call for 'Canter'," said Crook looking confused.

"Exactly!" said Finch, with a broad grin, as if this explained everything.

A look of understanding spread over Cpl Scott's face as he recalled the earlier events. "So there you are, standing by the newly appointed Brigade signalling officer, Cornet Willoughby, and the Colonel on the dais with us, all formed up in Squadrons for the ride past, and he orders you to sound 'walk march', which you did." Finch nodded, happily. "So we start forward at the walk, and then he asks you to sound the 'trot', which you did."

Finch nodded again, an even bigger grin spreading across his face. Unable to contain his story he interrupted. "And then he asks me to sound the canter. Well, I can't tell him there ain't no call for the canter, can I? 'Specially not with the General there. So I look at the Cornet and I'm not sure he knew there is no signal for canter either and he nods for me to go ahead, and looks cross that I haven't. So I improvise and sound the next best thing."

"So you sounded the 'gallop'," said Cpl Scott, a grin spreading across his face.

Finch shrugged, "Well, what else could I do?"

A look of realisation was spreading over the section. "So we start to gallop," said Cpl Scott.

"Yes, and that's too fast for the salute, so the Colonel looks at Willoughby and tells me to sound the canter again. So I don't know what to do. I look at the Cornet and practically beg him to say something but he just glares at me,…. so I sound the 'gallop' again."

"So we think he wants us to go faster," said Crook, grinning.

"So we let everything go and thunder past the dais at full chat and cover them in clouds of dust!" said Cpl Scott, laughing with the rest of the men. "Best salute we've ever done! What did the Colonel say?"

"Well, the Colonel was totally calm," replied Finch. "He turns to the General with a huge smile, and puffing out his enormous chest, said: "There, sir! You never saw a Brigade gallop past like that before." The General, being completely ignorant on the subject, took his cue from the Colonel and said: "No, that is splendid; I never saw anything so good in my life!"

"So you and Willoughby got away with it then?" asked Cpl McIntosh.

"I'm not sure about that. The Colonel gave Willoughby quite a look," replied the Trumpeter.

"And now our Troopy, Lord Binning, is the Brigade signalling officer," stated Cpl Scott.

There was silence for a while, the men staring into the fire as sparks climbed into a clear night sky.

"Do we know how the officers and men were selected to go to Egypt?" asked John.

Cpl Scott considered a moment. "As you may have heard, General Wolseley is very keen on volunteers. He believes they make the best soldiers. So that was a key criteria. Single men were also preferred to those with families. Then they wanted the best riders and marksmen. So, you lot are the elite of the elite." As the men grinned with pride, Scott paused before continuing ironically. "God help us!" They laughed.

"Were the officers selected on the same basis?"

"Ah, no," answered Cpl Scott. "Otherwise Colonel Burnaby would be leading the Household Cavalry. He knows the region well, speaks Arabic and, as we know, is as brave as a lion and has loads of fighting experience. All the officers were raring to go and prove themselves so they were appointed on the basis of seniority. That is why the composite Regiment is being led by Colonel Ewart of the 2nd Life Guards, even though he has never seen action."

The following day the Brigade paraded for Colonel Baker Russell again. This time they were formed up in review order and John was able to see the man properly for the first time; yesterday all he had seen was a blur as they raced past. He was a very big man in his mid forties with a commanding, loud voice and a long drooping walrus moustache that set off a determined face. He was tall, with exceptionally long legs. Clearly a fighting man, there was something about him that, like Colonel Burnaby, commanded respect.

They sat motionless in the large sandy clearing. In the distance the dais was empty of the dignitaries of yesterday, the only witnesses were the fir trees and gorse. The mounts twitched their heads and whickered with impatience to be on the move again. In front of the Troop, Cornet Willoughby made some comment to Lord Binning who chuckled. Colonel Baker Russell gave him a withering glance then pushed his helmet down on his head and spurred his charger towards Willoughby as hard as he could go. His big charger thundered across the sandy ground, teeth bared and moustache plastered back across his cheeks. When he was within a yard of Willoughby, that unfortunate officer jammed one spur into his horse and made it leap to one side, which resulted in the Colonel missing him completely and charging directly into John with a terrific thump. John and Alfie were sent sprawling, John banging the back of his head on the ground and momentarily lost consciousness. He came around a few moments later cradled across the Colonel's knee and staring into eyes filled with concern. The Colonel's voice was surprisingly soft. "My poor, dear man, I am sorry. I didn't mean to hurt you."

"I'm alright, Sir," he replied, slowly getting to his feet. "A bit bruised but there is no way I am missing this trip." He looked across at Alfie who was being checked out by Cpl Scott, but fortunately looked none the worse for his spill.

"That's the spirit! Just what we need in Egypt."

Detailed reports, accompanied by multiple etchings of the bombardment and aftermath, appeared in the Illustrated London News on 29th July, fuelling the imagination of the public and adding to their sense of purpose. John poured over the pictures and every detail, eager to understand more.

With all the preparations complete, amidst great excitement, on Monday 31st July they were back on parade at Albany Street Barracks. Alongside the Squadrons from the 1st and 2nd Life Guards, and dressed in their expedition uniforms, they were inspected by their Colonel in Chief, the Prince of Wales. In a short speech, Prince Albert wished them every success, declared his satisfaction at their turn out and disappointment at being unable to join them. He had, after all, been to Egypt before on a tour to build relations with Said Pasha in 1862, but the Queen had ensured his application was declined. He was particularly envious of his brother, Prince Arthur, the Duke of Connaught who would join the expedition in command of the Guards Brigade.

Colonel Burnaby addressed the Blues contingent alone, his high voice carrying to those in the Regiment who were not about to go to war. "You may have seen the story circulating in Vanity Fair that the Minister of War, concerned at our cost and lack of recent battle honours, wishes the Household Cavalry to be abolished? It is said that being well aware of the unsuitability of heavy cavalry for operations in Egypt, he expects to be provided with an argument as to your uselessness in time of war." He grinned. "This is, of course, neither true nor particularly amusing, but that has not stopped some of my acquaintances foolishly repeating it in my presence. I have noted those who choose to bait me with such nonsense and have purchased several copies of Vanity Fair that I look forward to feeding them, personally, when you return victorious with everyone's praise ringing in your ears." He paused to allow the ribald cheers to die away. "You are the elite of Her Majesty's Army. Do the job I have trained you for, with pride, and I may even allow you to watch them eat their words!"

"I am, of course, hugely disappointed that I am unable to join you for this expedition. My wife lobbied long and hard for me to be included, but to no avail. However, I have every faith in Colonel

Ewart, who despite being 2nd Life Guards," he paused to allow the ribald cheer to subside, "is a sound officer who, ably supported by our own Major Milne Hume as his second, will, I'm sure, lead you brilliantly. Remember, it is not your job to die for your Queen and Country, but to ensure the other chap dies for his. Good luck and may God be with you."

"Three cheers for Colonel Burnaby and the Blues," called the RCM. "Hip, hip, hooray…."

As the echoes of the cheers subsided and the officers departed the parade ground, more cheers and celebrations could be heard across London.

That evening the Prince gave a dinner for 23 of the Blues officers at the Marlborough Club. The men spent the night with friends, relations, sweethearts and old soldiers who came to bid them a last farewell. John, like several others had no sweetheart and spent the early evening roving the streets in search of potential candidates and enjoying the attention in his expedition uniform. All night long, hundreds of people crowded outside the Barracks singing popular hymns, comic songs, "God Save the Queen" and "Rule Britannia".

On the morning of 1st August reveille was sounded to a long loud cheer throughout the barracks that the longed for hour of departure had come. After a sleepless night, John mounted Alfie at 0345, and paraded in service marching order with the rest of the Troop, and others of the composite Squadron. At 4am they left the barracks to a rousing march played by the Regimental Band. With the detachment led by Major Milne Hume, they proceeded passed Bedford Square and down to the Strand. Passing down Ludgate Hill, St Pauls Cathedral was barely visible in the pre-dawn gloom. He was surprised that even at that hour, the streets were lined with well-wishers who cheered and clapped as they passed. At 0530, as dawn broke, they arrived at the troopship *Holland* moored alongside in the newly opened Royal Albert Docks. Stood at ease in formation, they waited until 0630 before leading their mounts up the gangplank.

It was the first time any of the horses or men had been on a troop ship and a few of the mounts, picking up on the trepidation of their riders, needed considerable encouragement to be led on board. Wooden stalls had been specially built for 30 horses on the central section to each side of the upper deck. These had a lean-to roof that discharged water overboard with enclosed back and sides, the chargers close together, separated by a rope and facing out to the deck. In front of each horse was a trough for feed and water.

The remainder were stabled in similar stalls built to each side of the wooden main deck below the upper deck. With all the chargers facing into the centre line of the ship, air and light was provided via a deck well that could be covered during inclement weather.

The men were accommodated in a large open mess on the lower deck. Wooden tables and benches were fixed down each side and at night the men slept in closely strung hammocks over the tables. Light streamed through the portholes and down the companionways from the decks above, but the place was still dim and smelled of tar and close humanity.

Once aboard, the rest of the Squadron joined them. The dismounted party had paraded at 0600 and travelled by the 0625 train from Portland Road Station to Galleons Station and then marched to the loading area in the docks. The dock was full of troop ships in various stages of loading to a timetable that must have taken considerable planning. Troops were arriving from all directions, on foot, by train and by steam launch from Westminster Bridge. Everywhere there were scenes of great enthusiasm.

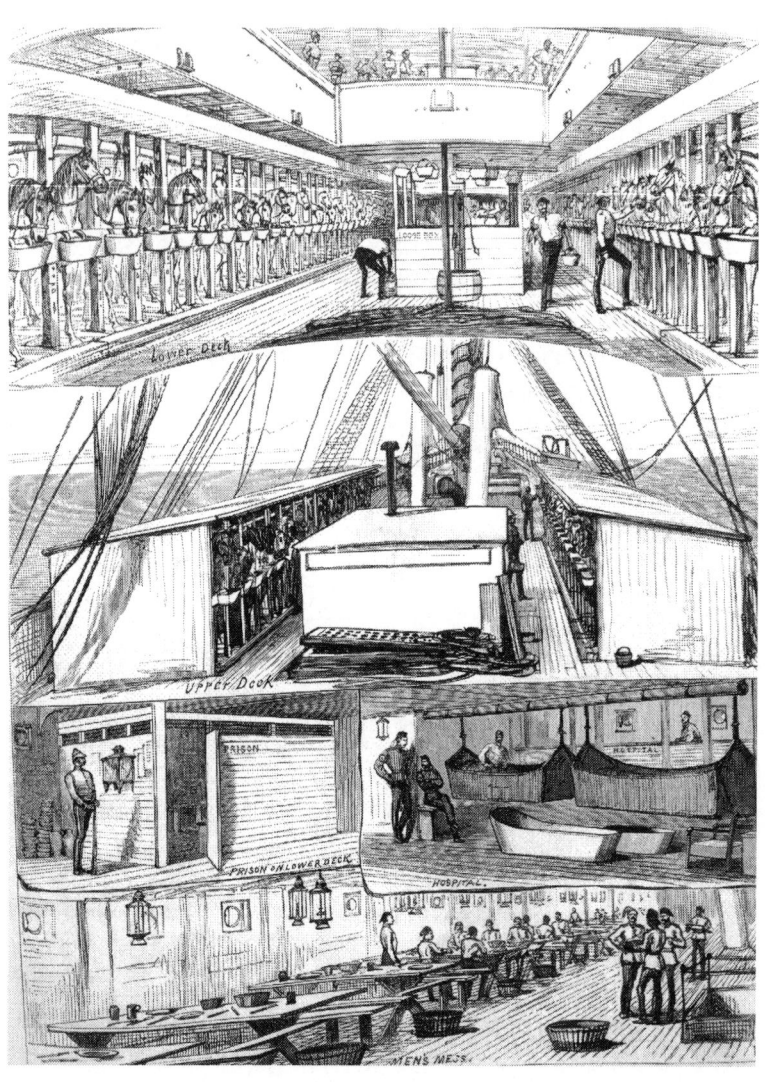

Holland departed in the afternoon, seen off by the Duke of Cambridge and both the Secretary and Under Secretary of State for War. There were encouraging cheers from the crowd on the dockside and also from the steamboats and other small craft that accompanied them down the river. Navy cadets on the training ships manned the yards, three boys sitting on the very tops of the masts. The excitement was at fever pitch among both the men and the horses, few of whom had ever been aboard a ship before. As they steamed passed Gravesend on their way out to the North Sea it did not occur to any of the men that they might never see England again.

They stopped briefly at Deal to take on ammunition from a lighter. The excitement swiftly reduced as they left the Thames Estuary and turned into the different, rolling motion of the English Channel. To the amusement of the sailors, many of the men clung to the sides of the main deck with pale clammy skin waiting for the nausea to pass. Some of the horses were affected too, and only the men with the most robust constitutions were able to clear up the sour half digested mash without needing to dash up to the side of the main deck.

The Queen was at Osborne House on the Isle of White and was disappointed to be unable to see her Household Cavalry off from the docks. She therefore requested they pass through Cowes Roads at 10am on Wednesday 2nd so she could communicate farewell. The men lined the side and imagined they could see the diminutive Empress as the ship steamed slowly past. The last they saw of England was the Eddystone Lighthouse, winking farewell.

Every officer and man had his hair cut almost to the scalp, so they resembled the rats that, in the absence of a main cargo to eat, patrolled the upper decks of the ship in large numbers and soon became targets for sword practise. Amidst much discussion as to the best type of edge to be used, all swords were sharpened and then browned by burning the blade, hilt and scabbard.

The shipboard routine was almost the same as in barracks, though without the ability to exercise the horses that grew increasingly restless. The heat climbed steadily so that five days later as they passed Gibraltar, temperatures below desks frequently rose to 100°F even though the sailors rigged air scoops above the stairs and gratings to channel air below. The horses' hair came off in handfuls and some had to be taken up to stalls on the main deck, where the breeze made it marginally cooler, and pumps could be used to spray seawater over them.

As they neared their destination, each man was issued with a Martini-Henry carbine, to be carried as usual in a leather bucket at the right side of the saddle, as well as their Enfield revolver. All trappings of metal were allowed to rust so as to avoid reflecting the sunlight. Targets were erected to enable pistol shooting to be practised, and on one day, when Africa could be dimly seen in the distance, small barrels were thrown over the side and the sections competed to sink their barrel using rapid fire from their carbines.

They stopped briefly at Gibraltar and Malta for fuel and dispatches and reached Alexandria on Monday 14th August; the *Holland*, slowly passing the partially destroyed forts and the British warships anchored in the inner harbour, to tie up alongside the pier. As the troopers waited to disembark they marvelled at the noisy, bustling waterfront with its over laden donkeys and the vibrant smells and colours that the illustrations in the papers could not convey.

The destruction was plainly visible, the skyline altered from the images they had seen in the papers by the missing roofs and hollow, partially collapsed, shells of buildings. Almost every European looking building was heavily damaged, gaping voids where windows once reflected a prosperous city.

The streets were now clear enough to pass, but rubble was piled beneath the remaining walls. "Blimey, the Navy must be lousy shots," said Tom Parris, making sure a sailor wearing the wide brimmed hat with '*Condor*' on the ribbon could hear him. "The city looks destroyed while the forts look like they could be back in action tomorrow."

The sailor took the bait and scowled. "All this destruction was down to the looters and arsonists who rampaged through the City after the bombardment. The buildings were so unstable we had to use dynamite to collapse the walls, and pay the natives to clear away the rubble. You should have seen it a couple of weeks ago. This is tidy."

They saddled their chargers who were as impatient to be ashore as the men, carefully arranging their weapons and equipment before leading them down the gangplank and on to the dusty quayside. They formed into a single body and in the late afternoon made their way eastwards through the City towards Ramleh.

As they passed through the European quarter and the Place Mohammed Ali, it seemed strange to be able to see inside once fine rooms that were now blackened hulks, missing floors, ceilings and at least one of the walls. They saw a huge unexploded shell from

Inflexible lying by the side of the road. Their progress was like a silent parade, the natives in their mainly blue or white dress, staring in awe at the giant horses and men, who absolutely dwarfed all the local people and animals. John had no doubt that news of their arrival would be with the Egyptian army by nightfall.

Leaving the Rosetta Gate behind, they trotted along deep dusty roads strewn with the broken and discarded spoils of the looting. As they passed once grand, and now derelict, houses they saw gardens littered with smashed furniture, gutted pianos, couches with their covers slashed and horsehair stuffing exposed. Books lay spineless across the lawns, pages fluttering and escaping in the gentle breeze that came from the sea. Occasionally they saw the remains of domestic animals, distended stomachs destined to explode.

There was beauty too. From a distance the houses, in a multitude of different colours, appeared untouched by the violence and lay set in delightfully manicured walled gardens that overlooked the stunningly blue sea. The horses, as happy as the men to be free of the confines of the ship, skipped and threw their heads despite the weight they now bore. Unlike the officers, the men had neither been abroad, nor had they had a holiday or experienced such fierce heat. They were drawn to the beach, where the equipment was carefully piled and naked men and horses rode through the surf to bathe in the clear warm water. The prospect of war was as distant as *Superb*, anchored a mile off and periodically sending shells into any of Arabi's earthworks built within range to the South.

That night they camped in the exotic walled garden of a fine yellow house and slept with nostrils filled with the warm, honeyed scent of mimosa under millions of stars, and the distant sound of the sea. John rose for an hour of guard duty at 2am, alert to the responsibility and the potential of the first real threat to his life that he had experienced. Adrenalin tingled down his spine as he cradled his carbine and explored the shadows with the corner of his eye. Overhead, shooting stars arced like shells in the dazzling sky.

Fingers of electric limelight swept out from the roofs of the taller villas towards the enemy lines, in Kafr-Dawar and Aboukir, highlighting any change in their disposition.

For the next couple of days they rode patrols along the deep sandy paths that exercised the horses rather than the enemy. They enjoyed picking white, almost transparent, grapes and sweet figs in the gardens. Many learned to swim in the warm waters that daily cleansed them from the clinging dust and sweat induced by the heavy serge tunics.

As more reinforcements arrived, Ramleh became a mass of white tents that covered more than a square mile. The rest of the Household Cavalry, who arrived on the *Calabria,* joined them on the 16th. For some unexplained reason their trip had taken a day longer even though they had not diverted via Cowes to be waved off by the Queen. The commander in chief, General Wolseley, had travelled with them rather than by rail, for the sake of his health, and had not wanted any further delay.

29
FEINT

General Sir Garnet Wolseley looked up from the map and out of the window of his stateroom on the wooden paddle steamer dispatch vessel, *HMS Salamis,* towards the ruins of Alexandria. He suppressed the anger that surged through him as he considered what he had learned. Outwardly calm he turned to his friend and protégé, Lieutenant Colonel Herbert Stewart, quartermaster general to the Cavalry Division, and the man who had refused to leave his side on *Calabria* during his illness.

"My intention is to split the Egyptian army. I will do this by convincing Arabi that the British attack on Cairo will be from Alexandria," he used his swagger stick to indicate locations on the map as he spoke, "while seizing the neutral Suez canal, landing at Ismailia and attacking via the shorter route from the East. If the enemy stand and fight we will achieve a decisive victory against the Egyptians at their entrenched defensive position of Tel-el-Kebir, here, before it can be reinforced by the troops currently holding the line at Kafr-Dawar."

"I understand that General," replied Stewart. "It is a bold plan that requires us to ensure the Egyptians neither take control of the Suez canal, nor block the Sweetwater Canal water supply to Ismailia. I am not clear how this latest news from Turkey affects the plan? Surely their troops will help?"

Wolseley considered his response. "Yes, the Sultan has belatedly decided to send 20,000 troops to Egypt, which is what we hoped he would do. But that was many months ago, when we were sure they would support the Khedive and before we committed to this expedition. If he sends troops now, Arabi will surrender to the Porte who would then declare order had been restored and demand British troops withdraw from Ottoman territory, placing us in an impossible position. We have therefore insisted that the Porte issue a statement to the effect that Arabi is a rebel before the troops depart Turkey."

"I'm a soldier not a diplomat. How will that help?" asked Stewart.

"It leaves the Sultan with three options. If he sends his troops without declaring Arabi a rebel he will offend the British and risk a war with us that will further weaken his position with the Russians. In addition, if he does not declare Arabi a rebel then there could be a chain reaction of rebellion throughout the Ottoman Empire. If he declares Arabi a rebel, when the Khedive can be argued to be in the control of the British, a non-Moslem power, he will outrage the entire Moslem world. His third, and I believe most likely option, is to delay and send the troops when it is too late."

"So it is another factor, but not a major one?"

"And not one we can influence, manage or control. We can leave that to our political master, Sir Edward Malet, who has recovered his health remarkably since British troops arrived." He gave Stewart a look that left no doubt as to what Wolseley thought of Sir Edward. It was a rare display of emotion from a man who hid his true thoughts from all but his wife.

"What concerns me more are three things. Firstly, how can we get the Navy to work with us rather than pursue their own glory seeking agenda? Secondly, what this news that Arabi has occupied Nefiche, near our proposed landing point at Ismailia means, and finally the effect that General Alison's fighting reconnaissance on Kafr-Dawar ten days ago has had?"

"I read the reports of the reconnaissance on Kafr-Dawar," replied Stewart. "Fifteen companies of infantry, a 200 strong Naval Brigade and a further six companies in the second wave, all supported by this new 'armoured train' idea. Seems like a lot of men for a reconnaissance."

"Exactly. To the Egyptians it must have looked like a full-blown attack, which they repulsed. Heaven knows what it has done for their morale to appear to defeat regular British troops."

"I understand we lost one officer and 3 men killed and another 27 wounded, General. Mainly from the Naval Brigade. Private Corbett of the Mounted Infantry has been recommended for a VC, for remaining alongside his officer, Lieutenant Howard-Vyse who was dying of wounds received from a sniper. I understand the rounds were hitting all around them, but he refused to take cover or leave his officer's side."

"Hmmf, did not save him though." Wolseley considered a moment before softening his stance slightly. "But I admire his loyalty and

VCs have been awarded for similar acts of selflessness, regardless of the outcome."

"And what have we gained for their sacrifice?" he continued. "We estimate the Egyptians lost 200 killed and wounded. We now know Arabi will not pull back in the face of a British assault on his position and that armoured trains are very effective platforms for artillery and machine guns. We can hope Arabi is now further convinced this is our line of attack. I have instructed General Alison to keep the Egyptians in a state of constant alarm. So, why has Arabi sent more troops to Tel-el-Kebir, and worryingly, to Nefiche?"

"We don't know how many troops he has sent, General," Stewart replied. "From what I have seen, Arabi is a capable commander. Despite the French assurances that the canal is neutral and will not be used by the British, there is always that risk. If you were entrenched at Tel-el-Kebir, would you not send a reconnaissance force East to keep an eye on the Canal? You would need to be careful not to upset the French or threaten the canal's neutrality, for fear of giving us an excuse to use it, so Nefiche, two or so miles South West of Ismailia is the logical place to send your recce force. What is more it is on the railway line, so they can reinforce or pull back at pace."

Wolseley nodded, reassured and pleased at his protégé's argument. "Sound reasoning, Herbert. So, what more do we need to do to convince him of our intent to attack from the North rather than the West? By positioning our troops at Ramleh we have cut off 4,000 Egyptian troops in the forts at Aboukir from Arabi's main body at Kafr-Dawar. If it really was my intent to attack South, I would first want to neutralise that threat to my rear."

"What I need is the support of Her Majesty's Navy. While they are not under my command or even obliged to support me, the Admiral is an old friend who has fought alongside me before, so I am hopeful of his help. My first task is to let the Press know my plan to attack Aboukir." He smiled, knowingly, at Stewart.

"You had better join your Cavalry Division and see they have all the water, stores, equipment and accommodation they need. Don't make them too settled though. They will be back on board ship soon."

30
ISMAILIA

The Household Cavalry returned from Ramleh on Friday 18th August. John Waterston re-boarded the *Holland*, with a distinctly unimpressed Alfie, and spent the night anchored in the Alexandria outer harbour. At midday on the 19th, 17 troop ships escorted by 8 ironclads weighed anchor and steamed for three hours before anchoring in Aboukir Bay to the East. There, the Blues watched the warships strike their yards and lower topmasts in preparation to bombard the forts. Wolseley's ruse worked perfectly with the Press, most of his Generals and the Egyptians expecting an assault on Aboukir. The Egyptian gunners stood by their guns, though a white flag flew above each fort. The troopers wondered what would happen next, but did not have long to wait. In pitch darkness they weighed anchor again and steamed to Port Said at the Mediterranean end of the Suez canal.

Port Said appeared, grimy from the gloom, as the sun's first rays peaked over the horizon on Sunday 20th August. John Waterston stood before the Regimental padre and the neatly piled Regimental drums for the Church of England field service on board *Holland*. Overhead, sailors were rigging the canvas awnings that in a few hours would provide some shelter from the blazing sun. For the first time, other than the Regimental church parades, the whole section was present. John Crook and Ted Ankers both looked slightly embarrassed when the padre saw them and smiled welcome, as new participants.

The previous night, and to the surprise of all, the padre had joined them around the section table on the lower deck to enquire about their wellbeing. After a little small talk the conversation had turned to faith and its value in battle.

"I'm sorry that I don't believe in God," Ted Ankers was unusual in a society that was resurgent in evangelical Christianity. "Does that make me a bad soldier?"

"Perhaps the better way to think about it is, with faith, could you be a better soldier?" replied the padre. "Trooper Waterston, you are a regular attender at my services; what do you think?"

John looked uncomfortable at being singled out, unsure what to say. LCpl McIntosh chuckled, "Waterston is certainly not lacking in faith, he attends all the services, though I believe those with a prettier congregation particularly benefit from his presence, Sir." The men laughed at John's discomfort, though he smiled wryly. The padre looked quizzically at him.

"You attend the Catholic service, too?" he asked, surprised.

John nodded, "and the Methodist if I can, Sir. I was raised in the kirk and there are no Presbyterian services in London or Windsor that I have found yet." He noted the padre's slightly shocked look, and felt an explanation was necessary. "I was raised with the word of God; in the psalms, not in a faith's interpretation of that word." He looked at his friends who appeared to be seeing him for the first time. He grinned. "Though an attractive congregation also helps and it gives me something to do in what little free time we have."

The padre looked slightly mollified. "You are a man of faith then. Does that faith give you strength in facing these Egyptian Mohammedans?"

"I have faith that my God has a purpose for me and will watch over me in battle, yes. But I also have faith in my horse, my weapons, my training and most of all, my friends." He indicated the rest of the section, several of whom smiled and bowed. Noting that the padre seemed keen for him to continue, he realised he had not answered the full question.

"If you are you asking, Sir, if my faith is stronger than the Mohammedans, I did not realise that this was a holy war. I am not familiar with Islam, but from what little I have read and heard, our beliefs stem from a shared belief in the same God."

"Well, it is a factor, is it not? Arabi's followers, the Nationalist rebels, are attacking European influence in their country and that influence is Christian. The rebels have carried out appalling crimes against Christians,..... and Jews." The padre was warming to his task.

"I thought they were just criminals who were caught and severely punished, Sir?" asked Cpl Scott. "Opportunists and people too stupid to realise they were being manipulated into criminal acts by those whose motivation is the pursuit of personal power and wealth. Religion is used as just another lever, like jealousy of those with wealth."

The padre did not look at all happy at this reasoning. Cpl Scott changed tack to more comfortable ground. "So how can you help Trooper Ankers, Sir? Can you help him find God?"

"In my experience, most soldiers find God on the battlefield," replied the Padre. "Particularly when all hope is gone. I hope to see you at my service tomorrow."

That Sunday morning, as first light filtered through the rigging and the Padre led them in prayer, John felt the familiar tingling he associated with being close to God. He looked at John Crook and Ted Ankers, eyes closed in supplication. Perhaps they all drew faith from the realisation that generations of soldiers had come closer to God in similar services in war zones throughout the world.

The Navy had already seized Port Said and Ismailia and had cut the telegraph wires, allowing the troopships a free passage down the canal to Ismailia. At midday, *Holland* raised anchor and steamed South. Port Said slid by them, low storage sheds and shacks interspersed with the occasional more solidly built three storey structures. Jetties extended stubby fingers from dusty yards toward foreign shipping waiting to use the Canal. As they passed they received a rousing cheer, particularly from the American ships.

The passage down the canal, conducted as it was without any pilots from the Canal company, was very slow; the trees and rushes that lined the edge of the canal creeping past and occasionally concealing the flat featureless land beyond. Frequently they had to drop anchor to avoid running into the ship in front, if it had run aground. Fortunately these groundings were not serious and the ships easily towed off. Only one ship, the *Catalonia* with the West Kent Regiment aboard, ran badly aground in the shallows 7 miles North of Lake Timsah. 300 men had to be disembarked to lighten the ship, while the soldiers watching from the other ships as they crept past, sang "Who ate all the pies?" to much amusement.

Fortunately there was no enemy resistance, an omission on the part of the enemy that was the cause of much speculation since artillery on the bank could have stopped the British in their tracks. Had Arabi believed Lesseps' assurances that the British would not abuse the neutrality of the canal, or were the Egyptians afraid that positioning forces near the canal would be seen as a threat to that neutrality and create pan European support for an invasion? As the light faded, every half hour they heard a single cannon fire from the South. The following day they discovered that as part of the operation to take control of Ismailia, *HMS Orion* and *HMS Carysfoot* had bombarded the enemy position at Nefiche from Lake Timsah 4200 yards away, causing the Egyptians to abandon the camp and retreat back towards Cairo. They continued to pound Nefiche every half an hour until daylight the following morning, the 21st, when the advanced guard landed in Ismailia.

In darkness the *Holland* finally arrived at Lake Timsah, now crowded with British warships and troop transports. As dawn broke the steady firing ceased and Ismailia appeared out of the gloom. Nestled on the North Western shore, Ismailia was a pleasant little town that had been founded 17 years before as a half way point on the canal. Stone built villas, shops, cafes and hotels clustered around the railway station that provided a means for canal passengers to travel to Alexandria, Cairo and Suez.

A huge Swiss chalet, overlooking the vivid blue lake, belonged to the Lesseps family and was swiftly requisitioned to be Wolseley's HQ. The wooden palace built for the Khedive Ismail to facilitate the grand opening of the canal, was turned into a military hospital a few days later.

Logistics would play a pivotal role in the British plan. Wolseley needed to secure the Sweetwater Canal, which was the sole source of fresh water for Ismailia and Suez, before the enemy could damage it. The single line railway, in the roadless desert, would also be vital to the campaign and the British had been fortunate to capture a single locomotive during their initial night assault. General Graham disembarked first at 10pm on the 20th with a force of 800 men and a small naval contingent. At first light on the 21st, with soldiers already dropping in the heat, they marched to Nefiche and found it to be occupied only by an elderly woman who berated Graham for the shelling. They were able to capture 30 railway trucks of ammunition and stores.

The small wooden jetty at Ismailia was now in semi-organised chaos as boats of all sizes approached to disgorge loads from the ships. Everywhere, sailors were offloading stores; rolling barrels, or carrying crates and bales.

General Wolseley immediately issued a proclamation to the effect that the British were only in Egypt to re-establish the Khedives authority and were only fighting against those who were in arms against His Highness. All peaceable inhabitants would be treated with kindness, their religion, mosques, families and property would be respected, and all goods would be paid for. When a few local traders tentatively opened their stalls and discovered they could sell their goods to soldiers at exorbitant prices, business was soon booming.

A few Greek and Syrian locals took advantage of the confusion to steal stores from the quayside. After ten of them were caught and summarily executed in the main square, this practice soon ceased.

Eventually the Household Cavalry disembarked. This was a far from simple process as the large ships were unable to dock at Ismailia and the horses had to be lifted down into smaller boats that were then towed to the shore by steam launches. This was not an activity that the Household Cavalry had experienced before, and Alfie, for one, felt that having strops placed under his chest and being lifted over the side into a small boat was beneath his dignity. John climbed down into the craft to calm his horse, stowed his kit, and once several were loaded they pushed off from the ship and were towed to the shore. The water was thronged with craft heading in all directions, and they steered to a holding area to wait before being called forward to the jetty. The normally calm water was disturbed by the wakes of all the craft heading in different directions, and John found it hard to keep his footing at times. So did Alfie, though John was able to reassure him and keep him calm. Trooper Evans was far from happy, and his charger was drawing on that concern to become increasingly agitated.

A steam launch filled with officers impatient to be ashore, and that was therefore travelling too fast for the congested water, had to rapidly change direction to avoid another craft. Amidst 'cheers' and 'whoops' from the officers, the launch cut close to their bow before veering away at the last second. The boat lurched in the resulting wash and Evans charger reared before deciding to make a dash for the side. Another charger decided to follow suit and the next thing John knew the boat had capsized and they were all in the water. Kicking up towards the light in the murky water, John broke the surface and looked around. He still had hold of Alfie's reins and the big charger was snorting with pleasure at the opportunity to swim. It was beautifully cool after the heat of the mid morning sun, but he was kicking quite hard to remain afloat given the weight of his clothing and boots. He recalled the first time they had been swimming with their chargers and was grateful when he saw Evans' head near his mount. Evans had clearly learned to swim, probably during their stay in Ramleh. It was carnage, the boat had settled upright in the water with its gunwales just visible and items of equipment bobbing around inside. John wondered briefly if his kit was still there or if it was now at the bottom of the lake. He lay along Alfie's back and gently directed him to the shore; while behind and around him, boats salvaged both men and equipment, and tried to herd the horses towards the quay.

Water streaming off him and to the amazement of the locals, John rode out of the Lake and up the shallow bank into Ismailia. Under a blazing sun and amidst clouds of flies, he rode his out-of-condition horse to their temporary camp. He was surprised to find the streets to be tarmacadam, though once out of the town the desert was light shifting sand that Alfie sank into up to his fetlocks. The surface was generally smooth, interspersed by low hummocks and mounds of camel grass. To the North the ground slowly rose and from there it was possible to see the violet tinted hills of Geb-el-Attakeh. There was no sign of the enemy, though a few Bedouin were seen in the distance.

John discovered that his weapons and equipment had stayed in the transport boat when it capsized, though Evans had been less fortunate and local boys were diving to recover the items that had sunk. The kit dried rapidly, but John spent a considerable period oiling and polishing to return it all to a serviceable condition. He found the carbine and revolver were easier to keep clean and free from dust if they were not oiled, and later discovered that locals made a point of never oiling their weapons. He was particularly glad to have recovered the small cookset he had purchased in London. It was a luxury that became a necessity in the days ahead.

While the stores were offloaded and consolidated, the troopers tried to acclimatise to the intense heat and re-condition the horses after their long sea journey. Those who had travelled on the *Holland* were in better condition than the 1st Life Guard horses on *Calabria*, which had not fared well. Two chargers had even died, their bodies thrown overboard before arriving in Alexandria.

31
MAGFAR

24 August

The Sweetwater Canal was rapidly dropping, threatening both the water supply and their means of transporting stores as they moved towards Cairo. It was clear that Arabi's forces had built a dam upstream or had broken down the banks of the canal.

On the 22nd August General Graham made a reconnaissance south towards Suez. The next day he pushed on to El Magfar, 6 miles west of Ismailia on the Sweetwater Canal. Ahead, he could see the enemy had erected a dam that now blocked their water supply. The stores were not offloaded and the horses were neither fit nor acclimatised after their sea journey but they could wait no longer.

At 4am in the coolest hour before dawn on Thursday 24th August, the Blues and the 2nd Life Guards, whose horses were the most fit, joined a company of mounted infantry and pushed west along the line of the Sweetwater Canal, to the right of the railway. The 2nd Life Guards took the lead with a troop forming a screen to the right flank. John was in the centre with a company of Mounted Infantry, whose locally procured horses were both smaller and fitter than the huge, black, sea weary chargers. The Blues were joined by General Wolseley, General Willis and the staff, who took a position at their head. It was the first John had seen of the legendary commander; riding a fine charger, and seemingly relaxed, as though out for a morning ride.

A morning ride was the way this had been presented, perhaps to dilute the concerns of those who wondered about the prudence of advancing to contact without the support of the Royal Horse Artillery, whose 13-pounder guns had still not been unloaded. Back in Ismailia, a troop of the 1st Life Guards waited to escort as many guns as could be made ready and catch them up, hopefully before they were needed.

The going was slow as hooves sank through the heavy, soft, energy sapping sand. The sun rose behind them, shining into the eyes of the enemy concealed somewhere in the desert plane ahead. The lack of artillery was not the only problem discussed the previous evening. The second troop of the 1st Life Guards was assigned to guard the baggage train. The heavy regimental carts were designed for European roads, not soft sand, and the 44 old artillery horses assigned to pull them were too few and too weak. To reduce weight, all the officers' baggage had been left behind and each cart was only half loaded. Each trooper had to replace their personal equipment, normally carried with them on their charger, with 2 days basic rations and 20lbs of forage. All they were left with for personal comfort was a cloak.

The sun rose at 5am, beating through the serge tunics to boil their backs; the temperature, at this hottest time of the year, swiftly climbing above 80°F. Peering through the small blue goggles that gave them the appearance of beetles, they drank in the stunningly dreadful desert that extended ahead and to their right. By midday it would be almost 100°F in the shade, and there would be no shade. Wind had scoured the sand into a stunning static sea of soft ridges, gentle valleys and curious cones, any of which could conceal the enemy. Here and there clumps of rocks and scrubby course grass flotsam threatened to wreck the unwary foot. Overhead a cloudless azure sky faded to a blue white horizon.

Their eyes constantly scanned for signs of the Egyptian forces, but they saw none.

Ahead, the red tunics of the Life Guards, though dulled by the sun and dust, were plainly visible. Steps muffled by sand, only the creak of leather and the heavy breathing of the horses broke the sweltering silence of the desert.

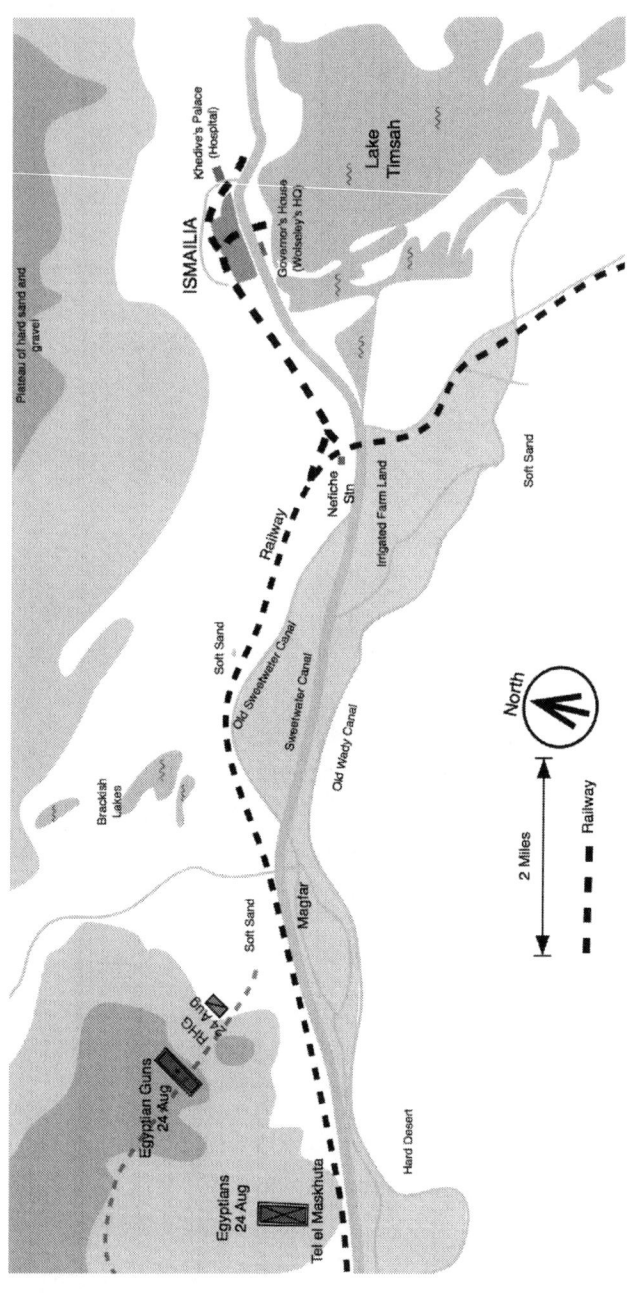

They joined General Graham and 1000 infantry from the York & Lancaster Regiment and the Marines at Nefiche. This body formed in a column, behind, and to their left; it slowly pressed on along the line of the canal. Here, west of Nefiche, the canal split into several irrigation ditches that ran parallel or as tributaries from the main canal, enabling crops to be grown in the sandy soil to create a greener belt perhaps a mile wide. During one of the rests the infantry fell upon one of these fields and spent several happy minutes decimating the crop of watermelons to slake their thirst. South of the green belt the desert rose in a steep escarpment of soft sand that any army would find very hard going, and which meant any threat was from the North or West.

Their journey west was necessarily slow but they reached Magfar at 7am and ahead could see the 70ft wide dam blocking the main Sweetwater Canal. The infantry rested briefly and then, moving in sections that provided cover for each other as they advanced, rushed silently toward the dam in the valley below them; still no enemy. The cavalry pressed on towards Tel-el-Mahuta.

Suddenly shots were fired and John saw a flurry of movement as the Life Guard chargers accelerated towards enemy infantry skirmishers. The British infantry quickly took up positions along the line of the canal and, protected by sandy hillocks, returned fire.

"Form Line!" the Blues bugle sang and, without thinking, John swept right to his position. His breathing quickened and an excited tingle spread through his chest, making him shudder. They continued their advance, sweeping the land. Ahead, and at the gallop, the Life Guards fanned out in fours and sections to pursue the enemy skirmishers who, heavily outnumbered, ran in groups back toward their lines. One group, chests heaving, stopped and turned to fire a volley at the cavalrymen. The shots all missed and in the next moment the group was put to the sword. Another group, surrounded, refused to surrender and it was only after a couple were shot that they gave up. Riding hard, Colonel Ewart suddenly pulled up as he reached an irrigation ditch and a trooper behind jumped into him, sending them all into the muddy water. John recognised Colonel Ewart's soldier servant pull them out, but not before the Colonel had lost his sword in the deep water.

Alfie's nostrils twitched at the scent of the blood as, moving more quickly now, they passed a handful of Egyptian infantry sprawled dead in the sand. Flies were already flocking to feast on the bodies. Further on, a pale faced Life Guard John vaguely knew, lay back against a cone of sand clutching his right arm as blood oozed through his fingers. His charger lay dead by his side.

"Bad luck, mate, that looks like a nasty nick," said LCpl McIntosh as they passed. "What happened?"

"Bloody Gippy officer shot my horse and when we both went down, tried to cut my head off. I put my arm up to deflect the blade and this happened." He indicated his arm.

"You were lucky to get away with it. What happened to the officer?"

"I managed to draw my sword and cut him in half." Through the pain, he smiled grimly.

John looked behind him and a short distance away saw the bloody mess for the first time. He almost gagged and looked away, but found his eyes drawn back to what had, a few minutes before, been a man.

"The bandsmen with the hospital litters should be with you shortly," he said. "I don't think they will be able to sew your prisoner back together though." He nodded at the corpse and the Life Guard grinned through the pain.

They continued the advance and were suddenly aware of bullets spinning through the air above and around them like angry bees. Artillery shells passed overhead and started landing around the dam, where the infantry had already started to dig shelter trenches. 1200 yards ahead on a slight rise, in what John presumed was the village of Tel-el-Mahuta, they could just make out entrenched Egyptian

Infantry, now suspended beneath a cloud of powder smoke. Behind them, and a large embankment that blocked the rails of the permanent way, a train disgorged more soldiers. The bugle sounded the 'retire' and they wheeled about to find cover behind the low sand hills. They dismounted so they were out of sight and to conserve their horses. John was sent forward with a few other marksmen to take up a prone position at the top of the sand hill where they could observe and discourage any of the enemy from coming any nearer. John's eager eyes scanned the sand ahead, his carbine cradled on his forearm, searching for movement.

General Wolseley dismounted and passed the reins to his soldier servant. He climbed the low rise of the sand hill, wincing inwardly as the pain from the old wound in his thigh flared, and regarded the enemy position through his binoculars. Rifle barrels and bayonets glittered in the early morning sun. He could see the entrenched Egyptian infantry being reinforced by the trainload from behind. He cursed that the he did not yet have an operational railway of his own and hoped that sunstroke would not claim too many of his reinforcements as they marched from Ismailia and Nefiche.

Arabi seemed rather better prepared than he had expected, or hoped. Looking at the Egyptian position he realised they had built a second dam across the canal. There was a real risk that the drinking water would run out, and, if that happened, he would have rioting locals in Ismailia and Nefiche to contend with too. He knew he had been right not to delay, even though his horses were not yet fit and many of his troops, artillery and supplies were still on board ship. Speed now was of the essence before the Egyptians could reinforce the position further, or gain a sufficient superiority of numbers to successfully attack him. He was already outnumbered here; his trump card was overwhelming belief in the superiority of regular British troops. His troops believed in their superiority, but most importantly, so did the Egyptians. He could not afford for them to know how weak he was; how fragile his position. The sensible thing to do would be to pull back, to consolidate his beachhead in Ismailia and then smash through the Egyptian forces once he was ready. But that would mean pulling back now, giving the Egyptians the impression they had beaten the British, building their confidence and making the next steps far more difficult. Worse, if he pulled back now they could use their superiority in numbers to attack, and given the logistical chaos in Ismailia they might inflict a real defeat. There was no doubt in his mind, he needed to attack, and quickly. He needed to keep the Egyptians on the back foot. He needed to disrupt them and drive them back to Tel-el-Kebir, where he could deliver a knockout blow. He needed to determine his next steps and sort his supply chain, something his analytical mind was best suited to.

"General Willis, the field is yours, don't lose it! I don't think it in consonance with the traditions of Her Majesty's army that we should retire, even temporarily, before Egyptian troops, no matter what their numbers might be. I will chase up reinforcements, and now I know Arabi's position, will determine the strategy for tomorrow. Carry on."

There, it was done. General Willis was one of the Duke of Cambridge's chums. Someone who had not seen any action since the Crimea, 30 years before, and a charming fool who believed good manners, quiet understatement and breeding were all that was required to be an officer. He was only here because he should have been commanding the annual war games in Aldershot and was immediately available. Amateur. If Willis won the day, Wolseley would be able to claim the credit as a bold risk taker. If he lost, Wolseley would be able to deflect the blame on to one of Cambridge's lackeys and so strengthen his case for Staff College and professionalism. The fool probably even thought he was doing him a favour in giving him an opportunity!

Pushing these thoughts aside and carefully fitting his mask of charm and calm, he gathered his staff around him and dictated orders for the Duke of Cornwall's Light Infantry and the Duke of Connaught's

Guard's Brigade, together with all available cavalry and artillery to reinforce them.

He viewed the York and Lancaster Regiment, taking up their positions, and pondered what it would take to destroy the dam they already controlled? He sent his Chief Engineer to investigate and was not encouraged by the answer.

"General, the dam has been formed of alternate layers of strong reed and sand, and is so compressed below water level that tools will not touch it. It is all held in place by lines of piles and telegraph poles tied together with wire. Destroying that dam is not going to be a quick process. If the one at Mahuta is as well built we will not be able to restore the flow of fresh water, or use the canal for transport purposes, for several days."

"Damnation!"

Beyond the Tel-el-Mahuta embankment, black smoke climbed into the still air as more trains arrived with Egyptian reinforcements. At 9am two Egyptian cavalry regiments, including Bedouin, began to advance over the high ground to the British right with the intention of outflanking them or attacking their rear.

To counter this threat, the two Household Cavalry squadrons and the Mounted Infantry company remounted and moved about a mile north of the railway, where they were immediately engaged by extremely accurate fire from four old bronze rifled muzzle-loading' artillery pieces that had been located on the plateau and were now silhouetted on the skyline. They could see a further eight, modern Krupp guns, being moved into position near the bronze muzzle loaders.

Four shells burst in amongst them but miraculously nobody was injured. Slowly, they were now kept moving forwards and backwards in open column.

"Corporal Major, I'm up for a laugh with the rest of them but why are we out here in the open giving their artillery something to shoot at?" asked Trooper Evans. "I mean.... someone might get hurt."

"Stop whingeing, Evans," replied TCM Gwinnell. "It's only your mother's least favourite son they are shooting at. Besides, the Gippys are using percussion fuses so the shells are exploding so deep in this soft sand they would have to get really lucky to hurt you."

"But why give them the opportunity to get lucky, Corporal Major?" asked Evans, who did not sound scared, but slightly miserable. The men chuckled. John was not sure if it was an act. Evans did not strike him as someone who would be afraid in action. He wished his stomach was not so tight.

Four more shells burst amongst them, not 20 yards away, causing a couple of the horses to shy slightly before being brought under control.

"Cpl Scott, why are we giving the Gippys the chance to blow Evans up?" replied the TCM as the men laughed slightly nervously. "And I mean other than because he's Welsh and bloody ugly."

"We have no guns to counter their artillery, Corporal Major, so for now we will have to keep them distracted so they don't get a chance to fire on our infantry before they have a chance to get dug in," said Cpl Scott. "We can move about so their gun layers have a more difficult time of it."

"Very good, Cpl Scott, why else are we out here?"

"In order to shadow their cavalry, Corporal Major. We would not want them to think they can outflank us, would we?"

"Quite right, Cpl Scott." The TCM was enjoying the tutorial, particularly since it was distracting the men from the very real possibility of imminent death. "So now they are firing lots of shells at us, none of us are falling over, so the Gippys must be beginning to believe all the stories they have heard about us being big, bad and bloody immortal. We are playing with their tiny minds."

"What if they realise their mistake and start using timed fuses, Corporal Major," asked Evans.

Moments later 2 shells burst high in the air above them.

"Speaking of tiny minds, you just had to ask didn't you?" growled the TCM, looking up and thanking his lucky stars that the shots were too high.

Two more shells burst high in the air above them, and a lucky splinter killed a horse; its rider was on his feet in a moment, calling out, "Three cheers for the first charger in the Life Guards killed since Waterloo".

"Hoorah!" replied the men as a spare mount was brought forward.

Some Bedouin cavalry were manoeuvring into a position where they could charge the Mounted Infantry.

The bugle sounded "half right" and then "form line". They were getting ready to charge. John felt excitement fill the void which nervousness had occupied until moments before. He took a better grip on the reigns. "Draw swords" sounded. He drew the long, heavy sword, its blade dull despite the fierce sun, and ensured the leather sword knot was firmly around his wrist. Beneath his legs, he could feel Alfie quivering with excitement; adrenalin overcoming the weariness. Ahead he could see the Egyptian Cavalry withdrawing.

"Come back, Gippy, we only want to introduce you to Mr Wilkinson," taunted LCpl McIntosh.

"Just as well they are withdrawing," commented Cpl Scott. "They are on the hard gravel, while we are on this horrible soft stuff. I'm not at all sure Archer has enough energy to charge far."

The bugle sounded "draw swords" again and they returned their swords to their scabbards.

To their left about 50 of the Bedouin cavalry were unaware the Egyptian cavalry had withdrawn and were pressing on. "This should prove interesting" said LCpl McIntosh as the Mounted Infantry chased after them. Shots were fired and several Bedouin fell, while others were captured, the rest running back to their lines.

A mile to the South a shell landed with a shriek in front of General Willis, and another landed behind him, amongst the staff. Both disappeared into the deep sand before exploding harmlessly upwards.

General Willis regarded the shell crater behind before turning back to view the Egyptian lines as though nothing had happened. The men expected their officers to be fearless and he was not about to disappoint them. He nevertheless ordered the men to lie down and the Household Cavalry and Mounted Infantry to fall back as the Egyptian Artillery brought up another 2 guns.

As "retire" sounded, the Household Cavalry silently gave thanks and, still in extended line, headed back towards the railway. Back amongst the low sand hills they dismounted, the Mounted Infantry and the Blues' marksmen once again taking up firing positions towards the North.

"Here they come." General Willis watched as the Egyptian infantry began to advance down the hill toward the dam. The York and Lancaster Regiment opened fire from long range and several Egyptians fell, causing them to pause about 1000 yards from the British lines.

Finding their advance on the dam checked, the enemy extended a thin line of Infantry on the British right. The Mounted Infantry moved forward to engage the thin line that was trying to encircle them and their best 7 or 8 marksmen opened fire with their rifles at a range of 900 yards. Several Egyptians fell. Lying behind some course grass at the top of a sand hill John did not bother shooting at the tiny figures he could just make out on the skyline. With only a carbine, firing at anything beyond 600 yards would be a waste of ammunition and draw attention to his position. He watched, impressed, as a couple of Egyptian infantry ran forward, over 800 yards away, and were almost instantly killed by the hidden Mounted Infantry marksmen. After a few more of the bolder Egyptians were killed, the others decided to remain where they were.

"10.30 and despite outnumbering us 10 to 1 they have not driven us from the field." General Willis was incredulous. "Thank God they do not have a bit more pluck and skill."

"At last!" Two guns from 'M' battery of 'A' Brigade the Royal Horse Artillery took up a position in the shadow of a sand hill by the railway embankment and began engaging the Egyptian Artillery in a far from equal duel. Willis estimated the Egyptians had 6 guns in action; having switched fire from the cavalry they were currently pounding the area of the dam and now the RHA guns. Fortunately the Egyptian gunners, while having a good aim, still had not managed to fuse their shells correctly and the timed shells were bursting too high, the percussion shells too deep in the sand, to be effective. The RHA guns on the other hand were well practised and so accurate were their airbursts above the Egyptian gunners, that the guns were frequently moved to force the British to change their point of aim.

"Look at that, General, the navy have arrived!" The General's military assistant pointed behind them and looked at his watch. "12 o'clock."

General Willis turned to see a launch slowly steaming up the canal with its crew watching over a couple of Gatling guns and a Nordenfeldt. "Splendid, place them to the right of the Yorks and Lancs in the ground between the canal and the railway if you please." He turned back to continue his observation of the enemy, wishing he could get rid of the headache and dizziness that had been bothering him for some time. At least he was not sweating so much.

It was midday, there was no shadow thrown from the rocks and grass and the heat haze made it almost impossible to make out movement on the plateau ahead despite the blue goggles. Clouds of flies swarmed around and John was thankful for the net draped over his face that kept them from crawling up his nose and eyes. The occasional bullet buzzed over John's head but for now the enemy seemed to be staying put. He saw the Mounted Infantry pulling back, their places taken by 1st Life Guards who had arrived with the RHA guns. He envied the Mounted Infantry's opportunity to drink. He had long ago emptied his water bottle and his mouth was as dry as the sand that surrounded him. Now he was no longer moving he was not sweating as much, though that might be because he did not have much sweat left. His mouth seemed to be full of grit, his tongue strangely engorged, his skin crusty with dust. He was beginning to develop a headache, and adjusted the position of his helmet in the hope it would help; it didn't.

"How's it going, Trooper?" John had sensed but had not heard the man approach up the sand hill to his position. He turned and found he was looking at the Commander in Chief, resplendent in a sand coloured pith helmet with a pink scarf tied around it. This close up he could see Wolseley's face was scarred and one eye appeared to be blind. The good eye gave him a cursory glance, that seemed to have rather a lot of curse in it, before returning to the skyline and the clouds of smoke that marked the enemy positions.

"Hot, Sir, in every sense of the word. It's difficult to see the enemy through this haze but if they do get within range, we knock them down, so they've been minding their own business and relying on their guns to drop shells in our direction." His reply was longer than he expected, but Wolseley nodded appreciatively.

"Good man, keep knocking them down," replied Wolseley. He made his way back down the slope to where the rest of the section clustered by their mounts. "Men, you have a place of honour; the safety of your comrades, and the glory of your country is in your keeping; you must stand or fall where you now are, even though the whole army of Egypt come against you." He remounted his charger and continued his inspection of the Cavalry's position, where they later discovered he made a similar speech all along their front.

Half the 1st Life Guards had dismounted and were now moving forward and back to engage the enemy from long range and give the impression of a larger force. They also dropped their forage nets, which from a distance gave the appearance of prone troops and attracted artillery fire for a while.

When the Mounted Infantry returned an hour later, the Blues and 2nd Life Guards were able to withdraw a mile behind the dam to find water and, hopefully, rations. As they returned to the valley and the Sweetwater Canal, the Egyptians brought another 6 modern Krupp guns into action and the shells started to rain down on the British with greater frequency and effect. In the distance, John could just make out the RHA gunners, stripped down to their shirts and trousers, sleeves rolled up, toiling to keep the two guns in action.

They passed the DCLI who had marched at pace up from Nefiche and were now recovering in reserve. He could tell Alfie was not happy, though he noted several of the Life Guard chargers were in a much worse state. As they neared the canal, the horses could not be controlled and charged for the water, plunging into the canal up to their chests and drinking deeply. The men did not care that the water had been stirred up by their mounts and drank deeply too, filling their helmets and pouring the brown soup over their heads. Behind them there was a steady stream of infantry coming back from the front, a few of them wounded by the shrapnel, but most unconscious through sunstroke.

One officer with sunstroke was accompanied by a Lieutenant Colonel, and John realised it was General Willis. He wondered who was now commanding the battle and presumed it was General Wolseley.

The two squadrons remained in reserve, a mile behind the British front line, for the rest of the afternoon. At 3pm the RHA guns ceased fire and the Egyptian Artillery switched back to shelling the 1st Life Guards and Mounted Infantry whenever they moved forward. Shortly afterwards John saw RHA wounded being carried back. That evening he discovered the story of the action from Ted Ankers, who had been out scavenging. At 2.45pm the new Egyptian guns achieved two direct hits on the RHA 13 pounders, killing two men and several horses. By that time they had been in action 5 hours and had fired 280 shells, which under constant fire and in that heat was an incredible achievement. One of the gunners, Joseph Knowles, had been wounded in the face by shrapnel early on but had continued to fight his gun to the end. His example was inspirational and they were writing him up for a Distinguished Conduct Medal.

At 5pm the two Household Cavalry squadrons prepared to move forward again as Bedouin cavalry appeared to be threatening to envelop the Mounted Infantry and 1st Life Guards. However, it was at that point that Colonel Baker Russell, resplendent in a white tunic, arrived with 350 sabres from the 4th and 7th Dragoon Guards. They had only disembarked that day and rushed forward as fast as they could, their locally procured horses familiar with the heat and in far better shape than the huge Household Cavalry chargers. Their appearance put an end to all thoughts the enemy had of trying to outflank the British position.

An hour later the sun descended behind the Egyptians. Dusk brought out the mosquitos, dew and a deafening silence from the guns. The Guards Brigade under the command of the Queen's third and favourite son, the Duke of Connaught, arrived accompanied by the four remaining guns of the RHA and a battery of 16-pounders.

The Guards had marched through the deep, soft sand in 100°F, with totally inadequate water and were not in good order; many of them had become casualties of sunstroke. They nevertheless took advantage of the darkness to push through the York and Lancaster Regiment line to a position at the base of the slope up to Tel-el-Mahuta, where the Egyptian Artillery was located. They formed a semi-circular position and waited for daylight.

As total darkness closed in at 8pm the Household Cavalry retired about 3 miles behind the front line. As they withdrew they passed small groups of Guards still making their way forward. The guns had only made it through the sand by adding horses to the limbers and using soldiers to push the wheels.

All this was at the expense of the baggage and stores. The robust, regulation waggons had not made it through the sand. The Egyptians had removed the permanent way rails and the water in the canal was too low for the heavier transport boats, so there was no camp and no other supplies. The horses were fed from the forage nets they had carried all day. The men went hungry. Ever resourceful, Ted Ankers had carried a couple of tins of Australian mutton stew that he had acquired in Ismailia and which he was prepared to share. They soon discovered why. The mutton was revolting; the vile, rancid mixture closely resembling string floating in oil. The only man able to eat it was Evans, who said it reminded him of home and his mother's cooking. After 17 hours in the saddle under a baking sun they chewed on their sour, black and underbaked bread ration, which at least filled part of the hole.

Everyone, officers included, had an uncomfortable night without tents. At least the flies had disappeared in the cooling temperature, but mosquitos now plagued them. The temperature dropped so low under the clear skies that heavy dew formed and their cloaks were insufficient. It was Ted Ankers who discovered some respite by scraping a hole in the sand; wrapping himself in his cloak and then raking the sand back so he was almost buried. The horses were tied to sacks filled with sand from the holes they had dug then the sack was partially buried and used as the pillow. Finally a mosquito net was draped over the sack to protect the head. Entombed in the damp and cooling sand they stared through the mesh at the miasma of stars until exhaustion claimed them.

32
MAHSAMA STATION

John was woken from a dead sleep by Tom Parris at 3am on 25th August. He buried Parris in his sleeping pit and, cradling his carbine, made his way to the sentry post for an hour of guard duty. Through a thick mist he watched the KRRC moving up from Ismailia, the infantrymen taking turns to lift and turn the wheels on the Royal Artillery 16 pounders through the clinging sand. He learned they had left Ismailia at 9.30 last night and had been marching solidly through the night, with but an hour and half break to rest.

At 4am the Blues rose from their sandy graves and fed their chargers the last of the forage. They breakfasted on a little black bread and listened to a high level view of General Wolseley's plan for the day. It was to pivot the force around the infantry, now in position in front of the dam and to attack the Egyptians from the British right flank. The cavalry would march out far into the desert to the North before heading back in a great arc to the Sweetwater Canal. The movement would hopefully encircle the entire Egyptian force.

As the first signs of dawn glimmered on the horizon beyond Ismailia, they formed into squadron columns in echelon with General Drury Lowe at the head. The 7th Dragoon Guards took the lead and the right flank, the 4th Dragoon Guards the rear of the cavalry and the left flank. Between them, the Household Cavalry formed with the Blues in column on the right, the 2nd Life Guards in column to the left and 1st Life Guards between. The 6 guns of the Royal Horse Artillery and the Mounted Infantry followed the cavalry. They trudged up the hill and out onto the high ground on the British right flank. To John, his head fuzzy from too little water and only a couple of hours sleep, it all seemed rather surreal. To their left and below, concealed in the mist, the Brigade of Guards advanced up the slope to the Egyptian earthworks at Tel-el-Mahuta. At any moment they expected to hear the sounds of the Egyptian infantry engaging the Guards, but they heard nothing.

On breasting the slope they found the ground to be hard sandy gravel interspersed with flints and fragments of petrified wood. It was from here that the Egyptian Artillery had fired all the previous day, protected by both infantry and cavalry; but of the enemy there was no sign. They continued west along the high ground, parallel to the canal, searching for signs of the enemy.

At 5.30am it was daylight and the mists were fast clearing from the desert. A galloper arrived with orders from General Wolseley. Word gradually spread among the men as they picked up the pace. During the night the enemy had withdrawn from their position at Tel-el-Mahuta and was now falling back to Mahsama Station 4 miles further west along the line of the railway and canal. The cavalry brigade was to push on at once to work round the enemy's left flank and cut off his retreat if possible. Every effort was to be made to capture a train. They pressed ahead, but the Household Cavalry horses were far from fit so the pace was slower than hoped, even on the firmer ground. General Drury Lowe seemed to be using the slower speed of the Household Cavalry to enable the Dragoon Guards to push ahead to either side like horns in a move reminiscent of the way the Zulu's attacked.

After a couple of miles at a steady canter John was uncomfortably aware of the sweat pouring off him and Alfie's more laboured breathing. They passed a dilapidated and unoccupied fort with its smaller pair half a mile to the left, down by the railway line.

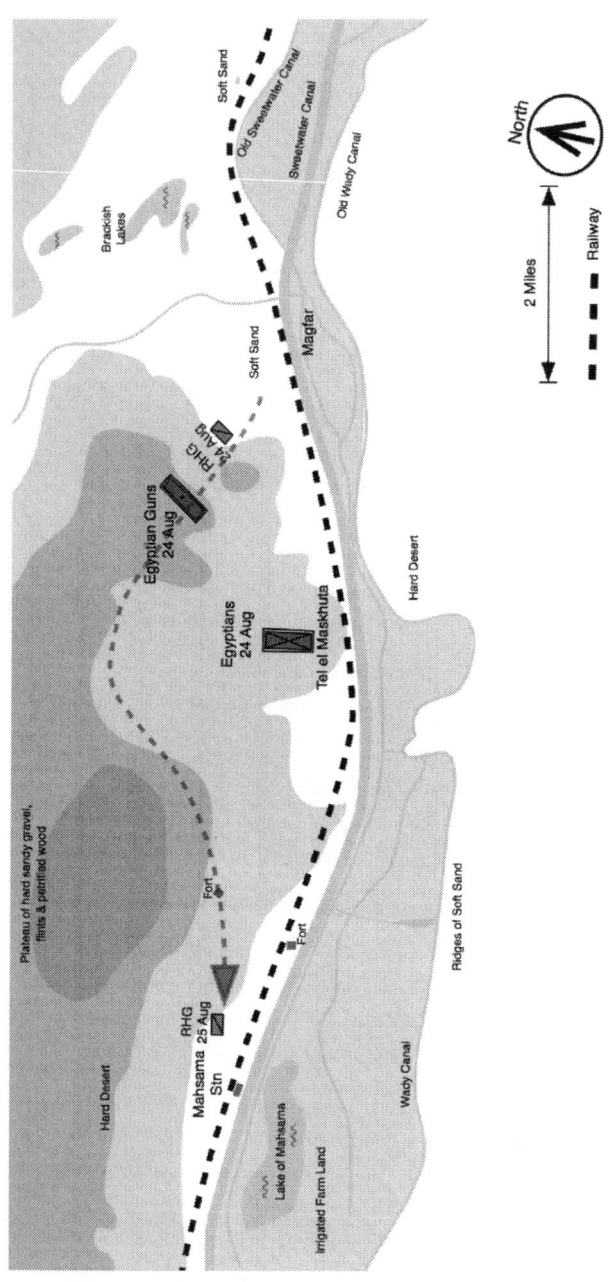

The 7th Dragoon Guards, far to the right, had disappeared into the desert. The 4th Dragoon Guards had spotted a train that was running at full speed West and nearing Mahsama Station and had galloped down off the heights to chase it. They were now 2 miles ahead of the Household Cavalry and approaching Mahsama. Just as they were about to catch the train a large body of Egyptian Cavalry charged them from the heights to their right. The 'gallop' sounded and the Household Cavalry urged their horses forward to intercept this new threat. The 4th Dragoon Guards veered away from the train to meet them, but just as they were about to clash, the Egyptians fired a wild volley and bolted; they may have seen the Household Cavalry about to hit them from the flank.

Suddenly, guns opened up on them from Mahsama and the heights to their front. At last, adrenalin washed away the fog in his head and surged through his muscles. To his left, John saw several horses and men fall as well directed shells screamed down and exploded on the firmer ground. He felt the blast of the explosions around him as the heavy horses continued to accelerate, keeping together in a solid wall of muscle and flailing hooves. Alfie was infected by the excitement and needed no urging to gallop towards the guns and groups of disorganised enemy infantry ahead. John was conscious that the ground was still firm as they descended the heights into the valley. Shells from the British guns were now landing in Mahsama and amongst the Egyptian guns, infantry and a tented camp. The Mounted Infantry galloped ahead and to the right on their fitter, smaller, Egyptian and Cyprian horses and now dismounted to engage the enemy with their rifles.

He could not remember drawing his long sword but now found it raised in his right hand, point down towards the white uniforms, guard twisted to protect his head. Shots fizzed past him and he ducked down behind Alfie's neck, an animal roar surging from his gut and past his bared teeth. Time seemed to slow. Ahead, the wild terrified eyes of the Egyptian soldier, tarbush askew, silvered rifle and bayonet glinting in the morning sun as it was reloaded and brought to bear; too late, arm straight, his sword slipped under the rifle, the guard pushing the bayonet out of the way and the point pushed through the man's chest with surprising ease. Shouts and screams rent the air. Twist the blade and allow Alfie's momentum to pull it free from the dying man.

Next target; moustache, scarred face, point, twist and pull. Slowing down, something tugging his sleeve. "Come on!" Gippy soldier aiming at Tom Parris. No time to correct his direction and point. Hack down across the man's shoulder, aiming at the ground. Jarring as the blade slices through flesh, sinew and bone and then nothing but blood as the man's head, and shoulder, and arm, falls to the flinty floor. The knees collapse and the body topples forward, blood gushing into the sand.

Keep going; momentum is the cavalryman's best friend. Through the guns. Alfie is blown. Sheath the sword; use the pistol. No matter that the Egyptian has his back to you, he is pointing his rifle at your friend. Aim low, squeeze the trigger, and watch the man throw his rifle away as the heavy bullet strikes between the shoulder blades. Constant vigilance, where is the threat? That man has thrown his rifle down and has his hands in the air. That man is still fighting, point, squeeze, miss, squeeze again. Dead. Two shots left. No more targets. Breathe.

Horses and men were milling around, bodies everywhere. Prisoners were already being herded to a central point for questioning. Rally to Cpl Scott. Check for casualties. He saw with relief that his friends in the section were all alive and undamaged. For the first time, John noticed the sweat trickling between his shoulder blades and down his back. Relieved laughter, though about what, John had no clue. Parris pointed out that John's jacket was ripped in the sleeve where a bullet had narrowly missed him. His breathing started to return to normal.

John dismounted and checked Alfie. The big charger was exhausted, covered in sweat but showed no signs of physical injury.

He reloaded his pistol and wiped his sword clean on a dead Egyptian. The fight had carried them down off the heights towards the deep soft sand at Mahsama. Here the Egyptians had built a well ordered camp with tents in neat rows about a mile from the Station. Some of them had been trampled by the 4th Dragoon Guards as they charged through, but most were intact. There were even a couple of well-provisioned hospital tents that the Regimental surgeons were already putting to good use, treating the surprisingly few British casualties. The Household Cavalry had lost their first man killed, Trooper Candy from 1st Life Guards, and there were 12 wounded. 16 more had been incapacitated by heatstroke the previous day and they had lost 11 horses. The other units had similarly suffered remarkably few casualties, only 6 killed and 27 wounded over the 2 days. The 4th Dragoon Guards, who had been in the thick of the fighting for the camp, had suffered none at all.

Everyone was jubilant, though the 4th Dragoon Guards were slightly despondent at having narrowly missed capturing the train General Wolseley so desperately wanted. Together they had captured 7 modern Krupp guns, large quantities of rifles and ammunition and 75 railway trucks full of stores, but no engine. The tents were often colourfully decorated and well provisioned with rice, barley, lentils, biscuits and beans, as well as large quantities of grain and chopped straw. Ted Ankers was beside himself, having also found cigarettes and coffee. Both they and their horses would eat properly for the first time in days.

The Egyptians had suffered a devastating defeat. Between the tented camp and the station were hundreds of dead, dying and wounded. Taking the horses down to the canal they discovered more bloated bodies floating in the muddy water. "Bastards!" cursed Cpl Scott. "These must be the dead from yesterday, soiling the water."

The Egyptian wounded were now suffering horribly in the blazing sun, crying out for water. The British fetched the water, and even carried some of them into the shade of the station house and railway trucks, but this practice stopped after an artilleryman was shot and killed by one of the ungrateful wounded. By 10am all firing had ceased as the British infantry arrived from Tel-el-Mahuta.

The few British dead were buried, without ceremony, in hastily dug graves by the railway line.

General Drury Lowe pushed forward with the 4th Dragoon Guards to survey Kassassin lock, which controlled the Sweetwater Canal, 5 miles further west. Ahead they could see the way was clear, but in the intense heat and after the exertions of the morning, nobody was in a position to advance further. Several more horses died of exhaustion and dehydration before they were able to drink in the canal and nearby lake.

That night, as he sewed the gash in his tunic sleeve, John was able to reflect on his first contact with the enemy. The act of killing was not something he wanted to dwell on, but he was glad he had been unafraid; that he had not fallen off his horse, let down his friends and that they had all survived without injury. They were the elite and had proved it.

They slept under canvas that night and for the first time in days awoke free from the heavy dew. At first light the 4th Dragoon Guards and a detachment of Mounted Infantry left to reconnoitre Kassassin. They returned after finding it abandoned and had left a detachment to await the arrival of an occupying force. Later that day, General Graham's brigade, comprising the York and Lancaster Regiment, Duke of Cornwall's Light Infantry, Royal Marines and Marine Artillery, as well as 2 guns of the Royal Horse Artillery, arrived and established defensive positions to both the North and South of the main canal. This disposition was not ideal as there was but a single bridge over the main canal near the lock house. While this would prevent the enemy over-running the position, it also meant that any forces pushed forward, or forced to retire would be unable to re-join the main body on the North side of the canal. To the North of the canal a tented camp was created between the main canal and the railway line. To the North of the railway line a redoubt was built and where the ground gently rose to a 100-160ft ridge, firing pits were dug in a North / South line. The British could move no further until ammunition and stores could be brought forward from Ismailia.

For the next couple of days, semi-bearded and their colourful tunics covered in grime, the cavalry remained in Mahsama to recuperate. The stench of death hung in the air as hundreds of bluebottle covered bodies, bloated in the blazing sun. Some attempts were made to bury them but, without tools and in the intense heat, it was a futile task. They did their best to drag the bodies from the canal. It was disgusting work, but necessary. John was glad to get away from the stink when the section was sent out to an outpost or to patrol the desert 3 or 4 miles north of the camp, and equally glad to return to vegetation and water in the marginally cooler canal a few hours later. The enemy seemed to be re-grouping at their Tel-el-Kebir camp, though a few Bedouin were seen keeping their distance.

The Engineers had already commenced work to relay the permanent way that would enable stores to be moved forward. Back in Ismailia, they were also extending the port facilities to enable the 113 vessels that now filled the lake to be unloaded. At Magfar and Tel-el-Mahuta the infantry were toiling to dismantle the dams and allow transport barges through. Wearing just their shirts and using entrenching tools the infantry soldiers hacked at the cut rushes and soggy sand in temperatures over 100 degrees. It was back breaking work and the first barges with supplies could not travel west of Magfar until the 27th; in the meantime the cavalry, recuperating in Mahsama, and General Graham's brigade in Kassassin, had to forage for food or starve. General Graham's men did not fare well and after 3 days without food even resorted to eating filthy dried out Egyptian biscuits salvaged from the canal.

Ted Ankers was in his element. His scavenging skills had ensured the Blues were less hungry than the rest of the brigade and he now assisted the quartermaster's staff to find local produce that could be purchased. Foraging parties managed to find 14 head of cattle as well as some sheep, chickens and turkeys. These were all brought in on the 27th, the day the first train arrived from Suez and the first barge arrived from Ismailia.

33
A MOONLIGHT CHARGE

At 9.30 on the morning of Monday 28th August, a large body of Egyptian cavalry was spotted advancing along the north side of the canal towards Kassassin and a couple of guns started firing from very long range, their shots all falling short. At 11am an outpost noticed a large force of cavalry, infantry and artillery moving behind the hill North West of Kassassin. General Graham did not have sufficient forces to occupy this hill and had placed the troops he had in a line of gun pits to defend an attack from that direction. There was nevertheless a risk that General Graham could be outflanked and an attack made on their logistics chain to Ismailia, cutting them off.

It was late morning and John was sitting with the section outside their captured Egyptian tent, cleaning weapons and wondering what they could add to the tin of Australian beef stew they were having for lunch to make it palatable, when they noticed the first flashes of the heliograph signalling. Shortly afterwards they were all ordered to mount up, ready to advance and support General Graham's brigade if needed. They moved north into the desert and a couple of section patrols were sent out further to look for signs of the enemy trying to outflank them. Nothing was seen.

There was no wind and the temperature had climbed to 104 degrees. The only sound was the occasional thump of artillery fire in the distance, beyond Kassassin. After a couple of hours patrolling the desert in blistering heat, they all dismounted a couple of miles from Mahsama. John spent the rest of the day sitting in the little shade available under Alfie, wishing he had a larger water bottle and that his tongue did not feel so large in his parched mouth. It was the middle of the afternoon when the distant guns ceased and with no sign of the enemy they were able to retire to their camp. By the time they returned to the canal at Mahsama the horses were mad with thirst and once again charged, out of control, into the muddy water up to their girths.

Alfie was fed and watered. Having missed the lunch that was normally the main meal of the day, John was looking forward to his evening meal, when he again heard firing from Kassassin and saw another heliograph signal flashing in the late afternoon sun. The Egyptians had made a bolder advance from the West, this time in greater strength with cavalry and infantry supported by guns. They had deployed their infantry in a mile long line of skirmishers that threatened to overlap General Graham's open right flank. This time the enemy's intent was more than a demonstration and they came on until they were within range of the British rifles, which checked the advance.

General Graham asked the cavalry to turn out again and protect his right flank. Two 16 pounder guns had been sent to Graham during the afternoon and now the Marine Light Infantry and another battery moved out to join him. The Household Cavalry, 7th Dragoon Guards and 4 remaining guns from the RHA wearily climbed back into their saddles and as twilight approached once again moved up the hill to the North West. It was 6pm. The 4th Dragoon Guards were left in reserve at Tel-el-Mahuta.

General Graham now saw that the Egyptian advance would expose the enemy left flank to an attack by the cavalry. He therefore passed another heliograph message to General Drury Lowe asking him to take the cavalry round by his right under cover of the hill and attack the left flank of the Egyptian skirmishers. Unsure that the message would get through, now the light was failing, he also sent his aide de camp, Lieutenant Pirie, with a verbal message. Graham's infantry and guns continued to engage the enemy where they showed. Artillery ammunition was now running short, though Graham was not concerned; he thought it unlikely the enemy would press their attack, particularly after dark. At 7.15pm when the Marines marched in with the additional artillery, and with total darkness only 30 minutes away, he ordered an advance that he hoped would coincide with the attack from the cavalry.

Pirie did not find the cavalry at Mahsama and, conscious of the urgency of his task, he grew increasingly worried as he galloped through the gloom and the soft sand. His horse foundered with exhaustion and it was only by good fortune that he happened upon an RHA battery returning from Kassassin, out of ammunition, and was able to borrow another mount. Aware of his commander's intent, he had some idea where the cavalry may have gone so he struck out into the desert and finally found them 4 miles north west of Kassassin. By now he was in a highly excitable state, his concern increased by the implications of the shortage of artillery ammunition. He hurriedly relayed his orders for Drury Lowe to attack the enemy left flank as quickly as possible because Graham 'was only just able to hold his own'.

Drury Lowe thought he might now be riding into a night action that could by now be already lost. He wheeled his brigade round and advanced in a wide sweep to come in on the enemy's left flank.

John rode Alfie at a walk through the deepening darkness. The Blues Squadron was formed in a column, 4 abreast and following the Life Guards. He estimated they had covered 5 or 6 miles, following the valleys between the sand ridges that ran parallel to the canal. Only the occasional order to trot or change direction broke the low sound of bits jingling and leather creaking. A thick haze now covered the desert as the temperature fell into the 70's, dampening the flash and sound of the firing around Kassassin to their left. The moon was rising over the horizon like a second, much duller, sun. In its eerie light he caught the occasional glimpse of the 4 guns of the Royal Horse Artillery as they rumbled over the solid sand, gravel and flint ahead of him. Up front of the guns, the 7th Dragoon Guards were a solid dusty body in the moonlight, just cresting a low rise.

Ahead, he heard the boom of a gun followed by the hissing of a shell that passed over him and burst in the air somewhere far behind. 1500yds ahead, at the high point of the ridge that dominated the area, he saw a rapid series of flashes as guns that moments before had been firing on Kassassin turned to fire at the cavalry threat that had come on them from their flank. Shells hissed over their heads, most bursting harmlessly behind. A few steel splinters spat around them and one sparked off a flint not far from his side.

The 7th Dragoon Guards quickly wheeled, left and right, to allow the guns to engage, and reformed in column of troops behind the Household Cavalry. Ahead, the four 13 pounders raced to the top of the low rise, rapidly unlimbered and opened fire from a point some 5 or 600 yards from the enemy guns.

The Blues followed the Life Guards forward and to the right of the guns. As John passed them at a walk, a mass of rifle shots crackled from the night directly ahead. Flashes rippled down blocks of white that he could now make out at his 11 o'clock; Egyptian infantry in very large numbers. The butterflies he had been feeling in his stomach for the past hour fluttered down his arms and legs as the adrenalin started to surge through his body.

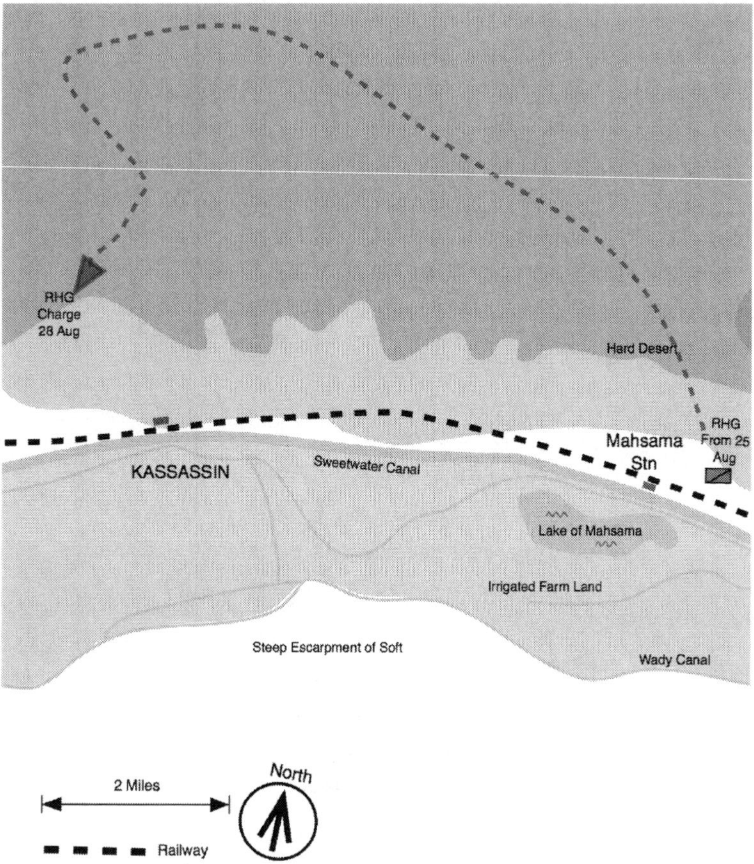

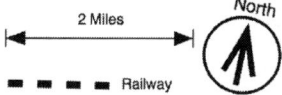

"The Household Cavalry will charge. Front form in two lines," roared Colonel Baker Russell, his white jacket making him clearly visible amongst the deep red and blue tunics.

John urged Alfie forward and to his position 100 yards to the left of Baker Russell and with the rest of the Blues, in the second line. John heard LCpl McIntosh quietly cursing. "Bloody Colonel Ewart, once again placing his Life Guard's in the van to get all the glory."

"Yeah, but he won't go down in history as the man who ordered the first charge of the Household Cavalry since Waterloo," replied Cpl Scott.

The huge charger's ears pricked with a palpable excitement that washed away all the fatigue of the day. Bullets fizzed about them, mostly high but there was an occasional thump and a cry from horse or man as a round hit home.

"Draw swords!"

The bronzed blades emerged from their leather sheathes, gleaming dully in the moonlight. Riders took a firmer grip of the reins and tugged the leather lanyard taught over their wrists. In moments they were in position and John was facing a formed body of the enemy for the first time.

"Household Cavalry, charge!" Baker Russell's command was like thunder and, cheering, they sprang forward; monstrous in the gloom. 20 yards ahead, the first line of Life Guards kicked up stones and dust as they accelerated towards the muzzle flashes that lit the sky like a firework display.

Hooves drummed on the desert, horses huffed and men roared to build a wall of sound that seemed to insulate them from the bullets and shells that cracked and burst about them. Ahead, the blocks of Egyptian infantry, white uniforms glowing in the gloom, fired rapidly as the cavalry tore across the open ground.

300 yards, John was dimly aware of John Crook, riding to his left, crying out and slumping in his saddle, his wild-eyed charger continuing as if nothing had happened. Ahead, the Life Guards were a solid black wall of thundering death. As they charged, Major Milne Home, who was leading the second line, was gradually leading the Blues to the right, and now John could see why. There were solid blocks of Egyptian Infantry to the right, who would be missed by the Life Guard's charge and who could then fire into their rear.

200 yards, Tom Parris cried out and fell from his horse. John could do nothing other than grit his teeth and carry on. Parris' best chance lay in destroying the enemy.

100 yards. The Egyptians stopped firing, turned and ran. The Life Guards charged through and over the white clad soldiers, intent on the guns behind. Bodies fell, only to rise again as the black beasts passed. John pointed his sword and took the first man between the shoulder blades. Alfie's huge hooves crushed the next as John allowed the momentum to pull the blade from the body. He flicked the bloody blade over Alfie's ears and leaning to his left took the next man in the neck as he part turned to face his tormentor. He switched to another white-jacketed target wielding a sword 20 yards away to his right. With a shock he realised that the white tunic was not an Egyptian officer but Colonel Baker Russell, on foot, his charger lying dead by his feet. Surrounded, the huge man was resolutely laying about the Egyptian infantry with his sword in one hand, while fumbling for his pistol with the other. John switched targets and ran through a large Egyptian with a fierce moustache who was about to bayonet the Colonel in the back. He wheeled Alfie on the spot, rage driving him to slash at another Egyptian, whose head toppled from his shoulders. For a moment, John and Baker Russell exchanged a fierce, determined look, and then he swung his leg over the saddle and dismounted; parrying a bayonet out of the way and thrusting his sword into its owner's chest as he dropped.

He had not considered the risks of what he was doing for a moment. His Colonel needed a horse, so he should have Alfie. Shaking his head, Baker Russell stared at John in disbelief for a moment, before grabbing Alfie's reins from John's outstretched hand. John parried another bayonet and stepped towards the Egyptian, smashing the hilt into the man's face; the Egyptian crumpled. In seconds the Colonel had stepped up off his dead charger's flank and onto Alfie's back and was now expertly turning the huge horse to face three more Egyptian's that were rushing towards them. In a well-practised movement, that had as much to do with Ted Ankers penchant for penny cowboy novels as it had the cavalry training manual, John pulled his revolver from its holster with his left hand and shot one of the Egyptians in the chest. Baker Russell skilfully stabbed another and John shot the third in the head before he could fire the rifle he had aimed at the big officer. The charge had carried on beyond them and the two cavalrymen were now alone amongst white clad bodies that were slowly rising from the dead.

"Are you bloody mad, man?" Baker Russell kept Alfie constantly moving around John, looking for the next threat. He guided Alfie to trample a wounded infantryman who was lying on the ground and fumbling to reload his rifle. He whirled in the other direction. Within 20 yards of their position, four Egyptians had got back to their feet and were reloading their rifles.

"I must be, Sir." John had 3 bullets left, though he knew that the pistol was of little use beyond 10 yards and took an age to reload, one round at a time. They were going to die. "Please be good to my horse, his name is Alfie." A bullet cracked past his head; the Egyptian who had fired the shot already reloading. John saw the cartridge being ejected and in a moment was screaming and charging towards the man, his sword waving above his head. As the man brought his rifle to bear John fired his pistol at him, twice, hoping to distract him as much as hit anything. To his surprise the man's nose exploded and he crumpled as the second shot hit him in the middle of the face. Baker Russell charged with him and ran through a second man in the gloom. How many bullets did he have left? He thought it might be one, but was far from sure. Another bullet tugged at his side and he turned to see another Egyptian, 15 yards away, reloading. He pointed the revolver and squeezed the trigger, missed. He squeezed again and heard the hammer clack against the spent chamber. The Egyptian smiled and calmly raised the rifle to the aim. John threw himself to the side and dived towards a rifle lying on the ground. The man would not miss him again. He braced for the impact he was sure would come next. Even as his fingers closed around the stock of the rifle he heard hooves thundering towards him and the next moment a dozen Dragoons rushed past and over him. He gripped the rifle awkwardly, his sword, still attached to his wrist, digging into the warm sand, and tried to get to his knees in a way that would enable him to go through the dead Egyptian's bandolier and locate a round to feed into the breech. Breathing heavily he was conscious of Alfie by his side and looked up into his Colonel's concerned face.

"We made it, Trooper. Are you alright?"

"I think so, Sir." Removing the lanyard from his wrist he sheathed his sword and brushed himself down before reloading his revolver. He saw his helmet lying on the ground nearby, dusted the sand off it, and replaced it on his head.

A line of 7th Dragoon Guards passed by them rounding up prisoners, and stabbing any wounded Egyptian who looked like making a fight of it, as they went. It was the only way to be sure. An occasional shot in the night mingled with the moans of the wounded and the dwindling sounds of battle at Kassassin. Deep shadows passed over white bodies as riders picked their way over the battlefield.

Somewhere to their left a bugle sounded the rally. It would no doubt take some time in the dark. Excited Troopers would have chased the enemy in all directions for some distance.

Baker Russell cleared his throat. "What is your name, Trooper?"

"Waterston, Sir."

"Have we met before? There is something familiar about you."

"Briefly in Aldershot last month, Sir, you charged into me by accident on parade."

"Ha, knew it, I never forget a face. Well, I am very glad to have run in to you again this evening, Waterston. I believe I owe you my life. Thank you."

"You just owe me a horse, Sir. Can you make sure I get him back? I get in loads of trouble every time I lose him."

Baker Russell chuckled again. "Come on, let's get to the rally point."

"I will shortly, Sir, I need to find my friend before the Bedouin do. He was shot from his horse as we charged. Could you pass my carbine, please, Sir?"

The Colonel sheathed his sword and pulled the Enfield carbine from its leather case behind his right leg. He opened the breach and passed it down.

"Come on, I will help you look, it's the least I can do." Now the adrenalin was dissipating, the Colonel's voice was low, concerned.

"Thank you, but you'd better go and take command again, Sir. The Blues will kill me if you are thought dead and a Life Guard takes over."

The Colonel chuckled. "Very well, Trooper Waterston. I would not want to get you into even more trouble." He touched his fingers to his helmet in salute, and disappeared into the night.

Sheathing his sword, and loading a cartridge from his pouch into the carbine, John carefully picked his way through the bodies that littered the battlefield until they petered out. In the bright moonlight he could just make out the churned up desert floor and the line of their charge. He was not alone in retracing their steps and was relieved when he discovered Cpl Scott and Robert Gibson also looking for Tom Parris. They finally found him leaning up against a small mound in the shadow of a straggly bush. His pistol was drawn and in his lap and he was trying to stem the bleeding in his left shoulder that dropped at an unusual angle; the arm dangled uselessly by his side. His charger, Altair, was nowhere to be seen and had probably carried on with the charge. Gibson bandaged the wound and strapped the arm before they helped Parris onto Scott's charger, Archer, and walked slowly to the rally point.

There, John found a spare mount and Parris was reunited with his horse. They joined the rest of the Squadron for the return to Mahsama. Walking back through Kassassin they could see that General Graham's brigade charge had defeated the Egyptians and was now returning to its original position. It was clear from the number of bodies that the Egyptians had suffered another heavy defeat. They arrived back in Mahsama at 1am.

The Household Cavalry were jubilant, excitement overcoming exhaustion. Colonel Baker Russell's batman returned Alfie, who was tired and cut in several places, but had not suffered any lasting damage. With Robert Gibson's help they sewed him up, treated the wounds and gave him a good drink. Finally the section was able to cook a late night meal and give their individual accounts of the action. Their mood was more sombre than most. John Crook was unconscious and did not look like he would live through the night. He was likely to be the only Blues fatality. Joseph Proudlock was severely wounded, though the surgeon was hopeful he would live. Tom Parris would make a full recovery but would not take any further part in the Egyptian campaign. They were about to be sent back to Ismailia via flat bottomed boats hauled by steam launch.

John was surprised to find that his personal battle had been unusually eventful and his friends were amazed when they learned that in the midst of it he had given his horse to the Colonel, saving his life, at great risk to his own.

"You'll get a medal for this, you mark my words," said Cpl Scott, and under his breath. "Mad bastard."

34
CONSEQUENCES

The following days were spent consolidating the British position at Kassassin and preparing for the assault on the main Egyptian defensive position at Tel-el-Kebir. The Blues took turns with the rest of the cavalry to patrol the desert by day and night, in part to further acclimatise the horses but mainly to keep an eye on the

Bedouin riders who continued to threaten the supply chain from Ismailia, and steal livestock whenever possible.

The following evening as they drank cocoa Ankers had obtained from somewhere he was keeping a closely guarded secret, he relayed what he had heard from a 19th Hussar who had visited the battlefield the day after the charge.

"A squadron of the 19th Hussars attached to General Graham's brigade were up on that hill at first light. The bodies were already covered with flies and carrion birds. They saw a few Bedouin looters who disappeared to watch from a distance when the Hussars appeared.

"There were bodies everywhere, as well as a large number of wounded that they tried to help, but who had to be finished off instead."

"Like the Egyptian wounded we found here?" asked Robert Laidlaw.

"Yes, they did not believe we would help them, and shot or tried to stab anyone who came close," replied Ankers. "After seeing what the Bedouin do to the bodies, I understand why."

The men leaned towards him, curious to know more. Ankers paused for effect.

"Who here is circumcised?" he asked. They looked at him curiously. "Nobody? Then you'd better hope you don't die out here. Or, if you do, make sure we find you before they do." He grimaced before continuing.

"The uncircumcised bodies were mutilated. Feet and hands chopped off. Abdomens ripped and gashes on the forehead........."

"And in the poor bastards' mouths.........were their wedding vegetables."

John realised his mouth was hanging open in surprise, and promptly closed it.

"So, no getting killed," said Cpl Scott after a long silence. He looked at John. "But if you must do something stupidly heroic and cop it, then be sure we can find you first to bury you properly."

That night, John found out first hand how difficult and dangerous the Bedouin could be. He was on foot at 1.30am, patrolling the line where the horses were hobbled. It was a clear cool night and the stars winked spectacularly in the deep indigo sky. Here, near the canal, a silvery mist reflected the remains of the moonlight. He loved this time, even if it did mean his sleep was interrupted. The temperature had dropped and, provided he kept moving, was comfortable after the oven-like heat of the day. It was peaceful and he had time to reflect on how different his life was from that of a railway guard. Sure, he had not impressed a girl into walking out with him, but he could not have dreamt of the excitement of the past week; nor the boredom or the terror.

The horses shuffled and sporadically snorted as they rested. John could hear human snoring from a nearby tent, too. 20 yards away he noticed a couple of the big chargers were slightly disturbed. Strange, what had they seen?

He felt, rather than heard the man approach his back and without thinking stepped suddenly to one side, bringing the butt of the carbine back, hard, as he stepped. He was rewarded by a grunt and caught the silvery flash of a long thin blade as he turned. The blade narrowly missed his shoulder as the man doubled up slightly with a grunt. Weapon at his hip, in one movement, he continued the turn, pointed the short carbine at his assailant's chest, barely a foot away, and pulled the trigger. The carbine roared and the flare of the powder exploding from the barrel ruined his night vision. The Bedouin was thrown back with the force of the heavy bullet exploding his chest and sprawled into the detritus of the desert floor. There was no way he was getting up again.

John quickly turned to where he had seen the original disturbance. One of the chargers was gone. He ejected the cartridge, cursing the bright light in the centre of his vision that perfectly replicated the flash from his barrel and prevented him seeing properly. Feeding a fresh round from his pouch into the breech and snapping it shut he extended his other senses to the threat. His heart thumped and pounded in ears that still rang with the sound of the shot.

The shot had alerted the camp and 2 roving guards came running across to him. "Thieving bastards," he said. "They have taken one of the chargers." He pointed at the gap in the line. They hurried towards the horses, ducked under the line and disappeared into the night.

John knelt down and scanned the horizon, the lighter sky all he could see now; everything nearer the ground a dark jumbled mass. Would the Bedouin make a dash for it? There, the silhouette of a man on a horse 75 yards away and trotting towards the desert. Vision returning he could just make out that the shape of the man was not that of a soldier. He raised his carbine, gave the shadow half a body width of lead to account for the movement, and squeezed the trigger. This time he kept his left eye closed to retain his vision. The carbine barked and he re-opened his left eye. The man was gone, but the horse was still there and had stopped, its back bare. John hurried over to it, reloading as he walked. He heard movement to his right but was relieved to see from the helmeted heads that it was the pair of guards. Alert, they scoured the area around the horse and soon found the prostrate robed shape of another Bedouin. He, too, was dead.

There were more people rushing everywhere now and the guard commander quickly organised a line to search the camp. At the camp perimeter, more troopers filled the gaps between the sentries and scanned the horizon for signs of more Bedouin. They would be out there, but nothing more could be done until it was light.

After first stables the following morning, Cpl Scott took John to one side. "It looks like you have been noticed. Cpl Smith was wounded in the charge so John McIntosh has been promoted to replace him. You have been selected to take Jock's place as my second." He paused to smile at John's incredulous look. "No need to look so shocked. I know you are barely out of the recruit's cadre but we both know you are far from wet behind the ears. You learn quickly, know your trade and are proven in battle. I cannot think of anyone I would rather have as my second. Congratulations."

"Thththank you, Corporal," John replied, lost for words.

"Thank you, Corporal," Cpl Scott smiled again, "and the name is George, though not when others are listening in. Don't mess up. Lance Corporal is an easy rank to lose, just ask Ankers. Now, I need to get to a briefing for this afternoon's patrol, gather the section together and clean the weapons. Remember, only dismantle half the carbines or revolvers at any time just in case we are surprised."

When they returned from the patrol later, John was surprised to be greeted by TCM Gwinnell, who looked unusually cheerful, and Lieutenant Binning wearing an enormous grin. "You are going to be famous, Corporal Waterston. For saving his life, Colonel Baker Russell has written you up for a Victoria Cross. The first medal for bravery in the Household Cavalry, and it's a VC. Better still, it is to a Blue rather than a Life Guard. Colonel Ewart does not know whether to rejoice or cry."

"It's not confirmed yet, Waterston," added the TCM. "Horseguards will want their say, but you meet all the criteria for its award. Congratulations."

John found himself surrounded by cavalrymen, some of whom he barely knew, slapping him on the back and congratulating him. That evening, after all the chores were done, Ted Ankers produced a couple of bottles of very fine brandy that had been liberated from somewhere; nobody cared to ask from where. The celebrations lasted until the bottles ran out. Cpl Scott had taken John's guard duty and returning in the early hours found the section were rather the worse for wear. Even the teetotal John was slightly affected as someone had 'added' to his cocoa. It appeared alcohol was rather more effective when you had not had a drink for weeks and were dehydrated in a hot climate. The section were unable to conceal the fact that they were not fit for duty first thing the following morning.

The TCM was beside himself with rage. Celebrating was no excuse in the field and Cpl Scott was to be severely punished for allowing his section to get into such a state. Lance Corporal Waterston was horrified. It was not Scott's fault; he was to blame for not standing up to Ted Ankers. He remonstrated with the TCM, pointing out that Cpl Scott had not even been there, and asking that he be punished instead. It was at this point that events became complicated, and escalated. The next he knew, Trooper Waterston, (Scott had been right about the difficulty in retaining that first stripe), was summoned before the Commander in Chief.

35
THE ADMINISTRATION OF WAR

General Sir Garnet Wolseley sat behind a folding desk in his tent, writing his daily telegram to the Queen and considering what he might add that would entertain her. He was glad that at this stage in the campaign he had time for such a daily missive. He suppressed an irritating thought; her letter of the 28th had contained not a single compliment. He was determined that she would finally see his worth.

He cursed the insufferable heat and contemplated the neat piles of paper. Letters and telegrams from Horseguards, the Foreign Office, the Royal family and, he smiled, the witty ones from his wife Louisa. There were now even messages passed by telephone from Ismailia; there was no way he would talk on the confounded new-fangled thing. Then the daily reports; intelligence updates, progress in the logistical build up, casualty reports and requests for his approval of more equipment, ammunition and stores. Yes, he had some capable staff officers who could analyse and summarise them all for him, but they might miss something vital.

One telegram from London angered him considerably; he glanced at it in the hope it might spontaneously combust. The Indian reinforcements had arrived in Ismailia on the 25th August, though he had prioritised the unloading of the British units that he was sure would be far more influential on both the military situation and his career. He could not forget the Indian infantry deserting the 66th to their fate at Maiwand. The Indian General, MacPherson, had the audacity to complain at the delay to London and Horseguards had now ordered him to unload the Indians. He cursed inwardly, then, appreciating there was nobody present to hear, outwardly. It was the right time for them to disembark anyhow, but General MacPherson would believe it was as a result of his complaint and would be even more insufferable.

He glanced at the personnel update. The 2nd Bengal Cavalry and 13th Bengal Lancers were now unloaded, with their baggage train, and would join Drury Lowe's cavalry in Mahsama on 2nd September. With the arrival of the Indians he now needed to reorganise the cavalry into a proper Division with 2 Brigades, and that meant he needed a Brigade commander. Colonel Ewart of the Life Guards was the senior, but Colonel Creed Baker Russell was the experienced fighting commander he needed, not some rich, well-connected popinjay. Creed was also a good friend who needed the money associated with promotion following a disastrous business loss. His charge at Kassassin had saved the day by destroying the enemy's will to fight, and Creed had led the charge like a man. It had also created another interesting opportunity, a VC in Her Majesty's Household Cavalry.

The Household Cavalry had done well; an elite formation he had created from a smart regiment that had not been tested in war for generations. The Press could laugh at them no longer and their performance would put paid to any thoughts of amalgamation or disbandment, a VC would seal it. Yes, their very survival was down to his insistence on bringing them to Egypt, in the face of Childers's doubt, and pushing them well to the front. Her Majesty must be grateful to him for saving her favourite Household Cavalry. Yes, it must be enough to swing her allegiance from her cousin, the Duke of Cambridge, to him and remove her objection to his elevation to the Lords. That would please his Louisa. The VC would seal it.

He would meet Trooper Waterston and see if he was the right stuff. He was already a little concerned about the VC won in Kafr-Dawar. There was something about Private Frederick Corbett that nagged at the back of his mind. What had induced him to remain by his officer's side while under sniper fire? Yes, he would meet Waterston and be sure. Was he a volunteer? Did he have a choice when he joined the army, or was it out of necessity? There were very few tramps in England who at some time or other had not been in the Army. Everywhere there were men who wandered all around the world. They would enlist in winter and desert in the summer, and each time with a free issue of kit.

Was Waterston young? He did not believe in old soldiers, young men did what they were bid, and went where they were told.

Did Waterston have a choice when he risked his life to save Creed? Almost anyone could appear brave if they were fighting for their lives. It took another type of bravery to deliberately place one's life on the line to protect someone else. Most interesting of all, was he a man of faith? Did he trust in God to protect him? He scribbled a note to his assistant to arrange an interview with Waterston, and better get Creed to come too.

He turned his attention back to reorganising his troops. He had now ordered Sir Archibald Alison's Highland Brigade, together with General Hamley and his staff, to move from Ramleh to Ismailia so they could join the assault on Tel-el-Kebir that would finish Arabi. General Sir Evelyn Wood's brigade would remain in Alexandria to defend the city. It was all coming together nicely, yes, Tel-el-Kebir on the 15th or 16th of September would be in accordance with the plan he outlined in Horseguards before he departed. He could be back in London by mid-October.

36
THE PRICE OF HONOUR

They fussed around him. His blue jacket was beaten and sponged until it could be cleaned no more, and almost half the dust and salt stains had been removed. Cpl Scott was all for re-darning the 2 bullet tears so they would be less visible, but the TCM said they demonstrated quite how lucky John had been so should be left as they were. An Egyptian razor, soap and a shaving brush were found so John's semi-beard disappeared, though a moustache was retained. Ted Ankers came up with a bath – digging a hole in the sand, lining it with a waterproof cape and filling it with cleanish water from the canal. Angus Duncan even peeled some of the dead skin from the back of his sunburned neck and tops of his ears. John looked almost respectable, and certainly unusually smart amongst the rest of the Regiment whose personal equipment had not made it from Ismailia yet.

He waited with TCM Gwinnell outside General Wolseley's tent. He was standing at ease but that was certainly not how he felt. He would almost rather fight on foot amongst a horde of Egyptian infantry than enter the unknown domain of his Commander-in-Chief. Officers bustled in and out of the tent, casting curious looks in his direction. John could not hear the muffled conversations within the tent, but could sense the tension that surrounded the great man.

Colonel Baker Russell approached with a warm smile that was only just visible behind the huge walrus moustache. The TCM and John came to attention and saluted smartly, noting that Baker Russell's batman clearly had access to better cleaning and darning skills than John as his tunic was almost white. It was not possible to remove all the blood and powder stains though, and the Colonel wore them like badges of honour. The salute was returned smartly. The TCM was acknowledged and then all attention was on John.

"Good to see you, Waterston. I hear you bagged a couple of intruders the other night, well done." The voice was deep and booming. John tried to maintain his gaze a few inches above the Colonel's forehead but found he was craning his neck, which was still rather sore after Angus Duncan's ministrations.

"Know why you're here?"

"No, Sir. At least, I'm not sure Sir. Is it to do with Cpl Scott and the section drinking all that brandy the other night? Because, that was my fault not his, Sir. He should not be punished too."

He was surprised when the Colonel laughed, his eyes twinkling in amusement.

"I had not heard about that, but no, the Commander-in-Chief has nothing to do with disciplinary matters." He made a mental note that here was a man loyal to his friends and clearly capable of taking responsibility for his actions. He warmed to him even further. "Come, let us see what the General has to say about the recommendation I have made." He exchanged a look with the

General's military assistant, who indicated that the Wolseley would see him now.

"Corporal Major, wait 30 seconds then march him in please; then return outside, there is not room to swing a rat inside." Baker Russell entered the tent and John heard the tones of a greeting between two friends.

TCM Gwinnell said quietly, "Nothing to worry about other than my guarantee to make your life a living hell if you fuck this up. At my command, right turn, quick march, halt before the General and salute." He waited another 20 seconds then gave the commands. "Right turn. Quick march. Halt. Salute." They both saluted. "This is Trooper Waterston, Royal Horse Guards, Sir."

"Thank you, Corporal Major. Please leave us." General Wolseley's voice was quiet but with a hard confidence about it.

John found himself at attention before the great man, who asked him to stand at ease. Out of the corner of his eye he could make out Colonel Baker Russell sitting to the side, relaxed and smiling reassuringly in the small space.

"Trooper Waterston, I have here a recommendation for you to receive the Victoria Cross for your actions during the moonlight charge at Kassassin. It says that 'without thought to your own safety, you gave your horse to Colonel Baker Russell after his charger had been shot from under him, and fought with great distinction on foot by his side whilst in the midst of a determined company of Egyptian infantry.' " He paused to look at John, measuring him up, gauging his reaction. "Before approving this I want to understand more. Why did you join the Household Cavalry, Trooper?"

John considered. 'To impress the girls' sounded so frivolous now; he could not say that. What would the General want to hear? No, he was over thinking this. Honesty was the best policy and to hell with the consequences. "Adventure, Sir." He unsuccessfully fought the desire to fill the silence that followed. "And a better uniform than my one as a railway guard. And a big black horse, Sir."

There was the faintest indication of a smile around Wolseley's eyes. "So, not to fill your belly then?"

"No, Sir"

"So, what were you thinking when you gave your horse to Colonel Baker Russell?"

"I'm not sure I was thinking Sir. It just seemed the right thing to do, Sir. Him being an officer."

"Did you not think that getting off your horse in the midst of the enemy would be tantamount to suicide?"

"Well, Sir, my blood was up. I just wanted to get at the enemy. I remembered what Colonel Burnaby told us before we left, that it was not for us to die for our country, but to make sure that the Gippy died for his. I did not think it likely that I would come across an Egyptian who was bigger or better than me, and God was on my side. Sir."

Wolseley smiled. Faith. Belief. There it was. Here was proof that volunteers with faith made the best, bravest soldiers.

"So, you are a man of faith then? You regularly attend church?"

"Aye, Sir. I attend all the services."

Silence. Wolseley, the staunch Irish protestant, bristled. The carefully controlled anger that was always within him rose to the surface. "What do you mean, you attend all the services? Church of England _and_ Catholic?

"Aye, Sir, and Methodist too. There are not any Presbyterian services I have found yet in London." John was confused. Where had this tension come from? He believed in the word of God, in the scriptures. It mattered not to him how that word was translated into a service or worship, and in his experience there was not much difference between a Catholic service and a high Church of England one. Besides, he stood more chance of meeting a nice girl by going to a different service each week.

"Any man who changes his faith is no man at all."

Wolseley's words quietly exploded into the compressed confines of the tent. Baker Russell's eyes widened with shock. John felt as though he had been punched in the chest and his blood suddenly raged as it had fighting the ghostly Egyptians. How dare this man, any man, question his faith, which was a matter between him and his God? Rocked back on his heals he stepped forward into the fight, his right fist drawn back to smite the General in the face. Baker Russell was on his feet in an instant, reaching out to restrain him. There was no need, John's self control re-asserted itself but the damage was done. In stepping forward in the confines of the tent, he had overturned the camp writing desk. Wolseley had leaned back in his chair and it had collapsed on the uneven ground. Papers, and the General, littered the floor.

Wolseley extricated himself from his chair and grimaced at the pain that shot through his leg from the old wound.

He cursed inwardly as his brain processed the implications. He, an officer, a General no less, had been assaulted by a soldier in a theatre of war. Assaulting an officer in a theatre of war was a hanging offence.

But questions would be asked. The Queen would become involved if one of her own Household was hanged. Why had a soldier, of renowned bravery, assaulted him? Was the soldier mad? If he was mad why was he meeting the General in the first place? If he were not mad, then what had he, Wolseley, said to provoke such a reaction? He was a General, he could not possibly be at fault, but questions would be asked, doubts raised, and those doubts could prevent his elevation to the Lords at best and, at worst, destroy him.

He needed to contain the damage. He could not deny it had happened. Baker Russell had witnessed the assault. Nor should he deny it had happened. The Trooper had to be punished or there would be a complete breakdown in military disciple. What to do?

All these thoughts cascaded his consciousness in the time it took for him to rise to his feet and right the chair. The military assistant and TCM appeared in the tent entrance. "Get out!" Wolseley shouted. "Not you," he quickly added as John did a smart about face. "You stay where you are."

Calm, and charm, reasserted itself and his voice returned to normal. "Well, this is a to do and no mistake. It appears you have a quick temper, Trooper Waterston. That may be fine for a battlefield but it has no place here. Some might think you just assaulted an officer, but that cannot be the case as, if it were true, or ever spoken of again, I would have no choice but to hang you, this being a theatre of war. Do I make myself clear? This incident will never be spoken of again, to anyone, under any circumstances."

He looked at his friend Creed, to be sure that he understood what was to come, and why. "I cannot support this recommendation for the Victoria Cross. Some may think this unfair, particularly when the actions are compared with other acts of valour, but I believe too many VCs have been awarded for acts that were undeserving. Trooper Waterston, you are to wait outside and speak to nobody until Colonel Baker Russell has spoken with you. Dismissed."

John did not know what to think, or feel. The events of the past few minutes had rushed passed in a blur. He remembered at the last moment to salute, smartly turned and marched from the tent, ducking his helmeted head to exit through the low flap.

He halted next to the TCM and waited in silence.

"What was all that about, Trooper Waterston?" asked the TCM. "It looked as though a bull had raced through the tent."

Waterston did not respond. He could not respond. He had been sworn to silence.

"Answer me, Waterston." The TCM's voice was now very dangerously low. He had to answer and hang the consequences. 'Hang the consequences' suddenly took on a new and very unpleasant meaning.

"I'm not sure what happened, Troop Corporal Major. Colonel Baker Russell will tell me what happened in a minute."

Inside the tent, Wolseley righted his desk and turned to his friend. "We will never speak of this matter again. You know why I have turned down the VC, even though it was well deserved. Waterston needs to know that he is clearly an excellent soldier in the finest traditions of Her Majesty's finest regiment. I see a bright and distinguished future for him, provided he is not hanged for assaulting an officer. He should tell anyone that asks, that his actions, while fine, did not meet my stringent standards for the award of the most sought after medal Her Majesty can bestow."

"Which is all very well, General, but should anyone ask, were his actions undeserving of any award? While I might forget the events of the past few minutes, I cannot forget that this man saved my life at great risk to his own. I am in his debt." Baker Russell appreciated the neatness of Wolseley's solution, but it needed to be watertight.

"A good point that needs a neat solution." Wolseley considered exactly what Creed had just said. He 'might' forget the events. Did he need inducement? No, Creed was an exceptional officer and friend. He understood. "What do you suggest?"

"Well, General, has not Her Majesty said that her Household Cavalry would display courage to the standard of recipients of the Victoria Cross, and therefore one would never be awarded?"

"A very good point that Waterston should understand." Wolseley was relieved, but of course had not shown that he was concerned in the first instance. "I am sure you will see he understands." He gave his friend a meaningful look. Now to seal it.

"You know, Creed, that you have always impressed me. You have been promoted Major, Lieutenant Colonel and Colonel as a result of distinguished service in 3 campaigns, rather than as a result of the privilege of birth. I propose that Egypt will be no different. With the Indian contingent due to arrive shortly I will create a second, Indian, cavalry brigade under the command of Brigadier General Wilkinson. Under General Drury Lowe you will be promoted Brigadier General and command the 1st Brigade."

He picked an order of battle from the detritus on the ground, blew dust from it and carefully smoothed it on the desk. "Comprising the 3 Squadrons of Household Cavalry, the 4th and 7th Dragoon Guards, Part of the 17th Commissariat & Transport and half of Number 1 Bearer Company. Drury Lowe will also get the Divisional support troops – the Royal Horse Artillery, Mounted Infantry, a detachment of Royal Engineers, the other part of the 17th and Number 6 Field Hospital. Congratulations, your promotion is richly deserved.

"I have no doubt Horseguards will kick up a stink in my promoting you over Colonel Ewart, who is your senior, but I will deal with that. We will destroy Arabi at Tel-el-Kebir and there will be nothing they can say on the matter. Now, General Baker Russell," they both grinned, "go and ensure Waterston understands."

"Thank you, General"

Baker Russell departed the tent. "Thank you, Corporal Major. I have a task for Trooper Waterston and will ensure he gets back to you. Waterston, follow me."

Once he was sure they were out of earshot he rounded on the young Trooper. "Waterston, I believe in the past few days you have learned some valuable lessons that will serve you well. I don't know precisely what happened in that tent and would counsel you to ensure you forget it. The General expects a great deal of everyone that serves him. We are all constantly being tested. I now understand my recommendation placed the General in a difficult position. Her Majesty has made it known that she expects all her

Household Cavalry to display bravery to the standard of the Victoria Cross at all times. For the General to single you out for your actions on that night, however deserving, would be tantamount to saying the rest of her Household Cavalry were not displaying courage to the standard required. I am sure none of us would want that given all they have achieved over the past few days."

"No, Sir." John was not sure he followed the reasoning or that it explained the events of the past 20 minutes, but he realised he was not going to be awarded the VC.

"Now as to the other matter. The General is of the view that the table collapse was an accident. Should anyone ask, the General fell off his chair when it wobbled on the uneven ground, and in falling caused the table to collapse. Any other explanation will get you hanged. Do you understand?"

"Yes, Sir"

"Good man. The General and I are of the view that you are clearly an extremely brave and capable soldier. I see a very bright future for you and will make sure your Officer Commanding is aware of our views. I owe you my life. Should you ever need anything, please do not hesitate to let me know." He smiled, the genuine warmth extending into his eyes. "Carry on."

John saluted and returned to the Regimental lines, pondering all he had learned, and what he should tell his friends. The only element he was totally clear about was the warning. If asked, and he hoped he was never asked, the General fell off his chair.

Baker Russell sighed, watching him depart. Had the young man done him a favour in saving his life? He had lost £5000 on that business deal and was ruined. Promotion would help, but it would not restore those losses and he was not getting any younger. No, perhaps it would have been better to die in battle.

37

THE SECOND BATTLE OF KASSASSIN

John returned to his lines deep in thought to find the TCM waiting for him. "Well, Trooper Waterston, what on earth happened? Is the VC approved?"

"No, Corporal Major. It appears that was the reason for the interview. Since Her Majesty expects every member of her Household Cavalry to display the courage of a VC winner, nobody in the Household Cavalry will ever receive one."

Disappointed, the TCM considered this for a moment, looking for the positive. The idea that the VC would only be awarded to other, lesser, Regiments was somehow appealing. He rehearsed the idea in his mind to use when challenged by one of those Regiments who had a VC. 'Of course the Household Cavalry display courage to the highest level at all times, there was a recommendation for the VC in Egypt but it was rejected not through lack of merit, but simply because Her Majesty has said she will never award one to her elite Household Cavalry.' Yes, that had a good ring to it, though it did suggest none of them would receive any medal for bravery, or the pension that accompanied it. It would make an interesting subject for discussion in the Corporal's mess when they returned to London.

"And what of the General's desk? All I could see was paper and the General all over the floor."

"An accident, Corporal Major. The General's chair collapsed. He was not happy about it." The lie would come easier with the telling, and become truth. Or so he hoped.

The rest of the Regiment mirrored the TCM's disappointment when they heard. John was still trying to recall what was said during the interview, not that he could repeat it. One phrase kept revolving in his mind "Any man who changes his faith is no man at all."

Wolseley had interpreted his desire to attend the services of multiple churches as a lack of faith, when the reverse was true. John's kirk centred on the scriptures, the word of God, not one church's interpretation of that word or how God was worshipped. It did not matter which church he attended to access the scriptures. The General's reaction had been extreme. Why? It came to him many weeks later when reading an article on the troubles in Ireland and a biography on General Wolseley's upbringing in Dublin and his protestant faith. Surely, any faith that encouraged the polarising of society for its own ends, was a contradiction of the scriptures? The General was wrong to have said what he had said, but at least John now understood why.

The British Commissariat and Transport was a joke, and not a funny one. All the ships had been loaded without thought to the order items were required in once landing began in Egypt. The stores that were required first were loaded at the bottom of the ships.

At least there were ships. An enterprising staff officer had ordered as many as he could find even before Parliament had belatedly agreed to invade, but that was the only positive in a catalogue of disasters that the British soldiers were paying for on the ground. With too many war correspondents, chasing too few stories, the Press was full of derisive articles ridiculing the Commissariat and General Wolseley for his inability to progress.

In contrast, the Indian troops had food and water. Ankers was drawn to the Indian logistics chain like sand flies to a body. He was curious to find out how their supply waggons were able to travel through the desert, while the British ones were completely useless. The Indians were very friendly and Ankers built relationships quickly. He soon discovered that the Indian staff had read an authoritative paper on the subject earlier in the year, and had acted on it, building new Maltese carts with 5ft diameter wheels and extra broad tyres; these could be pulled by a pair of the 2500 mules the Indians had brought with them. The British Commissariat, and Quartermaster General Wolseley, had ignored the paper, and as part of the political game the Turks had refused to allow the 1500 mules the British had purchased in Greece to be transported to Egypt in time. In addition to mules, the Indians had large numbers of packhorses, too – one cavalry regiment had 2 packhorses for every trooper.

Building on Ankers' connections, it was not long before the section was spending time in the Indian lines. They made delicious bread, chapattis, and the sikhligars could hone the Blues' swords to a razor edge. Ankers was soon doing a roaring trade that culminated in the whole squadron feasting on curried rice in a break from the usual fair of beef stew.

John greatly admired the tall warriors with their beards and turbans. Always immaculately turned out they were clearly very capable soldiers. He found the Indian humour, enthusiasm and inability to accept anything was impossible, inspiring and infectious. Their propensity to agree was a challenge though. They did not appear to have a word for 'no' and would agree to everything, worrying about the consequences later. John discovered this the hard way after learning that the answer to the question "Is this the way to the latrine?" would always be "yes" regardless of the direction one pointed. Everyone had suffered stomach problems brought about by the insanitary conditions. The 'Sweetwater' canal most certainly wasn't, having rather too many bodies in it. By day flies plagued them, constantly buzzing into ears, nose, eyes and mouth. By night, mosquitos took over. Sleeping in any building was to be avoided as these were infested with fleas, lice and other insects, including scorpions. Fortunately none of the men reported seeing snakes. The Indians were far more comfortable with the field conditions and John learned many lessons that would serve him well in the years to come. He particularly appreciated their observation that any fool could be uncomfortable as it resonated with Ted Ankers's ethos. It was the Indian Troopers who pointed out that the Egyptian millet in the field next to the Blues would make excellent forage, and then proceeded to cut it down for them.

The railway was the primary means by which the Egyptians could move large bodies of troops. The railway engines ordered from England only arrived at the beginning of September and this heralded the acceleration of the movement from Ismailia to Kassassin. By the 9th September, the British force build up was almost complete. It was an auspicious day for the Egyptians, a year to the day from their initial rebellion against the Khedive, and they marked it with a second determined attack on the British position. They had been encouraged to do this by the Bedouin who falsely reported to Arabi that they had cut off the British supply chain, and then gave the British a copy of the Egyptian plan of attack.

During the night of the 8th September the Egyptians carried out a skilful and highly risky night march, from Tel-el-Kebir in the West and Es-Salihiyeh in the North, with the intention of combining for a dawn attack on Kassassin.

The first John knew of this was at 6.45 am when the alarm was sounded and the Indian cavalry brigade was ordered out of the camp to delay the enemy attack. He later learned that Indian vedettes had discovered the Egyptian forces at 5am, just before first light, when they realised three squadrons of enemy cavalry had bypassed them during the night. Undeterred by being utterly outnumbered the lancers had charged through the enemy to sound the warning.

The first enemy shells started landing in the camp just after 7am, throwing dust high into the air and causing horses and cattle to break their halters and run through the tented streets. John, and the rest of the 1st Cavalry Brigade moved out to the North shortly after. In the distance, long lines of white clad Egyptian infantry could be clearly seen, framed by the early morning sun, as they descended the high ground to the North West of Kassassin.

The heavy cavalry's task was to ensure the two prongs of the Egyptian attack were kept apart. The approach was similar to the first battle with the two British cavalry brigades manoeuvring to prevent the Egyptians attacking the British flank, while at the same time attempting to attack the Egyptian Flank. This time, Egyptian cavalry, followed by a large mass of Bedouin, provided a mobile shield to perhaps 2000 infantry marching down off the hill in column of route.

Occasionally one or other brigade would halt to allow the horse artillery to engage. The British guns were particularly effective, forcing the white clad cavalry to break formation to avoid the fire, but as the nimble Indians charged to take advantage of the disarray, the Egyptians would run, outpace them and reform. It was a skilful game of cat and mouse played in extreme heat.

All this time thirty Egyptian guns were raining shells down on the British infantry and artillery positions with commendable accuracy, though once again much of the ordnance failed to explode. The British infantry advanced in short rushes into a hail of rifle bullets and vicious case shot, capturing guns and driving the Egyptian infantry back.

At 10am the 2nd cavalry brigade finally saw an opportunity to charge a large unwieldy square of infantry about 700 yards distant. They gradually increased their pace until they were about 300 yards away when they heard the bugle sound the recall. General Willis, concerned that they did not have a sufficient numerical advantage, had ordered them to halt and return to the lines.

Thirty minutes later the Egyptians were in full retreat, abandoning ammunition boxes and equipment to speed their withdrawal to Tel-el-Kebir. General Willis considered a general advance, to turn the withdrawal into a rout, but General Wolseley, who had arrived in Kassassin from Ismailia later in the battle, declared such an idea be abandoned as too risky. The heat was ferocious, the men hungry and thirsty after marching and fighting all day; while the Guards, in

Tel-el-Mahuta, and the Highland brigade were still en-route to Kassassin. There was a further factor General Wolseley kept to himself. His plans for the attack on Tel-el-Kebir had been formed on board ship from England and centred on a night march that would enable the cavalry to bypass the Egyptian position in the remaining fourteen hours of daylight, cutting the Egyptians off from Cairo. He was determined they would not destroy the city as they had Alexandria.

Casualties on both sides had been remarkably light, with the Royal Horse Artillery accounting for most Egyptian losses – some seventy men, though a large number of Egyptian prisoners were taken.

The following day, the build up in Kassassin continued; two hundred and fourteen men of the Royal Navy arriving with six Gatling guns. The next, Monday 11th September, saw the arrival of the infantry to complete the Indian contingent, and General Alison's Highland Brigade, who had relocated from Alexandria. The last to arrive was the 1st Battalion of the Royal Irish Fusiliers, augmenting General Grahams 2nd Brigade. The British force was now complete and General Wolseley, outwardly exuding confidence, finalised his plans for the attack on the great hill of Tel-el-Kebir.

38
REVERSALS

8 September 1882

Al Mahdi surrounded El Obeid, provincial capital of Kordofan in Western Sudan. He was furious. A few weeks ago he had suffered a defeat at Duem. It was not a heavy defeat, but each loss raised doubts about his divine right to rule and reduced his influence. He had hoped to remove the Egyptian rulers in El Obeid without bloodshed, well, without any of his Anṣārs' bloodshed. He had sent emissaries into the city to demand Pasha Wahbi's surrender, but the donkey had hanged them out of hand. His subsequent assault had failed. Thousands of his Anṣār had died and now he had no choice but to starve the Egyptian rulers out.

39
TEL-EL-KEBIR

Where was the blasted man? He should have been here over an hour ago. It was very dark. General Wolseley looked at his pocket watch in the light from the few stars and could just make out the hour hand near the 4. It was early on the 12th September and they waited at a rendezvous point on the low hill overlooking Kassassin from which the Egyptians had launched their attack on the 9th. An unpleasant smell suggested several Egyptian dead remained unburied in the vicinity. Around him, he ignored muttered conversations in the darkness as the officers made small talk while they waited. Leather creaked and bits jingled. He idly wondered whether the young trooper was among the escort of Royal Horse Guards that formed a dark mass fifty yards away. The Household Cavalry had done well, enough to silence their critics back home, which should please Her Majesty. This next action would be one for the infantry, but the cavalry would ensure a total victory by cutting off any retreat. The last thing he needed was a drawn out fight through the cultivated land behind Tel-el-Kebir, or worse a battle in Cairo, and the destruction of another major city. He still could not believe the mess the Navy had made of Alexandria. It was this factor that had determined his plan of attack, one that would encourage the Egyptians to stand at Tel-el-Kebir rather than undertake a fighting retreat through the cultivated lands.

At last, he made out a small group of riders approaching from the southeast. The leader, General Hamley, looked irritated at being late though General Willis' staff officer, who had been their guide, was the most flustered. It did not bode well for what was to come. He was going to ask them to march thousands of men and horses over this ground in total darkness and complete silence. It was vital they remain undetected and arrived on time in exactly the right place to start the attack. If they got lost and arrived late, or not at all, he could lose a great many infantrymen, and his reputation. There was a great deal that could go wrong in the dark; it only took one fool to fire by mistake, or in fear, to remove the vital element of surprise. There was one man he certainly needed to shield, Arthur, Duke of Connaught, commanding the Guards Brigade. He was a very active and capable Brigadier, but he could not risk pushing the Guards to the front. Her Majesty would never forgive him if anything happened to her favourite son.

He was confident they would win, but his staff had estimated they might lose as many as twelve hundred men. The thought worried him considerably, but he could not wait for more reinforcements from England. Every day, the Egyptians strengthened their position. Yesterday clouds of dust had been seen in the distance behind Tel-el-Kebir as more troops moved in, and last night he had clearly heard the rumbling and clanking of trains arriving and shunting back and forth; more reinforcements.

He could not afford for anyone to know how worried he was. Confidence was all. He took a deep breath and visualised his past victories and the euphoria he had felt.

"General Hamley, so good of you to join us. I trust you have not had too unpleasant a ride in the dark." There was no sarcasm in the tone but Wolseley had made his point, he was in charge, don't be late. Hamley mentally added the comment to his list of reasons to loathe Wolseley; he felt considerably ill used after being abandoned as part of the subterfuge in Ramleh. His nemesis continued, "I have called you here to enable you to see the enemy position that you will attack in just over 24 hours' time."

"Tel-el-Kebir is about five miles to the West of our position. It is an area that Arabi knows well as he was exiled there last year when his regiment first rebelled against the Khedive. The position is a 100ft high plateau gently sloping in all directions, except the south down to the canal and railway, which is steeper. The ground is generally barren with no cover to speak of and comprised of compressed sand and rock rather than the deep soft stuff the men have laboured through thus far. Arabi has created a defensive position on the top of this hill about four miles long and comprising a ditch 8-12ft wide and 5-9ft deep, behind which there is a breastwork 4-6ft high, protected from the rear by a small banquette and regular shelter trenches. Interspersed along this breastwork line are a series of well-designed redoubts. He has also built another dam across the Sweetwater Canal, which is why the tea tastes so bad. These positions are well established to the south near the canal and incomplete to the North. Arabi does not have sufficient men to defend such an extensive position, which is why our deception in the North was so necessary, and why we must attack now before more reinforcements arrive." He suppressed the irritation he suddenly felt. If Hamley were a better officer he would recognise how important his role in the deception was and be less angry. Idiot.

"My intent is to attack the position along the entire front and to send the cavalry around the northern flank to attack their rear. We will approach in total silence and by night. Surprise will be essential. Follow me, if you please." He spurred his horse into motion and they proceeded down the slope into the area he had visited on each of the previous two nights to supplement the intelligence gained from his reconnaissance officers.

He slowed his approach as they neared and brought them to a halt about eight hundred yards from the enemy defensive positions that were just about visible in the distance. They sat on their mounts in silence until the first streak of dawn appeared over the horizon and they could make out the enemy's mounted pickets making their way to their positions. "Gentlemen, note the time is 5.45. Our attack must be before this hour or those vedettes will detect our presence. Go straight in on them and then.... kill them all."

"Well, gentlemen, don't talk about it until the orders are issued during the course of the day. I wish you all good luck."

John shifted in his saddle to reduce the feeling of cramp in his right leg. As though in sympathy, Alfie snorted quietly and tossed his head. Fifty yards to his left the generals formed a line facing the enemy trenches, as though they were about to charge. Ahead of them he could just make out the enemy positions on the horizon. They ran along the top of a hill for about four miles in a line northwards from the canal. He could not see any trenches or other obstacles that might have been built to hamper an attack on the ditch and breastwork. His eyes continued to scan the arc he had been allocated, not looking directly at the shadows and using his peripheral vision. As the first glimmers of light appeared he began to distinguish darker areas in the shadows, and then he could see a pair of mounted sentries approaching from the Egyptian lines. He could not believe the Egyptians did not deploy their vedettes at night. He reached behind to pull the carbine from its sleeve behind his right leg, but felt someone touch his arm and stop him. He looked to his right and could just make out Cpl Scott shaking his head, slowly. They were well within artillery range and if spotted would draw rifle fire, too. It was far better to do nothing than to draw attention to their presence by firing. The sentries had not come closer, the reconnaissance group still hidden in the pre-dawn shadow. Fortunately General Wolseley and his group retired moments later and the Blues patrol followed. The assault was imminent, probably in the next couple of days.

There were fewer patrols and vedettes sent out that day and they were warned to conserve their energy and water. Perhaps the assault would be sooner than he thought? Seated on his saddle on the ground outside the section tent he wrote a short letter home but was rather at a loss for something to say. 'Hope you are well, I am fine but it is really hot here' did not seem to cut it. He was not much of a one for writing and he did not want his mother to worry. Besides, they would not be able to understand his new life, or the reality of war. He wished he had a girl he could write to. Perhaps when he returned home a hero?

"Well, the Royal Irish Fusiliers are now here. I don't think there is anyone else invited to the party so we can begin." Angus Duncan stirred the stew with his wooden spoon and suddenly pulled a face as though he had just seen something horrific floating in it, which was quite possible.

John laughed sarcastically. "Ha ha. That was quite funny the first time I saw it, but since coming here some of Ankers's stew augmentation ingredients have made me wonder if the horror is genuine."

"Well, thank you for the vote of confidence and appreciation," Ankers responded. "Next time, you can go hunting for vegetables in the Egyptian fields."

"I could kill for a proper potato and carrots to dilute the beef," said Angus.

LCpl McIntosh lay dozing with his head on his saddle in the dappled shade of his fly net, propped from the barrel of his carbine. He opened an eye lazily. "Well, it won't be long now but don't let the enemy know you are only chasing them in the hope they have some decent vegetables in their backpacks. They think we are huge scary cannibals rather than vegetable hunters."

"To be fair, Duncan probably is a cannibal," John threw another stick on the fire and took a peek inside the cooking pot. "Hang on, is that a human ear?"

"I hope not," said Cpl Scott appearing from behind the tent with a glint in his eye and an evil grin. "The last one got stuck between my teeth something rotten. I'm still not sure I have got it all out.

"Right, gather round, I have just received our orders for the night." He glanced at his notes. "Sir Garnet has had enough of this waiting about so the attack is tonight; well, at crack of sparrows fart tomorrow morning to be precise."

The section was suddenly attentive, the excitement clear. This was what the whole campaign had been building towards. Scott drew a simple map with a stick of firewood in the sand and then used it to emphasise his words and the plan.

"You know where we are going. Tel-el-Kebir, that hilly thing we visited last night. The infantry will set out once it is dark, form up in the desert, have a bit of a rest and then advance to contact as dawn comes up. They will attack across a broad front and surprise is essential. They have been ordered to march in total darkness and silence so will attack using hard steel only – they don't want to risk being discovered in the night by some Glocky Guardsman pulling the trigger by accident.

"We will leave at quarter to midnight, heading north for a mile before striking out to the north west. The plan is for us to hang back, wait for the infantry to make a mess of it, then charge around the north of the enemy position and save their arses by attacking the Gippy's from the rear. Once we have scared them stupid, we are to cut off their retreat and then race to Cairo for tea and medals." The section were grinning like madmen.

Scott continued "I'm afraid that after we bore the brunt of it at Mahsama and Kassassin the General has decided the Indians should get first crack at the enemy so we will be riding in everyone else's dust and bringing up the rear." They groaned with disappointment.

"I don't need to remind you that this will be the largest British engagement since Crimea almost thirty years ago. It will be fought against a modern, well-equipped army that has been trained by

American officers who learned their trade during their civil war twenty years ago. This won't be a walk over and when we have won, it will be a battle you can tell your grandchildren about, hurrah!"

"And mighty bored they will be," said Duncan sardonically.

John chuckled with the others before saying, "Crook, Proudlock and Parris will be devastated at missing it. Has anyone heard how they are?"

"Still alive. The last I heard they were being packed off to Gozo." answered Ankers. Seeing their confused faces he continued. "It's an island off Malta. They have established a hospital there, at Fort Chambray. Poor bastards will miss all the fun."

"Well, they have done their bit and will have stories they can tell, even if they miss out on the final act," continued Cpl Scott. "No preparations until after dark just in case the enemy are looking, then strike the tent. Ankers and young Waterston here can drop it over by the railway; with luck the commissariat will transport it to Cairo for us. Robert, give the mounts a final check over to ensure they are not going to throw a shoe. Duncan, keep the fire going and wander about so it looks like we are here for another night. Ensure you are all packed and ready to go by 11pm. No loading your weapons, make sure all the equipment is rigged for silent movement tonight. We won't be coming back."

Tents were struck at last light. They were carefully rolled, stowed in their bags and left with all baggage down by the railway lines. The fires were left burning, though the men had suffered a shortage of firewood for cooking throughout the campaign so there were only a few of these anyway. Rations for three days were issued and waterbottles filled with weak tea. Each man was issued one hundred rounds of ammunition with strict instructions not to load or use this until the enemy position had been taken at bayonet point.

Like spectres in the night, John watched eleven thousand infantrymen and sixty guns depart into the desert, their way guided by telegraph poles specially placed by the Royal Engineers to aid navigation. They marched for about a mile to a rendezvous where the ground became firm and they could ensure they were in the correct position and formation. They were to rest there, in silence, until 1.30am and then advance in formation to take the enemy position. South of the canal and railway line in the cultivated area, the Indian infantry moved out an hour later due to concerns that they would disturb animals, or perhaps farmers, during their advance and the noise would alert the enemy.

Drury Lowe's cavalry division moved out just before midnight with Brigadier General Wilkinson at the head of the column with the 13th Bengal Lancers and 2nd and 6th Bengal Cavalry, followed by two batteries of the Royal Horse Artillery and the Mounted Infantry. Brigadier General Baker Russell's heavy brigade brought up the rear with the 7th Dragoon Guards in the lead. The night was dark and still as they headed due North. High clouds obscured the stars so that only the Little Bear and the North Star were visible. Other than his friends immediately around him, John could see and hear none of the main force making their way across the desert to the enemy position on the great hill five and half miles away. It was a strange feeling, the tension palpable despite the Blues now being familiar with manoeuvres in the dark. The cavalry meandered across the desert looking for the flagpole that had been carefully placed in daylight to mark their first stop. Several officers and corporals were heard whispering how glad they were not to be in the van of a column of two thousand cavalry and charged with navigating by night.

There were few stars to go by and no means of illuminating a compass. The night was so dark that the flagpole could not be seen from fifteen yards away and took an age to find. It was not until 2.15 that they were finally sure enough of their position to advance properly, this time heading North West until they were on the extreme right of the British advance. There was so little light that shortly after leaving the flagpole they were drawn to a ghostly phosphorescent bluish light flickering in the sands. As they approached several of the horses shied away from a disgusting smell and the sight of a four-day dead man's skull grinning through the bluish vapour.

They halted at 3am about two miles from the Egyptian position to rest and await the sound of the gunfire that would be their signal to move around the right flank of the enemy line. It was going to be a long day. John dismounted and lay down with Alfie's reins in his hand and resting against his helmet. The big horse dropped his head and nuzzled him. It was cold but his eyes were heavy and in moments he had dozed off.

He awoke with a start an hour and a half later, aware of movement around him. Angus Duncan and Robert Laidlaw were excitedly talking in a low whisper about something on the horizon. John turned to look at the Egyptian entrenchments now illuminated by a large shaft of pale golden light, shaped like a sheaf of corn, shooting straight up into the sky. It was still forty five minutes until dawn and it took him a moment to realise it was a great comet – a phenomenon that had also alerted the Egyptians to the British attack. Moments later, just before 5 am, they heard the first rifle shots fired from the centre of the Egyptian lines and then a bugle was blown.

A shell whirred over their heads and General Baker Russell called out, "We shall be under fire in under three minutes." They quickly mounted and, riding in Squadron columns, started their advance at a slow walk that gradually turned into a trot. They were two thousand yards from the enemy position, behind which the stars were less easy to distinguish as the sky lightened with the dawn. The Egyptians were now very much awake and there was a line of fire that ran for miles along their entrenchments. Cannons roared and the sound of the muskets was a continuous crackle. Bullets zipped through the air around, and mainly above, them.

Ahead, John heard the first shells, fired from a redoubt on the extreme enemy left explode with a flash somewhere near the Indian lancers. They halted and the RHA batteries were brought forward. After a short duel, the enemy guns, firing into the dark, were silenced by the RHA guns firing into the flashes of fire. As dawn broke, the cavalry moved forward again. They swept past the northern end of the enemy entrenchments and within thirty minutes were well to the West of the northern redoubt and about level with it. They swung south and east, by this time travelling at considerable speed and into the enemy rear.

The sound of fire from the Egyptian trenches was incredible, but he had not heard any response from the British infantry who had been ordered to use bayonets alone until they reached the trenches. In the centre of the Egyptian position, the British had manhandled an artillery battery up the parapet where a couple of guns were now firing north and three guns were firing south into the Egyptian positions. It was in the South, nearer the canal where the Highland Brigade was attacking, that the main fighting seemed to be taking place.

The Egyptian infantry in the Northern section of the line were now being fired on by artillery on three sides. General Graham's infantry was approaching from their front and the cavalry was threatening their rear. Within minutes they were running from the breastwork in the face of the onslaught.

The Egyptian right, near the canal, fought a ferocious rearguard action. Attacked by the Highland brigade from the front and General Graham's brigade from the North, the black Nubian infantry, in particular, fought hard and well, despite being abandoned by their officers.

Resistance appeared to cease less than 45 minutes after the first shots were fired and now white clad fugitives could be seen running south and west down the slopes, through the camps, over the railway and across the canal.

The light, fast, Indian cavalry pursued, cutting and lancing their way through the fleeing troops. Initially they gave no quarter as they had been told about the Egyptian tactic of lying down and then hamstringing the horses as they jumped over them, or shooting them in the back as they passed. As the cavalry advanced, the artillery switched fire to the railway terminus where trains were preparing to leave, but they had to cease for fear of hitting the Indians. The Dragoons, following up behind the Indian brigade, killed a few of the enemy who continued to fight; however, as the scale of the rout became apparent, the Division was ordered to take prisoners instead.

By the time John reached the action, a few minutes behind the leaders, the remaining enemy had pretty much surrendered. As he cantered across the Tel-el-Kebir bridge over the canal at the southern end of the position, he saw General Wolseley meeting the other Generals amidst cheers from the Highland Brigade.

Angus Duncan, riding to his left, shouted at the Highlanders as they passed, "Bloody Jocks haven't left us the chance of a fight!" The rest of the troop were of a similar mind, in part relieved they had survived a major battle, but mainly deflated after the build up; their role had been mainly that of spectators.

They spent a happy half hour or so chasing terrified Egyptians and herding them into groups where they could be watched over by the infantry, still wielding bloodied bayonets, and then moved out to continue the advance on Cairo.

It was late afternoon. General Wolseley removed his uniform jacket outside the Egyptian Officers tent that would be his home for the night, and possibly longer. He was just rolling up his shirt sleeves when he noticed the slightly overweight man in his late thirties. Melton Prior, the war correspondent and artist for The Illustrated London News, approached him with a smile. Wolseley quite liked Prior who was a seasoned veteran of numerous campaigns, including the war in Ashanti, and South Africa. He drew quickly and well, often from close to the action, and reported accurately. He was also British, not one of the foreign correspondents such as the man from the New York Herald who seemed keen for the British to be slung out of Egypt merely due to the fact the Egyptians had modern weapons and had been taught by the Americans. He smiled back.

"Hello, General, congratulations on your great victory. I thought you would lose a great many more men than you did."

"So did I." He did not add that the day had gone far better than he had dared hope, even if his Aide de Camp, Wyatt Rawson, had been seriously wounded in the attack. The Naval officer had successfully navigated the whole force across the desert with just a few stars as a guide. He hoped he would live and made a mental note to do all he could to ensure he was promoted for his cool determination.

"I would very much like a plan of your attack if you could point me in the right direction, General." He could do better than that for a man like Prior. His attack had gone exactly to plan, and that was something he wanted the world to know. So much for the adage 'no plan survives contact with the enemy'.

"Come inside, Mr Prior, and I will show you."

They went inside and spread out on a colourful rug that covered the floor. The captured Turkish tent was beautiful; the Circassian Egyptian officers clearly lived well, even if they did not fight or lead well. He spread out his plan and watched as Prior copied it meticulously, every unit perfectly positioned and the Egyptian lines shown in detail. He even certified it for him. At that moment his Military Assistant poked his head into the tent to remind him it was time for the final briefing of the day. Prior thanked him and took his leave. Wolseley slipped his jacket back on, settled his helmet and walked to the bridge crossing the canal where the Generals and his staff were waiting for him.

The bridge was busy, but everyone knew where it was so it made a good meeting point. Egyptian prisoners, some of them walking wounded, were being escorted to the holding area. Native drivers were herding heavily laden camels across the bridge and signal officers and messengers on horseback crossed back and forth. Suddenly, a ferocious looking camel took a violent dislike to one of the Egyptian prisoners and lunged at him. Opening its mouth wide it crushed the top of the man's head between its teeth, biting the top of his head off and exposing the brain. The man collapsed, dead. It was quite the most sickening thing he had seen all day. The camel was beaten and moved on. He must move on. He approached the command group standing some way from the bridge and the camels.

"Gentlemen, thank you for coming, and congratulations on a well fought battle and a splendid victory. Before orders for tomorrow, I have asked for a brief summary of today. Chief of Staff, carry on."

Lieutenant General Sir John Adye glanced at his notes and then used a swagger stick to indicate points on a rough sand model laid out on the ground. "Thank you, General. Well, our intelligence was surprisingly accurate. The entrenchments were formidable but incomplete, particularly to the Northern end. They were manned by some six thousand five hundred well disciplined regular infantry, two thousand cavalry and fifty eight guns served by first class artillerymen. The remaining eleven thousand men were a well equipped but newly conscripted, untrained rabble that ran as soon as they saw our cavalry approaching.

"We were fortunate that during the night approach march we pulled to the right and as a result missed a formidable redoubt, hidden behind a hill that our reconnaissance had missed. You will recall, General, that it was artillery fire from this strongpoint that forced your headquarters to scatter briefly so we were not such an attractive target. Had we kept to our original path, we would have been discovered and would have had a very stiff fight to take it and then a twelve hundred yard advance across open ground.

"On our left, General Alison's Highland brigade was fired upon first and the Highland Light Infantry and the Black Watch, in particular, had a very tough time facing disciplined, courageous Nubian troops who had ample ammunition."

"Not to mention having to fight past a fourteen foot deep, steep sided ditch and two lines of trenches," commented General Hamley, convinced that his part in the battle had been entirely overlooked by General Wolseley.

"Quite," continued Adye. "In the centre, by 0520, the Artillery were able to manhandle three guns up into a redoubt captured by the Black Watch where they were able to fire south in support of the Highland Brigade and north in support of General Graham's brigade.

"On our right, General Graham's brigade started their attack 10 minutes after the Highland Brigade and from as far back as twelve hundred yards from the parapet, which they successfully took. The enemy withdrew fifty yards but gave way at 6am when faced by guns on their left and right, the infantry to their front and the Cavalry Division who had outflanked them and threatened their rear.

"The enemy right, by the canal, was the last to give way and the Highland brigade then captured the railway station, bridge and the camp.

"We are told Arabi escaped, possibly on horseback or by the first train. The second train was destroyed by artillery fire. The Duke of Connaught's prize for most innovative use of a camel has been awarded to the Bengal Lancers who shot one as it was crossing the railway track, thus preventing the third train from escaping." There were a few chuckles.

"General McPherson's Indian Contingent advanced along the canal tow paths supported by the Naval Brigade. They faced about four hundred infantry, four guns in trenches and a defended village, which surrendered at 6am. The Contingent pressed on to the town and major rail hub at Zagazig, twenty miles West of us, which surrendered this afternoon. By controlling Zagazig and lifting some of the track, the Egyptian lines of communication are now broken.

"The Cavalry Division now occupies Belbeis, twenty miles South West of us, and will advance on Cairo tomorrow."

"What happened to them? I had hoped they would be in Cairo by now," asked Wolseley.

"Well, General, the Division divided here, at Tel-el-Kebir. The heavy cavalry brigade and the Royal Horse Artillery batteries crossed the canal and followed its south easterly bank towards Belbeis. Progress was extremely slow as we had not anticipated that the cultivated land was criss-crossed by branch canals and irrigation ditches that were only served by very narrow bridges. The wheeled artillery had to be stripped down in order to cross every bridge. General Baker Russell sent the 4th Dragoon Guards and the Mounted Infantry ahead, but they did not arrive at the town until 4pm. There they found the Indian cavalry, which was not slowed by the artillery and had taken the north westerly branch of the canal, and then occupied Belbeis at noon. The Indian cavalry had a running battle with the fleeing Egyptian Cavalry for almost thirty miles, the last seventeen being over soft sand so were in no position to proceed to Cairo."

Wolseley's frustration showed briefly before he turned to his chief medical officer. "And what of the bill?"

"The Highlanders suffered 70% of the casualties. We still have thirty men missing, but the latest report is of fifty seven killed, including nine officers. A further twenty seven officers and three hundred and fifty six men are wounded, many of them seriously."

"It could have been a great deal worse had the Egyptians better eyesight, fired lower or had more competent leaders ," commented Wolseley. "I hear General Willis was hit?"

"Yes, General, he was unfortunate to have been hit in the left shoulder; more fortunately, by a bullet that was almost spent. He will be black and blue for a fortnight but otherwise fine. He has kept the bullet as a memento, noting that it did not have his name on it."

Wolseley smiled, ruefully. "And what of the enemy casualties?" he asked.

"We will not know for a considerable period. The Egyptian army organisation has completely broken down since all the officers have run. A couple we captured remarked that they knew they would run when we attacked, but hoped that their brother officers would not. We estimate they lost between fifteen hundred and three thousand men killed and we have about three thousand prisoners. We are treating the wounded where we can."

40

CAIRO

John and the rest of the heavies bivouacked for the night, amidst a dense cloud of mosquitos, by the side of yet another irrigation ditch about a mile short of Belbeis. It had been a long and frustrating day in which they had followed the rest of the cavalry division's dust cloud without making much of a difference. The Egyptians had pretty much surrendered by the time the Blues, bringing up the rear, rode through the enemy position.

He had spent half an hour or so chasing Egyptians through the fields and hamlets of the cultivated area; rounding them up at the point of his revolver and escorting them back to the camp. The further they had ridden into the farmland, the more abandoned equipment and uniforms they saw; 'soldiers' transformed back to farmers. The remains of the day had been spent queuing to cross narrow bridges over canals and ditches as they rode towards Belbeis.

He was thankful that as they headed towards Cairo the water was better than he had experienced elsewhere. It was still the muddy consistency of thin soup, but at least it did not have bodies floating in it. He was now suffering the gut ache that had plagued the rest of the men throughout the campaign. At first it had been amusing to see one of his mates fall out to the side as they marched and disappear behind a small bush or sand mound to dig a small hole and squat with a look of exaggerated relief. Now it was an all too familiar action that plagued officers and men alike, all dignity forgotten. More men had been incapacitated by sickness and sunstroke than by enemy action. Whenever they camped, the digging of latrines was the first task undertaken, its necessity reinforced by the sight of some of the revolting conditions found in sections of the Egyptian camps.

At 4 o'clock the following morning, the 14th September, the cavalry division advanced on Cairo. After their experiences in the cultivated areas the previous day the division crossed the canals and travelled at a brisk trot on the compact gravel desert to the east. As they rode, the banks of the west bank of the canal were crowded with Egyptians and they stopped frequently to read a proclamation from General Wolseley that had been prepared in Arabic to the effect that the war was over. Cries of "Aman! Aman! ("Peace, Peace!")" were heard passing from village to village.

They halted for two hours at the Es-Siriakus lock, twelve miles from Cairo, to water the horses and prepare for the final phase. They had seen no sign of the enemy but were conscious that Arabi was still at large and the Egyptians had not surrendered following defeat at their main defensive position in Tel-el-Kebir. Would they continue the fight to defend their capital?

They marched on without incident, the heat and the flies oppressive and familiar. To their left, the desert stretched seventy miles to the

Suez Canal. To their right, the Sweetwater Canal marked the eastern border of the cultivated lands that at this point extended ten miles further to the west and were bordered there by the great river Nile. When the Nile and the Sweetwater Canal converged, they would have reached their destination.

By the late afternoon the Nile was two miles to the west and the domes and minarets of Cairo could just be seen, tantalisingly close, through the haze on the horizon. Before darkness fell they established a camp out of range of the Abbassiyeh barracks, an outpost two miles north east of Cairo. Egyptian infantry could be seen swarming all around the barracks, digging defences. A detachment of 4th Dragoon Guards and some of the Indian cavalry were sent forward with Lieutenant Colonel Herbert Stewart, an intelligence officer, Captain Watson RE, and a couple of Khedival officers, to determine the situation. A Squadron of Egyptian cavalry, all carrying white flags attached to their carbines met them; the Egyptians had seen the British cavalry and intended to surrender. It appeared there would be no further fighting.

At 8pm, Captain Watson, three Egyptians from Abbassiyeh and one of the Khedival officers, escorted by a hundred and forty officers and men from 4th Dragoons and the Mounted Infantry, took an old desert road into the Citadel of Mehemet Ali, now known to be the location of the remaining Egyptian forces. The Citadel occupied an elevated position over Cairo, it's forbidding sandstone walls enclosed lofty minarets, domed buildings and doomed prisoners. As Watson approached he had no way of knowing what else it concealed. Did the occupants know how small the British force was? He steeled himself and told his escort to wait in cover outside so the enemy had no idea as to how few they were. With far greater confidence and authority than he felt, he roused the Citadel commander from his bed, demanded his surrender and that the garrison lay down their arms and disperse. The commander complied and Watson decided to spare his weary men and push his luck further by sending an Egyptian officer to the fort on the

Mokattam Heights overlooking the city to ask the garrison to surrender and leave too. He was then asked to lock the fort and bring him the keys. This was done and ten thousand troops surrendered without a shot being fired.

The Blues did not discover that Cairo had formally capitulated until very early on the following day, the 15th September. It was at about 2am that a brougham carriage, containing a couple of elegant Egyptian gentlemen, arrived in the cavalry camp. The first gentleman in particular was impressive. Tall and dark, with a large moustache and well-trimmed beard, he had a quietly confident and authoritative demeanour. The second gentleman was short, timorous and pallid from anxiety. He introduced himself as Toulba Pasha, commander of the Egyptian forces at Kafr-Dawar. The first gentleman spoke in cultured Arabic, translated into French by his companion, introduced himself as Arabi Pasha and asked to speak with General Drury Lowe.

Arabi Pasha impressed all who met him. He surrendered unconditionally and explained that he had not wanted war with the British, but had been unable to avoid it after Egypt was invaded. The war was over.

For the men of the Household Cavalry, Tel-el-Kebir and the advance to Cairo was all rather an anti-climax after the fighting at Mahsama and Kassassin. The whole character of the country seemed to change almost overnight and within days they were touring the capitol and taking in the sights more as tourists than conquerors. They found Cairo to be an unexpectedly modern city; much of it could even be described as European with electric light and telegraph cables apparent in some areas. They roamed the bazaars and took a ride out to visit the pyramids while the city gradually filled with British troops arriving by train from Zagazig. The unlucky were found billets in former Egyptian army barracks and forts, most of which were in a filthy, flea-infested state so the men continued to sleep outside on the parade grounds.

The Household Cavalry kept to themselves while Egyptian forces throughout the country were disarmed and disbanded. Finally it was felt a show of force was necessary to firmly establish the British as being in control of Egypt and to set the stage for the return of the Khedive. On Saturday 23rd September, the whole of the cavalry division marched through the native bazaar quarter dressed for war. The Household Cavalry, Dragoons, Hussars, Indian Cavalry and Mounted Infantry formed a mounted column three miles long that took forty minutes to pass. Crowds lined the streets and the latticed windows above were filled with women peeping out with curiosity rather than terror. To John, staring down from his huge charger, the native Egyptians appeared sullen, but he heard from his friends in the Indian camp that their faces were transformed into expressions of wonder as the Bengal Lancers passed by with their pennons fluttering and the sunlight reflected off the highly polished tips of the lances.

The scene was now set for the return of the Khedive from Alexandria. On the afternoon of Monday 25th September John found himself lining the approach to Cairo station for his arrival. Once again dressed for war they faced into the centre of the street with the crowd lined up behind them. Alfie did not seem in the slightest bit bothered by the crowds or the heat or the flies as the train chuffed slowly into the station at 3.15pm.

It stopped in a cloud of steam and the Royal Horse Artillery fired a royal salute. As the steam and smoke cleared, and the booms ceased their echoing progress through the narrow streets, the large detachment of Grenadier Guards presented arms and their Band struck up 'God Save the Queen'. The Khedive's hymn was not played. The Khedive carefully stepped down from his railway carriage to be met by the Duke of Connaught and General Wolseley.

Wolseley greeted the young man warmly; he was after all the key to maintaining legitimate British influence in Egypt and his restoration to power was ostensibly the reason so many men had lost their lives. Khedive Tewfik was not an imposing man. Of average height, at thirty he was already thickening into middle age, but his eyes sparkled with intelligence and his demeanour demonstrated none of the standoffishness of oriental rulers.

As the Khedive greeted the large assembly of Egyptians of rank, whose loyalty had so recently switched back to him, the Duke of Connaught said quietly to Wolseley, "He reminds me of one of the young snake charmers I've seen plying their trade in the bazaar, General."

"An interesting analogy, your Royal Highness. He walks a very narrow path destined by birth and determined by the complex and ever changing agendas of politicians in many countries," replied Wolseley. "He, and his country, are pawns in the great game. I almost feel sorry for him. Come, let us see him safely to his palace."

The Duke, Wolseley and the Khedive drove in an open carriage to the Ismailia palace, official residence of the Khedive. The streets were lined all the way with British troops and decorated with flags. Lanterns hung from houses ready for the night's illuminations. Banners with Arabic inscriptions of 'a loyal welcome' were strung from the houses of many of those who had only days before fervently supported Arabi. The crowd was large, enjoying the spectacle and the prospect of peace after so much uncertainty, but there were no signs of unbridled joy. Would the future bring a return to the disaffection of the past? For now, they needed to celebrate and give the people reason to give thanks that the British had brought stability back to their country.

41
LITTLE VICTORIES

Late September 1882

Al Mahdi tried to clear his head and focus on what had been said. Did it matter? It sounded important. The messenger was happy to tell him this news, other messengers recently had been less happy. What had he said? Rahma Muhammad Manufal was his faithful servant. Yes, he was. He had defeated three thousand Egyptian soldiers as they were making their way to Bara at a place called El Kona. He had captured a further eleven hundred rifles. This was good news. Welcome news to relieve the boredom of a siege.

The hashish must have been bad for him to feel so little. He was al Mahdi.

42
THE KHEDIVE'S PARADE

General Wolseley sat his charger in the square outside the Abdin Palace on Saturday 30th September. To his side, his Chief of Staff, General Adye, shifted slightly in his saddle, every movement resulting in a trickle of sweat. Trees provided little shade even in the late afternoon, and the heat was oppressive. Behind him the Khedive sat between Sir Edward Malet and Admiral Sir Beauchamp Seymour, and surrounded by his ministers of state in a pavilion grandstand shaded by colourful silks and banners. The stand was furnished with the Sultan's flag, the Khedive's flag and the Royal Standard of England, barely moving testament to the complexity of Egyptian affairs. In the adjoining compartments of the stand were five hundred specially invited guests, mainly Europeans, encouraged to return to their homes by the newfound stability. Looking ahead were several officers on horseback and the guard of Royal Marines, sent from Alexandria, resplendent in their red coats and white trousers. The streets and every rooftop were lined with thousands of Egyptians. The Khedive's wife, together with other ladies of rank, watched from the windows of the harem. This parade would be the culmination of several days of grand dinners, garden illuminations and magnificent fireworks displays, the most recent of which had involved two thousand rockets.

A faint aroma of smoke and the acrid taint of cordite lingered in the air to remind Wolseley that stability in Egypt was not going to be easy to maintain. Fortunately, it would not be his problem. Now the war was over the politicians would take over again and General Alison would command the remaining British military presence.

The bands struck up and the march past commenced. General Drury Lowe led the men of the Household Cavalry, who were no strangers to parades, and now, thanks to him, no longer strangers to war. He smiled at General Baker Russell, the first of the officers of his trusted inner circle, his Ashanti Ring, proven in multiple expeditions. As the Blues marched past in open column and the officers turned in their saddles, flourishing their swords in salute, a shiver of pride ran down his spine. These big, fierce men on their great chargers really were magnificent. He was impressed. What the natives felt, heaven only knew. Would they be encouraged to keep the peace rather than rise up at the behest of those who would use them for personal gain?

The cavalry expertly moved from open column to form fours as they passed him. Increasing pace they proceeded at a trot down streets lined with police and Egyptian cavalry. Next came thirty guns of the Royal Horse Artillery, colours rumbling over the hard ground.

So many troops to review, it would take an hour and a half and be dark before the Indian infantry brought up the rear. The sound of the crowd, the bands and the troops masked his thoughts and conversation. His eyes on the men marching past, he spoke to his Chief of Staff. Not one of his inner circle but a fellow Lieutenant General and a sound officer who had some interesting thoughts and insight.

"What do you make of the young Khedive, Sir John?"

"A capable man, My Lord, trying to do the right thing for his people and his country." Pleased that he had remembered to use Lord Wolseley's newly announced title, he paused to consider. "But he lacks experience and trusted advisors in a complex culture that loves intrigue and subterfuge."

Wolseley felt both pride and a stab of irritation. 'My Lord' had a fine and much longed for ring to it but he felt shabbily treated by the Establishment. Two days earlier he had received a letter of congratulation from the Queen, the only one he had ever received, yet the contents had been cool praise, as though he had won first prize in a worthless competition. He had always been ambitious but his highest aspiration was to see Britain great, and to lead in making it so. The Establishment merely saw his ambition and thought it self-serving and proof of his lack of class. He was useful but, regardless of rank and position, the Establishment would always see him as an outsider and treat him accordingly, a servant to be kept in his place. Bastards. Even the pleasure associated with the award of his barony had been devalued by the knowledge that Admiral Beauchamp Seymour had received exactly the same honour and bounty for stupidly destroying Alexandria from the comfort of his stateroom. Why had they not made him a Viscount rather than a mere Baron? He was brought back to the present by the arrival of the Guards brigade, led by the Duke of Connaught. At least Prince Arthur was a capable officer and a decent Royal. He had hoped he could make a good impression on the Queen's favourite son and that it would improve her opinion of him, clearly not. "And the Khedive as a leader?" he asked.

"Ahh, milord, I think you have put your finger on the root of the problem. The Muslim people need, nay, expect a strong leader; someone they can respect. But a strong leader presents a potential challenge to the Sultan, and to the European countries with vested interests, financial and otherwise. Strong leaders are difficult to control. Heaven forbid they might decide to do their own thing and then where would we be!"

Wolseley chuckled. "So, he has a narrow path to walk."

"Indeed, with crocodiles and bottomless pits to either side. I understand that historically, the Egyptian leaders have maintained supremacy through a first class intelligence network and by constantly shifting power to ensure no one person builds sufficient support to mount a challenge."

"And if they are challenged, have a strong enough personal guard to defeat any coup," added Wolseley. "But what if that protection is provided by a foreign power?"

"Hmm, I think that rather depends on the foreign power, don't you, milord?"

"Indeed. France was arguably at the root of the recent problems – with their annexing of Tunisia, links to Khedive Ismail and their highly paid officials administering the Egyptian debt and the Canal."

"Not to mention their inability to do anything militarily to put down the Arabi uprising. Their navy steamed away and they could not raise any support for intervention in their parliament," added General Adye. "Which leaves Turkey."

"Do you think the Sultan treads a path much wider than the Khedive?" asked Wolseley.

"I think if it were wider, he would have been more decisive in Egypt. As it was, I think our ambassador to the Porte, Lord Dufferin, was able to handle him and the situation admirably," answered Adye. "Once the Sultan realised his best course was to deploy troops to support our removal of Arabi, Dufferin managed through numerous guises to delay their deployment until after Tel-el-Kebir, making such deployment so pointless they never bothered. I have no idea how he did it."

"Indeed, with his experience of Russia, Afghanistan and now Turkey, Britain would do well to post Lord Dufferin to Egypt as the Khedive's advisor. He believes we should enable the Egyptians to govern themselves under the uncompromising aegis of our friendship." The inherent criticism of Sir Edward Malet was unspoken.

"Does that friendship include the long term deployment of British troops to support the Khedive?" Adye left unspoken the common knowledge that Gladstone's Government wanted to withdraw as quickly as possible and leave the Egyptians to it. They sat in silence until the Highland Brigade was marching past, kilts swinging and bagpipes playing.

"The march past of the Highlanders, with their reduced numbers, is a reminder to us all of the human cost of failed diplomacy and leadership. They took the greatest casualties," said Wolseley, making a mental note to ensure Generals Hamley and Willis were sent home as soon as possible. He briefly wondered if he had been a little petty in forcing them to take up billets in a couple of stone huts deemed too damp to be useful for vegetable storage, while more junior officers, members of his inner circle were assigned comfortable quarters in the various palaces. No, he would be glad to be rid of them.

Adye answered. "I fear the greatest casualties will be due to poor hygiene and water borne diseases. We had our first case of Typhoid this morning. Diarrhoea and dysentery are rife now we have arrived in Cairo. And there are hundreds of cases of Opthalmia. It is highly infectious and one of the reasons many of the Egyptians could not shoot – they simply could not see. It can cause blindness y'know. I just hope the Army Hospital Corps is up to treating them all."

"Hmmmffff." Wolseley gave a derisive snort. "The hospital in Ismailia did them no credit, and the only field hospital I have seen properly equipped was the Egyptian one we captured in Mahsama. I visited the field hospital at Tel-el-Kebir when they were bringing in the Arab wounded. It was no better than a butcher's shop with arms and legs being cut off by the dozen. I have little faith the Hospital Corps will perform any better in Cairo. They are no better than the Commissariat whose performance was woeful and caused no end of suffering for our troops."

"That may be so, General, but we have been able to discharge over two hundred Arab wounded to their homes and transfer another three hundred to the hospital here in Cairo, where they are well treated," replied Adye. "It contrasts favourably with the treatment handed out by the Bedouin."

Wolseley considered. "If we are to maintain order here we need to be seen to be fair as well as strong. Have all the prisoners been handed over to the Khedive?"

"Yes, milord," replied Adye. "We have made it clear that this is on condition they are not to be put to death without the express consent of the British authorities."

The last of the British infantry, General Sir Evelyn Wood's brigade from the Alexandria and Ramleh garrison marched past and then Wolseley noted the change in the demeanour of the crowd as the Indian contingent appeared. Muslim troops were clearly a source of wonder and he had been right to bring them. "The Indians, I regret to say, were far better prepared for this expedition. Their supply chain worked, their soldiers were fed and watered. Their khaki uniforms look no different from the day they disembarked. It is all rather a contrast with the filthy, salt encrusted, red and blue serge uniforms of our troops. The uniforms are totally inappropriate for this climate. We need to pull together a comprehensive list of deficiencies and lessons learned."

It was getting dark. The air stirred the banners into a final wave before disappearing for the night. The stillness brought with it an acrid whiff of smoke. Wolseley asked, "And what news of yesterday's fires?"

"As you can probably smell, they are still trying to douse them. We may never know for sure what happened. It could be arson and insurrection but we think it more likely one of the storemen dropped a live percussion shell as they were loading a railway waggon with shells and boxes of cartridges for return home. The trucks exploded in turn and also destroyed the end carriage of a train just arrived from Benha. We were lucky; it had only just been vacated by the KRRC wounded at Tel-el-Kebir.

"The fire spread to the Station buildings and the Commissariat stores. Several soldiers and natives were killed and wounded from the exploding shells and flying bullets. It could have been much worse. The Duke of Connaught personally led a detachment of Guards into the burning sheds to push waggons of ammunition away from the flames. It was quite touch and go for a time."

"I hope he does not tell his mother. I would never hear the end of it and be blamed for putting him in harms way," reflected Wolseley. He watched the last of the Indian contingent march past in the dark. The Beloochees carried torn banners and looked particularly exotic; fierce expressions under turbans contrasted with their vibrant green tunics and baggy red trousers. Last came the watermen, 'Bheesties' he thought they were called, who looked positively uncouth, but seemed to be making a considerable impression on the natives in the crowd. Good soldiers, but their 'followers' needed to be watched carefully as he had already received reports that they broke into houses everywhere, plundering left and right!

43

HOMECOMING

The Household Cavalry were the first to leave Egypt, before the big men and irreplaceable horses succumbed to disease. John, and a hundred and one men of the Blues, boarded the troopship Lydian Monarch at Alexandria and returned to London, arriving off Gravesend at 11am on the 19th October. By 2pm they were moored alongside the South West India docks and were met by Major Lord Kilmarnock who supervised the unloading and the preparations for the return to the Albany Street Barracks the following day.

That night, they slept on board the Lydian Monarch for the last time and then paraded on foot in No 10 shed in their expedition uniforms which had been brushed, cleaned and pipeclayed to the best of their ability, but still looked decidedly shabby compared to their normally spotless parade standard. John was particularly conscious of the darned tears in his jacket where the bullets had narrowly missed him. Their trousers and boots had been discarded as beyond use on leaving Egypt so they now wore new breeches and hessian boots. They all sported fierce moustaches, even Evans had managed to grow one that the TCM was prepared to allow out on its own in public. Colonel Milne Home, his face as tanned as the men, shone with pride. "Well chaps, this parade will be one you will remember for the rest of your lives. It will be like no parade you have ever done before. Enjoy it, your performance in Egypt deserves it and I could not be more proud of each and every one of you. Regimental Corporal Major, carry on."

The Life Guards were to take the train to Windsor, so it was only the nine officers and ninety men of the Blues who experienced the ride through London on that Friday, 20th October. The bugle blew 'boot and saddle' and they mounted their chargers, who sensed the excitement, ears twitching. Beyond the dock gates they could hear the sounds of a large crowd. At 9.30am, the band of the Blues struck up 'See the Conquering Hero Comes' and, to the cheers of the 2nd Life Guards, the ship's crew and the dock workers, they commenced their march down the long line of docks, following Colonel Milne Home. As they passed through the gates the band of the 1st Life Guards took over and played "When Johnny comes marching home", which was the signal for a tremendous outburst of cheering. Turning out through the gates, John could not believe his eyes. People lined the West India Dock Road as far as he could see, three or four deep, clapping and cheering and reaching forward to touch the men and horses as they passed. The houses were decorated with bunting and signs "Welcome Home", "Bravo Boys", "Kassassin, Tel-el-Kebir and Waterloo". At intervals across the street, spans of flags fluttered in the breeze. Every window was thronged with people, and carriages had been drawn up in rows two or three deep to form temporary stands. The two bands played alternately all the way, each tune greeted with more cheers and the crowd even singing along.

The crowd showed no signs of abating as they entered the Commercial Road and crossed Whitechapel. The men could not believe the reception, turning to nod and smile at friends and well-wishers. As they travelled through Shoreditch along Great Eastern Street into Old Street a pretty girl John recognised from the Methodist congregation reached out and took his hand, beaming at him and blowing a kiss before letting go. John was astonished, he had not yet plucked up the courage to so much as say hello to her. Several of the section helpfully proceeded to make lewd suggestions and remarks for some time afterwards.

Old comrades, and a few happy drunks, walked out into the road to walk by their side, some putting their hands on the reins as a groom would to lead the charger through the streets. Such was the euphoria and astonishment the Troopers did not object and the parade turned into a triumphal procession. All along the City Road to Angel, the crowd filled windows, stood on the top of the double decker omnibus carriages, or on the roofs of buildings, to gain a better view and cheer their victory and safe return. Outside Kings Cross Station and all along the Euston Road the crowd was, if possible, larger still.

Progress was slow, every man revelling in the sudden popularity and bursting with pride. They finally arrived at the Albany Street barracks at 12.20 to find that the 29th Middlesex Rifle Volunteers had posted a guard of honour. At the bugle command, they drew swords and entered the barrack gates to the music of the Grenadier Guards band playing "Inkerman", to which the Blues band responded with "See the Conquering Hero Comes". They were met on the parade ground by the Prince of Wales, his family and by their commanding officer, Colonel Fred Burnaby. Burnaby warmly greeted Lieutenant-Colonel Milne Home and then gave orders for a march past and a dismounted inspection in the riding school. The Prince walked forward and shook hands heartily with Colonel Milne Home and congratulated the Household Cavalry on their performance in Egypt. The Prince returned to the saluting base and a Royal salute was given, swords flashing simultaneously in the air and the band playing the National Anthem. They were home.

Gordon Wilson stood in front of the large crowd in the Windsor High Street dressed in his Eton College Rifle Volunteer uniform. He felt self conscious and proud in equal measure. It was 2pm and the crowd continued to grow in anticipation of the arrival of the 2nd Life Guards as they marched in from Slough railway station, three miles to the North. They had been standing at ease for almost an hour and his feet ached. He wished he could move but he was on show, and any discomfort he might feel was as nothing compared with what the Household Cavalry had been through. He wriggled his toes and turned his head to see if there was any sign of the troopers. All he could see was the triumphal arch across the high street, adorned with flags and laurel. "To the heroes of Kassassin" was written above the central arch and the smaller arches to either side were marked "Egypt" and "Tel-el-Kebir", now familiar names. He and his friends had poured over the newspaper reports and etchings from Egypt, imagining themselves in a moonlight charge or storming the entrenchments at Tel-el-Kebir. He could barely wait to see how the men had changed.

Suddenly, the crowd started cheering and clapping as the Life Guards came in to view, led by Colonel Ewart and his officers. The chargers looked thin, their coats out of condition, but their eyes were bright and their ears twitched as they walked up the hill. The troopers looked thinner too with brown faces that seemed incongruous in the cool overcast October day. Their helmets were stained light brown and he was sure a couple of them had bullet holes, though that may have been a trick of the light, or his imagination. Their red jackets appeared well used, more than a couple of them, slightly ragged and patched. Their swords were drawn and rested against their shoulders. They seemed duller than normal. Was that blood? Occasionally one would be brandished in triumph into the air, raising a cheer from the crowd. It was certainly not the turnout he had come to expect of the Life Guards, but they suddenly seemed like real soldiers. Oh, how he wished he were older and could be in one of those saddles.

The following day, Saturday 21st October, Field Marshal the Duke of Cambridge, who seemed to share Colonel Burnaby's delight and pride, inspected the Blues in their expedition uniforms. Walking down the line, dressed in the uniform of a Grenadier Guard, the Duke paused briefly every few paces to inspect the man and say a few words. Colonel Burnaby was pausing to speak with some of the other men. John was surprised when, at a signal from Burnaby, both men stopped in front of him.

"Pretty ragged jacket you are wearing, Trooper Waterston," said Burnaby, a smile twinkling in his eye and a finger drawing the Duke's attention to the holes. "Anyone would think someone had been shooting at you."

"Oh no, Sir, those Egyptian moths are something terrible, Sir," the joke that had been flying about since the first battle was out of John's lips before he could think. He heard a couple of suppressed sniggers behind him. The Duke remained stone faced.

Fortunately Burnaby grinned and turned to the Duke. "Waterston here is the Trooper I was telling you about, Sir. It appears he came to General Baker Russell's assistance during the charge at Kassassin and without a 'by your leave' ruined Baker Russell's sport by giving him his horse and killing several of the enemy while on foot by his side."

"Did he by Jove?" said the Duke, reappraising him. "Well, we can't have that, can we? Medal hunting were we, Trooper Waterston?"

"No, Sir, nothing like that. I thought he needed a hand Sir, and, well, he's an officer, Sir, so better on a horse. My fault, Sir. It won't happen again, Sir." The words kept coming even though he was desperate to stop.

"Recklessly endangering one of my valuable chargers by giving it to a Hussar in the middle of a battle, eh?" Burnaby was playing with him now, the twinkle in his eye more pronounced and the pride discernable in his voice.

Surprisingly, the Duke smiled, his mutton chops twitching towards his ears, but a real intensity appearing in his eyes. "So, a brave act. Why no Victoria Cross, Trooper?"

John's mind went blank for a moment in panic. He could feel the men around him listening intently. He paused to collect his thoughts. "Because I did nothing more than what any of the other men would have done, Sir." He paused hoping it would be enough. The silence suggested it wasn't.

"Her Majesty has said she expects all her Household Cavalry to fight with the bravery of a Victoria Cross winner and so she will never give one to us, Sir." John was feeling more comfortable now, the line that would save his neck oft repeated and now truth.

"Did she now. I have not heard her say that. Where did you hear it?" The Duke's brow creased, deep vertical lines appearing at the top of his large nose, bushy grey eyebrows twitching, eyes burrowing into John, searching for signs of the underlying truth. The subject had been the topic of discussion in his club, rumours flying of Wolseley being found in disarray in his tent and of a Blues trooper being recommended for a VC and then the recommendation being withdrawn. The truth, whatever it was, would be an interesting insight into the man who remained in Cairo, but was the toast of England, an insight that could be very useful. Wolseley was even more powerful now; he could promote his favourites, such as Baker Russell, with impunity. It was the source of considerable irritation in the War Office; Colonel Ewart of the Life Guards was the senior and should have been promoted to Brigadier General over Baker Russell. Ewart came from a fine family and had seen action in Egypt, so Wolseley's dangerous assertion that he would rather promote an officer whose rank was due to experience in the Indian Mutiny, Ashanti war, and against the Zulu, no longer applied. It was a point he had made to the Queen. Promotion on merit was the system used in the republican French Army and would probably lead to revolution in England. Confound the man.

"I don't recall, Sir." John's response was clearly not what the Duke wanted to hear. There was an uncomfortable silence as both the Duke and Burnaby continued to stare at him. Keep quiet. Hold your nerve.

"It might have been General Baker Russell, Sir."

The Duke's stare intensified for a moment, at his mention of the name. Was that triumph? Damnation, why had he said that? More silence.

"Or possibly General Wolseley, Sir?"

He was feeling really uncomfortable now under the gaze of the Field Marshall and his Officer Commanding. He would rather be fighting in amongst the Bedouin than facing these two. Burnaby broke the tension, the twinkle gone.

"I am sure we will speak of this again. Trooper, for now, well done. The country is incredibly proud of you."

That evening they were drinking coffee after evening stables when Tom Parris walked into the billet, left arm in a sling, grinning broadly. They all jumped up to greet the friend they had not seen since Kassassin. Once the excitement had settled down and they had established his shoulder was mending, his expression changed.

"I'm afraid I've some bad news."

He had their attention. "John Crook died at sea on 21st September on his way home." There was silence as each man reflected on the last time they had seen him. John closed his eyes in silent prayer. He remembered the man being hit and slumping in his saddle as they charged across the black sand towards the Egyptian infantry, his horse continuing the race as though nothing had happened. LCpl McIntosh had ridden alongside and pulled his horse up when they were through the enemy. Crook had been bandaged up and sent by barge to the hospital in Ismailia, together with Parris and Joseph Proudlock. That was the last they had seen and heard of him.

"When he survived the night after Kassassin I thought he would pull through." Robert Laidlaw was the first to speak. He had been Crook's closest friend. "Joe Proudlock was in a bad way, too. Is he alright?"

"Joe is recovering slowly. You can see him at the Herbert Military Hospital at Shooters Hill. It's where I have just come from," Parris replied.

"There was a comment about conditions on the hospital ship in the paper." Robert Gibson indicated an old copy of the Illustrated London News, a pile of which they were still pawing over. "It said they were dreadful, with only seven staff to care for one hundred and fifteen sick and wounded. Are they true?"

Tom Parris frowned. "The *Malabar* was rough. Not as rough as what we heard about Crimea, but rough. The hospital staff did their best, but there were nowhere near enough of them. I was lucky and could move around, work with others to change my own dressing and could feed myself, but John could not move. I tried my best to help him, feed him and the like, but his wound got infected and there was nothing I could do."

They looked across at John Crook's bed, folded away against the wall as he had left it back in August. Soldiers died in the Household Cavalry, but through illness and accidents rather than war. There had been no deaths in A Troop for a couple of years.

"Did he have any family?" asked Ted Ankers. "I could sell his kit and send them the proceeds." He looked at Cpl Scott for approval.

"He never spoke of anyone. We were as close to a family as he had," replied Laidlaw.

"Poor sad bastard. No different from the rest of us. Well, in that case Crook would not have wanted us to stay in and mope about it," said Angus Duncan. "I suggest we sell his kit and drink the proceeds.

"It's what he would have wanted," said Robert Gibson with a rueful smile.

"As for me, I intend to live forever." Duncan paused and grinned. "So far, so good. Right, a night out in the smoke it is." He started to put on his expedition jacket.

"Hold on Duncan," said Cpl Scott. "That jacket still has another parade to do. It may have been through a few battles but it won't manage a night out in London with your reeking body still inside it. We will wear our undress uniforms."

"But how will anyone know we have just come back from Egypt, Corporal? asked John.

"Have you looked in the mirror recently? replied Cpl Scott. "You look more Arab than English.

He was right. Even dressed in their normal uniforms their brown faces meant there could be no mistaking where they had been. As a result their reception in every pub they visited was remarkable. Everyone wanted to buy them a drink, even the Landlords who would have thrown them out not three months before. They were back slapped and generally feted as heroes wherever they went. Everyone wanted to know where they had been and what it had been like. For a while, John revelled in the attention but it paled when men asked him how many Egyptians he had killed. When he closed his eyes at night he could still see every one of them, and rather wished he couldn't. He took solace in the knowledge that his friends were the same, even Angus Duncan and Cpl Scott, and were there for each other.

A couple of days later a banquet was thrown in their honour at Holborn Town Hall. There were over a thousand people present, including five hundred civilian friends of the Regt. The food was excellent and the wine and beer flowed freely so all had a thoroughly enjoyable time.

After the loyal toast, Colonel Burnaby stood and made a short speech.

"Enthusiastic was the reception given to the soldiers who came back from the Crimean War. Enthusiastic as was the reception given to the men who charged at Balaclava, the reception given by the British nation to the men who charged at Kassassin has been equally magnificent. I do not wish to draw any comparison between the importance of these two wars; but I believe in my heart that the men who fought in Egypt are worthy successors to those who fought at Waterloo and those who charged at Balaclava.

"Some people fancied that the Blues could not fight now." He glanced at a couple of gentlemen who could not meet his gaze. "They have said the men were too heavy, and have even gone so far as to suggest that they could not keep up with Her Majesty's carriage." He grinned, enjoying the cheers and laughter. "I think it will be admitted that those statements are utterly erroneous.

"What feats have been performed by the Household Cavalry in Egypt! From the enthusiasm I have seen all around me I augur that future generations of Englishmen yet unborn will read with pride and pleasure the doings of the Life Guards and Blues in Egypt.

"A short time ago - perhaps even at this present period – non-commissioned officers and men of the army were not allowed to enter certain places of entertainment, not to take seats to which civilians had free access – that is to say, Her Majesty's uniform was a bar to their admission. It is my firm conviction that this banquet will do good not only to the Regiment but to the whole of the British Army. The civilians present, by their presence here, show that they consider soldiers quite as good as themselves, and they should determine that if a non-commissioned officer or a private soldier who behaves himself properly was not allowed the use of a public room at any inn or hotel, they themselves would not in future patronize that establishment."

John, feeling comfortably full and slightly drunk looked around the room at the smiling faces of his friends, his new family, and wondered how long the civilians would remember their sacrifice.

Colonel Fred Burnaby sat down and took a sip of his wine before turning to his second in command, Lieutenant Colonel Milne Home.

"A fine speech, Colonel Fred, I hope you are right. History suggests the public are quick to forget. The papers are already wondering why we went there, and at what cost, particularly since Arabi seems more powerful in his prison cell than he was in command of their army."

"Hmmf. The press will always look for a way to stir up their readership. It is what sells their papers. Now they are able to sell romantic supplements describing and picturing Tommy Atkins' return to his girl on leave, while on the next page asking where the £4m cost was spent and how we will ever get it back from the debt ridden Egyptians. Meanwhile the lawyers make merry defending Arabi. Have you heard the latest?"

"The last I heard, Arabi is to be prosecuted, not for treason, but for instigating the June massacres, having directed and taken part in the burning of Alexandria and having violated a flag of truce by withdrawing his forces and pillaging and burning the city whilst the flag was flying," replied Milne Home. "The problem is that the British counsel appointed to defend him have discovered numerous witness statements and written orders, but they are contradictory and insufficient to support the death sentence the Khedive requires. If he is guilty of anything it is overzealous patriotism."

"In which he is mainly guilty of a lack of success." Burnaby finished the sentence. "So what will the solution be? We have to ensure the Khedive abides by the law; no sneakily executing his enemies when we aren't looking, or we will have Muslims everywhere up in arms."

"Quite. Lawyers are already demanding an investigation into whether our soldiers killed Egyptian wounded after Tel-el-Kebir; while conveniently forgetting the hundreds we treated, that the Egyptian officers ran and that the Bedouin treatment of the wounded is barbaric." Milne Home shuddered at the recollection of the sights he had seen the morning after Kassassin. "Bloody lawyers. Crows aren't the only carrion who circle the battlefield in search of pickings.

"The Khedive needs to appear strong and dissuade others from repeating the coup. No doubt there will be some compromise. Arabi and his followers will probably be exiled to the outer reaches of the Islamic world – somewhere like Ceylon."

"Out of sight, out of mind." Burnaby emptied his glass and looked around for someone to top it up. "We just need to make sure everyone remembers how well you all did. By God, how I envy your opportunity to charge with the men. Who knows when there will be another one?"

EPILOGUE

On the 2nd October, Valentine Baker wearing the uniform of a Turkish General, arrived in Cairo from Constantinople for a meeting with the Khedive to discuss the re-organisation of the Egyptian forces. Egyptian soldiers could not be trusted. One option discussed was to recruit Muslim troops from India. In the meantime twelve thousand British soldiers would remain in Egypt to protect the borders and to maintain order. They would be paid for out of the Egyptian treasury. Baker was ultimately tasked with the reorganisation of the Egyptian police forces before playing a prominent role in the Sudan.

On the 14th October the dual Anglo French control of the Egyptian debt ended with all responsibility for this passing to the commissioners of the debt who were all British. The French objected to the abolition of their control, as did the Russians, who had no legitimate interest in the matter. Their objections fell on deaf ears.

'Lord Wolseley of Cairo, and Wolseley in the County of Stafford' arrived back in London on 28th October to be met be an immense crowd. He nevertheless felt the Royal family did not appreciate him. It is therefore interesting to note that, on his return, the Duke of Cambridge gave an honest appraisal of Wolseley to Queen Victoria. "Wolseley is a very pleasant man to deal with, when he likes it, and I am not at all surprised therefore at Arthur's (Duke of Connaught) liking him as a Chief. His great fault is that he is so very ambitious, and that he has only a certain number of officers in whom he has any real confidence. If we could, on his return, only modify these two feelings, he would be twice the value he is to his country whilst indulging in these views. I think a little hint from you on these points at the proper time, perhaps given through a third person, McNeill or somebody of that sort, might do him a world of good."

In December all charges against Arabi and other members of his war council were dropped in favour of a charge of rebellion. By prior arrangement, Arabi and his compatriots pleaded guilty and were sentenced to death with the sentence immediately commuted by the Khedive to banishment, with their families, to Ceylon. All their property was forfeit and instead an allowance was paid to support the wives and children who could not be punished for the crimes of others.

The British desired to get out of Egypt as soon as possible, but the country was not stable. Anti-European sentiment rumbled just beneath the surface and events to the South, in Sudan, were about to ensure John Waterston's return to the desert. At the end of October 1882, Abdel Kader Pasha, the Khedive's new Governor General of the Sudan, sent a telegram to Cairo reporting that the troops he had sent against the Mahdi had been cut off and asking for ten thousand troops to defend Khartoum. Al Mahdi has been an irritant to the reader throughout this book. In the next, he becomes the man around whom a new crisis develops.

John Waterston's story continues in The First Batman - To Protect and Serve.

EXPLANATORY NOTES

I have attempted to make this story as historically accurate while being as readable as possible. It has been derived from the information contained in the Bibliography, John Waterston's records and the stories passed down from his son, John (Jock) Waterston. These sources, when related to battles are sometimes contradictory or unclear so I have tried to describe the most probable events based on the consensus view, my own military experience and discussion with military friends and historians.

The Household Cavalry do not appear to have kept a diary of their actions in Egypt so this is possibly the first attempt to convey the life of a Royal Horse Guards trooper in the 19th Century. Officers, being better educated and literate, have documented histories and some, such as General Wolseley, have been the subject of detailed biographies. Others, such as Colonel Burnaby, were published authors and wrote their own recollections too. I have been unable to discover any information about the character of the other RHG officers so these are fictitious. The Cabinet meetings and conversations between officers are an attempt to convey the political and strategic positions taken by leaders at the time, rather than a record of events. If some of the speech appears to be a slightly different and dated style that is because it represents a real quote.

With the exception of John Waterston, the soldiers are fictitious. The Blues ranks and surnames have been taken from medal rolls, but their first names, characters and individual actions are unknown. It has been assumed that those who did not receive the clasp Tel-el-Kebir, were part of the rearguard, wounded earlier or sick and unable to take part. Trooper J Crook died on board ship on 21st September 1882 and Trooper J Proudlock was severely wounded during the Kassassin charge.

There is no definitive record supporting John Waterston's recommendation for a VC, and the reason why he lost it, merely the story passed down through the family. However, his citation for the Distinguished Conduct Medal (DCM) awarded in 1886, confirms he gave his horse to Colonel Baker Russell during the charge at Kassassin when that officer's charger was shot under him. This selfless act, cavalry were incredibly vulnerable when unhorsed, does meet the criteria for a VC. Other cavalry recipients of the VC in this era were for identical actions (John Doogan at Laings Nek, South Africa in January 1881 and William Marshall at El Teb in February 1884).

There is other circumstantial evidence to support the story. The award of the DCM, and bar for John Waterston's later actions in the Sudan was made some months after the campaign ended and similar awards had been made. The DCM was personally awarded by Queen Victoria in the presence of Sir Henry Ponsonby and the Khedives' sons at Windsor Castle. It is unusual for a medal for distinguished conduct to be awarded so long after the event, and Queen Victoria only personally presented 185 out of the 472 VCs awarded during her long rein, raising the question as to why she personally awarded a 'mere' DCM.

Certainly VC's that had been awarded for bravery could be removed for disciplinary offences. Private Corbett lost the VC he was awarded at Kafr-Dawar in July 1884 when it was discovered he had enlisted under an assumed name (not that this was uncommon then) and he was convicted of embezzlement and theft from an officer. There are eight other instances of VC winners losing their awards, mainly for theft, and it was not until 1920 and the rein of George V that the rules were amended so that only those convicted of "treason, cowardice, felony or any infamous crime" would forfeit their VC.

Whether John Waterston shot any Bedouin night raiders in Mahsama is unknown, but the Bedouin did slip into the camps by night to steal livestock and one did kill a wounded man in the Kassassin hospital.

It is more likely the 19th Hussars, rather than the Blues, provided the escort to General Wolseley as he took his command group to view Tel-el-Kebir on the night of the 12th September.

Why is this book series titled "The First Batman"? John Waterston's escapades continue in "To Protect and Serve" when his courage leads him to become the most distinguished Blues trooper in the Household Cavalry, and soldier servant to a wealthy young Australian officer, Gordon Wilson. The pair then travel the world in search of adventure and information of value to military intelligence. The term 'Batman' is used for a British Commissioned Officer's personal soldier servant in charge of the officer's "bat-horse" that carried the packsaddle with his officer's kit during a campaign. (from Old French bat derived from medieval Latin bastum 'packsaddle') + man. A batman's duties include:

- acting as the officer's bodyguard in combat
- grooming the officer's horse
- acting as a "runner" to convey orders from the officer to subordinates
- maintaining the officer's uniform and personal equipment as a valet
- pitching the officers tent or digging the officer's foxhole in combat, giving the officer time to direct his unit
- other miscellaneous tasks the officer does not have time or inclination to do

ROYAL NAVY SHIPS IN EGYPT

Ship	Date in Service	Characteristics	Armament	Crew
HMS Alexandra (Ironclad Battleship)	1877	9,490 Tons 325 ft long 15 Knots	2 x 11inch RML 10 x 10inch RML 6 x 13-cwt BL 4 x Torpedo carriages	694
HMS Sultan (Broadside Ironclad)	1871	9,439 Tons 325 ft long 14 Knots	8 x 10inch RML 4 x 9inch RML 7 x 20lb BL	633
HMS Superb (Broadside Ironclad)	1880	9,710 Tons 332 ft long 13 Knots	16 x 10inch RML 6 x 20lb BL 4 x Torpedo carriages	654
HMS Inflexible (Battleship)	1881	11,880 Tons 320 ft long 14.7 Knots	4 x 16inch RML in 2 turrets 6 x 20lb BL 4 x Torpedo carriages	440-470
HMS Monarch (Broadside Ironclad)	1869	8,456 Tons 330 ft long 14.9 Knots	4 x 12inch RML 2 x 9inch RML 1 x 7inch RML	605
HMS Temeraire (Ironclad Battleship)	1877	8,677 Tons 285 ft long 14.6 Knots	4 x 11inch RML 4 x 10inch RML 6 x 20 pdr BL 2 x Torpedo carriages	580

Ship	Date in Service	Characteristics	Armament	Crew
HMS Invincible (Audacious class ironclad Battleship)	1870	6,204 Tons 280 ft long 13.5 Knots	10 x 9inch RML 4 x 64 pdr	450
HMS Penelope (Armoured Corvette)	1868	4,540 Tons 260 ft long 12 Knots	8 x 8inch RML 3 x 5inch BL	350

RML = Rifled Muzzle Loading

BL = Breech Loading

HMS Invincible (1870)

BRITISH CAVALRY IN EGYPT

After 28th August, 1882 when the Indian contingent arrived, the Cavalry Division commanded by Major-General D C Drury Lowe comprised 2 Brigades and Divisional Troops:

1 Brigade commanded by Brigadier-General Sir Baker Russell and comprising:

> Household Cavalry Regiment (composite) made from a Squadron each of the Royal Horse Guards, 1st Lifeguards, 2nd Lifeguards
>
> 4th Dragoon Guards
>
> 7th Dragoon Guards
>
> Part of 17th Company Commissariat & Transport
>
> Half of No. 1 Bearer Company

2 Brigade commanded by Brigadier-General H C Wilkinson comprising

> 2nd Bengal Cavalry
>
> 6th Bengal Cavalry
>
> 13th Bengal Lancers
>
> Divisional Troops:
>
> N/A Battery Royal Horse Artillery
>
> Mounted Infantry
>
> Detachment Royal Engineers
>
> Part of 17th Company Commissariat & Transport
>
> No.6 Field Hospital

BIBIOGRAPHY

A Tidy Little War – The British Invasion of Egypt 1882 by William Wright ISBN 978-0-7524-5090-2

A History of the British Cavalry 1816-1919 Volume 3: 1872-1898 by The Marquess of Anglesey FSA ISBN 0-436-27327-6

Tel-el-Kebir 1882 Wolseley's Conquest of Egypt by Donald Featherstone ISBN 1-85532-333-8

The Egyptian Campaigns 1882 to 1885 by Charles Royle

The Life of Colonel Fred Burnaby by Thomas Wright 1908

The Life of Lord Wolseley by Sir F Maurice & Sir George Arthur 1924

Beyond the Reach of Empire, Wolseley's Failed Campaign to Save Gordon and Khartoum by Colonel Mike Snook ISBN 1848326017

Campaigns of a War Correspondent by Melton Prior 1912

The Victorians at War by Ian Beckett ISBN 1-85285-275-5

The Illustrated London News 1882

Printed in Great Britain
by Amazon